Rowan Coleman lives with her husband and five children in a very full house in Hertfordshire. She juggles writing novels with raising her family, which includes a very lively set of toddler twins whose main hobby is going in the opposite directions. When she gets the chance, Rowan enjoys sleeping, sitting and loves watching films; she is also attempting to learn how to bake.

Rowan would like to live every day as if she were starring in a musical, although her daughter no longer allows her to sing in public. Despite being dyslexic, Rowan loves writing, and her books include the *Sunday Times* bestseller, *The Memory Book*, which was part of the Richard and Judy Autumn Book Club, and the award-winning *Runaway Wife*.

www.rowancoleman.co.uk
Facebook/Twitter: @rowancoleman

Praise for Rowan Coleman:

'I immediately read *The Memory Book* and it's WONDERFUL . . . I'm so happy because she's written other books and it's so lovely to find a writer you love who has a backlist' Marian Keyes

'Oh, what a gorgeous book this is – it gripped me and wouldn't let me go. So engaging, so beautifully written – I loved every single thing about it' Jill Mansell

'What a lovely, utterly life affirming, heart-breaking book *We Are All Made of Stars* by Rowan Coleman is' Jenny Colgan

'Painfully real and utterly heartbreaking . . . wonderfully uplifting' Lisa Jewell

'Like *Me Before You* by Jojo Moyes, I couldn't put it down. A tender testament to maternal love' Katie Fforde

Also by Rowan Coleman:

We Are All Made of Stars
The Memory Book
Runaway Wife
The Home for Broken Hearts
The Baby Group
Woman Walks Into A Bar
River Deep
After Ever After
Growing Up Twice
The Accidental Mother
The Accidental Wife
The Accidental Family

Writing as Scarlett Bailey:

Secret Santa (digital short)
Two Weddings and a Baby
Just For Christmas
Married by Christmas
Santa Maybe (digital short)
The Night Before Christmas

ROWAN
COLEMAN

the Other Sister

1 3 5 7 9 10 8 6 4 2

Ebury Press, an imprint of Ebury Publishing
20 Vauxhall Bridge Road,
London SW1V 2SA

Ebury Press is part of the Penguin Random House group of companies
whose addresses can be found at global.penguinrandomhouse.com

First published in 2011 as *Lessons in Laughing Out Loud* by Arrow Books
This edition published in 2016 by Ebury Press

www.eburypublishing.co.uk

A CIP catalogue record for this book is available from the British Library

ISBN 9781785037917

Printed and bound in Great Britain by Clays Ltd, St Ives PLC

Penguin Random House is committed to a sustainable future for
our business, our readers and our planet. This book is made from
Forest Stewardship Council® certified paper.

For my children, Lily and Fred, who make
me laugh out loud every day

Chapter One

There are moments in every person's life when something as simple as a wrong turn, an impulsive decision, or a door softly drawing to a close can change everything for ever. Moments that, Willow Briars knew better than anyone, were impossible to turn back from; moments that if you weren't very careful could shape the rest of your life.

Which was why she was trying rather hard not to murder Lucy Palmer. Many words and phrases had been used to describe thirty-nine-year-old Willow, but not until that very moment would anybody have ever called her murderous.

'Efficient' and 'capable' was how Willow was often described by her boss, Victoria Kincade, chief executive officer of Victoria Kincade Talent Ltd. Also 'invaluable', 'resourceful' and 'a genuine treasure'.

'Good old Will', was how many of her colleagues referred to her. Fun, funny, down-to-earth Willow Briars; always up for a good night out; says-it-how-it-is Will. And Willow knew perfectly well that if any of them were asked to describe her physically, they would dwell on her lovely skin, beautiful blue eyes, shiny hair, great smile, and fantastic taste in gorgeous shoes, which made up for her rather limited choice in fashion.

Her identical twin sister, Holly, who was exactly twenty-six minutes younger, called Willow her rock, her darling, her soul mate, her other half, and Willow could use all of those words to describe Holly too. Her four-year-old twin nieces, Jo-Jo and Jem, called her cuddly Aunty Pillow, sweet Aunty Will and, nicest of all, best aunty in the world Aunty Will, which was a compliment with limited range as Willow was also their only aunt, but still, she loved it.

Depending on her mood her mother called her either the London twin or the disappointing one.

Willow's ex-husband had started off calling her darling, but after two years of marriage, had ended up describing her as a waste of space. And, for a very brief time, his daughter, Chloe, had not minded one little bit if people thought Willow was her mum.

Willow Briars was, and had been, many things to many people but so far never violent. Not until Lucy Palmer, graduate trainee and the daughter of a family friend of Victoria, had joined the agency six weeks ago and Victoria gave her the desk opposite Willow and instructed Willow to look after the barely twenty-one-year-old *ingénue.* From that moment on, to Willow's great surprise, she discovered she would most certainly be capable of bopping another human being over the head with a brick and then feeding them into a wood chipper.

'. . . Anyway, Will, *you* would have *died*!' Lucy informed Willow with some enthusiasm. 'I mean, you would not have been able to believe your eyes. It was fully out, under the table, right there in the middle of Nobu! *Lol!*'

And that was it; that was the thing about Lucy that brought

out Willow's homicidal tendencies. She ended nearly every sentence with the nonsense word 'lol'.

A lesser woman than Willow would have hated Lucy for her smooth skin, glossy hair, long legs and insistence on sharing every mundane detail of her vacuous life with everyone in one hundred and forty characters or fewer ('Lucy Palmer is eating a sandwich, lol.' 'Lucy Palmer is thinking about lunch, lol.' 'Lucy Palmer has got her period, lol.' 'Lucy Palmer's boyfriend got his dick out in the middle of a restaurant, lol'), but what Willow discovered that she could not abide was that Lucy Palmer said 'lol' out loud as if it were a word, as if it had any kind of meaning, as if it was actually a socially acceptable substitute for laughing out loud.

'So I told him, I said to him, if you don't put that away right now then there won't be any dessert tonight, if you know what I mean, lol.' For a second, Lucy stared at Willow who was doing her best to ignore her.

'I mean blow job,' she clarified. 'Lol!'

Willow bit her lip and stared at the Excel spreadsheet on which she kept a record of Victoria's expenses, wondering if the company accountant really would let Victoria claim for four nights on a yacht in Cannes with a young male actor-slash-model, who to date had not successfully auditioned even once, but who the normally ruthless Victoria kept on the books anyway, because he was terribly talented in areas that Lucy would have referred to as 'dessert'.

'Entertaining a client, darling,' Victoria had responded to Willow's raised eyebrow when she handed her the receipt.

'Don't you mean he was entertaining you?' Will had asked her.

'Well, somebody's got to,' Victoria had sighed. 'There is not enough Viagra in the world to get my husband standing to attention.'

'Poor Robert . . . perhaps if you tried being nice to him?' Willow had been living dangerously that day.

'Darling, you know perfectly well I married Robert for his money and the Suffolk house. By the time one gets to one's third husband being nice is definitely not on the agenda.'

Unable to question Victoria's particular brand of logic, Willow had shrugged and keyed in the amount under the column headed 'Entertaining'. Victoria liked her young men, and she didn't mind at all paying for them, sometimes in kind and sometimes with cash, but especially on expenses. Despite her own reservations on the matter, Willow couldn't help but admire Victoria's determination to get what she wanted from life, even if that meant ordering a young lover in exactly the same way she would order from a menu. She did sometimes wonder what Victoria's husband thought of it.

'Anyway he got dessert, all right. In the back of the cab on the way home! Lol!'

Willow looked at Lucy for a long moment, hoping that a mere glance would be enough to imprint her seniority and authority on the younger woman and shut her up. It did not.

'So what did you get up to last evening?' Lucy asked her. 'Anything?'

'Oh, you know,' Will said mildly. 'The usual.'

'Takeaway?' Lucy fluttered her lashes innocently.

'Orgy.' Willow did not glance up from her screen and she continued to key in figures.

'Wow,' Lucy said, wide-eyed, probably at that moment trying

to imagine Willow with her ample thighs wrapped around some man or men. 'Lol.'

The last time Willow had been out was, in fact, Saturday, on a blind date with Dave Turner, a friend of a friend of her brother-in-law, who had recently moved to London and didn't know anyone. Privately Willow objected to the assumption, often made by married people, that all single people over a certain age were so desperate about their mutual failure to find a life partner so close to imminent death that they became instantly compatible, but still she had agreed, because frankly she had nothing else on, and besides, Holly was only trying to be nice. And whatever else she might get wrong, Willow tried her best not to let her sister down because Holly cared about people. She worried about them, even people she didn't know, and it made Willow feel like a better person to do things to please her, partly because she'd do anything for Holly, but also because it sometimes felt like Holly was her living breathing conscience. Holly was the good twin, their mother said so often enough.

Dave Turner turned out to be far too good-looking to be a serious prospect, the sort of man who, in a year or two, would end up with a woman ten or fifteen years younger than Willow, who would giggle at his jokes, rather than raise a sardonic eyebrow. Now he was a confident bachelor, a man about town, who was not in need of a friend at all. Willow realised rather belatedly that Holly was actually trying to expand her own social horizons. It was soon obvious that Dave Turner was not hoping for anything serious. He had the look of a man who would soon get tired of all the effort of small talk, find a wife, put on five inches round his middle and spend the rest of his life trying to get them off. He'd been polite enough to flirt with Willow, though, and he'd seemed interested in her stories.

As the evening wore on, and after several glasses of wine, his gaze had begun to stray to her cleavage and his sentences were punctuated with much arm and hand touching. Willow sensed he expected some sort of pay-off for the four gin and tonics he had bought her. So they had parted company after several minutes of fevered grappling behind the wheelie bins in the pub car park. Dave offered to walk Willow home, but she had declined because, even drunk as she was, she found the prospect of an awkward and embarrassing Sunday morning, polite lies and empty number exchanges unbearable.

Willow liked to be wanted, she liked to feel a man's desire for her, but she knew – had known for a long time, even before her ill-fated marriage – that she could never be in a relationship. She just didn't have what it took to make another person happy.

'Oh, *lol*!' Lucy said to herself, reading something on Twitter, no doubt, prompting Willow to get up and pretend to go to the loo, just in case the urge to staple Lucy to the desk and hole-punch her carotid artery came to anything.

'Will, darling?' Victoria hung out of her office door, like a glamorous Nosferatu rising from her coffin, as Will passed. '*Uno momento, s'il vous plaît.*' She was never one to shy away from both misusing and mixing the languages of Europe.

'Marvellous,' Victoria said, as she gestured for Will to take a seat.

Victoria's Dickensian gothic office – the giant antique dark oak desk, scarlet velvet curtains, brass desk lamp, and, hanging on the wall, an oil painting of Victoria with both a cleavage and a blue silk gown, both of which came straight from the artist's imagination – seemed a little incongruous in the modern office building. Victoria liked it, however; she said it gave her authenticity. Willow had never really been sure what her boss meant by that, but neither was she really sure exactly how old Victoria was. Her face was held in permanent suspended animation somewhere in her late forties. Perhaps she'd had that desk since new.

'Super, darling. Love those.' Victoria nodded at Willow's heeled mules, which peeped out from below her wide-legged trousers. Once Willow had joked that she always wore high heels so that she was the right height for her weight, and everyone had laughed and rolled their eyes, and said things like, 'Oh, Willow, you *are* funny.'

But Willow had only been half joking. Shoes were the one fashion item that always fitted her no matter what her waistline was doing. Her feet were long and slender. She could walk into any shoe store in any city, and although the staff might look at her askance, they would not discreetly or politely tell her that they did not sell plus-size clothing. She would splash out on the kind of shoes that set off a sensible skirt; that would say to any observer, 'I am not frumpy, I am not past my peak, I am not just fat. Look, I have fantastic shoes that make me interesting, fashionable and show you that there is another side to me.'

'What can I do for you?' Willow asked Victoria, who was tapping her finger thoughtfully on her desk.

'Will, darling, I need you to get me something really marvellous. You know, special, exotic . . . really rare and expensive, OK?'

Will enjoyed working for Victoria – every day presented a different challenge – but she did sometimes have the knack of talking entirely in adjectives without ever actually saying anything.

'Can we narrow that down a bit?' Willow asked. 'When you say marvellous, exotic, expensive and rare, are you asking me to ring up that escort service again?'

'No . . . no darling, although . . . No, no time for sex today.' What might have been disappointment passed fleetingly across Victoria's mostly frozen face. 'What I *mean* is, you know, something delightful, sumptuous – an explosion of delight in your mouth . . .'

Briefly Willow thought of Lucy and her dessert.

'Chocolates, darling, *chocolates*! We need some really top-notch wonderful *chocolat* for this afternoon. India Torrance is coming in, and the poor little lamb needs a lot of cheering up. Apparently she's ever so fond of chocolate, although you wouldn't know it to look at her, thank God; I can't make money from a porker.' Victoria eyed Willow, whose affection for confection was burgeoning all too apparently behind her straining buttons. 'Normally I'd say something complimentary to make up for the fact that you're fat, but I haven't got time for social empathy today. We have only a brief period of calm before all kinds of shit starts to hit the fan. It's *most* inconvenient.'

'What sort of shit?' Willow asked as she closed the office door behind her and sat down, pulling her shirt over her waistband, and folding her hands over her stomach. 'Isn't India supposed to be in Cornwall in a wig and some stays, pining after a man she can never marry?'

India Torrance, twenty-something, had been a relative unknown until she'd won an Olivier Award for best newcomer at the tender age of eighteen, having taken first Stratford and then the West End by storm. In the following four years she had made a film a year that was both critically and commercially acclaimed and had become Victoria's favourite cash cow. Ethereal, beautiful, upper class but down to earth, India was in demand all over the world, and Victoria was on the verge of agreeing a string of endorsements for her, including perfume, a make-up range, a boho clothing line that India would take credit for designing, and all this while she was in the process of making her fifth feature film, a British costume drama that had, according to Victoria, Oscar written all over it.

'Yes, she fucking is,' Victoria said mildly. 'That's what she's supposed to be doing, but she has . . . transgressed, darling . . . been a teensy bit of a hiccup with my plans for her, and a little bit of "housekeeping" will be required.'

'Housekeeping?' Willow's eyes widened. That was Victoria's code word for covering up a really massive scandal and turning it to her client's advantage against all the odds. It was what Victoria was famous for, and most of the reason she was so successful.

'What's she done?'

'It's more like what she hasn't done.' Victoria paused, stabbing the nib of the fountain pen she liked to use into the blotting pad, which Willow was pretty sure was at that moment a substitute for India's lovely face. 'Anyway, she's coming in and I'm committed to treating her with kid gloves, et cetera, so I think we'll start with some lovely choccies, something that shows we really care about her, blah, blah, blah – OK?'

'Chocolate, OK, if you say so.' Willow started to get up, but Victoria stilled her with the flat of her hand.

'Willow, there is something else . . . something a little bit above the call of duty that I need to ask you, and when I say ask, I mean tell.' Victoria's brows furrowed about as much as the Botox would allow, always an ominous sign.

Willow waited, patiently confident, after five years with Victoria, that her boss would come to the point eventually.

'If this had happened next year it wouldn't have mattered, but she's just starting to get in her stride. Now is the crucial time, the time when she's really valuable. I'm this close to making me – *her* – some serious money, and this business . . .' Victoria thumped her desk with her fist, making Willow start back in her chair. 'Honestly, I don't mean to sound harsh, but the silly thick-headed little bitch, you'd have thought that the amount of money her parents spent on educating her would have meant she had a bit more sense than the average fuckwit on the street.'

'You don't sound harsh at all,' Willow told her mildly.

'She's fucked up, Willow. She's been having an affair with Hugh Cramner. They've been screwing and, now it's all come out, he's dropped her like a lead balloon and run back to his wife claiming he was seduced by a whore.'

'Hugh Cramner!' Willow gasped. Hugh Cramner, acting legend, his twenty-six-year marriage to his adorable wife often lauded as an example of how to be married. An adoring father of four, he was routinely referred to as 'a national treasure' and, it was widely rumoured, only a few short months away from being awarded a knighthood in the New Year Honours List. Willow felt queasy. 'But he's old enough to be her father, he practically is . . . Oh my God, doesn't he play her father in this film?'

'Yes, darling.' Victoria's face was immobile, which was the nearest she ever got to despair. 'Quite. India is absolutely distraught, as you can imagine, heartbroken, devastated, all the misery words. But the worst of it is that the press are about to blow the story wide open. They've got photos with more than a touch of nudity and some phone recordings – sex talk, that sort of thing. They want her side and they've given us forty-eight hours to agree to an interview before it goes nuclear. Of course, I've taken her off set, popped her into Blakes Hotel for a few days – they are very discreet there; that whole thing with me and that boy band went completely unnoticed – but she won't even be able to stay there to hide once the story is out.'

'But if she gives an interview, tells her side of the story . . .?'

'Oh, Will, have you learned nothing, *mon petite amore*? Of course I'm not going to let her give away her story for free to the blasted red-top whore-mongering scum. No, I'm going to *let them* think that's what we'll do, to buy her some time, and then I'm going to tell them to fuck off and make her disappear until, A, the shit's died down and, B, I can make some real money selling her story to the kind of magazine that pays big bucks.'

'Won't that make things a bit harder on India?' Willow shifted in her seat; sometimes Victoria's ruthlessness unsettled even her.

'Darling, I'm not here to make her life easy, I'm here to make her famous and rich.' Victoria shrugged. 'So when the story breaks on Sunday she'll be somewhere completely safe, where the press won't find her.'

'Right, and you want me to find somewhere, a cottage, maybe, in the country? Ireland?' Willow asked her, already mentally making a list.

'No, darling.' Victoria didn't miss a beat. 'I want you to keep her in your flat.'

'I beg your pardon?' Willow wanted to believe that she had

misheard but she knew Victoria well enough to know she had not.

'You have it,' Victoria said. 'Look, darling, I thought and thought about it for . . . well, a long enough time to make a serious decision. You know what the paps are like: when it becomes clear she's not going to play ball they'll hunt her down. They won't stop until they've got the woman who seduced Hugh Cramner.' Victoria squared up her padded shoulders, lifting her chin a little. 'I know I'm a monster, but I do care about the people who make me a lot of money, and India is one of them. And the thing is, she can be a bit fragile. You know how creative people are, all manic depressive and melodramatic. India went into months of decline over a bad review, so imagine how she will deal with heartbreak and infamy. Anyway, with her parents in Devon, I'm really *in loco parentis*, and I need to find a person – perhaps the only person who I can truly trust – to care for her.' Victoria pointed at Willow. 'By which I mean you. So if you could just pop her in your spare room for a week or two and make sure she doesn't top herself that would be marvellous.'

Victoria's smile was something to behold, something rather similar to the grimace of one of the mummified Egyptians in the British Museum, deathly and utterly lacking in warmth. Willow would not have been surprised if her face had actually creaked when she snapped the smile off again as quickly as she'd conjured it up.

'Victoria,' Willow said quietly and calmly, standing up to make her point, 'I am not moving India Torrance into my flat. This is worse than when you made me buy drugs for Simeon Burton. Have you any idea what it's like for a middle-aged woman in a trouser suit to turn up at an illegal drugs den at three a.m.?'

'Yes,' Victoria said with some conviction. 'And you are not middle-aged until you're fifty these days, darling. Everyone knows that. It was in the *Daily Mail*: fifty is the new forty, which makes me about thirty.'

'In donkey's years, maybe,' Willow muttered under her breath. 'You're putting me on suicide watch with a world-famous woman in my Wood Green flat? What about that makes any sense? Why don't you just rent a flat, or something? Get her a carer?'

'Willow, you know the sort of person I am.' Victoria gestured regally. 'I'm kind. I'm a kind person, which is why I'm asking *you* to keep an eye on India. You don't want to be responsible for the poor girl slitting her wrists, do you? I wouldn't want you to have that on your conscience.'

'Me!' Willow fumed impotently.

'Darling, just do this for me. As your boss – I mean, friend. OK – boss. Look at everything I've done for you. I've . . . well, I pay you quite well, considering. You'll have the weekend to prepare for her, tidy up, fumigate. And in a shake of a lambkin's tail I will have turned the whole situation around to our advantage, washed up that bastard Hugh Cramner for good and made us all a lot of money. Well, not you, to be fair, but you never know, perhaps I'll pop a bit extra in your Christmas bonus. Yes?'

Willow dropped her chin and looked at the pointed toes of her shoes. It was fair to say that there had been plenty of ups and downs in her life, to put it mildly. But, on the whole, working for Victoria Kincade had been one of the ups. Yes, Victoria seemed to think that she owned Willow body and soul, which Willow thought she might have signed over along with her weekends and evenings, when she agreed her contract in suspiciously red ink. But still, Victoria had been good to her and she didn't mind Willow's foibles; she actively seemed to like them. Besides, it was pointless fighting Victoria once she'd made her mind up. She was like the Black Death personified: there was no cure for her.

'Fine,' Willow relented. 'Fine. Whatever you say. I'll go out and get chocolate.'

'Thank you, darling.' Victoria didn't sound nearly as grateful as Willow thought she should. 'We'll discuss the details along with India when she gets here.' Victoria tossed Willow a credit card. 'Get yourself some while you're at it. You know you want to.'

Chapter Two

Many people would be a good deal more alarmed and overwhelmed by the prospect of unexpectedly putting up a dumped, internationally renowned actress than Willow Briars was, but for Willow it was almost as expected as it was unexpected. Or to put it another way, if someone had told her on her way to work that morning that she was about to be forced to cohabit with a celebrity then she wouldn't have been in the least bit surprised. Over the last few years, Willow had come to realise, and mostly enjoy, the fact that working for Victoria was a bit like following a white rabbit into Wonderland on a daily basis, where it was sensible to always expect the unexpected, and beware the Red Queen. In fact, as she swung her bag onto her shoulder and headed out of the offices of Victoria Kincade Talent Ltd and onto Golden Square to take the short walk to Liberty, the imminent arrival of India Torrance came pretty low on her list of worries.

Willow was irritated that Victoria hadn't given her time to think, but then that was Victoria. She didn't like to give her people time to think in case they took it upon themselves to think that they didn't like her plan for them at all and wanted to change their minds. Victoria wasn't a fan of people who changed their minds. It was a trait in her boss that Willow had learned to adapt to early on in her career by ceasing to think unless Victoria expressly asked her to, which was absolutely fine by her. Thinking, dwelling, wondering were all activities that Willow thought were exceptionally overrated.

No, it was not the prospect of having a celebrity to stay that rattled Willow. After all, she worked in one of the world's foremost talent agencies; part of her job was regularly babysitting people who either by accident, luck and, very occasionally, talent found themselves removed from the rest of the population by extreme fame. Having India Torrance slumming it in her flat would be no different from the time that Victoria made her go on a book-signing tour with a WAG who, at the age of twenty-four, had just finished the first instalment of her autobiography. It had been one of Willow's jobs to clear the toilets of any members of the public, and to make sure there were no offending smells lingering by the time her client arrived. And once Victoria had woken Willow up at four in the morning and sent her to Chelsea in a black cab to what could only be described as a brothel to pick out a suitable escort for a very shy married male film actor over from Hollywood for a few days. As Willow relayed the chosen girl (she had to be brunette, curvy and willing) back across London, she had been obliged to make her sign a series of watertight confidentiality agreements and, as Victoria had put it, mildly threaten her as to what would happen to her if she even thought about kissing and telling. Willow had felt sick to the pit of her stomach as she ushered the young woman past the hotel concierge and took her up to the actor's room, fighting her disgust at what Victoria had asked her to do.

'Why do you do this?' she'd felt compelled to ask the girl, who couldn't have been much more than twenty, shivering in a sequinned shift dress that skimmed the tops of her thighs, as they stood in the lift. The girl had shrugged as if she didn't really know.

'The money's good,' she'd told Willow with an absent smile.

'But doesn't it make your flesh crawl?' Willow had asked her, fascinated.

'It's only sex,' the girl had told her. 'It's no big deal. And sometimes something cool happens, like you get to fuck a film star.'

'That's nice,' Willow had said. She sort of understood, and there was a little part of her that was jealous of the bravado the girl displayed. Perhaps she meant it.

But still, Willow had felt no better as she stood on the other side of the locked door, making some final arrangements with the star's bodyguard before she finally went and found breakfast. It was the thought, just the thought, that that young girl might not want to be there, that she might be frightened, or feel helpless or sick that had made Willow, for the briefest of moments, think of going back through that door and rescuing her. But then she heard a peal of girlish laughter, like the tinkle of glass breaking, and she had removed her hand from the door and left. Not everyone wanted to be rescued.

What really gave Willow pause, as she pushed open the beautiful oak doors and made her way into Liberty, stopping briefly to inhale the delicious scent of polished wood, perfume and chocolate, was to have someone else, another person, staying in her home. Willow did not like people. No, that wasn't exactly true: she loved some people, approximately four, if she were honest, although she'd only openly admit to three of those.

She felt obliged to stay in touch with her mother, with whom she had not got on in years, and had a deep respect and affection for the largely terrible human being that was her boss. She enjoyed a friendly relationship with most of her colleagues, was always extremely personable with clients, no matter what their foibles or tics, and got on perfectly well with the friends of the one friend she had outside of work. But on the whole Willow did not like people, and she especially didn't like them too close to her, in her house, using her bathroom, quite possibly for crying and perhaps even slitting their wrists. The only person she'd ever been able to live with successfully was Holly, and she'd always known she would lose Holly one day. Since her divorce Willow liked to be herself in her own home. It was one of the few places where she could really relax, buy a KFC bargain bucket for dinner without anyone judging her, eat an entire box of Maltesers in an evening, sit about with her buttons undone, her bra slung over the back of the sofa and, most crucially of all, breathe out. And then in again, and out again.

Even breathing wouldn't be possible any more once India Torrance was *in situ*. Willow would have to be on high alert all the time, keeping India hidden and sane, the latter a task for which Willow was most definitely underqualified. And if something terrible did happen, if the press discovered India, or the girl did harm herself in any way, then the person who would get the blame would be Willow.

From what little Willow knew about her personally, India seemed to be a nice enough person, well brought up, well spoken. She was certainly very beautiful, in a fresh-faced way. She never seemed to need even a speck of make-up to gild those sparkling eyes and long light brown hair that framed her delicate features, although the stylists liked to glam her up for the red carpet and she took it well, an actress playing the vamp. India was still in that bloom of youth, that reign of beauty, that when you are in your twenties seems like your right, one that you never expect to lose.

Pausing in front of a mirrored wall punctuated with handbags of all shapes and colours, floating on glass shelves, Willow observed her own face.

For the last twenty years, perhaps more, Willow had been allowing herself to grow steadily fatter, adding a few pounds more every year and never quite finding the time or the will to make the necessary changes that could either halt or reverse the gradual increase in her waistline, hips and bottom. Willow met her own eyes, and regarded them for a moment, deep blue, almost violet, with a random fleck of black in one iris. They could be quite arresting, intense, intoxicating, someone had once whispered in her ear.

Everyone always said she had lovely eyes.

And Willow had great hair, she was a genuine blonde; no need for highlights or glosses or half a squeezed lemon for Willow. Her thick, golden, waist-length hair fell in soft curls. Always silky and soft to the touch, it was her crowning glory. Willow had it styled every six weeks by a celebrity hairdresser who owned a high-end salon in Covent Garden and gave her a massive discount for sending stars his way. He'd trim the ends whilst telling her that she had hair any star would envy.

Her skin was radiant, soft and smooth without a single blemish. Even at the age of thirty-nine, even after a horrible divorce, even after everything, she still looked a good ten years younger than she was. Willow would routinely get asked how she did it and she would reply, it was in the genes, although once, at some tortuous family occasion, one of her mother's friends had told her that big girls always have great skin.

'It's the fat, you see. Stops your face falling in,' she'd told her as if she were delivering excellent news.

'Fuck it, I'm having another piece of cake then,' Willow had said, enjoying the shock her casually dropped profanity had had on one of Mother's WI set.

'The fat' – as if it wasn't part of her, as if it were a separate entity all of its own that she could somehow absent-mindedly lose, or shed like a butterfly shrugging off a cocoon. But that wasn't going to happen. The fat was more than part of her. Sometimes Willow felt like it *was* her, all of her, marbling throughout her whole being, not just her body, but her mind, her heart and perhaps even her soul. Perhaps she had a fat soul.

Even so, Willow could never blame her weight on her genes or her metabolism or big bones or any other excuse. Her weight was all her own doing. A fact she was certain of because she had another reflection, one much crueller than any mirror she stood in front of could ever return. She had her own identical twin to look at, her very own genetic clone, to show in glorious Technicolor exactly what could have been if only she had been better at saying no.

Holly was almost her exact double, with the very same violet eyes, including the dark fleck, honey-golden hair and wonderful skin. The twins were the same in every respect except one. Holly was a healthy size eight and Willow was a large size eighteen. Whenever Willow looked at her beautiful sister, whom she loved more than anyone alive, and whom she knew loved her back equally, she had to confront on each and every occasion what she might have looked like, what she might live like, if only she could find whatever magic ingredient it was that would make her stop eating much more than she needed to every single day.

Willow stared at the woman who was staring back at her from behind a tangerine Mulberry bag, her rounded face, the gentle pouch of a double chin that billowed softly beneath her jaw, the buttons of her shirt that strained against the pressure of flesh building behind them, and the surge of fat that blossomed over the waistband of her wide-legged trousers. She could remember exactly the last day that she and Holly had looked identical.

It had been on the day of her stepfather's funeral in Christchurch. He'd been diagnosed with prostate cancer ten months before, and succumbed to his short illness, as the notice in the paper said, at home and at peace with his loving wife and doting stepdaughters. The twins had never known their real father and Willow's recollection of life before Ian shone in her memory like polished silver, despite the hardships they'd faced. Back then it always seemed to be summer, and she remembered being taken out for picnics on a school night, because the cupboard was bare and the bakers on the corner sold sandwiches at half price at the end of the day. They'd climb the side of the steep hill on a windy day, paper napkins sailing away on the breeze, and Willow and Holly, hands linked, would roll down the slope, laughing and laughing as the world spun out of control all around them, secure in the knowledge they would always have each other.

Then their mother met Ian, Mr Sinclair, the local bank manger. Imogene Briars had made her girls wait for her while she went in for her interview, careful to point out her needy charges, drumming their worn-down heels on the metal chair legs in unison, as she disappeared into his office. She'd gone in to extend her overdraft and came out with an invitation to dinner. After a whirlwind romance, during which Willow remembered her mother constantly smiling, they were married. Inside a year Ian had brought everything into their lives that had been missing before: stability, order, security. There weren't picnics on a school night any more, or evenings spent rolling down hills until after it got dark. But neither were there winters when the tips of their fingers went blue because the power had been cut off, or they had beans on toast for tea the third night in a row. From the age of eight Willow and Holly gained the closest they had ever had to a father, but it never occurred to Willow until they buried him, how much she loved him. And when she realised that was true, the only thing she could think of to do was eat.

On the day of Ian's funeral Willow's mother had been inconsolable, retiring to bed with a large gin and Valium, before the guests had left the wake. Holly, turned out so neatly in a black dress with a white collar, had done her best to step into their mother's shoes, and Willow, bereft and feeling a sudden empty crater open inside her, had sat quite alone at the kitchen table and eaten sixty ready-cooked cocktail sausages straight out of the packet, one after the other without stopping. Later, after everyone had gone and Holly had been upstairs to check their mum was still breathing, she had come down and found Willow still sitting in the kitchen.

'She's never going to get over this,' Holly had said, taking out of the fridge a chocolate cake that a neighbour had baked and putting it on the table. 'We're going to have to look after her now.'

'I know,' Willow replied. 'Well, we're almost fifteen now, anyway.'

'Just the three of us again,' Holly had said, her eyes meeting Willow's, full of apprehension.

'Just the three of us, yes.' Willow remembered feeling like the gulf inside her must reach through her toes and into the guts of the earth, the prospect of life without Ian had so terrified her.

From that day on she had drifted ever further from the life her identical twin lived. When Holly, size eight, went to university, Willow, size ten, moved into a bedsit over a chip shop and started at a temping agency, moving from job to job, quite happy never to settle anywhere. When Holly, size eight, started as a graduate trainee for a fashion house in the West End, Willow, size twelve, automatically went along as requisite flatmate and started working as a dentist's receptionist. For four years the two of them lived together; a perfect, happy period in Willow's life that always seemed to be full of fun. Holly and her boyfriend, Graham, were the sensible ones and Willow, curvier than her sister, flirty and sexy, was much in demand, dating an endless stream of men, never really able to settle on one. That all ended when Holly, twenty-five and size eight, married Gray, with Willow, size fourteen, standing at the altar in a bridesmaid's dress that had been dyed to match her eyes.

The following years were almost featureless in Willow's memory. Holly, size eight, had worked her way up in the fashion industry, travelled with Gray whenever she could, gradually spending more and more time visiting their mother and spending less time with Willow, who seemed to be trapped in a time warp, while everyone else's life moved on. Willow ricocheted from one ill-fated liaison to another, some of them lasting for months, others only hours, drifting from job to job that did nothing more for her than make ends meet, and in all that time finding no one or nothing that did anything to give sustenance to that constant gnawing hunger.

Then, at the age of thirty-two, Willow, size sixteen, found a new job working for a wine merchant underneath the arches in London Bridge. It took her entirely by surprise to discover how drawn she was to Sam Wainwright, her new boss, a man a little older than she, who had lost his wife a few years earlier and was now bringing up his seven-year-old alone. Willow was not certain whether she'd loved him, or his story, or his daughter at first, but love him she did, and it had seemed as if her life was finally resolving itself when a year after she started working for him he proposed. Holly, size eight, and Chloe, aged eight, had been her bridesmaids.

Which was why everyone was so upset when, at exactly the same time as Holly, size ten for two months, then size eight again, gave birth to her twins, Willow, size sixteen, left her husband and Chloe, never to return.

Holly, size eight, moved back to Christchurch to be near their mother, and Willow, verging on a size eighteen, got offered a job by Victoria Kincaid, who'd interviewed her along with ten other applicants, telling Willow she'd got the job on the spot because she was the only one there who looked like she wouldn't have a nervous breakdown after five minutes in Victoria's company. Her weight gain had slowed, but still it crept up, and Willow knew that, if not this year, then the next, she'd be looking at the next dress size up.

Now, brushing the thought aside, Willow picked up several packets of her favourite handmade 'Lick the Spoon' chocolates and reached into her pocket as her phone vibrated. That would be Victoria, probably asking her to stock up on wigs and various other disguises for India.

'You were thinking about me,' Holly said into her ear. 'Nice thoughts. That made me wonder how it went with Dave. I've been holding off asking, hoping you'd volunteer the details.'

Willow smiled. Holly was adept at playing up to the psychic twin thing, although half the time she would just hazard a guess about what her sister was doing or thinking, and mostly be right because she knew Willow so well. Sometimes, though, the two would get a sense of how the other one was feeling, as if another mirrored presence was passing through. It wasn't an exact science, though; it could never be predicted and it didn't always come at the right time.

'Ah, Dave,' Willow said, rather apologetically.

'What do you mean, "Ah, Dave"? He's gorgeous!'

Willow thought of Dave's half-hearted kisses and almost mechanical caresses.

'No, sorry. He's not for me. And I am not the one for him, either.'

'Oh, Willow.' Holly sounded quite cross. 'I had high hopes for Dave, too.'

'Sorry, sis.' Willow paused by a display of Liberty-print-covered notebooks, picking one up to flick through the blank pages. Since she'd been quite a little girl there had always been something about the neatly bound gilt-edged potential that comforted her. Other little girls had teddy bears, or age-old scraps of material to cuddle up to. It was a blank notebook that Willow always kept under her pillow. The world's most boring secret diary, Holly always said. But Willow knew what she would write in it, if she could, so she didn't have to spoil the beautiful pure white pages with words. Picking up a particularly lavish pink, purple and gold affair, she decided to add it to her purchases, and put it carefully in her drawer full of empty notebooks.

'Well, anyway, I've got to go, you ungrateful wretch,' Holly said, her affectionate tone belying her words. 'Jem seems to have taped Jo-Jo's hair to the underside of the table – but call me later to tell me about your big secret.'

'OK, that was a guess,' Willow said, and her sister hung up without a goodbye.

Willow caught her breath in surprise as the phone rang again and she saw Daniel Fayre's name on her screen. Daniel, the fourth person she would not openly admit to loving.

'What now?' she asked as she took the call, studiously careful to be flippant and brusque, as always.

'Nice,' Daniel laughed. 'Where's the hello, where's the how are you, Dan, what's up, it's been a few days? Did you get that assignment in Panama? None of that, then?'

'Dan, you and I both know you only phone me when you want something. What do you want?'

'I want you!' Daniel teased her, without knowing how, just by uttering those words even in jest, he made Willow's heart ache.

Daniel Fayre: photographer and Willow's former next-door neighbour, back when she had been married. Originally from Fort Worth, Texas, he'd come to the UK in his twenties and, upon discovering that British women could never get enough of his accent, never went back and never lost his accent. Willow had first got talking to him when she'd found him on the steps outside his ground-floor flat, staring bleakly at a smashed bottle of gin that had proved too weighty for the flimsy plastic bag it was in.

'Careful,' Willow had said as she watched him gingerly pick up the shards of glass. 'You might hurt yourself.'

'I might kill myself,' he'd said, directing a heart-melting smile at her. 'I had been planning to drink myself to death, but that was my last ten-pound note.' His American accent pronouncing those alien words had charmed her instantly and, taking pity on him, Willow went to fetch her dustpan and brush, before inviting Dan in for a glass of wine. When she told him her husband imported wine for a living he declared on the spot that she was his new best friend, and somehow that flippant remark had come true. When Willow was lost in the depths of divorce, Daniel had taken it upon himself to look after her. He'd given her a couch to sleep on, the night it all broke down, found her a place to live afterwards and generally patched her up and got her back on her feet, even bringing her a series of TV dinners every night for a month after she'd moved into her new flat, getting them both so drunk that they'd pass out every night on the sofa, heads lolling on each other's shoulder in snoring abandon. Willow wasn't sure exactly when, during all of that, she had decided she loved Daniel, but she was certain that it was a futile longing that would torment her for as long as it endured, which would quite possibly be for ever. Daniel loved her, in his way, and with steadfast loyalty. It was just not at all in the same way that she loved him, which was hopelessly, pointlessly.

'You're sighing – why are you sighing?' Daniel's voice interrupted her train of thought.

'I'm picturing you naked,' Willow told him.

'Then you should be laughing!' Daniel chuckled. 'I'm getting middle-aged, Will. I've got a paunch, an actual paunch, and I think I might be going bald. Will you look at the top of my head for me, because I've the distinct feeling that I'm getting a lot more sun up there than I used to.'

'You want me to look at the top of your head?' Willow caught herself smiling in the mirror as she toyed with the ribbon around the box of chocolates she'd picked up.

'No, I want you to come to dinner tomorrow night and perhaps between courses look at the top of my head, you know, if the conversation is running a little dry.'

'Dinner?' Willow was delighted. Daniel had recently started seeing someone regularly enough for her to be considered a girlfriend. Which meant he didn't require Willow's company for watching films, or eating out or drinking far too much on a week night, and Willow had missed him. Perhaps this invitation meant that this one, a leggy model he'd met on a shoot in Spain, had gone the way of the others and he'd already tired of her. Willow smiled; a night out before India moved in was just what she needed.

'I'm not sure . . .' Willow pretended to play hard to get, although both of them knew it was artifice.

'Willow, I need you. I'm working on something brilliant – real art, for once, instead of prostituting myself and my camera. But I need your thoughts. You know I can't make any decisions until I've talked to you.'

Willow knew she was being shamelessly manipulated, but still she glowed, preening under the caress of his voice. It had been too long since she'd spent time with Daniel, talking nonsense about nothing serious, lying on the decking of his roof garden, gazing at the stars.

'Don't deny me, baby,' Daniel complained. 'Please, Will, I need you.'

'Do you?' Willow asked him softly, each one of her heart-strings expertly tugged. 'I suppose I *might* be able to make it . . .'

Willow closed her eyes for a second. She was going at least to pretend for a few seconds longer; she liked the feeling of Daniel wanting her.

'Think about all of the times I've been there for you. Like that time I came and picked you up at three in the morning from that Australian barman's flat in Earls Court.'

'I know.' Will winced, remembering how she had drunkenly thrown herself at the much younger barman, until he'd relented, taking her back to a one-bedroom flat he shared with six others in Earls Court. Sobering up mid-mistake, Willow had told him she was popping to the loo, quickly dressed and sneaked out of the flat without saying goodbye, stumbling into the early hours of a wet October morning. Daniel had come to fetch her. Even though it was late, and he was drunk and there had been a girl in his bed, he had come. A lot of people, Holly especially, said that Daniel Fayre was no good for her, but, aside from her sister, he was the only person in the whole world who would always come.

'I'll try, I can't say more than that,' Willow told him, already knowing that she'd probably leave India Torrance alone with a cut-throat razor and a hot bath rather than miss spending time with him.

'Great. Kayla – you remember Kayla, right? – she'll be pleased to see you. Ah, and Serious James is coming, he'll be *very* pleased to see you.' Serious James was Daniel's other unlikely best friend, an archetypal accountant who dreamed of being a stand-up comedian. He persisted in this delusion despite so far only testing his talent for timing in a few flea-ridden pubs here and there. He seemed nice enough, with his permanently tousled blond hair, which he wore a little longer than you might expect for an accountant, and his greyish-green eyes, which crinkled when he smiled, were quite attractive; might even be considered very attractive if he wasn't standing next to Daniel Fayre. The trouble was that whenever Willow met him, he was always standing next to Daniel, and whenever he met her – which was getting to be quite frequently recently – he seemed to lose the ability to converse at all. Daniel was enormously fond of his only male friend, perhaps because of his geeky offbeat awkwardness, and he particularly delighted in teasing Willow about the fact that Serious James found her utterly beguiling. Yet somehow the more Daniel told her about James waxing lyrical about her, the less she liked him. Where many single women of a certain age would find his attentions very pleasing, if not something of a relief, it was his poorly closeted adoration for her that put Willow off. She followed the perverse logic that there must be something wrong with someone who could like *her* quite that much.

'Bring someone, if you like. Hey, bring that hot slutty one you hate from work. That will keep Kayla on her toes. The sex is always better when she's really insecure.'

Willow tugged absently at the ribbon on the box of chocolates, barely noticing it give way as she fought the disappointment of a rejection she hadn't even known she was in line for. She could still say no, of course, call him later with apologies.

But to pass up the chance to spend a whole evening in the company of Daniel, making jokes with him that his girlfriend wouldn't understand, laughing about Serious James behind his back, drinking so much that every nerve ending was lulled into a false sense of security, was hard to do, even if every moment of pleasure would be simultaneously blended with pain.

'If I lose my job over this you'll have to marry me, you understand that, don't you?' Willow heard the wistful edge to her voice too late, knowing Daniel had heard it too.

'Babe, you are the only woman I would ever marry, you know that, don't you?' he told her with practised sincerity.

'So you say,' Willow said with a mouthful of chocolate, which gave her pause. As she looked down at the box of chocolates, its lid askew, it became apparent that one of them had already found its way into her mouth. In fact, on closer inspection, it seemed that she had finished off three during the conversation and had barely even noticed.

'*Ciao, bello*,' Willow sighed, popping the last two chocolates into her mouth as Daniel hung up. Turning round, she found herself confronted by the watchful shop assistant.

'Are you planning on paying for those?' the woman asked, with more than a hint of accusation.

'Yes,' Willow said. 'And I'd better take another couple of boxes too, please.'

'Of course, madam,' the woman said as she bustled off to retrieve more chocolates, the look on her face giving away exactly what she thought of Willow.

Willow winced internally, brushing her long hair off her face and shaking her shoulders briefly as if she could shake off the darkness that sometimes engulfed her. Why had she picked

Daniel Fayre to be in love with? Because he was absolutely, totally, one hundred per cent guaranteed never to love her back, that was why.

Chapter Three

Without really thinking about it, Willow turned right when she left Liberty, choosing the back way to the office, rather than attempting to navigate Regent Street, thronged as it continuously was with tourists and day-trippers, intent on ambling along aimlessly exactly wherever she wanted to be. It was a sign of a practised city dweller to take the road less travelled, but it was more than finding a short cut for Willow, who was perfectly well aware that she chose to travel via the backstreets because there it was less obvious that no one noticed her. Once Willow would have put it down to the opposite: that she hated the thought of strangers judging her wobbly thighs or generous stomach, remarking to each other, 'Look at the state of *that*,' not quite under their breath.

But quite recently she had been compelled to walk the short distance between the office and the Athenaeum Club with Lucy on the way to a party being held in celebration of an elderly and slightly alcoholic actor's long and illustrious career in the theatre, although, as Victoria bitterly reminded everyone, in all that time he had never managed to break into film, not even to pay a requisite villain or a wizard in *Harry Potter*, and a knighthood was all very well but she didn't get twenty per cent of *that*.

Willow had been pretty pleased with her outfit, a black cotton full-skirted dress, with a sweetheart neckline that hinted at her deep cleavage, the skirt skimming the top of her knees, showing off her pleasingly turned fake-tanned calves, which were accentuated by the very high heels of her Prada sling-backs. And then Lucy emerged from the ladies in some tiny white Grecian-style frock that barely covered her modesty in any respect.

Cheerfully breaking the low-neckline, long-skirt rule with some aplomb, she bared about as much of her shapely slim frame as she could get away with, without being arrested for breeching decency laws, and sporting a pair of heeled gold gladiator sandals with straps that wound all the way up to her knees.

'Wow, Lucy, does your boyfriend know you're going out like that?' Marcus Blane, head of legal, commented, naked admiration all over his face.

'What he doesn't know won't hurt him, lol.' Lucy had winked at Marcus, who looked like he was only seconds away from actually salivating, which reminded Willow rather uncomfortably how, after working late one night last year, he'd offered to take her out for a drink and she'd ended up giving him a blow job in Victoria's office. An incident neither of them spoke of again.

Willow had never felt less attractive as she trailed along beside Lucy that evening, and never more conscious that everyone they passed – every man, woman and child of every sexual orientation – not only noticed Lucy, but even turned their heads to look at her. By the time they reached their destination Willow was hot, her brow beaded with sweat, her thighs rubbing together uncomfortably and her small swell of pride at feeling quite nicely turned out withering in the glare of Lucy's golden splendour. Lucy was a good deal younger than Willow, of course, but Willow was faced with the knowledge that if she had managed to stay a healthy size eight, like her sister, or even the size she had been during those happy days of flat-sharing, she certainly would have given Lucy a run for her money. Despite her wilful refusal to do anything about her shape or size, Willow was still a little vain, and it hurt her to realise that, at the age of thirty-nine, she had become invisible.

Lost in her thoughts, Willow stopped on the kerb to get her bearings. Somehow she'd taken a wrong turning. She'd routinely taken a little-known alleyway, charmingly called Portal Way, that ran parallel to Regent Street, branching off Carnaby Street, so narrow that if you didn't know about it you'd assume that it was nothing more than a side access to one of the fashionable shops.

Normally Willow emerged from Portal Way onto the north side of Golden Square but somehow she'd gone wrong in the hundred yards or so of alleyway, because now she found herself in a small square, really more of a courtyard, that was entirely shadowed from the glare of the midday sun by tall windowless buildings, which Willow assumed had to be the back of something. There didn't seem to be an exit from the square, which a dirty half-dislodged sign told her was Bleeding Heart Yard, W1, and Willow could not for the life of her work out how she'd never stumbled on this curious little corner of London before. The courtyard was covered entirely in cracked paving, infested with half-dead weeds, and in its centre stood a forlorn and ragged-looking tree, drooping over the circular iron railing that imprisoned it. A willow tree, Willow noticed wryly, picking up a crushed catkin from the ground and rubbing it into a yellowish powder between her thumb and finger. It was very quiet in the square, the din of London silenced by the surrounding buildings. For a moment Willow stood there, enjoying the peace, content to let the shadows bathe her in cool quiet calm, feeling almost weightless in this undiscovered inner space, and then something bristled the hairs on the back of her neck and forearms, and a sense of disquiet rushed through the air, along with a strong gust of wind that dashed yet more delicate catkins to the ground.

Unsettled, Willow was about to turn back when the jingle of an old-fashioned shop bell echoed around the square. For a moment it was hard to tell where it had come from, but then Willow realised there could only be one place: the three or four feet obscured by the tree's dishevelled canopy. Peeping around the tree like a little girl entering a forbidden room, Willow discovered a shop window nestling incongruously amongst the expanse of Georgian brickwork. Hesitant, she found herself looking over her shoulder. No one had passed her while she had been standing here and the dark, squat door that stood to the left of the window looked firmly shut, and yet she had definitely heard a bell ringing. And there was something else: her heart was racing, not from fear or anxiety, but something Willow recognised as a kind of prescient optimism. The certain knowledge that something really good was going to happen. Navigating the reach of the tree, Willow approached the shop, the echo of her heels ricocheting off the windowless walls.

There was no name over the door, which wasn't unusual in this part of town. Some of the more upscale designers seemed to think that the harder it was to find your store, the more exclusive it became, and there was certainly an element of truth in that. But even so, what shop could possibly survive here, where even the plant life struggled to exist?

Willow peered through the dirty glass. The window was bare except for a single pair of shoes, placed toes turned in on an upturned wine crate, as if they were just about to click their heels together and wish for home. Willow felt her pulse quicken again. Shoes, that made sense. This was not a shop, but a *workshop*, and in the window a single example of . . . Willow pulled the sleeve of her shirt over her wrist and rubbed a small clean circle in the centre of the film of grime. She gasped. They were quite simply the most beautiful pair of shoes that she had ever seen. Unwittingly, she pressed her palm against the glass, the tip of her nose grazing its surface as she admired them. Whatever material they were made from, Willow had never seen a finish like it. Black at first glance, a myriad of colours shimmered under the surface when you looked closely. Like a rainbow reflected in rippling water, they seemed to sparkle, somehow, deep set with an infinite universe of stars. Best of all, the high elegant heels, which looked as if they could have been made from crystal glass, resembled the stems of champagne glasses.

'Oh, I want *you*,' Willow found herself whispering out loud, the endless chasm in her chest opening up like a yawning mouth demanding to be fed again. She knew Victoria would be waiting for her back at the office, she knew that India Torrance was due to arrive any minute, and Victoria would be furious with her if she was late back with the chocolates. But stumbling across Bleeding Heart Yard, finding these shoes – this was what the good feeling fizzing in her veins was all about. This was fate. The universe had brought her here to find these shoes. These shoes were surely her soul mates.

Willow tried the door, expecting to find it locked, and was surprised when it opened with a jingle of a brass bell. She paused for a moment, some small dark memory nibbling at the edges of her thoughts holding her back for a second.

The shop smelled of dusty books, damp cheap paperbacks, which, even without seeing them, Willow knew would have yellowed pages, dog-eared corners and cracked spines. The sharply evocative scent left Willow feeling disconcerted, disjointed, as if she were missing something obvious and important. What books and shoes were doing in the same shop she couldn't fathom, but her longing for the shoes outweighed her instinctive reservations.

'Nothing ventured,' she whispered, stepping over the threshold, dimly sensing a point of no return.

The interior was dark, cool and quiet, except for the ticking of a clock somewhere. There were no other shoes anywhere to be seen, and she realised immediately she was wrong; this *was* a shop, a junk shop, hidden here, in the heart of everywhere and the middle of nowhere all at once.

Willow looked around. There was a glass cabinet half filled with an assortment of rings, a hand-written sign taped to the lid that read 'Second-hand Engagement Rings'. A rack of clothes hung along one wall, jam-packed with a collection of colours and fabrics that seemed to span decades of bad taste, including one flea-bitten ankle-length fur coat which looked like it should be hanging in the back of the wardrobe which led directly to Narnia. There were shelves of grubby paperbacks, piles of sheet music and possibly manuscripts stacked in precarious leaning towers all around the door; display cabinets laden with dusty ornaments: figurines of rosy-cheeked dancing girls, big-eyed begging puppy dogs and chubby-cheeked gurgling babies, which Willow knew, just by looking at them, had once been someone's pride and joy, a cherished object carefully dusted and admired regularly until somehow it had found its way here, this curious place.

Willow chewed her bottom lip. She was experiencing the oddest feeling of *déjà vu*, although she was certain she had never been here before.

'Hello?' she called out. There was no reply. 'Hello? I was just passing and I wanted to look at the pair of shoes in your window?'

Willow waited for a few moments, but there was no sign of life from behind the multicoloured plastic-beaded curtain, which hung perfectly still, shrouding off whatever mysteries lay behind it.

Serial killer, maybe, Willow thought. Maybe all these things are trophies, of the victims lured back here to be hacked to bits with a chainsaw, never to be seen again. Willow looked at the door. She could just leave. But on the other hand, those shoes were worth a skirmish with a psychopath. Besides, she was a pretty big girl; it would take a whole lot of killer to floor her without a fight.

'I'll just try them on, if that's OK?' Willow called out again, feeling a cloud of butterflies rise in her tummy as she approached the shoes.

'Please be my size, please be my size, please be my size,' she whispered as she picked one up, turning it over. The smooth leather sole was unmarked, and on closer inspection so was the velvet-lined interior of the shoe, with no sign of a size. They looked about right, Willow thought, wondering, even as she slipped off the shoes she was wearing, how much in denial she was prepared to be about how cramped her toes were, if it came to it. There was no seating, so, careful to avoid the piles of paper, she bent over and slipped on one shoe. Her foot slotted perfectly into the pointed toe, but Willow did not breathe out just yet. One of her feet – she could never remember which – was half a size bigger than the other one. What if the shoes fitted only the small foot? What if she'd put her small foot in first and bitter disappointment was still a certainty? Glancing briefly over her shoulder at the static bead curtain Willow put the other shoe on. It fitted perfectly.

'Oh,' Willow said, as she looked down at her feet, pressing her breasts out of the way with one hand so that she could get a better look. 'Oh, oh, I *love* you.'

'Would you like a mirror?'

Willow squeaked, whipping round to find an old lady regarding her from behind the counter, the bead curtain as still and silent as it had been a moment before.

'Pardon?' Willow croaked, feeling a lot like she had been caught out in some kind of act.

'A mirror, so you can get a good look at them? Without having to . . .' the old lady grabbed her own breasts in demonstration, ' . . . juggle.'

'Er . . . yes, please, if you've got one,' Willow said, unhanding her breasts rather sheepishly.

The woman was short and squat, with long dyed black hair, tied into a bun on the nape of her neck, an inch of white roots fanning either side of a centre parting. She was wearing something that looked like it had once hung on the clothes rack, a full-length kaftan dyed a multitude of colours in thick bands of colours, like a walking rainbow. She waddled out from behind the counter and pulled a tie-dyed sheet off a full-length mirror that had been hiding in the corner behind an assortment of odd Wellington boots.

'Keeps the dust off,' the woman told her, gesturing for Willow to look in the mirror. 'I like to keep the place tidy.'

Anxiously Willow made her way to meet her reflection. Trying on anything, particularly clothes, was always fraught with anxiety. Every shopping expedition was a double-edged sword. First there would be the fear that she wouldn't find anything that would suit her demanding frame, then the worry that once she had found something they wouldn't have it in her size, followed by the fear that even if they did have it in her size, it would be made for a different kind of her size, the kind without any bust or hips, and she wouldn't be able to get it on anyway. Finally there was always the deadly possibility that even if it did fit, she would look awful in it. This happened less with shoes, which was partly why Willow loved them so much. But it did happen. Sometimes she just looked at her generous figure teetering on the brink of ten centimetres of heel and acknowledged that she looked like a fat woman in a posh pair of shoes. Briefly Willow closed her eyes just as she approached the mirror. When she opened them she could not have been more pleased.

There was something about the shoes – something more than their style or finish – that suited her quite literally down to the ground. They seemed to be perfectly proportioned, making her feet look smaller, her calves longer and, as Willow hitched up her wide-legged trousers to her knees, maybe even just a little bit slimmer. In fact, as she turned this way and that to get a full view of the shoes, Willow thought that her bottom looked a good deal less tightly packed into the trousers then it had done this morning, when she'd seriously debated the risks of a seam malfunction on the tube, before leaving for work. It must have been some kind of optical illusion because now she felt almost weightless, hovering above the floor as if she'd discovered the secret to defying gravity.

'So these are second-hand then?' Willow asked the old lady, who leaned against the counter, her shelf of a bosom resting on her folded arms.

'Or second-footed,' the old lady chuckled. 'Yes, a young lady brought them in last week, or the week before . . . or possibly last year. Time doesn't mean much when you get to my age; you just wake up surprised to still be alive.'

Reluctantly Willow slipped the shoes off, feeling the traction of grit under her stockinged feet as she picked them up, turning them over, looking for some indication as to where they came from. Their basic shape was so classic that it was impossible to age them. They could be anything up to fifty years old, perhaps even older, and there were no identifying marks on them at all. Perhaps they were prototypes, Willow thought, feeling the same sort of excitement that she imagined Howard Carter must have felt when uncovering the steps to Tutankhamun's tomb. One-offs that never made it into mass production.

'They look like they've never been worn,' Willow said, stroking the smooth leather of the sole with the palm of her hand. 'Did the woman that brought them in tell you anything about them? The designer's name, how much they cost new?'

The old lady tipped her head to one side as if perplexed by Willow's questions. 'Nope, just that she didn't need them any more, and that she wanted them to go to someone who did, or something like that. I don't know, I forget a lot these days.' She gestured at Willow's prize. 'I can tell you they are shoes.'

Willow hugged them to her chest. 'Well, I'm going to take them. How much are they?'

The woman held out her hand, beckoning for them, and grudgingly Willow parted with the shoes, half afraid that this strange old lady in this strange little shop might change her mind about selling her the shoes at all. Mentally she calculated exactly how much she was prepared to pay and settled, rather extravagantly, on anything under five hundred pounds.

The woman sniffed, puckering her lips as she examined the shoes. 'Do you read?' she asked Willow.

Confused, but sensing that her fortunes relied rather heavily on her answer, Willow nodded noncommittally.

'Right, well, you can have 'em for twenty quid if you take twenty of them books. I can't shift them books and I've read them all now. None of them's worth a light.'

'Twenty pounds?' Willow repeated. 'Are you sure?'

'And them books.' The old lady nodded emphatically at the row of abandoned paperbacks. Willow wanted to bite her chewy old arm off, but her conscience would not let her.

'It's just, well, that doesn't seem like enough,' she said.

'All right, take that china dog then too. You drive a hard bargain, missy!' the old lady chuckled.

'No, I mean . . . it doesn't seem like enough for *me* to pay. How about I give you . . . fifty?'

'But you're still taking the books and the dog, yeah?' the old lady pressed her. 'And you can have that fur coat too, if you're going to give me fifty.'

'But I . . .' Willow caught the look in the old woman's eyes and didn't want to risk offending her by turning down a coat that she absolutely did not want.

'Ok,' she complied. 'Whatever you say.'

'You've made the right decision,' the woman said cheerfully, dragging the heavy coat off its hanger and stuffing it into a black bin liner. 'Funny, isn't it, how a wrong turn can change everything? You'll be a different person from today, you'll see, and when you're finished with them, bring them back and pass them on to the next one who's lost her way.'

'OK . . .' Willow humoured her. 'I suppose you don't get much passing trade down here – how do you keep going?'

'I don't need passing trade, love. This is a destination store.' The old woman winked at her as she took an indiscriminate wedge of paperbacks off the shelf and dumped them on top of the coat. Much stronger than she looked, she lifted the bag, testing its durability. 'They don't make these like they used to – all that global warming nonsense – but it should hold; you haven't got far to go.'

'Thank you so much. I'll tell everyone at the office about you. It's like . . . like a grotto of treasures!' Willow smiled warmly when finally the old lady handed her her shoes and she slipped them, toe first into her handbag, alongside her new china dog.

'You don't need to tell anyone about me, love. People find me when they have to. That's always been the way of it.'

'Well, then, thank you and goodbye.'

'I'll see you again.' The woman nodded at Willow's bag. 'When you're done with them, I'll see you again.'

'I don't think I'll ever be done with them!' Willow laughed, but the look of conviction on the woman's face didn't waver.

Feeling a little bit like she might be about to commit daylight robbery, Willow pressed her fifty pounds down on the counter, and headed for the door, her heavy burden toppling a hat rack just as she was about to make her escape.

'Oh God, I'm sorry. I'm so sorry!' Willow said.

'Not to worry.' The woman, surprisingly nimble, righted it again in one fluid movement. 'It wasn't your fault, you remember that.'

'OK, right. I will. Thanks again!' Willow waved awkwardly, suddenly very keen to be gone, dragging her unwanted fur coat and collection of books across Bleeding Heart Yard, past the wan little willow tree and back down Portal Way out into the noise and chaos of Carnaby Street. Autumnal rain needling her cheeks, she stopped, slipped off her old shoes and put on her new ones, immediately feeling elated with that particular kind of high that came from buying something. But it was more than that; as Willow finally started back to the office, she felt lighter, brighter. She didn't care that she'd been gone for over an hour and Victoria would be threatening to have her guts for garters. For the fourteen minutes it took her to navigate her way back to Golden Square, Willow Briars felt curiously invincible.

Chapter Four

'Where have you been?' Lucy asked her, wide-eyed, as Willow dragged her bin bag into the office, like the carcass of a mouldering beast, which in many ways it was. 'And what on earth is that stink?'

It had not become apparent until the lift doors closed on Willow that the coat actually smelled quite badly of mothballs and mould, and very, very faintly, haunting its musty folds and creases, the echo of someone else's perfume. Really, Willow thought, as she wondered where she could put it that wouldn't contravene health and safety regulations, she should have just dumped it with the other piles of bin liners that collected around the bottom of the streetlamps outside the office, but she couldn't bring herself to do it. The old lady had wanted her to have the coat and, for reasons that Willow couldn't put her finger on, she felt she ought to keep it, despite the stench, even if only for a night.

'It's a fur coat,' Willow said, with an insouciant shrug as if it was perfectly normal.

'A fur coat? Meat is murder, you know, lol!' Lucy giggled, between bites of a bacon double cheeseburger, that ordinarily Willow would have complained about her eating at her desk, but as she had trumped the stink with a virtual corpse she decided to let it pass.

'Hmm, not quite the same thing, but I respect your views, such as they are.' Willow's smile snapped on and off again. 'Have I missed anything?'

'Well, it's all cloak and dagger in there,' Lucy nodded at Victoria's office. 'What's going on, Will? Why is India Torrance in there in a hat and shades? Nose job? Nervous exhaustion?' Lucy made air quotation marks around the last two words. Everybody knew, even Lucy, that nervous exhaustion was the international celebrity code for a drug problem.

'Remember that watertight confidentiality agreement that you signed when you got this job? The one that, if you break it, means that Victoria can legally have you consigned to the bowels of hell for all eternity? Or worse, temping?'

'Yes?' Lucy's eyes widened.

'Don't ask, then. Unless Victoria tells us to, we see nothing, we hear nothing, we do nothing, we know nothing, which in your case is more true than usual.'

'Well, *you* must know something,' Lucy said, slightly offended. 'She wants *you* in there A-sap.'

'Lucy. "A-sap" is not a word, it's an acronym. Like "lol".'

Lucy blinked at her, not one iota of understanding registering on her face.

'So they're in Victoria's office, then?' Willow asked.

'Yes, have been for ages, and you are to go in right away and . . .' Lucy cocked her head to one side and examined Willow in a way that made her want to wipe her nose and check her teeth with her tongue. 'There's something different about you,' Lucy muttered. 'What have you done to yourself since you went out?

Is it your hair? Did you have cheeky spray tan? I swear you look like you've lost weight since this morning, lol! Maybe I've got a brain tumour.'

Willow eyed Victoria's closed office door, refusing to be irritated by Lucy's assertion that she'd have to have a fatal growth in her head in order to think that Willow looked good. Victoria's wrath versus showing off new shoes . . . A few more seconds wouldn't make any difference.

'Oh, I don't know,' she said nonchalantly, edging up the hem of her wide-legged trousers to reveal more shoe. 'It might be . . . these!' Willow pointed her toe with a flourish, gratified to see Lucy's eyes widen in delight.

'Oh my God, they are *lovely*. I need some of those! Where did you get them?'

'One-off, a vintage pair,' Willow told her, delighted by the dismay on Lucy's face. 'You won't find another pair like them anywhere in the world. Laugh out loud!'

'Can I try them on, please!' Lucy begged, and at that moment Willow wouldn't have been surprised if her colleague hadn't thrown herself round her leg. It was a wonderful moment of power that Willow wasn't especially proud of herself for enjoying, but enjoy it she did anyhow.

'No, they're mine, and I have to go now for a very important secret meeting.' Willow paused for one moment more, enjoying the naked envy on Lucy's face. 'You can try on my fur coat, if you like. You might have to kill it first, though.'

Willow had learned in her life that sometimes there was absolutely nothing you could do to prepare for what was coming next. You just had to keep your chin up, take a deep breath and get on with it. She had decided when she was really quite young that that was the way life worked: a test of endurance, punctuated here and there with exquisite little bubbles of happiness that burst too quickly, usually as a result of her own clumsiness. Contentment was an elusive concept, one she had difficulty understanding. She only knew that almost as soon as she allowed herself to be happy she was beset by fear and a quiet but resolute certainty that it would not last. It meant that she almost preferred her life to be a flat, empty, featureless landscape, with no mountain peaks or deep valleys for disappointment or regret to lurk in. She had no idea how her enforced relationship with India Torrance would go, but there was very little she could do to avoid it now. It was one of those things to be got on with.

As Willow put her hand on the door she thought of Daniel, dancing her around the bandstand in St James's Park at three o'clock on a Sunday morning, and then 'making' her stay awake drinking espressos with him in Soho, until he could escort her to work still in a sequinned dress and ripped tights. Such were the bubbles, tiny bubbles, she thought, that burst too soon. But like she'd always told herself, you have to have the bad stuff to deserve the good.

'There you are,' Victoria said, eyeing Willow over the rim of the glasses that she did not need and wore only when she felt the situation required extra *gravitas*.

'I know, I am so sorry.' Willow advanced, chocolates first. 'I just, well . . .' She turned to India Torrance, who was curled up in Victoria's armchair, a baseball cap drawn down over her face, her arms encircling her drawn-up knees, and still wearing an outsize pair of Chanel sunglasses, which made her look like she'd been in her mum's dressing-up box. 'Chocolate?'

'India's in quite a bad way, aren't you, darling?' Victoria said, gesturing for Willow to take a seat. 'As I told you earlier, Hugh's basically pissed all over her in a bid to save his career and a bankrupting divorce settlement. He's telling the press she set out to seduce him from day one, and that he is weak and fallible and an idiot, that he loves his wife and children, and India is a cold-hearted temptress who is basically trying to sleep her way to the top.'

A sob rose from the armchair, and India buried her head in her arms. Victoria looked at Willow, who discerned from what might have been a slight pursing of her artificially enhanced lips that she was expecting Willow to say something comforting.

'I'm . . . I'm so sorry,' Willow offered, leaning towards the younger woman. 'I've been through a divorce and I know what it's like to—'

'Have your husband whisked away by a slut?' India's head whipped up, her sunglasses sliding down her damp nose to reveal swollen, red raw eyes.

'That's not what I'm saying. It's just, this is painful. Losing someone you love. I know how that feels. It hurts but it does . . .' Willow wanted to say 'get better' but she wasn't entirely sure that was strictly accurate. '. . . it eases, after a while.'

'Darling, don't waste your tears on the cunt,' Victoria cut in impatiently, with a flourish of her scarlet nail extensions. 'Honestly, if you'd chosen to fuck anyone else on that set it would have been fine. Why, Indi? Why, darling? If you'd have called me I'd have said, don't touch that utter twat with a barge-pole! Sleep with the director, that makes much more sense;

even one of the writers at a push. Needy but often useful, writers.'

India raised her head, taking her glasses off to reveal a tear-streaked face.

'It wasn't about the sex, it was so much more than that,' she said on a ragged breath. 'He listened to me, he understood what it's like to be me, and that's so, so rare.'

'He manipulated and used you,' Victoria retorted, just about keeping in check her anger at the curve ball she'd been dealt. She took a breath, reaching into her bag for something, most likely Valium based, which she popped discreetly into her mouth and swallowed with a gulp of coffee. 'It's not your fault. You're green, wet behind the ears – of course you fell for his bullshit.'

India's bottom lip trembled perilously.

'Perhaps now's not the time to do the post-mortem thing . . .' Willow suggested, but Victoria was in full flow.

'What about the teen make-up range, the English Rose contract? They tend not to sign up slutty adulteresses as role models, you know.'

'Victoria . . .' Willow attempted to intervene again, her tone a fraction firmer.

Victoria took her glasses off and tossed them on the table so that they slid over the polished wood like a glass of whiskey across a bar in a Western saloon.

'I'm sorry, Willow, but one of the reasons I'm the best in this business is because I'm not afraid to tell it like it is. I don't do brown-nosing.'

'I know!' Willow said, pulling her chair closer to India's. 'I know you don't, but look at her. Despite all the fame, she's barely an adult and this is her first real heartbreak. You and I both know you'll find a way to spin it so her career isn't wrecked – you always do – and if I know you, you'll make money doing it. But for now can we just see the broken-hearted young woman sitting here who needs a shoulder to cry on, and stop dwelling on the more . . . commercial elements?'

Victoria paused, something akin to confusion settling on her faultless brow, as she pinched the bridge of her nose.

'Stunned as I am to admit it, Willow is right. We're agreed that you won't be grovelling to the tabloids over this. You have the weekend to indulge yourself at Blakes to take stock, get things into perspective, to start to *mend*, darling. And then when the story breaks on Sunday we'll need to squirrel you away for a bit. Willow's agreed to let you stay with her. It really is the best option.' In a move that was so out of character it was pure Victoria, Willow watched with mild horror as her boss got up, walked around her desk, kneeled at India's feet and put her arms around her, pressing the young girl's cheek into her silk-clad bosom. 'Don't you worry about a thing. You leave it all to Victoria, darling, I'll look after you. And when we've moved you out of Blakes, Willow will feed you up, let you watch as much telly as you like, give you plenty of girly chats, won't you, Will?'

'Yes,' Willow said, inwardly screaming in horror as she watched Victoria's talons stroke India's head. 'Of course. Or, alternatively, give you lots and lots and . . . lots of space. And time. To be . . . alone?'

'I don't think I can bear to be alone. When I'm alone that's when I start to think, and . . .'

Victoria smothered India's building sob with her bosom. 'Shush now, my darling, shush.' She rolled her eyes at Willow and released India's head abruptly. 'So we're agreed, I'll keep the vultures at bay for now and when the shit hits the fan you'll lie low at Will's place until the storm's passed. It's not The Ritz, darling, but I promise you no one will think to look for you *there*.'

Victoria clicked her fingers at Willow, who stooped to help her up.

India looked up at Willow, dragging her hat off and running her fingers through the tumble of brown hair that tangled round her shoulders. She sniffed and mustered a weak smile. 'Thank you for having me,' she said, like a well-schooled child.

'My pleasure. I've got chocolate.' Willow offered a box to India, who took it and hugged it to her chest.

'Right, well. Tell you what, you go and freshen up, and, Willow, you can take the rest of the day off, get India to Blakes, make sure she's settled. I'll get my car sent round the back in twenty minutes. Do you want Willow to come with you, darling?'

'No, I'm fine,' India said, dragging herself out of the chair, pulling her cap back down low over her eyes as she left the room.

'Any sharp objects in the ladies – shoe laces, bleach, anything that might prove a bit fatal?' Victoria asked, the moment that India departed.

'Not that I know of,' Willow said uneasily.

'Do you know,' Victoria put her hands on her hips and looked Willow up and down, 'you look marvellous. What's changed since this morning? It's me putting my faith in you, isn't it? You feel honoured, I can tell.'

'Are you saying I looked terrible this morning?' Willow countered.

'I'm saying . . . Will, learn to take a compliment, darling. And anyway, well done,' Victoria said with satisfaction. 'I thought you played that whole good cop, bad cop thing marvellously well.'

'I didn't know I was playing good cop, bad cop,' Willow frowned.

'Yes, darling. I beat her up, you comfort her. Now she trusts you. I'm quite sure that between the two of us we'll be able to keep her on the straight and narrow.'

'As opposed to what?' Willow asked.

'As opposed to her blabbing and blubbing all over the press. That skinny little scrap is my retirement plan and I will not let her fuck up my yacht in St Tropez.'

'You already have a yacht in St Tropez.'

'Do I? Well then, I will not have her fuck up my yacht in St Barts. From now on you are on call for India Torrance. Either you keep her under control and out of the limelight or I'll be forced to stage her suicide myself so that I can make money out the serialisation of the book about her tragic life.'

Willow would have laughed, but she wasn't entirely sure that Victoria was joking.

Chapter Five

Willow slid her front door key into the lock, but hesitated in turning it. Normally she felt pure relief to be able finally to shut herself away from the world, but she was uneasy about leaving India alone in her suite and she wondered if she should go back, her desire to be at home fighting with the splinter of discomfort that nagged at her.

India had seemed so fragile in the midst of all the black silk and gilded furniture, lost in opulence, out of place despite her acquired sense of entitlement. She was famous, world famous, but unlike many of the stars that Willow had dealt with since she came to work for Victoria, her celebrity seemed to sit uneasily on her narrow shoulders.

'All this crying has made me ugly,' India had said, in that perfect cut-glass English accent of an age gone by. As soon as Willow had unlocked the door to her room, India had crossed to a gigantic rococo-style mirror that hung over the dressing table to examine herself. Her fine fingers traced their way over her cheeks and down her neck, as she lifted her chin, peering down her arrow-straight nose at her reflection. 'I think I've aged ten years, at least.'

'Well, you looked only about eleven to begin with, so that's OK,' Willow said.

Victoria had told Willow to check the room for, and remove, anything that might be used to self-harm, but as there were enough swags and curtain ties to strangle a small army in a room inspired by Bedouin tents and *Arabian Nights*, she decided the task would be impossible without hiring a removal van. Besides, although India was certainly deeply upset, she didn't seem suicidal. Willow had once seen the look of a person who didn't care if they lived or died, and India didn't have it.

Willow hovered hopefully by the door.

'Anything you want me to organise for you before I go?' She silently prayed that India wouldn't ask her to stay.

Trailing over to the bed, India collapsed into its black duchesse satin depths, her alabaster-white skin contrasting starkly with the surroundings. She looked like a Pre-Raphaelite oil painting or one of the perfume ads she was lined up to star in, staring up at the canopy over her bed, unseeing. Willow suspected she was trying to think of some demands appropriate to a celebrity of her status.

India propped her head up on her hand and assumed a haughty expression. 'Yes. Some water, please, room temperature, and some fruit, not mango. I hate mango. I'd like some strawberries, organic, from inside the EU, keep down the air miles, and some grilled skate, with a side of samphire – but the fish must be fresh, caught this morning. I don't like to eat anything that has had more than twenty-four hours to rot.' She lifted her head and smiled apologetically. 'Is that OK?'

'This is Blakes; if you wanted chocolate-coated oysters served on a bed of kitten, that would be OK.' Willow smiled. 'Are *you* OK, though? Don't you have anyone – any of your people – to keep you company? A friend or PA or something?'

It was the inevitable truth that the more famous a person became the more they had to pay someone to be there for them.

India dragged herself into a sitting position, hugging a pillow over her abdomen. 'Victoria says no. She says that someone tipped off the press, that some hack might have got lucky and come across me and Hugh together with a long lens, but that it took an insider to get the phone messages, and the details of where we . . . met up. She says once she's found out who it is she'll arrange to have them disappeared . . . but that's just her idea of a joke, right?'

'Probably,' Willow nodded, noncommittal.

'So, no PA for me, for now. Although I'm sure it wasn't Martha. She's more of a friend than an employee, she just wouldn't. I'm sorry, how boring for you, to be dumped with all this.'

'Not at all, it's my job. I've done worse. Really.' India's gaze drifted away and she stared out of the window at the wet grey afternoon outside, the sky so low and dark it felt as if night might have fallen already. Willow cringed, thinking of her sofa. All the wonders that Blakes had to offer didn't compare to the thought of putting her feet up and falling asleep in front of the TV with a share-size bag of crisps and half a bottle of wine. But still . . .

'I *could* stay?' she offered reluctantly.

India shook her head, smiling weakly. 'No, I want to be alone, in the words of Garbo. I need to miss him, and if you're here I'll have to be keeping my chin up and going on about what a bastard he is. The sorry truth is, I don't feel that way, and I just can't believe he feels the way he's talking about me.'

'Right then. Well, you've got my number, so any problems at all and—'

'Do you think I disappointed him?' India lifted the neck of her sweatshirt and peered down it, before looking back up at Willow. 'Physically, I mean. Look at me, I have the body of a boy. You have very big breasts.' She cocked her head to one side as she unashamedly observed Willow's bosom. 'My head could fit in one of your cups. I've got no tits at all. Hugh said he loved my body. Untouched by life, he said. But he wasn't ever very . . . enthusiastic. I thought it was because our love was more spiritual than carnal . . . Do you think I'd look good with bigger breasts?'

Willow patted the door handle affectionately, and took a few steps back into the room.

'Well, it's easy enough to get to a G cup. I don't know why people pay thousands of pounds for surgery. All you have to do is eat double your own weight in KFC at least twice a week, and Bob's your uncle: a cleavage you could sink the *Titanic* in.'

India's smile was barely there but at least it was present. 'I would do that, but actually it doesn't matter what I eat, I can't put weight on. There was a photo of me in *Grazia* the other week, wondering if I had an eating disorder, but the truth is I'm just skinny. I could eat my own weight in KFC every day and all that would happen would be I'd die of a heart attack before the age of thirty.' India patted her concave tummy and then rested her palm on it, a deep furrow slotting between her brows. 'I wanted to say something, say I'm not anorexic, but Victoria says you must never say anything. Keep them guessing, that's what Victoria says.'

'To be honest, Victoria doesn't think that a spot of anorexia is necessarily a bad thing. The big fashion houses make a lot of noise about "healthy-sized" models, but really the thinner the better.'

'I've never understood that.' India tightened her squeeze on the pillow over her stomach, as if she were imagining a wider girth. 'Look at you, you're not skinny and you're gorgeous. If I were a man I'd much rather be in bed with a woman like you than a woman like me. You've got bits and bobs to fiddle with in all the right places. But you've definitely lost weight since that awards thing Victoria made me go to.'

Willow thought about what had become both her Nemesis and her obsession: the digital scales in her bathroom. They had steadily crept up by three pounds since that event.

'I don't think I have. I think it's these shoes – they must make my legs look longer or something.' In one fluid and entirely uncharacteristic movement, Willow left the refuge of the doorway, popped her shoe-clad foot onto the lacquered bedside table and pulled up her trouser leg.

India gasped, her eyes widening. 'They are perfect! I've never seen any shoes that are so . . . just lovely, but then I'm normally a trainers sort of person.'

'They're one-offs, a vintage pair. I found them in this weird little junk shop. Just sitting there. They fit me perfectly and they must do *something* for me, because ever since I've put them on people keep complimenting me, and no one ever compliments me.'

Finding it slightly more challenging to remove her leg gracefully from the table, Willow half stumbled, half hopped across India, collapsing on the bed next to her, gratified to hear the young woman chuckle as she landed with an audible puff of air being expelled with some force from goose-down pillows.

'Show me again,' India commanded, and Willow cheerfully

obliged, lifting her leg up slightly and pointing her toe as she displayed one shoe and then the other.

'Perhaps that's what I need – shoes,' India said wistfully. 'If I was more sophisticated, if I dressed like an adult, then maybe . . . maybe Hugh wouldn't have just left me. Have you seen his wife? She looks so proper, like a proper person. Not like me, I don't look proper at all. Perhaps if I have better shoes . . .'

'New shoes can cure almost everything temporarily but it would be very rare for them to manage so much.'

'Maybe, or maybe I can substitute shoes for love, and be happy. Like you.' India realised what she said the second it came out of her mouth, clapping her hands over the offending orifice, her green eyes widening. 'I didn't mean . . .'

'No, it's fine.' Willow was not offended. 'Maybe I have substituted shoes for love. I'm fifteen years older than you, I've had plenty of lovers, I've been married, and still . . . well, still there isn't anyone who appears to love me. And maybe that and some wonderful shoes is just my life.'

'But that's so sad,' India said, impulsively putting her hand on Willow's knee. 'And so not true. No one is meant to be alone. There is always someone for everyone.' Her head alighted unexpectedly on Willow's shoulder.

'Only one, you think, in the whole world?' Willow smiled, touched by the unexpected gesture of girlish affection. 'And what if he doesn't live in Wood Green? What if he lives in Kathmandu and he's a . . . goat herder or something. If there's only one person for me in the whole wide world then the odds are that I will never meet him. I don't believe in true love. It's just not practical.'

'I know you don't mean that. I know that true love exists, just as I know that I will never love again,' India informed her solemnly.

'Oh, you will,' Willow promised her. 'Only next time he will be young, have hair and no intermittent erectile dysfunction.'

'How did you know?' India gasped, sitting up and staring down at Willow with wide eyes.

'It's an open secret. Although probably not a secret for much longer if Victoria's got anything to do with it.'

'It didn't matter to me.' India sighed. 'I told him our love was more than just an erection.'

She said it so seriously, so dramatically, that it took a second or two for her to catch Willow's eye and to match her smile with laughter.

'Besides, you've got your whole life ahead of you,' Willow reassured her, privately surprised by how raw, how visceral India was, her tender heart beating furiously away on her sleeve. No, she wasn't the sort of person who endured fame very well at all.

No sooner had Willow closed her front door, leaning back on it for a moment, with the sigh of contentment of one friend greeting another, than her mobile rang. Holly.

'It's India Torrance staying in my flat to avoid the press. If you tell anyone I will lose my job,' Willow said, cutting out the small talk that simply wasn't necessary when you spoke to a person four or five times a day.

'You're having India Torrance to stay at your flat?' Holly shrieked in a tone so high that luckily only dogs and any passing dolphins would have heard what she said. 'You'll need to clean out your fridge.'

'How do you know my fridge needs cleaning?' Willow asked

as she plonked her keys on the table and went to the fridge, peering gingerly into its depths.

'Because I haven't visited you for over a month and you never do it yourself. Wow, Willow, India Torrance and new shoes! Your life is so exciting.'

Willow smiled. Holly did that from time to time; it was her way of being kind, pretending that she didn't adore her husband and children, or her picture-perfect house by the sea, and that Willow's life, which bounced between the office and her flat, was much more enthralling than hers. Then again, she also pretended that she didn't mind bearing the brunt of caring for their mother, who'd been diagnosed with multiple sclerosis almost twenty years ago, although Willow knew that Holly thought of it as some kind of penance. By no means did Holly have it all, but she was the only one of the sisters who could still look their mother in the eye.

'I do feel like something has changed, like something's—'

'About to happen,' Holly finished her sentence for her. 'As long as it's got nothing to do with that Daniel.'

Just as Willow was about to protest, the doorbell buzzed loudly.

'Who's that?' Holly asked her.

'Don't you know? Look, I'd better go.'

Willow's doorbell never rang unexpectedly. It only ever rang if some sort of takeaway was expected, or on the rare occasions that Daniel visited. Willow turned round and regarded her closed door suspiciously.

The buzzer sounded again and cautiously Willow approached the entryphone. Without knowing why, she got the feeling that whoever was calling was important. Perhaps it was India;

perhaps she'd been lonely in the hotel after all and hopped in a cab to come over. Except Willow was certain India didn't know where she lived yet. Maybe it was the press; perhaps whoever leaked the story of India and Hugh's affair *was* an insider, but one at Victoria Kincade. Perhaps Lucy was the culprit, Willow was momentarily distracted. Perhaps Victoria would have Lucy disappeared, proving that there was rarely any situation that didn't have some kind of silver lining . . .

The buzz of the doorbell vibrating for a third time snapped her out of her brief reverie.

'Hello?' Willow spoke into the entryphone receiver, but all she could hear was the rush of traffic through puddles, and static bristling in her ear. 'Hello?' she repeated but there was still no reply. Perplexed, Willow replaced the phone and went to her window, pulling back the aged net curtain, which she hated but had never mustered the energy to remove. She pressed her palms against the cool glass, slick with condensation, and peered down at the street below. Cold, tired people, each huddled in their own private cocoon, swarmed by, but there didn't seem to be anyone waiting to come in.

A knock at the door spun her round. Whoever had been ringing the bell had got into the building somehow. Maybe it *was* India, trying to hide from her adoring public. Or it could just have been Mrs Kuresh, from downstairs, thinking she'd forgotten her key again and then finding it in her hand. Telling herself that the curious tingle that crept up her spine was more the product of an overactive imagination than anything else, Willow went to answer the door.

There was no spyhole in the door, so instead she slid the security chain on and opened the door a tiny crack. It was impossible to see anyone in the limited slice of hallway that the gap in the door afforded Willow, but as far as she could tell the landing was empty.

'Hello?' she called, although she was fairly sure that any lurking villains or axe-wielding murderers would not issue a cheery reply. 'Who's there?'

Nothing. Willow thought for a moment, pushed the door to and, releasing the chain, opened the door wide and stepped out into the hallway. The communal front door at the bottom of the stairs was open, the chill of the evening bowling towards her, raising goose bumps on her legs.

Sighing, Willow trotted down the stairs and out into the cold, fume-filled street. The fug of the day rose from the pavements, slimy with wet leaves and litter, the exhaust of the rush-hour traffic sitting thickly in the air, damp permeating everything. Her arms folded around her, Willow looked up and down the length of the street. There didn't seem to be anyone around who looked suspicious, or more suspicious than usual, just the normal Wood Green crowd thronging the street, busy people desperate to be in their own homes, with their own people. The only person who appeared a little out of place was a teenage girl in a skirt that was far too short and skimpy for the cold weather, wearing a massive outsized hooded top, with the hood pulled low over her eyes, a scarf wrapped around her nose and mouth. She was crouching against the railings, uncertainty framing every angle.

Probably lost, or a runaway, Willow guessed. Or another one of those skinny kids you see every now and then and you wonder why they aren't at school or in bed, but you don't think about it too much because it makes you feel uncomfortable. The sort of kid you can't do anything for, they wouldn't want you to anyway.

There was something familiar about her but, unable to put her finger on exactly what, Willow shrugged and started to go back in. The girl sprang up, startling her.

'That's it, walk away,' she said, in a faux street accent.

Willow stopped, turning round, her heart racing unexpectedly. It couldn't be . . . could it?'

'Sorry, can I help you?' Willow said, both shock and confirmation rippling through her in one fluid movement as her former stepdaughter, Chloe, pulled back her hood.

'Chloe!' Willow went towards her, more than ready to embrace her, but Chloe took two steps back, her eyes flashing a warning to back off. Willow halted, a confusion of emotion churning in her gut. Chloe, this was *Chloe*, the little girl she hadn't seen in five years. In that first moment of recognition, Willow ached to hold her, but quickly checked the impulse. The way they had parted meant she had no right to hug Chloe, who obviously didn't feel any enthusiasm about seeing her – and why would she?

'Hello, Willow.' Chloe stood there, caught between uncertainty and defiance.

'Chloe,' Willow repeated in a whisper, the roar and stink of the street around them receding to nothing in a moment. Chloe had been ten when Willow had left Sam's flat for good. In Willow's head Chloe was ten still. Not this hard-faced, beautiful, angry girl. 'What are you doing here?'

'I've left home.' Chloe shrugged as if further explanation wasn't necessary.

'Um . . .' Willow wavered, trying to process the statement at the same time as her brain tried to make a connection between the rosy-cheeked black-eyed little girl she had once known and this gangly long-legged creature with charcoal eyes and . . . and were those piercings? Things really had changed. Willow could never imagine Sam allowing piercings.

'OK, well . . . left home?'

Willow glanced back at the open front door, the glow of artificial light glimmering on the wet stone steps. What was she supposed to say? How was she supposed to act? 'Well, that's, um . . . is that good?'

'Good?' Chloe shook her head, her disgust confusing Will. 'I'm fifteen, Willow, I've run away, in the middle of London, and all you've got to say is good!'

'That's not exactly what I said . . .'

'Then again, your mothering skills were never all that special, were they?'

Stung, Willow looked briefly away, trying to find some footing in this freefall she had stumbled into, waiting for her feet to hit familiar ground again. Of course Chloe felt that way. Five years ago Willow had left Sam's flat knowing she was walking out on Chloe for good too. Chloe must hate her. God knew, Willow hated herself enough; no amount of rationalisation or resigning herself to the knowledge that she didn't have a choice in the matter had ever salved the wound that leaving Chloe behind had opened up in her. Of course Chloe hated her, which begged the question: why was she here?

'So, if you know that it's stupid and dangerous to run away, why have you?' The question came out as an accusation, and Willow bit her lip, desperate that Chloe should not disappear as quickly as she had appeared.

Chloe shook her head contemptuously, clearly signalling exactly what she thought of Willow.

'Dad hates me,' Chloe pouted, but her defiance was mannered, practised, almost as if she'd been reading tips on how to be textbook rebellious. 'And I hate his new girlfriend, if you can use the world "girl" for a saggy-titted old witch. I can't stay there any more, I can't. It's like . . . it's like, a violation of my human rights, right? He treats me like . . . like a slave. So that's it. I'm outta there.'

'Out of,' Willow said automatically, irritating both herself and Chloe in one fell swoop. She was caught between indecision and uncertainty. Willow hadn't been fully aware until this moment just how much she had missed Chloe. There was always the background hum of her absence, a constant undertone that Willow had grown used to, but its volume was suddenly amplified to deafening levels. But now Willow had no idea how to approach Chloe. Not only was the girl no longer ten, she was a stranger.

Sam had made it very clear that being out of his life meant being out of Chloe's too. Willow could almost have predicted the relationship would end with her packing her bags from the moment she'd stood at the altar – no, the moment she'd accepted his proposal. But she had no idea how much and how quickly she'd come to love Chloe, how close they would become. But Sam had wanted to cut Willow out of his life entirely – he wanted, needed, a clean break – and that meant cutting her out of Chloe's life too. Willow had taken her to school in the morning and had moved out before the afternoon bell had rung. She hadn't even said goodbye. Over the years Willow had told herself it was easier that way, easier than having to watch Chloe's dismay and disappointment emerge at awkward uncertain meetings in coffee shops and zoos, until eventually they'd drift apart anyway. Willow always failed at making people happy. She didn't want to witness the impact her failings had on Chloe, or see Chloe come to hate her. She had resigned herself to never seeing her again.

And yet here she was.

Willow caught her breath. How did Chloe even know where to find her?

'Will you . . . come up? Have a warm drink at least?' Willow offered.

'What, before I settle down for the night in a shop doorway? How magnanimous of you.' Despite her response, Chloe needed no further prompting, heading straight up the stairs, Willow following her.

'You've put weight on,' Chloe said as Willow joined her outside her front door.

'Yep,' Willow nodded. It was the truth, after all: a full dress size and a half since Sam had told her he'd had enough.

'Cool shoes, though. They Topshop? Can I borrow 'em?'

'No and no,' Willow said firmly, opening the door and letting Chloe in first.

Chloe looked around the flat, the aged open-plan kitchen tucked into one corner of the single living room, the dirty patterned carpet and woodchip on the walls.

'Well, this is a shit hole. Dad wasn't lying when he said you didn't ask for anything in the divorce then.'

Willow shut the door and went to fill the kettle.

'I'm going to decorate, take up the carpet, refit the kitchen when I've got some time.'

'Oh, you've only just moved in, then?' Chloe asked.

'Not exactly,' Willow hedged, wondering if Chloe knew this

was the flat she'd moved to after the divorce. It wasn't that she hadn't had the time, or even the money to make the place nicer, it was just that she had never had the inclination. It did for her.

What had Sam told Chloe exactly? If he'd explained the whole truth about Willow's abrupt departure then Willow was almost certain Chloe would not be here. He must have said something, but what?

Willow turned back from the kitchen to find that Chloe had disappeared, and her bedroom door was ajar. She followed the young girl into her room where she stood surveying the unmade bed, the assortment of unwashed clothes that were strewn over the floor, the half-finished packet of biscuits on the bedside table.

'Fuck, you live like a tramp!' Chloe exclaimed, her brow furrowing. 'Funny, you always used to be so neat and tidy, always telling me to put my shoes together . . .' She plonked herself down on the bed and looked up at Willow. 'You OK? You look like shit, yeah?'

'Chloe, what's going on?' Willow crossed her arms. It felt appropriate.

'I told you, I've left home.' Chloe reached for the packet of biscuits and took one, cramming it into her mouth in one go.

'But why? Have you fallen out with your dad?'

'You could say that.' Chloe nodded thoughtfully, as she munched. She swallowed and licked her thickly glossed lips. 'Yes, that would be a fair assessment.' Her accent lurched from street-level slang to privately educated West London girls' school in one fluid roller coaster.

'So you've run away to teach him a lesson?' Willow paced the carpet, dimly acknowledging that she really needed to vacuum soon, before the carpet actually changed colour.

'No, I haven't run away *to teach him a lesson.*' Chloe did an irritatingly passable impression of Willow. 'I'm not a twat. I know that a young girl on the streets of London is in danger of falling into drugs and child prostitution and worse, whatever worse than that shit is. I've left home and . . . I've decided to move in with you.'

'Me?' Willow uncrossed her arms and then crossed them again, unable to take in what Chloe was saying. 'You've come to *me*?'

'Yeah, right. I've been thinking about it and I think you owe me.' Chloe's conviction was absolute. 'And besides, there isn't anyone else, and I can't hide it from him any more.' The girl's voice wavered for a fraction on the last few words.

'Hide what?' Willow asked ever so slowly because she somehow sensed that she would never be ready to hear the answer.

Chloe stood up and in one fluid movement unzipped the tracksuit top, shrugged it off her shoulders and let it fall to the floor.

'I'm up the duff,' she said, putting her palms on her rounded belly. 'About six months, I think . . . and when Dad finds out he's going to kill me, so I'm moving in with you, OK?'

It was Willow's turn to sit down on her bed.

'Chloe . . . you're fifteen.'

'Nearly sixteen . . . ish,' Chloe said, as if that made everything fine. Willow stared at her. 'OK, yes. I'm fifteen and pregnant, yes. *And* I knew about contraception, and I knew the risks of what might happen but, you know, I'm fifteen, how sensible do you expect me to be? Anyway, the UK has the highest incidence of underage pregnancy in Europe, and like about fourth or fifth in the world, so are you really that surprised?'

'Yes.' Willow nodded. 'Yes, Chloe, I am that surprised. I haven't seen you for five years. The last time I saw you you had long black hair that you refused to get cut because you wanted it to be as long as Rapunzel's, and forty-three pink teddy bears called Pinky, Pinky One, Pinky Two, Pinky Three . . . and then you turn up here with . . . a . . . a . . .' Willow nodded at Chloe's swollen abdomen, unable to articulate further.

'Baby,' Chloe finished for her. 'Although, the technical term until it's actually born is foetus. I read that. Oh, and I got thrown out of school for drinking. Dad's supposed to be having me home-schooled until I can start at some boarding shit hole in January, but I'm horrible to teach, a proper bitch. So he's gone through more tutors than fucking Mr Rochester, and five years is a long time. A lot can happen in five years. Maybe if you'd kept in touch you'd know.'

Willow rubbed her hands over her face. 'So, you haven't told your dad about the . . .?' Willow still couldn't comprehend what was blatantly obvious. It wasn't only that her former step-daughter was standing pregnant in her bedroom. It was that Chloe had come *here*. She had gone to the trouble of finding out where Willow was five years after she had been abandoned by her. Which could mean only one thing: there really was nowhere else for her to go. And that was the kind of desperate dead end that Willow understood. The unexpected joy of hope and fear of failure blossomed in Willow's chest. Please God, don't let me mess this up, she prayed silently.

'OK.' Willow thought for a moment, choosing her next

words very carefully, getting the distinct impression that picking the wrong one would be like cutting the wrong wire on an unexploded bomb. 'OK, you know I have to call your dad.'

'No!' Chloe's protest was instantly detonated. 'No, I don't know that. I know that if you call my dad I'll be out that door in a second and into drugs and teenage prostitution before you know it. And when they dredge my cold lifeless body out of the Thames that'll be your fault, too.'

Willow glossed over the barbed comments, which weren't exactly undeserved. One thing at a time. Priority: what was the right thing to do with a pregnant ex-stepdaughter? Bracing herself, Willow tried again.

'He'll be worried sick, Chloe.'

'If he can get his head out of his new tart's cleavage for long enough to notice I've gone,' Chloe said bitterly. 'Which he won't, because it's only . . .' Chloe looked around the room, spotting Willow's alarm clock, '. . . six. He never gets home from work till gone nine, and by then *she's* there, hand-making fucking ravioli and decanting wine. She's such a bitch. Every fucking thing she cooks is covered in fucking rocket.'

'Oh, you poor neglected child,' Willow muttered.

Chloe sat beside her on the bed, a hand's breadth of cold air between them. Sitting that close, Willow caught, beneath a slew of patchouli and cheap deodorant, the faintest scent of the little girl she'd last embraced. This girl, this strange present-day version of Chloe, wasn't going to let her hug her, and run her bath and brush her hair and read her a bedtime story. This girl needed something altogether different. Something that, for some reason, she thought she could get only from Willow. The trouble was that Willow couldn't imagine what it might be, and all she could do was grasp at clues and hope not to come back always empty-handed.

Willow attempted to get control of the situation.

'Look, Chloe, you're not an idiot—'

'You don't know anything about me.'

'Well, I know that because you found me here, for one thing, so let's forget the attitude crap for a second. Let's stick to the facts and try and see the situation clearly. You're scared, you've somehow got in this huge situation that you can't get out of . . . not easily. You don't have to tell me what happened, but I'm guessing the baby's dad isn't around any more.'

Chloe shook her head, sniffing.

'Well, you can't run away from that.' Willow nodded at the bump, its soft round promise of life at odds with Chloe's skinny, childlike body. 'And you can't run away from your dad. I know you're scared of letting him down or how he'll react. But I also know your dad and, whatever might have happened between us, I know that he adores you. My God, how did you keep this from him for so long?'

'Baggy clothes, stayed in my room. Like I say, he never looks at me any more,' Chloe said quietly. 'It was actually quite easy.'

'Let me give him a ring. I'll take you home. We'll talk to him together.'

'You think I need you to talk to my dad for me? You of all people?' Chloe's dark eyes flashed. 'I don't need you to talk to my dad for me. I need you to give me a place to stay that is better than a shop doorway while I work out what to do next. Like I said, you owe me that much.'

'You can't stay here,' Willow said, closing her eyes, already anticipating the pain of losing Chloe again.

'Why?' Chloe roared back, so ferociously that Willow leaned away from her.

'Your dad would never allow it, and besides, you need to sort this out with him at home . . .'

'What you mean is, I can't possibly inconvenience *you* and your precious people-free world,' Chloe spat.

'No!' Willow stood up. 'I just . . . I don't know if I'm the right person to help you.'

'You're the only person,' Chloe said, her voice receding into a whisper.

'Things can't have changed *that* much. Sam loves you. No matter what's happened I know he'll be there for you, once he's had a chance to take it in.'

'No he won't. You *don't* know him, not any more. He's not the same. Not since you . . . he's angry all the time. He'll kill me.' Chloe nodded to hammer home her point. 'He will, and then when they—'

'Drag your lifeless body out of the Thames I'll be sorry,' Willow finished for her, running her fingers through her hair. 'Chloe, there's no alternative. We have to tell him.'

'Fuck you.' Chloe crossed her arms, dropping her head abruptly. 'Fucking fuck you, bitch.'

And then she burst into tears.

It took a long time for Chloe to stop crying. Willow considered putting an arm around her but withdrew it again, as the gesture felt superficial. How lost and lonely must the girl feel to come to her, of all people? Willow couldn't imagine the transformation that Sam and Chloe's life must have gone through for that to happen. Was it her fault? Had her failure to stay married to Sam started the cracks, five years ago?

Eventually Chloe fell back onto the bed, her sobs receding as she repetitively brushed away the onslaught of tears with the heel of her hand, wiping her nose on her sleeve.

'I know I've fucked up,' she told the ceiling. 'I know I've ruined my life. I know all that, Will. I just don't know what to do now. I wish Mum were here. If Mum were here then everything would be all right. Because that's what mums do, isn't it? They make everything all right.'

Chloe turned to look at Willow. 'Do you know, I don't remember her at all? Isn't that so sad? I see little kids with their mums and I see all the love and fun they have, and I don't remember it. Not one thing.'

'You do, somewhere you do. That love your mum gave you then is part of who you are now.'

Instinctively Willow's hand hovered over Chloe's long black hair, the hair she'd inherited, along with the black eyes and elfin chin, from her mother, a photograph of whom had always hung in the living room over the fireplace in Sam's apartment. Willow would sometimes stand in front of the photo of the laughing, sparkling-eyed, dark-haired woman and think that it would be difficult to find someone as different from Sam's first wife as she was. Often she'd wonder if that's why he picked her: because he needed someone, but not someone who'd remind him in any way of the woman he'd lost at the age of thirty-three.

Willow had no idea how to respond to Chloe's pain. When she looked at the girl she felt like she had emotional dyslexia. She could see the pain in Chloe's face, but she couldn't make sense of it. She couldn't let herself feel it.

'How about a hot chocolate?' she offered lamely, in lieu of anything better.

'Yeah, OK then.' Chloe's reply was hoarse. She held out a hand and Willow pulled her up into the sitting position and handed her the remote control for the TV.

Grateful for an excuse to leave the room for a moment and take a breath, Willow went to reboil the kettle.

As she leaned into the gathering steam Willow tried to remember how long it was since she'd first met Sam. Probably eight years; she'd still felt young when she met him. She remembered sitting in his office while he was supposed to be interviewing her, a wine merchant in need of an assistant, which was blatantly obvious because the phone had kept ringing every five minutes, interrupting them.

Willow had watched him pacing up and down mid-conversation. She'd liked the look of him. He was tall, broad-shouldered, with dark hair that was greying slightly around the temples; stubble that darkened in the creases of his skin when he smiled. It seemed incongruous, somehow, to find this northern, working-class man in the midst of such a refined upper-class industry. But he owned it. Willow liked that about him too.

'Sorry,' Willow remembered Sam apologising. 'I'm all at sea here. My last girl went off on holiday and never came back. I'm a widower, you see, got a daughter. Chloe, she's seven. I'm not complaining – I know women have to juggle kids and work all the time – it's just . . .' he looked embarrassed, '. . . I'm not as good at it as I let on. I need someone who'll muck in from the start. Who'll work long hours for no extra pay, but all the wine you can drink.'

'I can drink a lot of wine,' Willow had quipped.

'Then you're the girl for me,' Sam had grinned, and Willow had fallen in love.

The longer she worked for Sam, the more she did for him, the more she adored him, content to love him from afar, knowing that she was fast becoming indispensable to him – which was almost enough. She started picking Chloe up from school every now and then, making dinner so he'd have something hot when he got in. It must have been blatantly obvious the way she felt about him but he never seemed to notice, until one night when they had been hosting a wine-tasting evening for their special clients at the office and he'd sent Willow off to get something from his car. As Willow was about to go, one of his clients said right out in front of everyone, 'Sam, when are you going to stop taking advantage of the fact that Willow is in love with you?'

Willow smiled faintly as she remembered the look on his face. He really had no idea how much she adored him. Until that moment he'd just never thought of her that way. But then the cat was out of the bag and everything changed.

Suddenly he couldn't talk to her the way he had or even look at her. Everything was awkward and terrible, and Willow had dreaded going to work every morning and gone to bed crying every night, certain that he was so appalled at realising the truth about her feelings for him that he couldn't bear to be near her any more. Unable to face another day of Sam ignoring her, Willow had decided to hand in her notice. She went to his office with the letter and . . . Willow caught her breath as she remembered what had happened next. Sam had taken the letter out of her hand and looked at it for a second, and then he had ripped it in half. Bemused, Willow had stood there as he came around the desk and, taking a deep breath, kissed her. She remembered the thrill of it, the firm grip of his fingers on her arms, the heat of his body pressed against hers. It was the most sensual moment of her life.

'I'm sorry,' Sam had said to her as they broke apart, his eyes roaming over her face. 'I'm not good with words, with romance and all that. I never thought you'd . . . you're too good for me, Will.'

'I'm not,' Willow had assured him. 'I'm not good enough.'

'I fell for you the moment you told me how much wine you drank,' Sam smiled. 'I just never thought you'd feel the same.'

They had laughed, embracing each other. Willow remembered the warmth, the sensation of comfort, the thrill of the unknown.

'You make me feel happy again,' Sam had told her. Knowing that was the most wonderful feeling that Willow had ever had.

They had got married inside a year. Every morning Willow would wake up, look around at her life and wonder how she came to be here, in a comfortable West London apartment, the wife of a wealthy man who adored her. Stepmother to a charming little girl who she grew closer to day by day. But even then, even in her happiest moments, that familiar sense of foreboding, the one that had been stalking her since she was a child, never left her. Even then she knew her happiness couldn't last, and she was right.

Willow poured hot water onto the chocolate powder and stirred, probably for a minute longer than she needed to, while she tried to think about what to do about Chloe. There had been several months, possibly years, of barbed-wire chaos after her marriage to Sam fell apart. Years of drinking too much and stumbling from one to another of too many men she barely knew. Stability, if not happiness, had finally emerged in two ways: by being employed by a woman whose lifestyle made hers look like a Benedictine nun's, and her friendship with Daniel. The lost love she had once focused on her husband now became Daniel's alone to enjoy. He'd never grabbed her and kissed her like Sam had, he'd never had a moment of epiphany, and although when she daydreamed on the tube Willow always imagined that perhaps one day it would come, she knew deep in her heart that she'd almost prefer it if he didn't ever love her back. That way she'd get to love him for as long as she wanted and she'd never have to see the disappointment in his face when he realised he'd made a terrible mistake.

Chloe being here brought back a lot of things that Willow had successfully managed not to think about for some time now, things she had become an expert at consigning to the past even though the consequences were still so tightly woven in the present. At least cut off from Chloe and Sam she didn't have to acknowledge the truth, which was the way that Willow preferred it. The truth was a terrible burden that never seemed to lead to anything good.

When she went back into the room it was silent. Chloe was lying on the bed with her back to the door, her arms wrapped around her, her fingers tipped with the obligatory chipped black nail varnish, clinging on to her clothes as if she were desperate for a hug.

Willow sat down on the bed, setting the steaming mug of chocolate next to her alarm clock, and began the speech that she had practised between the kitchen and the living room.

'Look, Chloe, I have to phone your dad. Believe me, I don't want to. I haven't spoken to him since . . . well, anyway. I understand why you're frightened and worried. You must have been going out of your mind, trying to hide this for so long, but I can't let you stay here without your dad knowing. And I can't let you get involved in child prostitution and drugs, and end up drowned in the Thames, even though it would save me a lot of grief. I have to call your dad.'

Willow put her hand on Chloe's shoulder and, feeling the steady rise and fall of her breathing, peered over to find that she was asleep, her mouth open, her thick black eye make-up disintegrating on her cheeks.

'So, anyway,' Willow said, brushing a strand of her deep black hair from her cheek, 'I'm sure when you think about it you will understand. That's settled then.'

'*Who* is coming round?' Holly asked Willow to repeat herself.

'Sam Wainwright, my ex-husband, is coming round to discover that his daughter is pregnant.'

'What are you going to say to him? What are you going to wear?'

'Holly, I can't really talk now . . .'

'But . . .'

Willow hung up, silently apologising as she paced the room and waited.

The doorbell rang about twenty minutes later. Willow steadied herself and prepared to come face to face with Sam for the first time since he'd asked her to move out.

Chloe was still asleep, knocked out with the kind of exhaustion that Willow had seen in Holly when she was pregnant with the twins. It was as if the body got to the point when it just couldn't take a minute more of activity, and shut itself down automatically, no matter where or what you were doing, like a sort of prenatal narcolepsy. And, to be fair, Chloe was probably more stressed out than most pregnant mothers, even secret teenage ones.

Phoning Sam after all this time had been nerve-racking, to say the least, but it was the kind of absurd torture that Willow seemed to dredge up for herself, so once she had got over the initial shock she really wasn't surprised by the turn of events. This, after all, was her life. Of course this happened; really, she should have seen it coming a mile off.

Willow had discovered Chloe's phone, which was a good deal more expensive than her own, in the pocket of her outsized tracksuit top and scrolled through her contacts until she reached 'Dad', only there hadn't been an entry under 'Dad', so she tried again and settled on what seemed to be the most likely candidate: 'Twat'.

Willow had been about to call from that phone, realising just in time that a call from your ex-wife from your daughter's mobile might be one thing too many to process, and Sam had a lot to process already, even if he didn't know it yet. So she went to the landline and dialled the number stored under 'Twat' from there instead.

'Yeah-lo?' Sam said. This was the way he always answered the phone. At first it had driven Willow mad, then she had found it terribly endearing, and *then*, for those last few awful phone calls, almost painful: an acknowledgement that the demise of their marriage had not been significant enough to alter his cheery, cheesy phone greeting.

'Hello, Sam. It's Willow.' Silence. 'Willow Briars? You know, we were married for a bit?'

'I know who you are, Willow.' Sam's voice was flat, unreadable. 'What do you want?'

'Sorry to phone you out of the blue like this but . . .' Willow trailed off, wondering at what point in the first conversation you had with your ex since you'd told him to shove his maintenance up his arse it was appropriate to drop a pregnant teenager daughter bombshell.

'Willow? *Willow?*' Sam repeated her name twice, forcing Willow to feel the tone and timbre of the voice she'd once so adored. He'd grown up in Sheffield, and lived in London for more than twenty years, but it was still there: traces of a childhood running riot amid the dark satanic mills of a decaying industrial city. Willow had liked that about him, that ounce of grit in his voice that turned each word into a pearl. Or at least that's what she used to think.

'I've not got time for this, Willow,' he all but growled.

'Sam . . . Look, this is weird, I know.' Willow took a breath. 'It's just that Chloe turned up here about an hour ago.'

'Chloe? With you? How . . . *why*?' Sam wanted the same answers Willow had.

'She's run away, apparently. She said you wouldn't have noticed yet.' Willow couldn't help the edge in her voice.

'What? This is nonsense. Put her on. Honestly, I'll—'

'She says she's been going through a hard time,' Willow interrupted him. 'She says she was excluded from school, that you don't take any notice of her, that she's contemplating a career in child prostitution and drug abuse.' It was a risky tactic, but Willow figured if she went in hard now then the whole six months' pregnant thing might not come as quite such a blow.

There was an exasperated gasp. 'Why has she come to you, of all people?' Sam exclaimed.

'Resourceful, I guess,' Willow said. 'So, is all that true? She didn't get it off the latest episode of *Hollyoaks*?'

'Look, I don't know what she's told you, but there's nothing wrong between Chloe and me, nothing more than the usual teen thing. She thinks she hates me, she blames me for everything, we don't talk, I never see her. She's fifteen, this is how it's supposed to be.' Sam stalled as if he'd just remembered that he didn't like Willow any more. When he spoke again his voice had hardened considerably. 'Where are you? I'm coming to get her.'

'Sam,' Willow took a breath, 'there is no easy way to say this. Chloe is six months' pregnant.'

Willow was not ashamed to admit that after hanging up on Holly, and during the twenty minutes she had been waiting for a knock on the door, she had brushed her hair, slipped on her new shoes and sprayed her cleavage with perfume. Of course, Sam had ceased to be interested in her that way a long time ago, if he ever really had been, but pride made her determined to show him that she too had moved on in the last five years, even if she didn't have a girlfriend who handmade pasta and liked an excess of rocket. She wanted him to see that she wasn't merely the flunky of a PR guru and talent agent, who went through a series of emotionless one-night stands with virtual strangers because she couldn't have the man she wanted. No, Willow was most determined that he shouldn't think that.

Closing her eyes and taking a breath she opened the door.

'Willow.'

Sam hadn't changed that much. He looked tired and,

unsurprisingly, stressed but he was still pretty much the same tallish, handsomeish man that Willow had loved so inexpertly. She was disappointed by the butterflies in her tummy when she looked at him and the increase in her heart rate, her body betraying her head with the memory of passion that had long ago been extinguished.

'Sam.' Willow managed to keep her voice even as she stepped aside and let him into her flat.

'Well, where is she then?' His hands were stuffed in his pockets, his jaw clenched. He would not look directly at her.

'Asleep. She conked out just before I phoned you.'

Sam shook his head with contempt. 'This is typical of you, Willow. You waltz back into my life like a time bomb. Wherever you go, shit follows.'

Willow took a breath. 'Actually, your pregnant daughter waltzed back into my life. I could have just shut the door in her face.'

'I'm surprised you didn't,' Sam shot back, his blue eyes thunderous.

'That isn't fair and you know it,' Willow said. 'I'm letting it pass because you are in shock. And you should be. How did you let this happen, Sam?'

'How did I . . . ? This has got nothing to do with you. Chloe!' Sam tried to barge past her, but Willow blocked him.

'She's my daughter. I'm taking her home!' he yelled, his impotent rage boiling over.

'I don't want to go home.' Chloe appeared behind Willow. 'So fuck off.'

'You . . .' Sam lunged at Chloe, barging Willow out of the way, and for one stunned second Willow expected to turn and see

Chloe knocked to the floor, blood trickling from her lip. But in the moment that it took her to turn round she found Sam with his arms around Chloe, holding her as best he could, which was tricky because of her not inconsiderable bump.

'How *did* you miss *that*?' Willow said, only realising she'd spoken aloud when Sam looked at her.

'Have you ever told a teenage girl she looks like she's gaining weight?' Sam snapped back. 'It never goes down well. Best to keep out of it.'

'That's your motto, isn't it? Keep out of it.' Chloe prised herself out of his arms, her childlike relief at seeing him evaporating in a second. 'I'm serious, Dad. I can't come home. I don't want to be in that flat any more. It's suffocating me!'

'Whose is it?' Sam ignored her, nodding at her belly. 'Is it that Ryan kid's? It is, isn't it? I swear to God I'm going to knock him from here to next week and then back again.'

'No! It's not that loser's.' Chloe looked affronted.

'Whose is it then? Who's done this to you? I'll kill him.'

'It doesn't matter whose it is,' Chloe shouted. 'Why won't you listen to me?'

Father and daughter both saw red at exactly the same moment.

'What do you mean, it doesn't *matter*? It *matters* all right. For one thing, it's a *matter* for the police. You are underage—'

'I won't be in that flat with you and that awful bitch any more. I've got this baby to think about now and you don't want me there anyway!'

'I'm going to prosecute. First I'm going to prosecute and then I'm getting a solicitor. No, first I'm going to beat the shit out of him and then I'm going to prosecute and then . . . I bet he got you drunk, didn't he? I bet some idiot kid got you drunk. I'll show him—'

'No one made me do anything I didn't want to. You're the idiot! I'm a screw-up, Dad. I'm a fuck-up, a big fat mistake!'

Sam wasn't listening. 'We'll need a nanny. You can go back to school until it's born. It'll have to be the local high school now – they've probably got a programme for teenage mums – and then we'll get a nanny.'

'Don't you see, I've thrown away all the opportunities that you've given me? I'm nothing like Mum. You always said I was just like her but I'm not. I got myself knocked up at fifteen. I disgust you. You hate me, admit it!'

For the first time Sam stopped talking and looked at Chloe, who was staring up at him with hot dry eyes.

'I don't hate you.' He looked utterly lost, so bewildered that for a second Willow wanted to reach out to him, to reassure him. 'I love you. I'll always love you, Chloe, no matter what.'

'You don't, Dad.' Chloe shook her head, adamant. 'I annoy you, I let you down. You can't wait for me to go to boarding school and stop disappointing you.'

'I don't hate you, Chloe. I'm just . . . I'm knocked off my feet. This is a huge shock. You don't know, you can't understand, what it's like to see your baby girl . . .' He gestured at her stomach. 'But we'll sort it. We'll cope, together.'

'I don't want to cope together.' Chloe spoke with quiet determination. 'I don't want to come home.'

'Chloe –' Willow tried to intervene but Chloe went on, her gaze fixed on her father.

'You don't know a thing about me any more. You haven't for years. You don't know that I started drinking vodka when I was twelve to try and help me get to sleep. You don't know that I'd been having sex for almost a year before I got pregnant. You don't know that last New Year I climbed out of my window at eleven and went out until dawn, even though you'd grounded me. You don't notice that I'm *pregnant.* I just live in your home and get on your nerves.' Chloe's expression was tight with fury. 'You might not hate me, but I hate you. And we don't have to cope because there won't be anything to cope with. I've decided what I'm going to do already. I'm going to stay at Will's until the baby's born and then I'm having it adopted. Then I'll go back to boarding school and as soon as I'm old enough I'll look after myself. You won't have to worry about me any more.'

'P-pardon?' Willow stammered, but she went unnoticed.

'You don't mean that.' Sam was staring at Chloe as if he didn't recognise her.

'Which part?' Chloe asked him.

'You don't hate me, you don't want to move out.'

'But you're OK with the adoption bit?' Chloe questioned him.

'Well, I mean, you need time to think things through – we both do – but if that's what's right for you –'

'For you, you mean. That's why I'm not coming back. If I came back then it would be for you. But it's not.' Chloe put her hands over her belly. 'I'm having it adopted for her or him. I want to stay here until it's born.'

'With me?' Willow couldn't stay out of it any longer. 'Really?'

'Yes, obviously it's your choice.' Chloe eyed her scathingly. 'Either I'm here with you, or on the street with the human traffickers and drugs dealers. Your choice.'

'Or at home.' Sam tried again.

'No.' Chloe was adamant. 'I'm not going there. And as I've

got no grandparents, no aunties, no friends who are still talking to me, the only place left is here.' She looked at Willow. 'You're it. You're Plan B.'

'Story of my life,' Willow said.

She looked at Sam. He suddenly seemed much smaller, much older, like the air had been let out of him and he'd deflated a little. She'd seen him look like that once before and the memory ignited an unexpected rush of sympathy.

'Can she stay here for a bit?' Willow said hesitantly. 'At least over the weekend, give you both a chance to take this in, see how things are then?'

'You are not a good influence,' Sam said.

'While you've done a brilliant job of keeping her on the straight and narrow so far.' Willow gestured at the bump. 'Look, Sam, I'm not offering to let her stay to annoy you. But, like it or not, she found me and I think a bit of breathing space, a chance for you both to calm down, is a good idea. I promise not to have sex or take drugs while she's here. I will need to drink alcohol, though, starting in about five minutes. Have you got any samples in the car?'

Her flippancy might have been a little out of place, but it was all that Willow could muster at that moment.

Sam shook his head, looking at Chloe. 'Is this really what you want?'

She nodded.

'Why her? Why here?' He jerked his head in Will's direction.

'Because I'm just like Willow. We're the same.'

Chapter Six

Willow wasn't usually a fan of Fridays. Friday meant the end of the week, the end of being purposeful, having a reason to get dressed and speaking to people. But as she forced herself out of bed that morning, the after-effect of far too much wine still swimming around her head, she was actually looking forward to the end of the week. Admittedly it had been less than twenty-four hours since Chloe had turned up, but so far her new role as sheltered housing for unmarried mothers hadn't been so bad.

Climbing out of bed and remembering at the last minute not to be naked, Willow pulled her dressing gown around her and wandered into the living room to put on the kettle. Carefully she pushed open the door to the spare room to find Chloe beached on her back, still snoring.

Sleep was good when you were heartbroken or battered by life. It was a refuge from the pain and there was always the gift of those few carefree moments just as you woke up before the world came crashing in again and the memories of all the bad things came flooding back. Who didn't need that every now and again? Gently, Willow pulled the door to, determined to let her sleep as long as she could.

Having made her coffee, Willow felt her heart lift as she spied her lovely new shoes by the sofa and slipped them onto her bare feet. As she walked into the bathroom for a shower she let the dressing gown fall to the floor and caught sight of her naked body in the full-length mirror that had been glued to the back of the bathroom door when she moved in.

Looking at herself without clothes on was something that Willow never did if she could help it, but as she glanced over her shoulder and caught sight of her bottom, for a fleeting moment she wondered whose bottom it was. Steeling herself for another look, she craned her neck over her shoulder to see herself from behind. It must be because she still had the shoes on. Her calves were stretched and shapely, smooth and creamy white, which Willow wasn't all that surprised by. She had always been fond of the lower half of her legs, particularly her ankles, which were persistently slim even when the rest of her body was piling on pounds of fat in all directions. Her thighs, though, were another story. Willow usually hated her thighs: the dimpling of lard that puckered under her skin, the thick pads of fat that collected at the tops and, worst of all, her inner thighs, which scraped and jostled each other, especially in hot weather. She despised her enormous arse, which exploded over the tops of her legs like an unruly soufflé, and was disgusted by the saddlebags that swathed her hips in wanton flesh. Usually looking at herself unclothed filled Willow with such a swell of self-loathing that she'd have to sit down, trying vainly not to feel the folds of her stomach pushing against each other. She'd have to give herself a good talking to, tell herself to get some control back over her life, remind herself that this weight was nobody's fault but her own. Usually that was when the great ache, the empty hole that was always there pulsating, oddly enough not in her stomach but in her chest, would open up and demand feeding. And whenever Willow was presented with the choice of changing things or carrying on the same way she'd realise just how far she'd have to go to turn back now, and she'd reach for some comfort food.

But today was different. Her thighs seemed smoother, somehow, and firmer. Her bottom looked a little rounder, possibly even a tiny bit pert, although much bigger than many considered socially acceptable. Still, it rose like a full moon from the curve of her waist. It was . . . statuesque. Willow admired her back for a moment longer. Maybe taking in waifs and strays was good for her metabolism, or maybe she'd invented a new diet, the pink wine and Maltesers diet . . . or maybe it was the shoes.

If these shoes could transform her posture and appearance from behind then what about the front? She snapped her head round and looked at the tiled wall. There were many, many things that Willow hated about her body, but nothing more so than her stomach. Could she stand to look at that if she didn't have to, even in the magic shoes? Slowly, holding her breath, Willow turned to look at herself in the mirror. Her sleep-tangled blonde hair trailed lazily over one shoulder, her eyes, a little more heavy lidded than usual, observed her from the other side of the reflection.

'Go on, I dare you,' Willow whispered to herself as she allowed her gaze to travel from her ankles upwards, as if exploring an undiscovered country. Her tummy, which she always felt hung like an apron from her hips, was still there, but somehow, now she was wearing these shoes, it looked smaller, if not flatter. Round and sort of sweet, like a ripe apple. Willow knew she had a good waist, that she'd have an amazing waist if she could only be more like her sister. Even now, even carrying all these extra pounds, her thighs and belly tapered into an approximation of the hourglass figure that could be hers. Finally her gaze reached her breasts. Large, of course, and always too heavy, Willow thought. She couldn't remember them ever going through a perky phase. In her head they hadn't been there one minute and then the next they had, along with a whole lot of attention. Still, her breasts were the only part of her body she felt confident about. They were the thing that men noticed first about her, that they were intrigued by and desired. Willow's breasts had been her currency since her teens, but even so, she wished they were less weighty, that free from the constraints of her bra, they'd plummet a little less earthwards. Observing them as she stood naked, but for a pair of junk-shop shoes, Willow felt a little flutter somewhere just below her stomach, something almost like desire. The cut, build, height of these beautiful shoes did something wonderful to her disproportionately unwieldy body, as if with them on her feet all the disparate parts of her that she hated so much individually lined up to make what was actually quite a pleasant whole. Which was, Willow thought as she let her eyes travel the length of her body once again, actually quite beautiful. She bit her lip, trying to pin down the unfamiliar sensation she was experiencing, and then she realised: she was feeling good about herself.

Just then the door burst open and her opulent reflection was replaced with Chloe in an outsized Little Miss Naughty nightshirt.

'Fuck me!' Chloe clasped her fingers over her eyes. 'I thought you were at work. Jesus, now I'll need therapy or something.' She turned round, bumping first into the door frame and then backing into a little metal rack of shampoos and soaps, sending it clattering to the floor.

'Oh, shut up,' Willow retorted mildly, picking her dressing gown off the floor and swathing her body in it. 'I was just about to take a shower, but I'm decent now!'

'I need to pee. I always bloody need to pee. It's a nightmare,' Chloe grumbled, before catching sight of Willow's heels. 'Wow, do you always shower in shoes? Kinky!'

Willow glanced down at her feet. 'No, but there's something about these shoes that makes me never want to take them off. I think they might be magic or haunted or something,' she said wistfully.

'Menopause?' Chloe eyed her suspiciously.

'No, I mean look at them: they really suit me. And I mean me; it's like they were made for *me*.'

Chloe stared at Willow's feet. 'They are shoes, Willow. It's really a shame you never got pregnant, then you'd have something to think about apart from shoes.'

'Whereas a girl your age really should only be thinking about shoes,' Willow snapped back, more stung by the careless jibe than she cared to admit. 'Pee, and be quick about it.'

'You have no idea what a pain in the arse it is to be knocked up,' Chloe said, sinking onto the loo with an expression of pure relief on her face as Willow hurriedly closed the door.

'So?' Victoria demanded as soon as Willow walked into her office. 'How's India this morning?'

'I went to check on her. She's not much better, I'm afraid. She looks so lost in that room. I left her in bed, sobbing and sipping from a macrobiotic smoothie.'

'Hmm, well, it looks like she won't be in that room for much longer. I think we might have to resort to operation secret shit hole today. There's been a coup. One of the bastard red tops has scooped the scoop. The cat is well and truly out of the bag.'

'Out?' Willow asked.

'Will, I'm sure I've mentioned to you once or twice that it's your job to keep up with the press, darling,' Victoria said, her tone deceptively mild, a sure sign that she was truly angry.

Willow thought about mentioning the unscheduled arrival of her former stepdaughter, and how it had taken her much longer to leave her flat than usual that morning, because it was just too hard to leave Chloe alone there, resting a plate of toast on her bump, watching reruns of *Friends* and complaining about the lack of satellite TV. For the first time in a long while Willow didn't want to go to work. But Victoria wouldn't understand any of that. She didn't do family life or personal stuff. She always made it clear when she recruited new staff that if they had sick children, or needy spouses or any kind of personal crisis it had to come second to the job. What surprised Willow was that there were more than enough people quite willing to take on those terms.

'Well, somebody has breached the terms of our agreement,' Victoria said, tight-lipped. 'Somebody will have to pay, but I'll take care of them later. For now we have to do a spot of fire fighting. Look at it, it's ghastly.'

She threw open a double-page spread of grainy photos interspersed with type, phrases like 'Ambitious young temptress' and 'No-holds-barred sex' singled out in bold.

'This has got Cramner all over it. I think he's engineered this because he knew that India was considering an interview. These cunts have really gone to town on her, as if Hugh had no say in the affair at all. It's going to be tricky, Willow. We've got to get her out of Blakes and into yours today.'

'No!' Willow said compulsively, thinking of Chloe, who'd already made herself at home in the one spare room.

'I beg your pardon?' Victoria whispered.

'I mean, I'm not ready. It's too soon.'

'It is what it is, darling,' Victoria told her, her voice diamond hard. 'Go and get in a cab and fetch India and take her to your flat. And once you're there, dig around, interrogate her a bit. There's got to be something we can pin on him. Anything, anything at all. If he liked it a bit rough then we'll say he raped her. If it was the massive age difference that attracted her to him then we'll suggest he's a paedo. He's messed with the wrong person this time. I'm going to crush him. '

As she slammed her clenched fist hard on the desktop, all Victoria was lacking to complete her portrayal of an evil genius was a white fluffy cat to stroke.

Willow was static, caught with indecision. She thought she had a whole weekend with Chloe, a chance to get to know her again, even if it was fleetingly, to make up, just a little, for leaving her. But if she had to take India back now . . . well, if Victoria knew there was anyone else in the flat, let alone a pregnant teenager, she'd be furious, and she'd tell Willow what she always told everyone: Get rid of her, the job comes first.

Whatever happened Willow knew she couldn't let Chloe down, not again.

'You appear to still be here,' Victoria remarked.

'Er, I know. I'm sorry,' Willow stalled. 'I'm just . . . how best do you think I should handle India? She's heartbroken, she loves

Hugh – with her delicate mental state I'm wondering the best way to play this.'

'Yes, I remember how first heartbreak feels,' Victoria said, doodling a rather large erect penis emerging from the forehead of a photograph of Hugh Cramner. 'My first real affair, I was seventeen, terribly well-to-do, obviously, and packed off to Cornwall in the summer holiday with friends of the family. I won't say I was innocent; girls' school, darling – we practically shagged everything that moved and quite a lot of things that didn't. But my heart was tender then. Still beating. He worked the fairground, a thoroughly bad lot. Swarthy, dirty, older and obviously giving every girl he came across a free ride, if you know what I mean. And then we met and for a few weeks it was so perfect, so romantic. He didn't look at any other girls, he treated me like a princess, we kissed under the stars, the sound of the waves crashing against the rocks – he'd even sing to me. He had a lovely voice . . .'

Willow sat down, intrigued by the faraway look in Victoria's eye. 'Then what happened?'

'He got stabbed, darling – horribly murdered – and left me alone, pregnant with his little girl. But sometimes I got the feeling that he was still there, in spirit, singing to me . . .'

'Victoria!' Willow impulsively reached across the desk to take her boss's hand and then snatched it away. 'Hang on, isn't that the plot of the Rodgers and Hammerstein musical *Carousel*?'

'Is it, darling?' Victoria looked unabashed. 'Well, it just sounds so much nicer than fucking my dad's best friend in his summer-house until his wife found us and I got banished to Switzerland. My point is, I do know how she feels. I *do* know. We just can't let her feelings get in the way of her make-up endorsements.

Girls aged fifteen to twenty-five don't buy mascara from a slag. Drug habit, fine; sleeping around, not OK. Unless she *did* happen to have an out-of-control coke habit . . .'

Willow frowned, catching glimpses of the dark monster that Victoria mostly hid rather well behind the Botox and wrinkle filler.

'Victoria, are you saying you want me to encourage her to develop a drugs habit?'

'Kill two birds with one stone. Make her look cool *and* take her mind off things.'

'I'm just going to pretend that you are joking, for your sake as much as mine,' Willow said.

'Very well.' Victoria attempted an approximation of contrition. 'Obviously I was joking. I care about India, that's why I've asked you to look after her. There aren't many people in this business who have the heart, kindness, wit and wisdom that you do.' Victoria looked a little nauseous. 'There, you made me be nice and you know how much I hate it. I'll have indigestion for the rest of the day now. It's going to ruin Nobu for me.'

'Right.' Willow stood up and went to the door. 'It's just, I'm the most irresponsible person I know. I always mess up my own personal life, all of the time, without fail. I'm just not sure I will have anything helpful to say to India.'

Victoria flipped open her laptop, her very particular way of telling someone they were dismissed.

'Sorry, darling, are you still talking?'

When she told Lucy that Victoria was sending her out for the rest of the day, Lucy demanded that she take the fur coat with her.

'I'm sorry, Will, I can't sit near that. When I went home

last night I had to have two showers to get the stink out of my hair. Marcus wouldn't come near me until I tipped a whole bottle of Coco Mademoiselle over my head. It stinks like a badger, lol!'

Willow ignored her as she briefly checked her emails.

'So how was your first night chaperoning the latest celebrity slut?' Lucy's high-pitched voice interrupted both Willow and the activities of several dogs within a five-mile radius.

Willow sat back in her chair and focused on Lucy, her glowing skin, her shining eyes and messed-up hairdo that had probably taken at least half an hour to create. It must be so nice to be Lucy, to be one of those people for whom life was just a breeze, an endless, mirror-smooth surface to glide over. No married men using and abusing you, no frightening pregnancy to deal with, never feeling lost or alone. No one ever threw a curve ball at Lucy . . . until now. Willow had an idea.

'I'm putting you in charge,' she said. 'Cover for me, OK?'

'Me? Cover for *you*? Willow! Have you cleared this with Victoria?'

'No,' Willow said. 'But she will be fine about it. All you have to do is answer the phones, try to be coherent, finish this expenses claim, review those contracts, sort out the catering for Victoria's networking bash tomorrow, go through the publicity requests, and keep Victoria supplied with enough caffeine to keep her heart beating until she can get to some drugs.'

'Willow!' Lucy looked panicked. 'I'm not very good at being in charge of things, lol.'

Willow put her hands on her hips, and noticed that in her magic shoes she seemed to have a waist that went all the way round, without losing its way in the mountains and valleys of her belly.

'Don't be silly, it's about time you showed Victoria exactly what you're made of. Lol.'

Willow left, dragging her coat behind her, thinking she would have enjoyed her dramatic exit considerably more had she not been accessorised with a bin bag that smelled like roadkill.

Once outside Willow snapped open her phone and dialled India's room. It rang persistently for almost a minute before India picked up.

'Hello?' she said uncertainly.

'It's Willow. Slight change of plan. I'm coming to get you now.'

'I know I've been on *This Morning*. They've been discussing the affair. My mum loves *This Morning*. On a Friday she goes to a quilting circle. They take it in turns at each other's houses; they quilt and watch *This Morning*.'

'Ouch,' Willow said. 'I'm sorry, India, Victoria is livid. Heads will literally roll over this, if that helps. Victoria's instant messaging an assassin as we speak.'

'Mum hasn't called,' India went on. 'Not since I phoned her to warn her about what was happening. I haven't heard a word. What do you think that means? Do you think she hates me? Have you seen the paper, is it bad?'

'It's not as bad as it could be,' Willow lied. 'It'll be old news by Monday.'

'Monday is when Hugh is going on TV to tell everyone what a terrible mistake he made being led astray by a grasping gold-digging slut like me. That's what the presenter on *This Morning* said.'

'Shit.' Willow hesitated outside a dry-cleaner's, half a thought forming in her head. 'Pack a bag, I'll be there soon.'

The young man in the dry-cleaner's looked at her as if she were clinically insane when she dumped the coat on the counter. 'Is there anything you can do for this?'

'I think the kindest thing would be to put it out of its misery,' he told her with the air of a person who did not plan to be working in a dry-cleaner's for long. Willow raised a brow. 'But there is a special treatment for fur I could try on it,' he added reluctantly. He quoted her an extortionate figure, which, even though she suspected he'd hiked it up to try to get out of the job, she accepted, opted for the express service, and climbed into the first cab she saw.

Once installed in the taxi, Willow was still haunted by the ghostly aroma of the fur coat, perfuming the air with the musty scent of the past. Lives already lived, dreams already surrendered, hearts already broken; memories like darkened rooms, curtains drawn in the daytime, shards of daylight piecing the gloom. Willow didn't dwell on her sudden impulse to have the coat cleaned and maybe even wear it, rather than dump it somewhere. In that moment it had just felt like the right thing to do. She sat back in her seat, willing herself to enjoy what would probably be the last few uncomplicated moments of her life for some time. She stretched out her feet and looked at her shoes. She got the distinct feeling that if she just let them, they would take her exactly where she needed to go.

Her mobile rang.

'So?' Holly asked her.

'So what?' Willow teased her gently.

'*So what?* I've been waiting since last night to find out what happened to Chloe, how it felt to see Sam again, if you've cleaned the fridge out, now that the scandal over India has broken.'

Willow was about to answer when she caught something in Holly's voice. Something she wasn't saying.

'How's Mum?' she asked.

Holly was silent.

'Has there been another episode?' Willow asked. The MS could strike at any time, wiping out another part of their mother's body and brain in one cruel sweep. Imogene was lucky, if it could be called that. She had the strain of the disease that struck and then quite often went into remission, but when it did hit, it hit hard, and the older she got, the harder it was for her body to take it.

'Her sight's gone – not completely, but almost. It was a few days ago. I didn't want to say anything. I wanted to see what the doctors thought first. She's home now. I've got the nurses coming in, one for day, one for night. But you know what she's like. She just wants me. Really she deserves me, a relative, to take care of her, but I can't . . . I can't face it, Willow. She gets so dark, so bitter in that house . . . I'm not strong enough.'

'You are, Holly. You do it all. I should do more.'

'Not really. There are the nurses . . .' Holly paused. 'Look, she's asking for you, but I don't think you should come. She's delicate and you . . . well, you should concentrate on you at the moment.'

'Actually, it's a relief to be concentrating on someone else, for a change,' Willow said.

'So? Tell me, I'm waiting to hear *everything*.'

'OK, I don't know who got Chloe pregnant. Seeing Sam was odd and . . . confusing. Oh, and I haven't cleaned the fridge. But some bacteria's good for you, isn't it?'

Willow got India as far as her front door without ever quite managing to break the news to her that Chloe was inside, afraid of jinxing herself. Afraid that if she went to the lengths of explaining the whole complicated situation to India then by the time she got home the complicated situation would have moved out and decided to go back home and make it up with her dad. But as India followed her up the stairs the overly loud pounding of Lady Gaga, which was certainly not being played by Mrs Kuresh from downstairs, told Willow that Chloe was still very much *in situ*.

As they reached the top of the stairs India pushed her shades into her hair and looked around at the cracked ceiling, the spider web strung between the ancient lampshade and the dusty cornicing, wrinkling her exquisite nose.

'It's not exactly Blakes, I know,' Willow said, pretending that she was unable to find the key, in a desperate delaying tactic.

'It's OK, it's fine.' India smiled. 'It's your home. I would never be so rude as to suggest that it was anything less than lovely. One just gets used to five stars, that's all. And yet, it's all just a fantasy really. A home like this is real, at least.'

India waited.

'India, the thing is . . . something personal came up and—'

'Fucking hell, it's India Torrance. Shit!' Chloe flung open the door, immediately unsheathing her phone and taking several photos. 'Wait till I Twitter this shit. I'll definitely be back in.'

'Give me that right now!' Willow snatched the phone out of Chloe's hand as India was already retreating down the stairs.

'What the fuck . . .?' Chloe protested.

'Go back in!' Willow told her furiously. 'India, wait, please!'

India stopped at the bottom of the stairs, her hand on the latch. Heavily she dropped her hand by her side and turned round, backing into the door.

'I don't know what to do,' she shrugged.

'I'm sorry, she's an idiot – well, she's a teenager, same thing. I didn't warn her you were coming. I didn't warn you she'd be there because Victoria will kill me if she finds out, but I don't want her to go – she's only just arrived – so I was trying to find a way to tell you. I thought if I could explain – and it's not like she isn't good at keeping secrets; she's been secretly pregnant for months . . .' Willow faltered to a stop, seeing that India wasn't really listening to her.

'I mean, if I don't have Victoria, or my PA, or a stylist, or the assistant director or you or someone telling me where to go or what to do, I have no idea what I'm doing. I was going to run away just then but . . . I don't know how. Pathetic, aren't I?'

'Do you want to call Victoria?' Willow asked tentatively.

India shook her head, looking up the stairs. 'So that's . . . ?'

'Chloe. She's fifteen. I used to be married to her dad. I haven't seen her in years, but she's having a bit of a crisis and she's come to me. I can't turn her away, I just can't. You see, I've let her down before . . .'

'Did you say she's secretly pregnant?' India's brow furrowed.

'Yes, well, not so secretly now,' Willow admitted.

'I don't mind, Willow, of course I don't,' India said carefully. 'It's just she already almost blew my cover in five seconds flat.'

'I know, but to be fair to her I hadn't prepared her for a world-famous actress of such incredible talent turning up on the door-step. I mean, Chloe is your demographic; she's your fan base. She adores you.'

Willow was rather going out on a limb. She had no idea if that was true, but her main objective was to get India back up the stairs. She'd consider the details once she had her safely inside the flat.

'Is she?' One corner of India's mouth crept upwards, just a fraction. 'That's nice.'

'Isn't it?' Willow said. 'So come on, come up. I'll make tea and you can meet Chloe and see what you think. If you don't think it will work out then we'll call Victoria.' Shortly followed by the Job Centre, Willow added silently.

Chloe was sitting on the sofa when Willow opened the front door again, her arms crossed. She didn't speak as Willow showed India in, only tutted and shook her head.

'Right, let's just get this out of the way,' Willow said. 'Chloe, I work for a talent agency. That's a business—'

'I know what it is,' Chloe snapped.

'Do you? Well, anyway, I have to hide India here for a while. No one can find out she is here. You can't tell anyone, and by that I mean text, Twitter, Facebook or anything, anyone. And I really mean that. Treat it like . . . well, like a secret pregnancy.'

Chloe looked India up and down, and Willow prayed she wouldn't say anything too offensive.

'Because you fucked that old man like they said on *This Morning*?' Chloe asked her.

Sighing, India dumped her handbag and slumped on the sofa next to Chloe. 'Yes, pretty much.'

Willow braced herself for inappropriate questions, comments, anger, possibly some object throwing, but Chloe just sat next to India.

'Getting dumped sucks,' Chloe said. She glanced up at Willow. 'I don't want to get her into trouble, but if you're cool with me being here I promise I won't tell anyone, even though it would make me the most famous person I know, next to you.'

'Well, if you're sure . . .' India also looked up at Willow. 'It will be nice, some company for me. We can share our woes.'

Willow breathed out. 'Really – are you sure? I've only got two bedrooms, but you can have my room and I'll stay on the sofa. I don't mind.'

'Sounds . . . well, I would say perfect, but that would be a lie.' India's smile was wan. 'But then, nothing is very perfect at the moment, so it is all very . . . *fitting*.'

'I'll make tea,' Willow said, turning her back on the young women as she filled the kettle. 'You two get to know each other.'

So far, so good. Things almost seemed, if not exactly to be working out, then at least to be not *not* working out, which in her life was a marked improvement.

Willow looked down at her shoes, gleaming darkly, as she waited for the kettle to boil. It was foolish to feel so superstitious about a pair of shoes, but the truth was that her life *had* improved since she'd found them. They were like an instant lucky charm, secretly sparkling in Bleeding Heart Yard. Willow smiled. It sounded like a place from the world she had created as a child, full of cities, valleys and mountains, and, most importantly, the endless possibility of adventure, which would carry her away whether she was staring blankly out of a window during the day, or into the darkened corner of her bedroom at night, when she couldn't sleep. It was comforting now to get just a sense of that belief in happy endings that she had invested so much hope in as a child. And probably, given her collection of footwear, rather fitting that it came in the form of shoes.

Still, even a hopeless romantic wouldn't put Chloe sitting in her living room chatting to India Torrance, down to a pair of second-hand shoes.

'So does the photo they've got show your tits?' Willow heard Chloe ask India outright.

'Yes, so lucky, really, I haven't got much. It's just like looking at a boy,' India said mildly.

'Mine have got massive since this,' Chloe said. 'Do you want to feel?'

'Really?'

Willow had studiously not looked up to see if India had taken her up on the offer as she found a packet of biscuits to accompany the tea.

Of course, Victoria would string her up by her intestines if she ever found out that India's secret hideaway had been violated by a mouthy teen, but Willow thought she could probably keep a lid on it, at least until India was ready to go out in public again. By which time Victoria would be making so much money from her notoriety that she wouldn't mind.

Chapter Seven

Willow put down the phone to Victoria and finished changing the sheets on her bed. Thankfully Victoria had only wanted to know that India was *in situ*, safe and well, and that she was now free to unleash hell on Hugh Cramner without having to worry about India getting mobbed by the press for free. Willow wasn't exactly certain of the true extent of Victoria's control freakery but her boss had once joked that she had all of her employees' home phones bugged. Everybody had laughed politely and then gone home and unscrewed their light fittings. No proof had ever been found, but Willow wouldn't be in the least bit surprised if Victoria had some extra surveillance keeping an eye on her most precious asset, so she was relieved that the phone call had been no more than an interrogation on the actress she was secretly harbouring.

'Well, keep her happy, darling. Get her whatever she wants, money no *objet d'art*. You know the drill.'

'I'm going out,' Willow told the two girls, who were watching reruns of *Friends*, linked arm in arm already, India's head on Chloe's shoulder as if the relative proximity of their ages and plights had immediately bonded them. Willow felt a pang of jealousy that the international movie star and pregnant fifteen-year-old had found common ground already.

'I've met her,' India told Chloe, nodding at the screen, as they both ignored Willow.

'Really?' Chloe was suitably impressed. 'Is she that beautiful in real life?'

'More beautiful.' India nodded. 'That's her real hair colour.'

'Hello?' Willow persisted, wondering how it was she felt like an outsider in her own home already. 'I said I'm going out. Get some provisions, stuff to keep you entertained so that you don't spend your entire time sitting there moping, banging your head against walls, not eating and crying until your eyeballs look like chopped liver.'

'Can you get Sky while you're out?' Chloe asked, without taking her eyes off the TV. 'Not chav Sky, but posh Sky, with the movies and shit.'

'No, I cannot.' Willow wondered about joining them on the sofa, but they looked so settled, she didn't think there was room for her. 'I'm getting DVDs, an iPod dock, crisps, chocolate, alcohol. Any requests?'

'No films with Hugh in, please,' India smiled weakly.

'Nothing under a certificate eighteen,' Chloe demanded. 'Get zombie films – I like zombie films. Or some of that vampire shit, but not the soppy one. The sexy one.'

'Oh, I know him too, the sexy one – he asked me out,' India added.

'No shit, what was he like?' Chloe's make-up-heavy eyes widened.

'I didn't go. It was when my affair with Hugh had just started.' India's face fell. 'I thought I'd found the love of my life.'

'You had a choice between sexiest vampire ever and that old twat?' Chloe looked appalled. 'You are a fuck-wit!'

'Chloe! I'm so sorry, India. She seems to think she can say what she likes . . .'

But India was giggling. 'I am, aren't I? I chose a fat, old, bald man with sporadic erectile dysfunction over over an anaemic Adonis!'

Willow smiled as the girls giggled together. The nine years between them seemed like nothing at all. She was torn; she wanted to sit down, to join in, to be part of it, but she didn't know how. And besides, she wanted just a little time with Chloe, just the two of them.

'Chloe, come with me,' Willow tried again. 'India's in hiding, but there's no reason why you should be cooped up. You can help me choose.'

'I'm busy,' Chloe said, staring at India with new levels of adoration.

'Come on, come with me.' Willow tried hard not to sound like she was pleading. She hadn't really had a chance to talk to Chloe since she turned up. She knew nothing about what had happened to the girl over the last few years, except the obvious, and as much as she dreaded finding out, she also needed to. She had to know if the way things were between Chloe and Sam was her fault. 'It'll do you good not to be cooped up.'

Chloe eyed her suspiciously. 'I like being cooped up. I like India, she's cool. I want to stay here.'

'You could do with some fresh air,' Willow persisted.

'There is no fresh air in London, and anyway I don't like going out. People look at me.'

'Put your big top thing on; no one will ever know. Come

on, Chloe,' Willow added, well aware of the note of desperation in her voice. 'You came to me, for some reason. Let's hang out.'

'I told you, there was no one else,' Chloe said darkly, turning her face back to the TV. 'It doesn't mean I want us to be best friends for ever.'

Defeated, Willow went to the table and picked up her bag, the magical shiny morning suddenly rather dulled.

'You should go,' India said, catching Willow's expression. 'If you go I know you'll choose really cool stuff for me.'

'Really?' Chloe said. 'You think that about me?'

'Yeah.' India nodded. 'Don't leave our movie-viewing choices up to Willow. We'll end up with the soppy vampire instead of the sexy one.'

Chloe chewed her bottom lip for a moment and then held her hands out to Willow for a pull-up. 'Fine, OK – I'll go. Just don't make out that you're my mother, OK?'

Their first stop was the dry-cleaner's.

'How is this shopping?' Chloe asked, as she draped herself over a plastic chair, next to a bald shop dummy decked out in a cheap-looking wedding dress, with a square of cardboard propped up against it that read, 'Preserve your dreams for ever – antibacterial too!'

Willow handed over her ticket and waited expectantly for the coat.

The same young man who had taken the coat in went to fetch it for her, laying it out on the counter and smoothing his hand across the fur. The smell was completely gone, and its colour had lightened to a dark amber.

'Do you know it's fox fur?' he asked her. 'A proper vintage piece too. My uncle out the back says that the cut and style probably date it to post-World War Two. Apparently it was hard to get hold of mink back then. Fox was pretty much the best you could hope for. An upper-middle-class woman's special treat from her husband, maybe an anniversary gift.'

'Really?' Willow asked, intrigued, almost as interested in the sea change in the young man's attitude as she was in the history of the coat.

'Or maybe it belonged to a hooker,' Chloe said, fluttering her eyelashes dangerously at the boy.

'No, it's still in pretty good nick, but this was once a quality item. See this hand-stitched label? It shows it was tailored at a furriers called Camille's, Conduit Street, London W1. This is too much of a quality item for a lady of ill repute.'

He smiled at Chloe, who instantly went pink and clammed up in a sulky resentful silence.

'So not all fur coat and no knickers, then?' Willow smiled.

He shook his head. 'I just think this coat belonged to a real lady, someone who would treasure it. I mean, look at it – it's sixty years old but it's in pretty good nick. Someone's resewn the hem here and here . . . it's meant a lot to the owner.'

Willow couldn't help but smile at the young man's expression as he tried to imagine who the coat had once belonged to. Where the uninterested, bored person was she had left the coat with, she didn't know, but it seemed almost as if he had fallen under its spell.

She looked down at the coat. 'That's a lot of dead fox, poor foxes. I hate fur really, but as this is vintage and they'd all have died of natural causes by now anyhow, then I suppose it's OK?'

Willow ran her hands over the fur, stoking it one way and then the other.

'Put it on.' Gently, the young man picked up the coat and brought it round the counter, holding it up by the shoulders for Willow to slip it on. The silky lining had torn and frayed in some places, but it felt cool on, like she was stepping into the shadows, out of the glare of unbearable heat.

'That actually looks quite OK,' Chloe told her, her brow furrowed in consternation. 'Although I think wearing murdered fox is vile, by the way.'

'It really suits you,' the young man told her, looking her up and down in a way that Willow wasn't entirely sure was appropriate. He couldn't think she was attractive, could he?

'Does it?' She was sceptical but he ushered her behind the counter to where a full-length mirror was screwed to the back of the staff toilet door. Seeing her reflection, she hugged herself on impulse, as if she'd just been reunited with an old friend. There she was standing in someone else's shoes, someone else's precious treasured coat, and not only did she not look like herself, she didn't feel like herself either. What came as something of a shock to Willow was exactly how much of a relief that was.

'There's something else too.' The youth opened the till and took a small clear plastic bag out from the tray. 'We found this in the pocket. There's a small hole in the hem and it was sort of wedged in it.'

He put the bag in Willow's hand and she felt a thrill of anticipation as she popped it open and tipped the contents out into the palm of her hand. At first she thought it was a coin, a small dull lump of blackened metal, about the size of a ten-pence piece. On closer inspection Willow realised it was a crude locket. It looked as if it was home-made out of two silver coins, the value and the date of which she couldn't make out through the tarnish.

'May I?' he asked her very politely. 'I have some cleaning fluid here.'

She handed him back the locket and watched as he rubbed it over with a cloth. He looked at it for a moment and then returned it to her.

Willow turned the locket over and over as she examined it. It seemed to have been made from two old sixpences, from what she could make out, although they had both been beaten into a convex, and a crude hinge meant so much of the original detail was lost, although on one side she could make out the silhouette of a king's head and the date 1915.

Willow looked at it lying in the palm of her hand, and she seemed to feel it vibrate with an untold story, a history of someone's hope and heartbreak that she would probably never be able to guess at and yet now it was hers to curate. She didn't know why but somehow she felt that was exactly the way it was meant to be.

Magic – not witchcraft or fairy-tale magic, but more the psychic resonance of old things, objects that had already lived a life – carried a once-told story that had somehow become hers to curate. Willow felt the shoes, coat and the locket were urging her to listen to what they already knew about life, what they had known long before she had even been born.

Her head knew they were just disparate random items from a junk shop that an eccentric old lady had off-loaded on her in a bid to shift some stock, but in her heart her ownership of them now felt *right*: a coat from about 1945, the little silver locket from 1915, and her shoes, her beautiful shoes. For most of her life Willow had often felt that there were large parts of her missing, qualities she only knew she was lacking because she saw them in her sister. Not simply vague or ephemeral notions like her failure to love or be loved, or her sense of impotence at the lacklustre job she was making of living her life, but actual physical holes like a second-hand puzzle with pieces carelessly lost long ago. It was a shallow and probably temporary solution, but for now at least the little mystery that surrounded these objects made sense of her, turning the reflection that she so often couldn't bear to look at into someone she thought she could actually like.

'He fancied you,' Chloe said as she hurried up Regent Street as if there might be some chance that Topshop wouldn't be waiting there on Oxford Circus if they didn't go fast enough, which was pretty fast, especially for a pregnant girl.

'Don't be silly,' Willow said breathlessly, as she trotted after Chloe. Although there had been something in the air, something quite different about the boy from when she had first met him that she couldn't explain. 'He probably fancied you.'

'No one fancies the pregnant girl, for some reason. The pregnant girl never gets asked to parties or out on a Friday night. I can't think why.' Chloe dug her hands into the pockets of her outsize hoodie. 'But anyway, he was mooning all over you. Rank!'

Willow smiled. 'I'll have you know I look good for my age, actually.'

Chloe glanced at her briefly before all but elbowing some

poor unfortunate soul who happened to be standing between her and her destination into a lamppost.

'You do, actually,' she said. 'You do look good. You look better than that old slapper Dad's with. Much better.'

Willow basked in the glory of the moment. Here she was shopping on a Friday afternoon with Chloe, who was even almost complimenting her. Perhaps this is what it would have been like if she had stayed married to Sam, if everything had worked out. Shopping trips with Chloe, exchanging banter and insults. A mother and her teenage daughter, close but pretending not to be. Except if she had stayed with Sam, then maybe Chloe wouldn't be so angry. Perhaps she wouldn't hate her dad and maybe she wouldn't be fifteen and pregnant.

'I don't know why people make such a fuss about age differences anyway,' Chloe said out of the blue.

'Really? I thought you were horrified by India and Hugh?' Willow was grateful to have a chance to catch her breath as they stopped at the crossing, Chloe's beloved temple of fashion now only yards away.

'I was, but now I've had time to think about it . . .'

'All of thirty seconds . . .'

'Age is just a number,' Chloe said. 'I mean, look at India. Everyone's all angry because she got it on with an older man, but she's legal, he's legal. What's the big deal?'

'I don't think there is a big deal, not about their ages. Although the fact that he's thirty years older than her is a bit creepy. It's more that he's married with children that people don't like.'

'So say he wasn't married, and he was only fifteen years older than her, then that would be fine, wouldn't it?'

'Yes, I can safely say that wouldn't be news at all. Or at least not this kind of news.'

'So age differences aren't always wrong, are they?' Chloe went on. 'A much older woman with a much younger man, like you and the dry-cleaner, and a much younger woman with a much older man. Not if everybody knows how they feel and what they want.'

Willow wasn't especially intuitive but she would have had to be made of stone to miss the subtext.

'So how old is he?' she asked as she guided Chloe through the throng of people, releasing her into the shiny sparkling glory that was Topshop's flagship London store.

Chloe was silent for a while as she considered a rack of rather rakish trilbies available in every conceivable colour. When she did reply it was posed as a question.

'Eighteen-ish?'

Willow bit her lip. Eighteen; three years older than Chloe. An eighteen-year-old boy and a fifteen-year-old girl. He should have known better. Yes, boys were stupid and girls matured quicker, but still – they both should have known better. Saying nothing, Willow was content to let Chloe try on hat after hat, relenting almost immediately when Chloe asked if she could have one.

'We're supposed to be buying stuff for India, not you,' Willow protested weakly as Chloe filled her arms with an assortment of clothes that Willow didn't have the heart to mention wouldn't fit her for a few months yet. It was just so nice to be with her, to watch her face light up as she smoothed some tiny gold sequin number over her bump, swirling a net-lined ra-ra skirt around, even though she couldn't get it past her thighs. She was almost ten-year-old Chloe again, that little girl who delighted so much in all things feminine, the girl who Willow had found the fluffiest, pinkest, most princess-like bridesmaid dress for, a dress which she wore and wore until the seams split and the buttons popped off, parading up and down the hallway with her nose in the air whilst Willow followed her around, her loyal subject. It made Willow's heart beat faster to see Chloe smile, to catch glimpses of the past that she had longed for so desperately. She had to be careful, Willow warned herself, she had to be careful not to care too much.

Once Chloe's insatiable desire for tiny dresses and skirts seemed to be finally met, Willow had let her lead her around HMV while she dropped one inappropriate DVD after another into the basket Willow was charged with holding.

'I'm not sure you should be watching this when you're pregnant,' Willow said, picking up something that looked particularly nasty, featuring an angle grinder. 'Or fifteen, for that matter.'

'Everyone watches eighteens,' Chloe said. 'I've been watching eighteens since I was twelve. Besides, it's good for the baby. It'll toughen him up for the big bad world.'

Chloe stopped for a minute, halted by thoughts and feelings that Willow could only guess at. Then she shook her head and marched on, tossing her next DVD into the basket. Willow decided not to mention that this time it featured a Disney princess.

Eventually Willow managed to steer Chloe away from Oxford Street, guiding her down the backstreets to the rear entrance of Liberty for lunch. As they passed Portal Way, Willow thought about the shoes that were so effortlessly embracing her feet. She had been walking on the five-inch heels for three hours now, and there was none of the pain that usually came with wearing heels for anything else than lying down in. The coat swirled around her almost with a life of its own. Willow never thought she'd suit anything quite so extravagant, but when she had it on she felt a little altered anyway. As she walked she felt the little locket, in its plastic bag, in her pocket. Once it had been someone's talisman – why couldn't it be the same for her?

Chloe studied in dismay the chicken Caesar salad and bottle of water that Willow had bought for her.

'This isn't a bacon double cheeseburger and a Diet Coke,' she complained, but she began to eat anyway.

She always was very good at eating her greens, Willow recalled. There had been a time, just before the first Christmas that they had been a family, when Chloe was obsessed with Brussels sprouts, mainly because Sam had persuaded her to try one by telling her they were elf cabbages. Chloe had practically eaten her own body weight in the things on a daily basis, labouring under the belief that if she ate enough of them she might be able to catch a glimpse of Santa on the big night. Willow smiled fondly. Sam, who could not bear the sight or smell, let alone the taste, of the humble sprout, had been on the point of heaving at every meal for most of December. But he had never let on that he wasn't as passionate about sprouts as Chloe was, and he had gone out and paid a fortune for the very best Father Christmas costume he could find, being ever so careful when he delivered Chloe's presents on Christmas Eve not to notice that she was waiting up, wide-eyed, peeping out from under her covers. That had been the most wonderful Christmas that Willow could ever remember.

So not everything about Chloe had changed, after all. As Willow watched her diligently chew her way through quantities of iceberg lettuce she wondered when she had stopped believing in Father Christmas. Invoking her new watchword she decided to tackle the subject of the baby's father again.

'So does he know, the eighteen-year-old?' she asked carefully as she poked at her own salad with a fork. 'Does he know that he's about to become a father?'

Chloe sighed, and nodded without lifting her eyes from her plate.

'There was never any chance you and he would . . . stay together?' Willow asked.

Chloe shrugged, a study in indifference. 'It wasn't meant to be serious. We always said it was just for fun. I knew that from the start.' She sounded like she was reading from an often recited list that she had learned by rote.

'And what does he think about your plans to have the baby adopted?' Willow pressed on ever so gently, aware of how uncomfortable Chloe was looking. Was it just the enormity of her condition that was making it so hard to acknowledge it, or was there something else, something so painful she couldn't bear to bring it up?

'He didn't want me to keep it. He thought I should get rid of it. He was worried that he'd get into trouble if anyone found out about us.' Chloe paused, composing herself. 'Besides, he never signed up for any of this. It was just a bit of fun.'

He'd broken her heart, this mysterious boy, Willow realised. Chloe's hard-as-nails front was a fragile edifice at the best of times, but now as Willow watched her face, her lashes downcast, an expression of pain etched around her mouth, she knew this was about more than being fifteen and being in trouble. Like India, she had opened her heart in good faith and, like India, had had it returned to her considerably damaged. Loving and losing was part of growing up, but it shouldn't be like this at fifteen. There should be a boyfriend, an angst-ridden poem and a miserable song on repeat for twelve hours a day, at least once every couple of months. Poor Chloe, the teenage years that were rightfully hers had been brutally curtailed.

Forcing herself to be brave, Willow reached across the table, putting her hand over Chloe's wrist. She felt her blood pulsing beneath her fingers for a moment as she gently squeezed, a silent gesture of solidarity that Chloe accepted by not drawing her hand away.

'I'm sorry that you've been so hurt,' Willow said.

'I'll get over it.' Chloe lifted her chin, defiant. 'He wasn't . . . he wasn't the way I thought he was, anyway. He wanted me to get rid of it, said he'd sort it all. I said no. I mean, it's not the kid's fault, is it? I didn't ask for this mess. And I saw this film about this woman who really wanted a kid, and it ruined her life. Every day she was sad and lonely and just wanted to be a mother. And you hardly ever get babies given up for adoption, so there'll be loads of people who want it. Loads of really good people, who will really love it.'

Willow wondered exactly how much Chloe had thought about her choices, if at all. She had the confidence of youth, an unwavering certainty that those who didn't know much about consequences were often blessed with. She certainly seemed happy with her decision, but Willow wasn't confident that she knew what it actually meant.

'And you haven't heard anything from this boy since you

decided to have the baby adopted?' Willow asked gently, noticing a woman sitting across from them alone at a table for four, having seated all her expensive-looking shopping bags around her. She was staring at her paper, but obviously listening to them. India would be pleased to know that unplanned, underage pregnancy was apparently more interesting than the sordid and largely made-up details of her affair.

'No.' Chloe's chest rose and fell in a determined sigh, and her chin sank towards her chest. 'He's got someone new now, anyway. Another girl at school. I don't care.'

'Hmm.' Willow stared at the top of Chloe's head. Looking at her sitting there, it felt like that was Chloe all over: the little girl, hidden by trappings of adulthood, some self-assumed and others forced on her. It was a look Willow remembered from her own teen years, a feeling of loss and isolation that she recalled with a jolt. She had so desperately wanted to be something, someone other than she was, to banish the little girl from her life completely and be free, just once. Perhaps that was how Chloe was feeling too.

'So have you found out how to have the baby adopted?'

Chloe shook her head, looking up, her face etched with her own brand of courage. 'I saw it on *Casualty*. They just phone some people and they come and get it. You have to sign something and you can decide if you want to hold it or not. I'm not going to. I don't know how to hold a baby; I'd be worried about its head. Did you know they have this massive hole in their skulls when they're born? I read that.'

'Really? I think the adoption process might be a bit more complicated than that,' Willow said. 'I think you might have to put the wheels in motion now, talk to Social Services, probably. Do you want me to find out and call them for you?'

Chloe stared at her, uncertain. A vague notion about what might happen on a forty-five-minute-long medical drama all nicely tied up by the time the credits rolled was clearly all that Chloe had allowed herself to consider.

'I don't know,' she said. 'What do you think?'

'I think that if this is really what you want then you need to be prepared, you need to really understand what it means. Talk it through with someone, make sure you know all your options. I'll call them on Monday, find out what the first steps are.'

Chloe swallowed, sucking her lips inwards over her gums. 'Yes, OK. OK then.' She mustered a smile. 'Thanks, Willow. I knew you'd know what to do, that's why I came to you. I tried to think about who would know what to do and there was only you.'

'Really?' Willow asked. 'I'm so glad that you came to me, but don't you have a friend or a teacher to turn to if you couldn't talk to Sam? Are you that lonely, Chloe?'

'You know the girl at school who's never in with the in crowd? That's me. I'm the loner, the one who hangs out with a bad lot and starts a rock band. Only I can't play any instruments. And Dad . . .' Chloe held Willow's eyes. '. . . Dad was devastated when you left. He was heartbroken. I don't think he ever got over losing both of the women he loved. He wasn't the same. When he did start seeing women, he never brought them home . . . not until Carol. And Carol hates me. Mainly because I replaced her moisturiser with Deep Heat.'

Willow repressed a smile. Chloe's life had been so full of people when she was younger. Her dad adored her, his staff were practically her aunts and uncles, there had been countless numbers of tousle-headed, overconfident school friends who'd parade through for tea on a seemingly endless rota of play dates. How had it happened that she'd become so isolated from all the people that cared about her, that, after living at the hub of human warmth, when it came to the crunch the only person she could think to help her was her one-time very bad stepmother?

'And how is the baby's health?' Willow thought that while they were having this moment together she might as well ask. 'Have the scans been OK? Is your blood pressure all right, all that stuff?'

Chloe shrugged. 'I've not exactly been to the doctor yet.'

'Not at all?' Willow wasn't surprised. She wasn't even sure an underage girl could see a doctor without a parent or guardian present.

Chloe shook her head. 'But I think everything's fine because I can feel the baby moving all the time, and I don't feel like I've got anything wrong with me. I feel OK. I bought a book. I look stuff up in it. I thought I was going to die of liver failure because I got all itchy, but it turned out I just needed moisturising.'

Chloe's face was so serious, that Willow couldn't help but smile.

'What?' Chloe smiled uncertainly in return.

'I don't know, it's not funny. You secretly reading a book under the covers about your secret pregnancy. Do you remember when you used to stay up secretly reading bloody awful *Mallory Towers*? I'd have to tuck you in about five times before you went to sleep. It was getting on for midnight sometimes. I'd think, your dad'll be in soon, he'll kill me if you're still up. But you had no regard for my personal safety. You just kept on reading.' Willow grinned at her but Chloe's returning smile faded as quickly as it had blossomed.

'I'm surprised you remember,' she said, forcing Willow to hold her gaze.

'Of course I do.' Willow shifted in her seat uncomfortably. 'Right, OK. Well, you need to get checked out. I'll take you to the GP too, or maybe the hospital. I'll find out which one.'

'But not today.' Chloe looked up, her expression flowing from anger to anxiety in one fluid movement. It was clear that despite the bump that was permanently attached to her front as a reminder, she just wanted another day of not having to think about her pregnancy, another day of just being fifteen.

'OK,' Willow nodded. 'So how about I buy you some clothes so that you stop stealing mine.'

'You already bought me a ton.'

'I know, but they're . . . for later. How about we find you something for now.'

'Fat clothes, you mean?' Chloe asked.

'Well, yes, a few things to keep you going. You've got to keep your image up. How are the kids of Wood Green going to know what to wear unless you show them?'

'Fuck, you're lame.' Chloe smiled nevertheless. 'Thanks, Will.'

'Typical,' the woman on the other table muttered under her breath.

Frowning, Willow looked over at her, her hackles instantly raised. 'I beg your pardon?' she asked with the kind of confidence that only an aged fur coat can give you.

The woman looked up. 'I didn't say anything.'

'I heard what you said,' Willow challenged her. 'If you are going to make a comment then at least have the guts to stand behind it.'

The woman pursed her lips, and sat up a little. 'Very well, I will. The trouble with young people like *her*,' she stared at Chloe as if she were a piece of dirt, 'is that there are no consequences. Look at her. She's gone and got herself pregnant *for a laugh*, by all accounts, and you're rewarding her with gifts. With a mother like you no wonder she got herself into trouble.'

Before Willow could respond, Chloe crashed out of her chair, advancing on the woman until her bump was almost in her face.

'She isn't my mother,' Chloe growled at the woman, 'and if you say one more word about her I'll rip your head off, bitch.'

'Oh my God. Help!' The woman scraped her chair back, shielding herself with the stiff yellow cardboard of a Selfridges bag.

Stunned by how rapidly her bid to defend Chloe had reversed, Willow scrambled up, taking hold of Chloe's upper arm to stop her lunging at the woman. Security guards were already bustling over.

'Come on, Chloe,' Willow said, putting her other hand on Chloe's shoulder. 'Remember your blood pressure.'

'*Her* blood pressure! She should have an ASBO, she should have a tag!' the woman screeched, emboldened by the arrival of staff. Still glaring at the woman, Chloe let Willow begin to lead her away.

'It's a good job that baby's being adopted. It wouldn't stand a chance with you!'

Willow felt Chloe's arm stiffen but she kept a firm hold of her, taking her out of the shop and guiding her round a corner until she found a quiet spot. Chloe leaned against a brick wall, her fists clenched, her foot tapping furiously.

'Are you OK?'

'No, I'm not OK. I want to go back in there and kill that

bitch.'

'She's just a busybody,' Willow said. 'If it's any consolation I think you did shave five years off her life, at least. You were like knocked-up Wonder Woman. You should have seen her face!'

'People like her, they've got no idea. They live in their nice little world, with their nice little hedges and nice little . . . stuff, and they don't know what the real world is about,' Chloe spat, gesturing furiously.

If she had been prepared to chance it Willow could have pointed out that Chloe too had lived in a nice, privileged, safe little world, but it didn't seem fair, or especially safe.

'You're very angry, aren't you?' Willow said, rather stating the obvious but she felt it needed to be said.

'Of course. Of course I'm angry. I'm the one who's got to do this. Who's got to feel it living inside me, who's got to get it out and then give it away. Of course I'm angry. I'm such a fucking idiot. I trusted him. He used me!'

'It's OK.' Willow put her hands on Chloe's shoulders, but she shook them off.

'It's not OK. How is it OK?'

'Because you will get through this. It will be OK in the end.'

Chloe sunk down the wall, winding her arms over her swollen abdomen.

'But it won't be, will it? What happens next will never, ever go away, will it?'

Willow crouched down beside her, desperately trying to think of something to say to comfort Chloe, but she couldn't because, after all, the girl was right.

Chapter Eight

'You look like a proper *femme fatale* in that coat,' India said as Willow prepared to leave her charges home alone once again, and head to Daniel's house for dinner. She'd briefly weighed up how sensible her decision to go out was. It wouldn't take much for the situation to get quite out of hand: one particularly persistent journo to decide to keep tabs on all of Victoria's staff, or for India to decide to pop out just for a breath of fresh air. Really, Willow thought, she should be there all of the time to micro-manage the situation. That was, after all, what Victoria expected of her. But something powerful had a hold on her at the moment. Even in the midst of all the heartache around her, including her own, Willow had suddenly acquired a sense of Romance with a capital R.

In the space of a few hours her confidence and self-esteem had risen like mercury in a barometer from lukewarm to red hot, as if, by slipping the shoes on, all the toxic waste that had been poisoning her had been cleansed from her system, and she was flowering again. No, not again – she was flowering for the first time. It was a kind of madness, it had to be: a combination of an impossibly glamorous coat and wonderful shoes, which gave her a persona she could step into and a fragile glimmer of that rarest of commodities, happiness. Willow felt happy and romantic, and if that little bit of magic could bring Chloe back into her life, then who knew? Perhaps Daniel was in reach too.

Willow's yearning to see Daniel outweighed all the practical considerations, like a near-suicidal starlet and a pregnant fifteen-year-old with a track record for terror, partly because she felt that one sort of cancelled the other out. She was going for only a few hours, she told herself – what was the worst that could happen?

India was under strict instructions not to let Chloe leave the flat. Chloe was under strict instructions not to let India anywhere near the windows. No one was allowed to answer any phones, send any text or socially network. Willow had secretly resolved to call Sam on the way over to Daniel's and update him on what limited progress they had made: the decisions to find out about how to have a baby adopted and to get Chloe to the doctor. She thought she'd leave out the bit about Chloe nearly decking the bitchy shopper.

'Do you know, I do feel a bit glamorous?' Willow said, smoothing her hands over the newly fragrant but still rather tatty-looking coat.

'If anyone asks you how much, say fifty for a blow job, hundred for full sex,' Chloe called, peering over the back of the sofa, but with a smile in her eyes.

'Is that the going rate?' Willow pretended to be shocked.

'It is for an old bag like you.'

Willow ignored her, instead taking India just outside the front door with her.

'I can still hear you, you know!' Chloe shouted.

'Yes, but I can't see you,' Willow retorted.

She looked at India's worn and tear-eroded face. She looked thin and gaunt.

'How are you doing after your first afternoon in flatsville?' Willow asked her. 'Because I'm very aware that I haven't done an especially good job of looking after you so far.'

'You haven't been on round-the-clock suicide watch, you mean?' India smiled.

'Pretty much that. Victoria expects me to be here popping Valium into your mouth on demand.'

India didn't look surprised as she wound a large cable-knit cardigan around her meagre frame, sheltering from the piercing draught that rattled up the stairs to greet them.

'Willow, don't be silly. Chloe's situation is far more pressing than mine. You needed some time alone with her. And besides, you've done a great job. You've got me through today undiscovered and actually it's nice to be distracted by mini Madonna in there. There is just one thing . . . I'm embarrassed to say, really, but . . . I forgot to ask you to pick up some mineral water for me. I don't drink tap water. It's full of chemicals, you know, and I don't like that taste, the . . . taste you get when you brush your teeth in hotel bathrooms. It makes me gag, so I always have litres of the stuff around.' India rolled her eyes. 'Listen to me, I'm such a prima donna. Honestly, I'll be asking you to arrange for me to have only orange M&Ms next. Actually, though, talking of food, you are rather short of vegetables. How risky would it be to ask my chef to drop off a few meals? I'm not fussy normally, but it's my skin, you see, it can't take processed foods. Although why I'm worrying about my skin when here I am cheerfully drinking myself to death I don't know.'

'Don't do *that*,' Willow said. 'Victoria will kill me if you die before she's got a double-page spread in *Hello!* for you. I don't think they do evening gowns and stately home photoshoot post-mortems, although I'm pretty sure Victoria would do her best to book it.'

The ghost of a smile hovered around India's lips for a moment.

'You know, she hasn't realised that I'd probably be worth more to her dead. "Tragic young actress dies before her full potential can be reached." I'd be her very own James Dean.'

'We'll know when she figures that out. She'll send you round a bottle of vodka and a value pack of Paracetamol,' Willow reassured her. 'Shall I stay in? I think I've got Trivial Pursuit somewhere, we can play that. I can pop over to the all-night garage and buy you some frozen peas and make you a risotto, dairy free. It will take your mind off everything.'

'No, no, I don't want to take my mind off everything.' India shook her head, her slender fingers burrowing into the cardigan as she held tightly onto herself. 'I want to dwell on it, I want to feel it, feel the pain, understand why this happened, how it happened. It's not just me – my mum and dad are under siege from a pack of journalists who are waving nearly topless photos of me in their faces. They're knocking on my neighbours' doors, asking them what I was like at school, when I lost my virginity, if anyone knows my ex-boyfriends, or has a photo of me in a bikini!'

'How do you know?' Willow asked her, anxiously. 'How do you know that?'

'Oh, I phoned an old friend while you were shopping.'

'India, you know you're not supposed to speak to anyone. Did you tell this friend where you were?'

'Yes, but don't worry, I can trust her.'

'Fuck. You'd better hope so.' Chloe really had made her take her eye off the ball. Victoria would string her up and then sack her if she knew India had been talking to anyone.

'Not everybody is evil, you know,' India said, tears springing suddenly into her eyes. 'Don't tell me that my oldest friend would betray me, because I couldn't take it. I'm already ripped in two, guts pouring out all over the place, heart smashed to smithereens. And that's even before I get to thinking about my career being over before it's begun. All I ever wanted to do was act. I never, never wanted *this* . . .' India set her jaw. 'Look, go out, have a break from the waifs and strays. You deserve it. I don't really do frozen veg anyway. Maybe tomorrow you could pop to an organic market.'

Willow hesitated. 'OK, if you're sure . . . Look, for what it's worth, this part doesn't go on for ever, it only feels like it.'

'And then?' India asked.

'Then, well, then I go into a sort of free fall. I pretend I'm someone else and I . . .' Willow hesitated, '. . . I fall. It usually ends up horribly messy and with an expensive cab fare home, but it takes my mind off things.'

'What things?' India asked her, her eyes locked on hers in the moment of stillness.

Willow's eyes dropped under her scrutiny. 'Oh, you know, my job, my fat thighs, the lack of a man in my life, all your usual sad, middle-aged woman crap. Stuff you will never have to worry about. Look, I'm going to leave you to your dwelling in the Slough of Despond. What sort of a dreadful bitch am I, trying to cheer you up with competitive board games and frozen peas?'

‘A fucking witch!’ Chloe called from inside. Willow and India exchanged looks.

‘Is it wrong that I like her being here? It’s nice to have a companion in my misery.’

‘Well, if you get sick of the companionship you can always get into my bed and watch TV in there. There are some emergency cupcakes in the bedside drawers.’

‘I’ll be fine. As long as there are emergency cupcakes, I’ll be fine,’ India reassured her. ‘And what about you?’

‘Me?’ Willow looked confused.

‘Will you be free-falling tonight?’ India asked her softly.

Willow shook her head. ‘No, not tonight. I need to come home and make sure you haven’t overdosed on butter cream, and that one in there hasn’t got herself pregnant again.’

‘Ha fucking ha,’ Chloe called.

‘Are you sure you will be all right?’

‘Fine,’ India reassured her. ‘Totally fine.’

Willow knew even as she swished down the stairs and out into the damp chill of the evening that that last statement would come back to haunt her, but she couldn’t resist spending time with Daniel, no matter what might happen. Her lack of willpower always had been her downfall.

The communal front door to Daniel’s apartment building was on the latch when she arrived, a habit that Daniel persisted with, despite the protestations of his neighbours, who weren’t quite so keen on random passers-by dropping in. But, as Daniel had explained to the Petersons, who owned the ground-floor lease, he was either always far too drunk or far too hung over to be up and down those stairs like a butler. Willow had felt sorry for the

Petersons, who were both too polite and too Swedish to take the matter any further, but it didn't stop her loving Daniel's belligerence, his insistence that the world was there for his enjoyment entirely.

Willow pushed the door open and breathed in. There was something about the scent of Daniel's place that she loved – not just his flat but the whole building. Perhaps it was the scent of polished wood, or the musty dried flowers rattling around in a vase that stood on a table just inside the door. Either way, it reminded her of just after Daniel had moved here, a short while after she and Sam had split up. Willow had spent a lot of time here then, most of a cold wet February and all of an unforgiving March, helping Daniel, who had gone away on an extended shoot somewhere warm, to unpack, waiting in for various things to be delivered or for workmen to connect or disconnect something or other. She'd unpacked and put away his surprisingly large collection of clothes and shoes, many of which she'd never seen him wear, some still with price tags on, the result of flirting with the fashion industry, she supposed. Occasionally she'd pull out something that had once belonged to some woman who had passed through his life, and she even made a little collection, which she had tipped into a drawer, taping a label on to it that read 'Trophies'. She'd unpacked all of his pictures and photos, hung them on the wall in the spots she judged most fitting and even organised and then reorganised his kitchen cupboards, whiling away her evening cooking meals and freezing them for him. Usually she hated to cook, she found it utterly boring, but at that point in her life boredom was a welcome refuge. Thinking about tablespoons of this and half teaspoons of that was so much better than thinking about the wreck of her life that was waiting for her outside Daniel's front door.

Willow hadn't dwelled on exactly what she was doing hiding away in Daniel's new flat back then. She'd only known at the time that being there was better than being in her own place, where she was officially alone and single, divorced and childless, where the remnants of the normal life she had attempted and failed at so spectacularly were still taped up in boxes. Sorting out someone else's life, if only their possessions, was exactly the kind of methodical escapism she'd needed from the mess she had churned up for herself. It had been not a happy time, but it was one of relative peace where Willow had lulled herself almost into another existence entirely.

And then the night before Daniel was due to fly home she realised exactly what she'd done. He'd asked her to check in on his place from time to time and she'd gone all obsessive psychostalker on him. She'd organised his pants; she'd bought him scented candles and a special earthenware jar just for balsamic vinegar . . . All she needed was a bunny to boil and the scenario would be complete. Horrified, Willow had imagined the look on Daniel's face when he walked back into his flat to find it had been taken over by his very own imaginary wife. She had scrambled out of bed, taking a very suspect-looking mini cab over to Daniel's place in the dead of night. For all of the hours that remained before he was due back she repacked his clothes, taped back up everything she could in bubble wrap, reboxed his kitchenware and finally threw out all her frozen meals in the bins in the alley out the back. She even scattered the contents of the trophy drawer randomly through the bin liners of clothes that she had restuffed, hoping he wouldn't notice that everything wasn't exactly as he had left it.

For two or three days after getting back Willow had been worried sick, bracing herself for the tirade of justifiable anger Daniel was bound to unleash upon her eventually. But when he did call he hadn't noticed a thing.

'Everything OK at the flat?' she asked him hesitantly.

'What? Oh, yeah, thanks for hooking the phone up. Everything's still packed but I'll probably leave it that way for at least another couple of months. Hey, I should have got you to unpack everything for me or you know what, I might throw it all away and start again. Who needs stuff, right? Anyway, I brought you back a Toblerone.'

Willow should have been, and to a great extent was, relieved that her intrusion had gone unnoticed, but she also realised two things. She realised exactly how she felt about Daniel Fayre; that what had started out as a diversion and had grown into a friendship had very quickly become much more for her. She also realised that there was something wrong with her. Something even more wrong than metaphorical bunny boiling. All those things she had done for Daniel while he'd been away she'd never done for her husband, or even herself. Her own possessions *were* still in bin bags and boxes. All the love and care she was able to lavish on an absent person became impossible in real life. In real life, Willow just wasn't capable of loving anyone, at least not well enough to make them happy. It was then, after leaving Sam's flat whilst Chloe was at school, after secretly living in Daniel's place in some bizarre fantasy, that Willow had been forced to acknowledge she was broken, and, more than that, she was fairly sure she was unfixable.

Now, as she reached the top floor and Daniel's flat, the scent of barbecued meat and the sound of boozy conversation floated down to greet her. Only Daniel would decide to barbecue in this weather. Taking a breath, Willow was about to go in when her phone rang. The screen told her it was Sam. She had forgotten to call him. Hesitating, she thought about not taking the call, but if he couldn't get through to her he'd go round, and if he went round then he'd discover she was out and . . . Willow answered the call.

'Sam.'

'So?' he asked her. 'Have you found out who did it? Is she ready to come back?'

'No, and I don't think so, not yet,' Willow replied turning longingly towards the sound of laughter and clinking of glasses coming from somewhere within Daniel's flat.

'Willow, what's the point of her being with you if—'

'The point is, she isn't sleeping in a doorway because she can't stand being with you,' Willow snapped before she could stop herself. 'Look, Sam, what happened? How did she go from that little girl to . . . to this?'

There was a long silence.

'I don't know,' Sam said eventually. 'I just . . . I suppose I wasn't there. I suppose I . . . I've been busy with the business.' It was nothing like an explanation but Willow supposed it was the nearest she was likely to get just now.

'I know she sounded like she knew what she was doing, but I think the whole reason she's ended up in this situation is because she's been trying really hard not to think about anything. It's early days, but I'm not sure if she really knows what adoption means, if she's ready to deal with it.'

Sam barked a mirthless laugh. 'But she's ready to deal with becoming a mother?'

'Maybe, if she felt like she wasn't alone.'

'She isn't alone. I told her, I'd get a nanny, sort out school . . .' Sam sounded frustrated. 'Why would she think that she's alone? I'd never force her to do anything she'd always regret. I live with enough regrets of my own.'

Willow was silent for the moment or two it took her to absorb the tacit insult.

'I'm going to take her to the doctor's on Monday and see if I can't make an appointment for her to meet with a social worker—'

'But you can't. Surely she needs a parent to be there for that.'

'Well, I thought I could say I'm her step—'

'No, you can't say that. You aren't.' Sam sounded adamant.

'She won't let *you* take her.' Willow was just as forceful. 'For whatever reason, she really doesn't want to be around you at the moment, Sam.'

'Then we'll both go. And that's that.'

'Fine.' For a frozen second Willow wondered how Sam and his daughter had come crashing back into her life so completely. How two people that she had considered ruled out of it were now so firmly back in, to the point where they were making arrangements. Perhaps that was down to the shoes, too. Ever since she'd put them on she'd felt her heart beating, ticking like a clock. The trouble was she had no idea what it meant, if anything. She only rather hoped it wasn't the ticking of a clock counting down to detonation.

What would Sam say, she wondered, if he knew where she was standing right now? He never had liked her friendship with Daniel. Sometimes she speculated, hoped even, that he might even feel jealous. She should have known better.

'Babe!' Daniel caught sight of her, on a run to the kitchen for more alcohol, no doubt. 'What are you doing loitering on the doorstep like Mata Hari, and what the fuck are you wearing?'

'I've got to go,' Willow said to Sam hurriedly. 'I'll call you.'

'Is that—?'

Willow cut him off.

Slipping her phone into the pocket Willow shrugged the sound of his voice out of her head at exactly the same time as she dropped the coat sexily off one shoulder, framing herself in the doorway, shamelessly vamping it up for her friend.

'Wow, I don't know who you are, but I know I like you,' Daniel whistled as he looked her up and down. 'What have you done with my boring best friend, you animal-murdering fiend?'

Willow's smile faded just a tad and then, taking a breath, she pushed Daniel aside and strutted past him, twirling first one way and then the other, her confidence growing as she saw him laugh, his eyes sparkling.

'Actually,' he said as she turned around, 'that moth-eaten old thing really suits you. You were obviously born for old-style glamour. You look great, honey.'

He picked up one of the numerous cameras he always had lying around and took some shots of her as she struck as many over-the-top glamour-girl poses as she could think of, careful not to look like she was taking herself too seriously.

'There's something else though, something different about Miss Willow Briars. What have you done? Have you done your hair?'

Willow beamed and then gracefully slipped the coat off to reveal a chiffon dress she had found in Monsoon on her shopping trip with Chloe. It was a pale lemon yellow, the sort of yellow that only a natural blonde could really wear, with silver beading under the bust and along the hem. As soon as she had seen it Willow wanted it, but the size eighteen had already gone. Nervously she had tucked the sixteen over her arm, unable to look in the eye the assistant who handed her a tag for a changing room in case the woman laughed out loud at Willow's hopeless optimism. Willow felt a little, well, not thinner exactly, but more shapely, but still there was no way that she could have dropped a dress size in a week. Maybe, though, just maybe, if the cut was right, the material a little stretchy, there weren't any buttons to pull or a zip to get stuck . . . she might be able to squeeze herself into it and not look too terrible.

No one was more surprised than Willow when the dress slipped over her head and seemed to fit her like a glove. It was probably a little tighter on her than the designer had envisioned, but she liked that it gathered in under her bust, neatly framing her cleavage, skimming her waist and thighs to the knee, showing off the bottom half of her tanned legs, which looked so much longer in her magic shoes. Willow had been careful to keep the shoes on as she slipped the dress over her head; while she had her shoes on she was lucky.

Willow pouted at Daniel as he took one last photo. Who knew exactly how far these shoes could turn her luck?

'It's great to see you looking so good, Will,' Daniel told her. 'Have you met someone?'

'No, I've met some*thing* – new shoes. Well, new-to-me shoes. Take a photo of them, please!'

Obligingly Daniel dropped to one knee and took a shot of her pointed foot.

'Wow, even I can tell those are good shoes. You need to be

careful, looking so hot. Serious James is on the roof trying to work out what to say to you.'

'Oh, no,' Willow groaned, her delight at soliciting several minutes of undivided attention from Daniel dimmed by the prospect of struggling through a conversation with sweet but shy James.

'You could do worse, you know,' Daniel teased her. 'He's got a good job when he's not trying to be a comedian, which, considering he finds social situations mostly horrific, is something I'll never understand. He's a decent guy and Kayla says he's got the whole sexy geek chic thing totally down. One of her model friends had been trying to get him to date her ever since they met at some do or other – I forget which – and he's driving her mad by not being in the least bit interested.'

Willow thought she might remember the girl, back when Daniel and Kayla were quite new as a couple, and before the autumn had set in so thoroughly. He'd had one final summer roof party. Holly had come down for it, and as far as Willow could remember they'd sat on a step drinking far too much Chardonnay while she lusted after Daniel and Holly glared at him. James had briefly come over to speak to them but had left hurriedly after saying something along the lines of, 'Wow, hot twins. Every man's dream!'

Willow and Holly had giggled like girls after he'd left red-faced and shamed by their stone-cold expressions of maidenly disapproval. Willow did vaguely remember a girl in a hot-pink dress, doing her best to flirt with him, which was difficult because no one had ever taught James how to flirt. It seemed that his discomfort and embarrassment translated into model language as 'playing hard to get'. Maybe that wasn't fair, maybe this girl liked him because he was nice, technically too nice to be Daniel's friend at all.

'*And* he is smitten with you. That's why he's turning down hot model action.'

'Who says so?' Willow questioned him.

'He does.'

'Exactly,' Willow said, trying not to show how she felt about Daniel doing his best to fix her up with his friend.

'Exactly what?'

'Well, you are a man, right?'

'All man, baby.'

'And you'd rather go out with a model, any model, than me.'

'Um, is that a trick question?'

'Of course you would. So why? Why is he pretending not to fancy this model girl and pretending to fancy me? The fat chick?'

'Er . . . because he fancies you?' Daniel looked perplexed.

'No, because he thinks he can get me. Because he knows that a model is out of his league, but that I'm not.'

'Darling, you've got that wrong. James knows he can get off with a model. She keeps asking him out. It's not that he can't get her, although how that happened is one of the great unsolved mysteries of the universe. It's that he doesn't want her. He wants you.'

'Well, he can't have me, the cheek of it!'

Daniel looked perplexed. 'I really don't get women, even you sometimes, and you're the coolest woman I know. Hardly like a woman at all.'

'Thanks!'

'That's a compliment! Anyway, come up, come up. I've got lots to tell you and something to ask you, and Kayla's up there hinting about moving in and I have no idea how to tell her I don't like her *that* much. By the way, you're going to need that thing out there. It's brass monkeys, as you Brits inexplicably say.'

'If you want Kayla to stop thinking that you're in a relationship, you could try stopping sleeping with her. That might help,' Willow whispered as she followed Daniel out of a casement window and onto his roof terrace. 'The thing about women is that they tend to think if you have loads of sex with them, spend all your free time with them, make them breakfast and let them wear your shirts, that you do like them that much, that you might even love them. It's deluded, I know, but it's the way we're brought up.'

'Well, it's just plain wrong,' Daniel whispered, pausing to pretend to examine one of his potted tomato plants. 'I don't want to finish things with her, I do like her, but I don't want to live with her. She rarely has anything interesting to say and if she stays up too late she gets these bags . . . It's like all the fat in her body collects under her eyes overnight.'

'Sometimes I actually think you hate women,' Willow muttered, forcing herself to smile at Serious James, who was leaning rather self-consciously on the low brick wall that surrounded the roof terrace, and waving at Kayla.

'Well, that can't be true,' Daniel said, patting her fleetingly on her bottom, sending a thrill up Willow's spine. 'I love you.'

'Willow, how nice to see you!' Kayla, who had been turning prawns on Daniel's barbecue while the light drizzle of rain beaded her hair, came to greet Willow, like a good girlfriend and, therefore, co-host should, Willow thought.

'A barbecue at this time of year, crazy, right? The things we girls do for love. I'm freezing! You look lovely, though. Fur is very on trend.' The poor girl really had no idea at all that she wasn't Daniel's girlfriend. And Willow knew from past experience that he wouldn't tell her either. When he got bored of her he'd just leave her to come to that conclusion herself, after a series of missed calls and unanswered texts.

'It's only while I'm cooking. We can go inside in a sec. But seriously, I thought the English loved the outdoor life,' said Daniel.

With her long legs – she was even taller than Daniel – and her burnt-umber hair, Kayla was everything the average person on the street expected of a model, *and* she was nice, despite Daniel's protestations. That was the trouble: she was too nice. She wanted things from Daniel that, when you added them all together, constituted a future and, despite being forty, Daniel still wasn't ready to think past next week. He really was incredibly immature. He was the sort of man that any sensible woman would avoid with a bargepole, but Willow had never been a sensible woman. In fact, she was so stupid that she let him unwittingly torment her without even getting any of the sex that he was so prone to spreading around. She consoled herself with the knowledge that he liked and respected her in a way that he never did his lovers.

'You look great, Willow. That dress is amazing – it really suits you. You are so lucky being able to wear yellow.'

'You are so lucky being a catwalk model!' Willow countered.

'I'd trade in these legs for those boobs any day,' Kayla went on in her usual sweet ritual of trying to show lesser beings that she was just like them, even in the rain, which she obviously hated.

'Shame, really, you never get long legs and big breasts in one package,' Serious James said out of the blue, cupping his hands in front of his chest in an ill-advised mime. Willow and Kayla looked at him. He was wearing a sort of parka, with the hood up, which make him look like a vaguely menacing sex pest. 'I mean, I suppose you could. I expect there are women with big breasts and long legs, but probably not real ones. Not real breasts, I mean. Probably implants, and I don't think implants are sexy at all. I mean, they're not supposed to point straight out when you see them naked, are they, and I think that the whole sex with a big-breasted woman thing would be spoiled because I'd be feeling them and all I'd be thinking about would be that little silicone sack in there, and that's not sexy. What I mean is that a naturally shaped woman, whatever that shape might be, is better than one that's been surgically enhanced—'

'James, shut up, mate.' Daniel clapped his friend on the shoulder and handed him a beer. 'Stop talking before these two have you arrested.'

'It's the cold. I've got hypothermic delusions,' James complained, and yet he was out here too, waiting for Daniel's unseasonal cooking. Daniel really did have a knack of getting anyone to do anything for him.

'Is that your routine?' Kayla asked James. 'Is that what you're doing on Thursday? Only it's not really very funny.'

Willow repressed a smile. Sweet-natured and beautiful as Kayla was, she had a natural talent for tactlessness that Willow liked about her, even when it was directed at her.

'No, honestly, it's me not being able to talk . . . around women that I . . . admire,' James confessed, dipping his head so his hood slipped back, revealing his tousled blond hair. 'I've always been the same since school.'

'Apparently you told Lexi the name of every star in the sky. She said you were the most interesting man she's ever met. You didn't have any trouble talking to her!' Kayla said, adding a touch bitterly, 'And she's just got *Sports Illustrated*, swimsuit issue.'

'Lexi is very nice. She's very . . . tall. I like her, but I don't, you know . . .' James flushed crimson. 'I like her as a person.'

'I know. I think that's why she's in love with you,' Kayla giggled. 'No one ever liked Lexi as a person before, which is hardly surprising – she's a bitch.'

James smiled at Willow before examining the top of his bottle of beer. 'That's why I'm still single. I'll either have to marry a beautiful deaf girl who can't hear the offensive drivel I come out with, or someone I don't find attractive at all but can enjoy witty banter with. It's my only hope. How's your hearing, Willow?'

'Willow's not deaf, James!' Kayla shook her head, rolling her eyes at Willow. 'Just try to relax and be yourself, like you are around Lexi. Apparently that person is a dream date. OK?' Kayla patted him, just short of on the head, and wandered off to where Daniel was incinerating shellfish, leaving Willow and James alone, each one furiously fumbling for something to say to the other.

At a loss, Willow watched as Kayla draped her long arm around Daniel's shoulders and rested her head against him, a sweet casual gesture of affection. It must be nice to be that relaxed with another person, even if it was an illusion. Kayla really didn't deserve the way that Daniel talked about her.

'So,' James said out of the blue, having clearly geared himself up for a conversation, 'how's work?'

'Oh, the same self-serving narcissistic cannibalistic frenzy that it always is,' Willow remarked.

James laughed, a little too enthusiastically. Then there was silence again. After one more excruciating moment of awkwardness Willow took pity on him.

'So how's the stand-up going?'

'Not bad, actually.' James hazarded a rather sweet lopsided smile, which gave him a boyish air. 'I've got my first ever paid gig next Thursday. When I say paid, I mean fifty quid and a couple of pints, but still, it's come out of all the open mic stuff I've been doing, so it's a step up, of sorts. It's in a pub near Battersea Bridge. Maybe you could come along, a bit of moral support? With everyone else, I mean?'

'Well, I could do with a laugh,' Willow said politely. 'It's just I've—'

'Oh, that's brilliant, I'd love it if you were there. I think it would make me really go for it—' They both spoke at the same time, James realising that Willow was turning him down seconds too late.

'But of course if you're busy . . .' James's neck flared scarlet.

'No, no, I *will* come. If I possibly can I will,' Willow found herself saying because she couldn't bear his discomfort and disappointment any more. 'I do have this complicated work thing and this other complicated sort of family thing that might get in the way, but providing the situation is stable and doesn't look like it might go nuclear then I will be there.'

'Right.' James nodded. 'Right. Well, thanks. I mean, it's no big deal, one way or the other. You do work in a talent agency, right? Not a bomb disposal unit?'

'Fair point,' Willow said, her wry smile rendering him

unable to look at her, opting to study the horizon instead, where London's jagged edges were tearing at the soft pink evening sky.

'I do get a bit caught up in my work sometimes,' Willow said. 'But honestly, I'm not making it up. It is a really delicate situation. I can't tell you about it . . . which makes me sound like I think I work for MI5, I know. But my point is I'm not trying to think up an excuse because I don't want to come.'

'Really?' James asked her.

'Really. I will be there if I can. I actually think you are very brave. If a bit mad. It's a fine line, isn't it, between people laughing with you or at you.'

'I'd settle for near me,' James said. 'Well, if you can make it then we're all going for a drink afterwards – that's assuming I'm not in A&E with a serious head trauma from all the objects that will be thrown at me.'

Willow smiled, which gave James the courage to look at her again.

'I almost made you laugh,' he said, holding her gaze for a second or two before dropping his eyes to the floor.

'Almost,' Willow replied.

'It's a start.' James nodded, that sweet smile slowly returning. 'I'd really like to be the one to make you laugh, Willow.'

There was silence between them while Willow tried to work out what he meant by that comment, and he tried and failed for some time to think of something else to say.

'Those are stunning shoes, by the way,' James said eventually, gesturing at her feet. 'You have the most beautiful ankles, like . . . like . . . oh, I really didn't think about where I was planning to go with that sentence.'

'I tell you what, let's just leave it at that and say no more about it,' Willow said, repressing a smile.

'Talking to you is just like talking to Annabel Fisher,' James said.

'Who?'

'This girl at school. She was in the year above me, a real warrior queen, pink hair and attitude – you know the sort. I had the hugest crush on her, only she didn't like me because I wasn't cool. I was last of the boys in my year to have a growth spurt and I had a bit of a stutter back then. Didn't stop me, though. I was like a little kamikaze Romeo. I'd be there every break-time trying to have a conversation with her. It never worked, but I'm nothing if not persistent.'

Willow looked at him thoughtfully for a moment. 'Brave, more like. You must be brave to want to do stand-up. I'd never have the guts.'

'Perhaps,' James shrugged. 'Courage in all things, that's sort of my motto. If I lose in life, I never want it to be because I was too afraid to try.'

For the briefest of moments the two held each other's gazes, and Willow got the feeling he was about to say something more.

'James, I thought I told you to stop talking out loud to women,' Daniel called from inside, where he was laying out prawn and chicken kebabs. 'Come inside and eat. I need to ask Willow about you know what.'

'You know what?' Willow looked at James, who instantly looked guilty.

'What? *What?*' Willow followed the others inside and went to hang her coat up, awkwardly sidestepping James, who was waiting behind her for the coat hook, so that the side of her bosom brushed the back of his hand.

'Oh God, I didn't –'

'I know,' Willow smiled at him.

It really did seem that he couldn't do anything right around her. It was like looking at the reverse image of Daniel, with all his dark good looks and smooth talking. James was blond, Celtic-looking with his greenish eyes, although totally lacking a silver tongue to go with it. He was tall and unruly, where Daniel was compact and neat. He was one of those people who was born to be untidy, with his white shirt buttoned up wrong and his hair giving the very strong impression that he'd recently been through a hedge the wrong way.

Willow leaned in closer to him, enjoying the paralysis of uncertainty as she whispered in his ear, 'Your buttons are done up wrong.'

Leaving James to defluster himself, Willow followed Daniel into his living room and slid onto a chair, conscious of the James-sized space that Daniel and Kayla had left next to her. 'What do you want to ask me?'

'*Venus at a Mirror*,' Daniel said, leaning over so that he could remove a piece of folded paper from the pocket of his jeans. 'Painted in 1615 by Rubens. He was in his late thirties at the time.' Daniel spread an image of the painting out in front of Willow. 'This gorgeous big blonde girl is featured in much of his work from that time, which is why people often describe larger women as Rubenesque.'

'Code for "fat", you mean,' Willow said, taking the colour photocopy that Daniel handed her and smoothing it out on the table. It showed the image of a porcelain-skinned woman from behind, her large bottom topped with generous hips nestled into velvet cushions, ripples of flesh shimmering down her back. Her long blonde hair was tossed over one shoulder and you could see only the reflection of her face in a mirror that was being held by a rather knowing-looking boy, possibly a cherub, whose gaze was most certainly not directed at her face. To the right of her, a black male servant looked rather bored.

'You have no idea how risqué it was in those days for the nude to be looking directly at the viewer, even via a reflection. That seductive, flirtatious look she's giving you, that's practically the invention of porn.'

'She's gorgeous,' James said, as he took his seat, now properly buttoned. 'Perfect.'

'She's got awful cellulite, though,' Kayla added.

'Pah, cellulite was invented by cosmetic companies to give you women a new complex to spend money on,' Daniel said dismissively.

'I, for one, like a woman with curves,' James repeated, pouring himself a large glass of wine.

'I think we are all aware of that. Now I suggest you hush your mouth before Willow has to take a restraining order out on you.'

'What has this got to do with me?' Willow asked him, well aware that he was skirting around something.

'I'm putting together an exhibition. I'm reimagining old masters through photography. These paintings were about so much more than just the subject; they were full of hidden meanings, symbolism that was as easy to read to the people of the time as Twitter is to us. But over the centuries that meaning has become lost. I want to shoot these images, with the amazing lighting and texture and sexiness of the originals, but make them relevant, ironic, irreverent. So maybe I'll include some anti-cellulite cream, maybe I'll have a folded copy of a celeb magazine. At first glance you see a straight reproduction of a famous painting, but look again and it's a comment on modern life. Just as the original artist meant.'

Willow studied the painting. 'It's a good idea, Daniel, it's a really good idea. But I still don't see what it's got to do with me.'

Daniel hesitated. He had the look of a naughty schoolboy who'd just drawn a penis on his desk with indelible marker.

'James is going to be both the Ambassadors in my version of Holbein's masterpiece, but instead of an anamorphic skull, I'm going to have an anamorphic iPhone.'

'Is he?' Willow looked interested. 'I think I know that one . . .'

'Kayla is going to be all three Graces, the 1531 version by Lucas Cranach the Elder. That involves full-front nudity and a total wax.'

'Which isn't a problem because I already have a total wax,' Kayla told her casually, turning Serious James bright red again in an instant.

'Wow, Kayla – you're brave.'

'Not really. And it will be good for my portfolio, plus I've done full nudity loads of times before, so it's no biggy.'

'Well,' Willow smiled at Daniel, 'I'm impressed. You actually have a grown-up and very interesting idea. How do you want me to help? Hook you up with some publicity-hungry celebs?'

'Not exactly . . .' Daniel said, looking like he was waiting for the penny to drop.

Willow glanced back down at the image of the big naked blonde woman and the penny clattered noisily to the ground.

'No. Oh, no, no, no, Daniel. No.' Willow was firm. 'No,

Daniel. I'm not getting my fat arse out for you or anyone else to mock. Get a model – get two; they might add up to a normal-sized person.'

'Not to mock, Willow, to adore,' Daniel insisted, as passionate about his idea as Willow had seen him about anything in a long time. 'The whole point is I need ordinary people to do this. That's what's going to make it so real, so touching. And look at her. She's radiant. In her time she was the very pinnacle of what was considered beautiful. I started with this image; the whole idea came from this because I was thinking about you. The first clever, brilliant thing I've come up with in months came from you.' Daniel leaned across the table a little, looking into Willow's eyes so that for a moment it felt like they were alone. 'I never told you, because I knew it would piss you off. But the first moment I met you I thought of Rubens' Venus. That's kind of my own private nickname for you. There isn't another woman in the world I'd put in this picture, and without this picture I'd have to scrap the whole idea.'

Willow looked at him and in that moment a silent communication passed between them that both Kayla and James registered but neither understood.

'Things are different now, now I know how much you mean to me,' Daniel said out loud. 'I'd never do anything that put that at risk.'

Sitting back to break the spell that Daniel had so expertly cast between them, Willow looked at James. 'Do you think I should do it?' she asked him, quite unfairly.

'I think you should if you want to,' he said carefully. 'I think it's the best idea Daniel's ever had. I think . . . I think if you do, he will do you and the painting and the Rubenesque lady here justice. He'll show the world how truly beautiful you are.'

'Oh, go on, Willow,' Kayla cut in, rather to Willow's relief. 'We can do ours together, and I promise you when you're naked in front of a photographer it's not embarrassing at all. They don't even see you. They just see shapes, shadows and light. You forget you've got no clothes on after a bit.'

'But what about the cherub and the other guy?'

'Shop mannequins,' Daniel told her. 'To signify our obsession with self-image. In the seventeenth century it was a status symbol to have slaves wait on you; in the twenty-first century we are all slaves to self-image.'

Willow thought for a moment, aware of three pairs of eyes on her. Three things she knew for a fact. A day ago she would never, never ever have had the courage to do something like this, and in a few days' time she might not again, but at that magical moment, she thought she might. Daniel always said what he had to in order to get what he wanted; he could charm birds out of trees with a look or a smile. But the way he'd looked at her just then, he had never done that before, not even when . . . well, not even in their closest moments. For those few seconds Willow felt like he knew her utterly, and that in his eyes she was a whole person. And she knew that she had to find out if that was true, because there may not be very many more, if any, moments, when she could.

'Fuck it, OK then,' she said, feeling a rush of adrenalin surge through her. 'OK!'

'Brilliant! When?' Daniel asked her, anxious to seal the deal before she backed out.

'Soon, before I change my mind. Monday, but it'll have to be evening. There's some stuff I've got to do.'

'Oh, I can't do Monday evening, I've got a shoot,' Kayla said.

'Doesn't matter,' Daniel said. 'I'll do you earlier. That way I can really concentrate on Willow. So Monday evening here, at the studio. You, me and the camera.'

'And several bottles of wine,' Willow said, the idea of posing naked for Daniel thrilling and terrifying her all at once. To be near him for any longer now would be too difficult. Either she'd change his mind, or something about him would change, something that showed he had really meant all those things he'd said just now. Looking for an out she glanced at her watch; it wasn't even ten yet.

'I've got to go, actually. Thanks for the wine and the food . . . although I didn't get round to eating any.'

'Really? Do you really have to go?' James asked her, dismayed.

'Don't go yet, Will,' Daniel said. 'I don't see you enough.'

'I've got to. I've got this . . .' she smiled at James, '. . . couple of unexploded bombs I've got to look after. It's a long story.'

'I'll see you out,' James said, before either Daniel or Kayla could offer to do the same, although Willow got the distinct feeling that they both wanted to. Disappointed that it wasn't Daniel who was escorting her down the stairs, she had nevertheless warmed a little to Serious James and his odd mix of awkwardness and sincerity.

'So I'll maybe see you Thursday, then?' he asked her as they reached the front door. 'At the gig?'

'Yes.' Willow nodded. 'Yes, I'll try and be there, I will. Bye, then.'

James made no move to leave.

'Or . . . if you like – if you *wanted* – I could come along to the studio on Monday evening and sort of chaperon?'

Willow could not hide her mirth. 'James, look, if you do fancy me then I think that really we should go on at least one date before you see me naked, don't you?'

'Oh God.' James looked mortified. 'It's not that. I don't want to see you naked. I mean, I do, but that's not why I . . . Daniel can be terrible. And sometimes he doesn't really care how terrible he is.'

'James, I know that already. Daniel is my best friend. I know everything about him. You don't have to worry, I can look after myself.'

'Willow . . .'

Willow waited.

'I think you are really very nice. Quite the nicest person I know.'

'Thank you. I think you are very . . . you. I'll see you Thursday, then.'

'And . . .'

Willow had walked a few steps before turning back. 'And?'

'I'll see you Thursday.' James nodded, and Willow knew he was watching her as she walked down the street, probably only going back inside once she had climbed into a black cab.

It was a cold evening, and once she was ensconced safely in the back of the cab Willow drew her coat even more tightly around her, trying to imagine the woman who had once worn it, the arms of her husband or lover around her the first time she had tried it on, that sense of loving or being loved. Willow opened her eyes and slid the little locket out of its bag, turning it over and over in the palm of her hand. It looked like nothing, just a little dull grey grubby disc, but to Willow it seemed like a key, a small mundane mystery, a window into a life that was probably not all that different from a million other lives but which crucially would be so different from hers. Without thinking she pressed the locket to her lips and kissed it before slipping it back into the pocket where it seemed to belong, just as her phone started to vibrate.

'Tell all,' Holly said by way of a greeting.

Chapter Nine

When she got back from Daniel's, her head full of what it would be like to be with him, alone, naked, Willow found, not exactly the sort of trouble she'd feared when she went out, but a very close approximation of it.

The first thing she smelled when she got in was cigarette smoke.

The living room was empty but, seeing the flicker of the TV under the closed door, Willow checked her own bedroom, hoping against hope that not only did India smoke, she found it acceptable to indulge in the habit in the bed of her host, unlikely as it seemed, considering her objection to frozen peas.

India was not smoking, though. She was asleep in Willow's bed, the TV on some trashy channel, an empty bottle of garage wine on the bedside table, no glass apparent and a halo of cake crumbs surrounding her head on the pillow. She must have gone to sleep clutching her phone, which now lay loosely in her fingers, as if she had only recently surrendered to sleep. After a moment's hesitation Willow picked it up and checked the call register. There were sixty-eight missed calls, almost all of them from unrecognised or withheld numbers – probably the press –

and certainly none that read 'Mum' or 'Dad'. Willow noticed a few from someone called Tally, who she guessed was the trusted best friend, and one from 'H'. After a moment's hesitation Willow checked the dialled calls. 'H' had been dialled a total of eighteen times, which suggested that he had not picked up until someone had been forced to return her persistent calls, probably a publicist . . . or maybe his wife. Willow wondered what had been said and if it had anything to do with the other empty bottle of garage wine, the neck of which poked out from under the bed. India stirred as Willow put the phone back, scooping up the empty at the same time.

'Wha . . . oh, you're back. Sorry, I'm in your bed and there are crumbs.'

'Don't worry,' Willow said. 'It's your bed for now. Besides, I am the opposite of a princess: I can't sleep *unless* there are crumbs.'

Willow looked at India huddled in the sheets, the empty bottles of wine. The eighteen calls to 'H'.

'How are you feeling? You look a little lost.'

'I certainly do feel lost,' India said, wincing as she moved her head. 'I make a terrible alcoholic. I don't usually drink, you see, not really. Actually, I think I might have to be sick . . .'

In one movement Willow took a pot plant out of its planter and handed the pot to India. It wasn't the first time it had doubled up.

'Tomorrow I'll buy you as much mineral water and vegetable matter as it takes to max out Victoria's card. I can't have you going to pieces on my watch. There'll be a heroic wronged-starlet photoshoot any time now.'

'Am I a starlet?' India's delicate features seemed to fall

inwards. 'I never wanted to be a starlet.' She looked around the room. 'I think vegetables are a good idea. I've eaten all the emergency cupcakes, anyway.'

The stench of fresh smoke rose in the air.

'Have you been enjoying a cigarette with your cake?' Willow asked hopefully.

'Oh, no. Sorry, Willow. I did say I thought it was a bad idea, what with the baby and everything, but after she went to the garage to buy me wine it did seem like a terrible double standard to lecture her.'

'Right. Well, I'll leave you . . .' At that point India retched violently and Willow made a tactical withdrawal. '. . . to it.'

Chloe was lying in the bed in the spare room, plugged into her iPod, watching the TV, tapping cigarette ash into the saucer that was resting on her swollen abdomen, half a glass of wine on the bedside table.

Willow watched her for a second, trying to pair up this alien creature with the little girl she had once known, unable to make any coherent comparison.

'What the fuck are you doing?' she said, but Chloe seemed intent on ignoring her.

Suddenly furious and unable to stop herself Willow marched over to her and yanked the earphones out of her ears.

'Oi!' Chloe protested as Willow snatched the cigarette out of her hand and threw it out of the partially open window. '*What the fuck . . . ?*'

'What the fuck? What the fuck? I'll give you what the fuck. How about what the *fuck* are you doing smoking and drinking when you are six months' pregnant? How about what the *fuck* are you doing smoking and drinking when you are fifteen years old? You might not want that baby, but that's no reason to try and fuck it up before it's born!'

Willow stopped mid-rant, pointed finger frozen mid-air, belatedly realising that she may have gone in a little heavy-handed.

'Fuck this,' Chloe said, heaving herself off the bed and barging past Willow.

'Where do you think you're going?' Willow asked her, following her into the living room.

'I don't know and I don't care, as long as it's not here,' Chloe said, pulling a coat on over her nightshirt and slippers. 'I'm not staying here to be talked to like that by *you*, of all people.'

'What the hell is that supposed to mean?' Willow bellowed at her.

'It was just a couple of fags. I'm stressed, all right? I thought they might calm me down!'

Willow just stared at her. 'But you know – *everybody* knows – that drinking and smoking can hurt an unborn baby.'

'Yes, yes, I know – but what about me? I am still here, I am still a person, I haven't turned into a baby carrier overnight. I still get stressed. It's not even going to be my baby anyway . . . so what do I care?'

Willow ran her hands through her hair, at a loss. It was hard to find reasons to tell the girl to care, when for most of her life she'd been struggling and failing to do exactly the same thing.

'You care. If you didn't care you wouldn't be six months' pregnant. You'd have had a termination. You wouldn't have thought about adoption.'

'That's not true,' Chloe said, her voice dropping. 'I would

have. I would have got rid of it, but I couldn't, not without Dad finding out. I tried but they won't let you when you're under sixteen. And I couldn't . . . I just couldn't tell him. I wasn't ready to see that look on his face. So you see, I'm not a good person, I'm not a caring person, I'm not thinking about the baby or the woman out there who really wants a kid. I just couldn't face talking to Dad, that's it. And when it got too big to hide it any more, well, this was the only place I knew where to come. So . . . there. That's the truth.'

Willow closed her eyes for a moment, she was in danger of getting this all so wrong.

'It's the thought of seeing a doctor and the Social Services, isn't it?' Willow guessed. 'That's what's freaked you out.'

Chloe nodded, unable to look her in the eye, fiddling with the hem of her dressing gown sleeves.

'I'm sorry, I didn't think. You seemed to be taking it all in your stride. I just thought you were OK.'

The two stood for a moment and then Willow held out her arms. After a second's hesitation Chloe walked into them and let Willow hold her. It was an awkward, uncertain embrace for both of them, but they persisted, each aware that the other one was something of a beginner at hugging.

'I'm not very good at this,' Willow confided in her. 'Knowing what to do, or say to people. Sometimes I think I could be good at it, but then I mess up. I always mess up.'

'That's not true. When you came to live with us, you were brilliant,' Chloe said, into her shoulder. 'At first, when Dad told me he liked you, I was pissed off. I didn't want you around. I liked it being just me and him. But then, after a while, I liked it. I liked getting to say what the other kids said at school. I liked getting to say, "I'll ask my stepmum", "My stepmum said . . ." I liked you being there.'

Willow was silent, battling the quiet rent that was ripping open inside her chest, the uncharacteristic ebullience she had felt earlier ebbing away as she was faced with a reflection of her past, a version of her that she hated to face at all.

'I couldn't believe that Dad took you away from me; I couldn't believe it. I came home from school and you . . . you just weren't there and he wouldn't say anything except that he didn't love you any more.' Chloe looked up at Willow. 'I wasn't even allowed to call you.'

'Chloe . . .'

'And you didn't try to call me, did you?' Chloe went on, her dark eyes searching Willow's. 'I mean, I looked, I thought maybe you'd written and Dad had intercepted the letters and hidden them, I don't know why. I saw it in this film once. So I looked for them, but I couldn't find any. You never called, or came round, did you? You never turned up at the school gate. You didn't try to see me at all . . . did you?' Chloe's tone was finely balanced between heartbreak and hope.

'I . . . well . . . it was what your dad wanted. He thought a clean break was for the best,' Willow said, engulfed in cowardice.

'I hate him,' Chloe said flatly.

'Why? Because of me and him splitting up?'

'Because he hates me,' Chloe said simply.

'Chloe, you might feel like that, but it just isn't true. You are everything to Sam.'

'It is, it's so true. He used to love me when I was cute and funny and never did anything wrong, but now I just wear him down. I know it's true because I heard him telling bitch-face.

That's what he said. He said I wore him down. She was the one who suggested boarding school. "You need to give yourself a break, darling. Don't let her drag you down too." ' Chloe's face contorted as she mimicked the woman. 'He didn't stand up for me, not even a bit.'

'That doesn't sound like your dad,' Willow said, guiding Chloe back to the spare bedroom and slipping her coat off her shoulders. 'Your dad would move mountains for you.'

'Not now he wouldn't,' Chloe said as she sat wearily on the bed. 'Even bitch-face doesn't make him happy, she just makes him look old. Nothing makes him happy any more. The business is failing, he can't really afford to send me away to school. And I just make things worse.'

Willow sighed. 'I'm not going to lie. Getting pregnant at fifteen isn't helping. But this isn't a new story. Millions of people have gone through what you're going through, and got through it. You will too. Look, let's just take this one step at a time, together. Somehow, between us, we will work it out.'

'Do you mean it?' Chloe asked her as she lay back on the bed.

'Of course I do.'

'There's just one thing I don't get,' Chloe said. 'If you're prepared to do all this for me now, when I'm like this, why didn't you stick around for me then? I needed you then, too.'

'I . . .' Willow opened and closed her mouth, looking longingly at the open bedroom door. 'I just wasn't . . . aren't a good enough person.'

'Bollocks, that's not it,' Chloe muttered, but before Willow could respond she was asleep.

Chapter Ten

Willow hesitated – hovered, more like – a few yards down the road from where Daniel Fayre was waiting for her to take her clothes off. She wrapped her coat around her and stood stock-still in the middle of the pavement. Until this moment she hadn't given this very particular event a second thought, her life had been so full of other people, and then all of a sudden here she was. About to be naked in front of Daniel.

Seeing the typically fashionable people of Hoxton eye her suspiciously as she loitered in her fur coat and shoes, looking like she'd been transported to the present from a black-and-white film, Willow made a point of going to the nearest shop window and looking in it. For several minutes she stared unseeing before she realised that it was a small art gallery, that was currently displaying an exhibition of watercolours of vaginas.

Willow checked her watch. In three minutes she would be late and she had a pathological inability to be late for anything. No matter how she tried, no matter how she might dread whatever appointment fate had in store for her, from root canal surgery, to her yearly appraisal with Victoria, or holding the world's neediest soap star's hand during a bikini wax, she was always exactly on time.

Her stepfather had once told her that lateness was the ultimate insult. 'If you are late,' he explained reasonably when she and Holly had once returned from the park just as the sun was setting and just before her mother had sent out a search party, 'you are wasting the precious moments of another person's life. Moments that they can never get back. Do you see?' He hadn't been cross, just worried and tired-looking. Pleased to see them home safe, he'd patted them on the heads and then left it to their mother to do all the shouting and angry crying. It was Ian's words that had stayed with Willow, though: the legacy Ian had left her. The idea that another person could eat away minutes of your life without a second thought appalled her.

Which meant that she had three minutes both to ask and answer the question that she had been studiously ignoring, even though it had been following her around in ten-foot-high flashing neon lights since the moment she'd agreed to Daniel's request. What exactly did she think she was doing taking her clothes off for Daniel, especially after everything that had happened earlier that day?

There had been numerous occasions over the weekend when Willow considered calling Daniel and backing out. She'd even kept her phone on her at all times, certain that he'd think the proposal through, realise it was a terrible idea for many obvious reasons and call it off. But he didn't call, and in the fuss and bustle of keeping two young women from killing both themselves and each other, Willow put the whole ridiculous business out of her mind.

Tugging up the collar of her coat and nuzzling her mouth and chin into its soft warmth as she procrastinated, Willow smiled to herself, briefly distracted as she thought of the last chaotic few days.

Having Chloe there again, even as she was, was like going back in time. Willow had forgotten, or rather struggled hard not to remember, how much they had laughed together. How Willow would make up preposterous stories about wolf-eating monster pigs or nasty prince-stalking Cinderellas and tell them to Chloe on the way to school and back. Sometimes Chloe would be doubled up with laughter; sometimes they'd have to stop in the street, holding gloved hands, leaning on each other while they gasped for air, their giggles materialising as vapour in the frosty air. Making Chloe laugh had fast become Willow's main objective in life. Every night as she went to sleep she'd think about things that would elicit that lovely gurgling giggle from the little girl, that would make her eyes light up and sparkle.

Chloe wasn't quite so willing to laugh at Willow's jokes now, but in the midst of the terrible horror-movie marathon, all kinds of junk food and home-made style makeovers, she had seen Chloe's tired worried face transform with laughter. Her smile was like a balm, like a miracle salve that eased any pain. Willow had watched her as she plastered India's perfect English rose complexion with about as much gothic make-up as it could take and wondered if that was what it was like to love your own child, that aching mixture of joy and anxiety. Did Chloe have any idea of what she might be giving up with her baby? How could she possibly know what it was like to miss a child you had no rights to any more?

But Willow had only wanted to see Chloe laugh, so she didn't say anything. In fact, the three of them had whiled away the weekend in splendid isolation as if the world outside their door was a universe away and had nothing at all to do with them.

There had been one intrusion from reality: a phone call with Victoria.

'How's the suicide watch going, darling?' was her greeting. Sensing it was best not to have this conversation where India could hear one side and Victoria might hear Chloe, Willow retreated into what had become India's bedroom, sitting on a bed strewn with tear-soaked tissues.

'Not bad,' Willow said, picking up a fraction of a photo of Hugh, which looked like it had been torn out of a magazine and then ripped to shreds. Peals of laughter chimed from the other room; Chloe was no doubt showing India what a spot of back-combing could do for an international superstar. 'She seems quite upbeat, actually.'

'Good, perfect.' Victoria inhaled sharply. 'I think I've cracked it, brokered a deal that means India's going to come out of this smelling like fucking roses, darling.'

'Really? That's great news,' Willow replied as she found a single man's sock stuffed under the pillow. She didn't have to get too close to it to realise it had been worn recently, and not by a fragrant young woman. India's scratch-and-sniff keepsake of Hugh? Gingerly Willow tucked it back into its hiding place.

'Trouble is, it's going to be hard on her. She's going to have to tough it out. Be prepared. Long and short of it, I want you to prepare her.'

Willow's heart sank at a rate of knots. What deal with the Devil had Victoria made this time?

'Prepare her for what?'

'The others, darling. His other women. A whole string of them waiting to kiss and tell. All much younger, impressionable, in his evil thrall. One of them was a bit famous for a while, had that recurring part in *CSI Whatever.* Met Hugh when she was working with him in the West End, where he gave her repeat performances night after night, if you know what I mean.' Victoria morphed into a passable Mae West impersonation.

'Isn't he a bit impotent?'

'Yes, but not for the purposes of this story. For this story he's a heartless fucker. Literally heartlessly fucking his way through innocent young women. So I've got her, wossername, and also two others, for starters. A make-up girl with a four-year-old, who let's just say looks terribly Hugh-like, and another actress who hasn't worked in years and will say almost anything for a walk-on part in *Casualty.*'

Willow sighed as she realised what she had to prepare India for. Not only were the most intimate details of her personal life about to be discussed in public, she was also going to discover that the special love she thought that Hugh had for her was nothing but a pastiche, a much-thumbed script that he'd read from over and over again. Theirs was not a great love torn apart by circumstance. She'd fallen victim to a dirty old womaniser.

'So India wasn't his one mistake, the love he couldn't ignore. She was one in a long line of lovers. That's going to hurt.'

'I know, but it's cruel to be kind. These girls sell their stories to the red tops. The red tops lay off India, Hugh gets what's coming to him and India is the victim, the innocent recovering from escaping the grasps of a sex addict. I've already got *OK!* and *Hello!* in a bidding frenzy, darling, and I can organise a *hoard* of close personal friends to let a few things slip to *Grazia.* Of course, she'll have to go back and finish the film, and so will he. Neither of them can afford the lawsuit if they don't. But the curiosity of the public will make it a hit and everyone's happy.' Victoria paused for breath. 'What I might do is get her a boyfriend, darling, someone young and wholesome. Maybe the gay one that's not out yet from . . . oh, what's that band called? You know, the fat one? Although, according to his manager he's not fat, he's a lazy bulimic. Actually, I might call him now . . . Prepare away, darling. Prepare away.'

Willow sat on the edge of the bed for a moment or two, listening to Chloe shriek with laughter as India fashioned her a red-carpet gown out of some bed sheets, and wondered how it always seemed to be her job to do the preparing. What good would it do, she wondered, to tell India now, when she was verging on some loose version of happy, about Hugh's other women? How would it help her? Surely it would be better to let her spend the rest of the day, and as long as possible, keeping the cruelty of the world at bay?

Willow thought she had at least another twenty-four hours' worth of terrible horror films. Factor in some sleeping, eating and a news blackout unwittingly imposed by Chloe, who refused to watch anything 'boring', then she thought she could keep India in her nice little bubble for a good while longer yet. It wasn't a good idea to disobey Victoria but perhaps it was having Chloe in her home again, perhaps it was seeing quite how fragile India was, but anyway, Willow decided not to prepare her. She had decided to protect her instead.

'All right, love?' A man in a denim boiler suit and fashionably thick-framed glasses winked at her. 'You the artist's model?'

'Me? The artist's model?'

He nodded at the display of delicately painted female organs.

'Oh!' Willow blushed, hurrying a little further down the street where she found a newsagent's to loiter in. If she left now she could be there in less than a minute. Daniel's studio was big and cold, but he'd promised her a minimum of four electric heaters. Willow shivered just thinking about it. Still, she had to decide.

Maybe if she'd followed Victoria's orders and prepared India she would be thinking about this less and just going for it, going for naked time alone with Daniel. It was a bona fide dream come true. It was the textbook situation where boy kisses girl and girl relents. It was the way it was supposed to happen.

But Willow hadn't done as Victoria told her and the consequences had led her to realise that perhaps her scatter-gun approach to life wasn't always the best plan.

Sam had arrived at ten that morning, to take Chloe and Willow to Chloe's first antenatal appointment. Willow had been uncertain where to go with her, in the end booking her directly into the local hospital antenatal department, where the receptionist had sounded decidedly bored by Willow's brief recounting of Chloe's age and her own lapsed step-parent status. She had texted Sam the details, too afraid to speak to him in person, and he'd arrived in his big black Audi 4x4, exactly on time. As Willow settled India in front of another movie she wondered if he remembered how particular she was about punctuality. A tiny thrill that he might still think of her at all, even in passing, fluttered uncomfortably in her chest.

Chloe clambered into the front seat, next to Sam, and Willow had rather awkwardly hauled herself up into the back, her fur coat slippery on the cream leather upholstery, taking a seat behind Chloe.

'This is a lot of car,' she said. 'Have you taken up farming?'

Sam ignored her, blowing away the last thrilling flutters in a single well-placed puff of indifference. Instead, as they pulled into the sluggish traffic, he glanced at his daughter, who, a perfect mirror image of her father, was doing her best to blank him.

'How have you been?' he asked her tentatively.

'Fine,' Chloe said, without tearing her gaze away from the window.

'I tried calling . . .'

'I know.'

Sam shifted slightly in his seat; Willow saw the hurt in his profile. He was trying, she knew him well enough to know that. He was just as desperate and as sad as Chloe to discover this gulf that had opened up between them. It was as if he and Chloe no longer spoke the same language. How could these two people, who had been so close, have ended up this way? Silent, Willow returned her gaze to the window. If she could find a way to reconcile them, then she would do something. Something to make up for the past.

'Have you been looking after yourself, at least?' Sam said rather crossly, his eyes meeting Willow's briefly in the rear-view mirror. Willow thought about the glass of wine and cigarettes, not to mention the processed sugar and saturated fat they'd all consumed in the last few days, and she prayed that Chloe would put her before her compulsive desire to wind up her father.

'No,' Chloe said. 'Willow's been looking after me. It's been great. Like old times.'

Willow breathed a sigh of relief that was short-lived as she watched Sam bristle at the mention of old times. Once, on a cold winter's morning, before the central heating had come on, and the air in the room was still chilled with frost, Sam had gathered Willow into his arms, burying his face in her hair, and whispered, 'I'm over the moon that I love you. Loving you is the second-best thing that could possibly happen to me.'

'The second-best?' Willow had exclaimed, trying to pull away but not struggling very hard when Sam contained her within his embrace.

'The first-best is that Chloe loves you too. I couldn't ask for more, I really couldn't.'

How long, Willow wondered, how many days was it from that moment to the moment when he threw her out? How long had it taken for her to turn his happiness and contentment into anger and resentment, because it obviously still endured all these years later?

Sam had looked distinctly uncomfortable in the clinic waiting room, his long legs at odds with the rows and rows of chairs upholstered in pastels, his eyes roaming image after image of pregnant women, diagrams and cross sections. He sat, his fingers interlocked, one forefinger impatiently tapping the back of the other hand. Chloe had made a point of not sitting down at all, choosing instead to pace up and down, pausing now and then to study a leaflet, look at a poster or press all the buttons on the drinks vending machines even though she didn't have any money. Willow watched her as she scuffed the toes of her Uggs against a beanbag, wondering if she was purposefully behaving like a bored child to wind her father up, or if after all that was just exactly what she was.

Willow had wanted to keep her coat on. It felt less of a coat and more like armour now. She felt safe ensconced behind it, masked from public view, but they seemed to have turned the heating up to full in the antenatal waiting room. Warm dry air blasted through the vents directly above her head until eventually she could bear it no more and slipped the coat off her shoulders, arranging it around her like a sort of nest.

Sam eyed her across the aisle, and Willow found herself wishing that she'd put some more time into thinking about what she had put on this morning. She'd still been in weekend mode when she'd got dressed, thinking that it didn't matter if her muffin top billowed over her waistband, or that her shirt was a little tight. She'd got dressed in a hurry, pulling on a pair of jeans that she'd actually set aside for the charity shop because they hadn't buttoned up in months. Realising her mistake only after she had done them up and discovered there was room to run a finger around her waistband, Willow had been so pleased with their miraculous looseness that she elected to keep them on, pulling on a red shirt that had been in the too-tight pile too, without even thinking about it. Now she thought that perhaps she didn't look as good sitting down in the jeans as she had standing up, and that not being able to do the top three buttons up on the shirt might look good from a fashion point of view but three inches of cleavage wasn't exactly the look she was going for when it came to being the responsible adult elect.

Sensing Sam watching her, Willow looked away. It was strange to feel his eyes on her again. Once he'd looked at her with such love; it was a look that Willow hadn't thought she would ever see, and one she knew she would probably never see again. Now when he looked at her it was with repressed fury.

Obviously the clinic was running late, so they were almost an hour behind time when Chloe finally got called in by a stout, capable-looking midwife in her fifties.

'You can wait out here,' she instructed her father, who half rose from his chair, as the midwife gestured for Chloe to follow her.

'I will not!' Sam protested. 'I'm your parent, and you are under –' He stopped himself just in time, looking around.

'Ashamed of me, are you?' Chloe said gesturing around her. 'Ashamed of your underage pregnant daughter?'

'No, I . . .' Sam stood up. 'Chloe, let me come with you.'

'Wait here. Come on, Willow.'

'Sam . . .' As Willow set off after Chloe, she sent Sam an apologetic look. He shook his head and turned his back on her.

'I'm having it adopted,' Chloe told the midwife as soon as she shut the examination room door behind her. The woman, whose name badge revealed she was called Joy, looked over the rim of her glasses at Chloe, her face impassive.

'OK, well, let's just check you and baby are doing well and then, if you like, I can make you an appointment with a social worker to come and see you and talk it all through.'

'Good.' Chloe nodded, surrendering her arm while Joy took her blood pressure, and asked her a host of questions.

Willow sat there trying to take it all in so that she could report back to Sam, until finally Joy got up, spread what looked like a giant sheet of kitchen roll on the bed, and told Chloe to lie down so she could scan the baby.

'Willow,' Chloe's voice suddenly sounded very small, 'I don't want to look at it. I don't have to, do I?'

'Not if you don't feel you want to,' Joy told her gently when

Willow looked at her. 'Maybe you'd like your mum to look for you?'

'Oh, I'm not—'

'Yes, will you look?' Chloe said before Willow could correct Joy. She reached out and grabbed Willow's hand. 'Will you?'

Willow had waited, listening to the ultrasound, finding that she was holding her breath in anticipation.

'There,' Joy smiled, and Willow looked at the image of the baby, his or her profile in perfect relief. The baby had Chloe's nose and chin. As she watched it bucked and bounced a little, one tiny hand floating upwards. Willow bit her lip, squeezing Chloe's hand.

'Is it OK?' Chloe asked.

'Beautiful,' Joy told her. 'Now I've just got to take some measurements and do some checks on baby's health. You should have had two scans by now, so it will take some time. I might go a bit quiet, but don't worry. I'm just concentrating on what I'm doing.'

Chloe nodded, keeping her eyes on the ceiling tiles, and her fingers intertwined in Willow's.

Willow watched in awe as she saw a cross section of the baby's heart beating away furiously, the formation of its brain and then, without warning, quite obviously what sex it was.

'Oh!' Willow found herself gasping. 'Oh, wow!'

'Oh, oh, what? Is it deformed?' Chloe propped her head up and looked at the monitor. 'Is that a baby?' She looked horrified.

'That's a cross section of the baby. I'm checking the organs. Here, wait a sec . . .' Joy readjusted the scanner so that Chloe would see the baby's profile.

'Oh.' Chloe stared at the image. 'It doesn't look deformed.'

'No, it's not, and I think your mum just spotted what sex baby you are having!'

'Sorry,' Willow apologised, unable to keep the grin spreading over her face. 'I had no idea it could be so obvious!'

'Really?' Chloe looked at the monitor, her gaze fixed on it. 'He's a boy! Bloody hell, Willow – look! You can see his . . . thingy.'

'I know,' Willow chuckled. 'Isn't it amazing?'

Joy waited patiently as Chloe took in the image, her dark eyes hooded as she came face to face with the life she was carrying for the first time.

'That's . . . like . . . fuck!'

'It's an incredible thing, I know,' Joy said, glancing discreetly at the clock. 'Are you ready for me to stop?'

'Oh . . . oh, yes, OK. Whatever.'

Joy removed the scanner from Chloe's belly and handed her a rough piece of paper to wipe away the jelly.

'Well done. You have a very healthy baby in there. The scan dates your pregnancy at about twenty-eight weeks, your due date, believe it or not, is Christmas Day, the twenty-fifth of December.'

'Mental,' Chloe said, shaking her head as Joy printed out two photos.

'A boy!' Chloe giggled. 'There's a boy in there.' She looked at Willow, laughing. 'That's weird, right? Mental! I've got a *boy* inside me . . . ! Willow, why are you crying?'

Willow shook her head. 'It's just . . . it's a baby. Oh, Chloe, it's amazing!'

Pulling her top down over her bump, Chloe eased her legs off the gurney and put her arms around Willow.

'Don't be thick,' she said. 'It's nothing to cry about. A healthy baby is good. The fags and booze haven't mutated it at all!'

'Exactly,' Joy said, assuming Chloe was joking. 'I'll make you your next appointment for a month from now, and I'll arrange for a social worker to contact you . . . at this address?'

'Yes.' Chloe nodded when Joy indicated Willow's address. 'What will happen?'

'It might be a few days before you hear anything. They're backed up, up there: a lot of children who don't have a place to go to. It's hard to find foster parents for most of these kids . . .' Joy looked a little weary. 'Firstly, they'll talk through the adoption process with you, the practicalities, and then if you are sure it's what you want, you'll be offered counselling while they find the right family.'

'Well, I don't want counselling,' Chloe said, crossing her arms. 'I'm not mad. I know what I'm doing.'

'Chloe,' Joy said gently, 'giving up your baby is not an easy thing to do, not even if it is the right thing for you and for him. So if there is a little bit of free help in this world that might just ease that pain a little, you take it, OK?'

Swallowing, Chloe nodded, suddenly subdued. 'OK.'

She was silent as Willow put her arm round her and guided her back out to where her father was waiting, standing legs apart, hands behind his back. Like a soldier on guard.

'Well?' he asked her.

Chloe said nothing, so Willow stepped in, struggling to keep her own voice bright and relaxed.

'Well, she's twenty-eight weeks gone, the due date is Christmas Day, can you believe, and mother and baby are doing really well. Oh, and . . . it's a little boy.'

Sam quickly looked away, but not before Willow caught the bright promise of tears shining in his eyes.

Just as they got back to the car Chloe stopped.

'Dad, I've got something to say,' she said firmly.

'Yes?' Sam waited, his eyes fixed on Chloe.

'I know what to do,' she said. 'I've worked it all out, just now actually.'

In the second before Chloe spoke Willow had felt a moment of prescience as the ground undulated beneath her feet.

'Willow can adopt the baby. It makes perfect sense. She wants a baby and I've got one. I'm going to give Willow the baby for Christmas.'

Standing outside the newsagent's in Hoxton, Willow saw the faint orange light of a black cab approaching and she knew exactly what she should do. She should grab the cab, go home and face the mess that she had walked out on. That was exactly what she should do, but she couldn't. It had all been too much: Chloe's decision, Sam's utter rage, and India. Willow winced as she thought about India. She'd left all of that mess behind her without a second thought.

Steeling herself, and with thirty seconds to go, Willow headed to Daniel's studio.

Sam had said nothing after Chloe's revelation. His jaw had tightened, his fists had clenched but he'd said nothing, so Willow thought it best to say nothing too. Not that she could think what to say. She was utterly stunned. Why? Why would Chloe pick the woman who'd more or less abandoned her to look after her baby? It was a crazy idea, wasn't it? She couldn't look after a baby . . . could she?

So Willow was silent on the journey home too, letting Chloe talk and talk, trying to fill the void of reaction with words.

'And the best thing is I'll still know the baby, because I know Willow. So I know he'll be OK and—'

'Don't be ridiculous,' Sam said finally as he pulled up outside Willow's flat. 'Chloe . . . Christ. Just as I think I'm getting my head round this you act like such a bloody child.' Sam's laugh was mirthless. 'Of course you do – you *are* a bloody child! Willow is not going to adopt your baby. It doesn't work like that.'

Before Chloe could respond he got out of the car, narrowly avoiding being flattened by a speeding bus as he slammed the car door shut, walked round to the passenger side and flung open Chloe's door, taking hold of her upper arm. 'Get out. I've got a good mind to drag you home right now.'

'You lay one finger on me and I'll have you arrested for assault,' Chloe said loudly enough for passers-by to glance at them, as she shook off his hand.

Willow climbed out of the car, finding her keys in her bag, hoping to move the conversation into a little less public setting. 'Sam, calm down. I just think Chloe's trying to be kind—'

'Kind! To you?' Sam shook his head, his hands on his hips as he looked up at Willow's flat window. 'You know what? I'm done with pussyfooting around. I admit I don't know what to do. I fully admit I never expected my fifteen-year-old daughter to get pregnant and run away to live with my ex-wife. I didn't prepare for that! But what I do know is that I am your father,

Chloe Elizabeth Wainwright, and until the law says otherwise you are under *my* care and no one else's.'

He looked at Willow. 'Let us in. I'm getting her stuff and taking her home.'

'No!' Chloe protested, but Sam took the keys out of Willow's hands and before she could stop him, marched up the steps, trying each of her keys in turn until he opened the communal door.

'No, no, no!' Chloe screamed, hitting him repeatedly on the back with a clenched fist. 'I know what I want. I want Willow to have the baby. She needs a baby, she needs someone to love her and for her to love . . .'

Sam pushed open the door and marched up the stairs towards Willow's flat.

'She had that,' he told Chloe as Willow followed. 'We loved her. You and me, Chloe. We loved her and all she had to do was love us back.'

'She did,' Chloe said. 'She loved me.'

'No, no, she didn't. She . . . didn't.' Sam stood there, shaking his head, fury, sadness and confusion filling his face. 'She left.'

'You made her leave,' Chloe accused him.

'And have you ever asked yourself why?' Sam shouted at her.

'Because you weren't good enough!' Chloe retorted, making Willow gasp and clap her hands over her mouth. She expected Sam to explode, to call her all the names he could think of, and worse. But he didn't. He just stood there staring at Chloe, like a man defeated. In Willow's mind he was always so strong, so capable. Seeing him this way frightened her.

'I don't know how this has happened,' he said, his voice edged with tears as he gestured futilely. 'I don't understand it . . . I'm a grown man and I . . . I don't know what to do.'

He looked at Willow, utterly lost. After a moment she went to him and gently took the keys out of his hands.

'Look, come in. Have a cup of tea.' She hesitated. 'I've got a guest. You might recognise her. Please, just pretend you haven't seen her.'

She opened the door and let Sam and Chloe go in first. India was sitting on the floor, her head in her hands. There was a bottle of wine open next to her.

'You didn't tell me,' she said, looking up at Willow, her eyes raw and swollen from crying, her face pale, almost grey. 'Look!'

India tossed a paper at Willow's feet. 'Cramner's Sex Shame Scandal'.

'Where did you . . . ?'

'A whole bundle of them came this morning after you left. I thought your neighbour must have left them . . . does it matter?' India sobbed. 'Willow, I never meant anything to him. I've ruined my life, my career, everything, everything for a man who just wanted to use me all along. There is no way back from this. I might as well just . . . just *die*!'

'Look, India, you've been dumped. It could be worse,' Chloe said, pointing at her belly and raising her brows. 'Yeah?'

'Oh, you're India Torrance!' Sam said, his jaw dropping, his unhappiness temporarily punctuated by finding himself standing in front of an A-list celebrity, albeit a snot-nosed drunken weeping one. Nevertheless he was star struck. 'Fuck!'

'And now! Now you bring in strangers to gawp at me! I mean, I thought Victoria made me come and stay in this shit hole because you are the best she has! How incompetent are you, exactly?' India stood, stamping her bare foot as she spoke. 'Oh my God, Willow, why don't you just hand me a knife and watch me slit my wrists?'

'That's India Torrance,' Sam repeated to no one in particular, utterly confused, like he'd woken up in a dream.

'I am not a sideshow freak!' India screamed at him, snapping him back into the moment, whirling round and heading for Willow's bedroom. 'I'm phoning Victoria and I'm telling her to get me out of here, now, this minute! You are utterly unprofessional, irresponsible and . . . and . . . *fat*!'

'Fucking prima donna!' Chloe said as India slammed her door. 'Was she talking about me? Bitch!'

As Willow was potentially being put out of a job, not to mention added to some death list in the other room, she stood between father and daughter, at war with each other.

'Chloe,' Willow said, 'I know I don't have the right to say this, but I . . . I care about you so much. And I love that you want me to adopt your baby. It's the nicest thing I think anyone has ever wanted to do for me. But, darling, your dad is right. I'm not the right person. I'm always at work, my flat is a mess and I don't know the first thing about being a mum –'

'You do,' Chloe protested. 'You were a good mum to me.'

Willow and Sam looked at each other, each trying to read the other's face, which each had briefly known so intimately.

'Not good enough, though,' Willow said eventually. 'Your dad was right: I had a chance to be happy and I screwed it up, not him. I saw what a wonderful life I had and I ruined it. And I . . . I knew what I was doing, Chloe. I was trying to hurt your dad and . . . and you, before you hurt me. And I succeeded. I'm not the kind of person you want to adopt your baby.'

'You didn't walk out, Dad threw you out and he wouldn't let you come back, would he?' Chloe said. 'You tried to come back, didn't you? But he wouldn't let you. That's what happened, isn't it? Because you wouldn't just leave me, would you? You wouldn't do that!'

'Chloe . . .' Sam spoke her name softly, desperate to spare her hearing the answer, 'come home, darling. Come and sleep in your own bed tonight. I'll make you spag bol and treacle pudding for dessert, your favourites. Not a leaf of rocket in sight. Come home, and you and me – we'll work it out. We're a team, Chloe. Team Wainwright. We can do this.'

Chloe didn't take her eyes off Willow.

'You wanted to come back, though, didn't you?' she repeated slowly.

Every day, Willow wanted to say. But she didn't. She didn't say that there hadn't been a day since when she hadn't ached for Chloe or the life that she had once had with Sam; when she hadn't cursed herself for what she had done. And she didn't say that she had tried to see Chloe, tried to write to her, but that Sam simply refused to let her anywhere near his daughter again and that she had given up all too soon because, after all, she didn't blame him. Willow knew if she said any of those things then it would be Sam that Chloe would never forgive and he didn't deserve that.

'No,' Willow said. 'I . . . thought it was for the best not to.'

Chloe bit her lip, tears springing in her eyes. 'But you were so happy to see me. I saw it. I saw it in your face.'

'Yes, I was – I *am* – but . . .'

'I'm not coming home.' Chloe looked at Sam, pointing at Willow. 'She's lying. She wanted to come back and you didn't let her. She's lying to protect you. And I'm not coming home and I am giving Willow my baby.'

'I don't want your baby,' Willow said slowly, carefully, quietly.

'I'm not coming home,' Chloe repeated. Without looking at Willow she turned her back on her father and ran into her bedroom.

There was silence.

'Thank you,' Sam said after a moment, exhausted, defeated, his strong shoulders slumped. 'Thank you for not blaming me.'

Willow ached to touch him. He looked like he needed to be held and there was nobody else there to do the job but her.

'How could I possibly blame you? It was never your fault,' she said softly.

'I know now that I could have . . . I could have dealt with it better,' Sam said. 'Maybe there wasn't any hope for you and me but . . . I didn't give either of us a chance to find out. Angry, stubborn, I cut off my nose to spite my face. That's what my mum always said about me. She was right.'

Willow shrugged. It seemed bad-mannered to agree.

'I was just trying to hurt you, the way you hurt me. I didn't have to freeze you out of Chloe's life too.'

'Maybe you did.' Willow took a step closer to him. 'Look at me, look at the mess I make of things. I'm not the sort of person who's good for other people. Sometimes I think I can be, I try, but . . . I always end up making things worse. You were right: it's better that I keep myself to myself.'

'No, that's not true. You're the one who put a smile back on Chloe's face after her mum died. You did both of us the world of good. I was just so angry. I still am. I'm furious,' Sam said bitterly. 'I'm boiling with this rage and I don't know what to do with it.'

'Really?' Willow's face fell. 'You still hate me that much?'

Sam watched, shaking his head. 'No, no . . . you don't get it, do you? It's not you, Willow, it's me. I knew, didn't I? I remember that night, after I'd asked you to marry me. That night we sat up until dawn, talking. I knew everything about you. I knew how much you needed me to love you and I failed. I couldn't love you enough to make it better or to forgive you for what wasn't really your fault.' He shrugged. 'Chloe's right, when it came to the crunch I wasn't good enough for you. I will always be angry about that. There's no one I can blame except myself.'

'Oh.' Willow pressed the palm of her hand over her mouth, willing the sob that ached in her throat to stay suppressed. 'Don't say that, Sam. Be angry with me, but don't say that.'

Sam looked at Chloe's closed door. 'Right now, I'm not angry with you at all.' He let his arms fall to his sides. 'Listen, do you want a hug?'

Willow nodded mutely and Sam crossed the room in two steps, putting his arms around her. Willow pressed her cheek into his chest and listened to the rhythm of his heart. After a minute, perhaps a little more, she moved her hand away from her mouth and rested it on his shoulder.

'How have you been, anyway?' Sam said into her hair.

'OK. Working, mainly,' Willow replied, wondering at the absurdity of making small talk with one's ex-husband whilst locked in a tight embrace.

'Never met anyone else . . . important?' Sam asked.

'No,' Willow said. 'But Chloe tells me you've got someone new. Makes her own pasta and everything.' Willow felt a single breath of laughter in her hair. Sam rested his chin on the top of her head, his stubble tickling her scalp.

'Carol. She's nice. Decent. Funny. Kind.'

'Sounds perfect,' Willow said, feeling the tension in her shoulders flood away as she relaxed into Sam's arms. It had been a long time since anyone had held her that way. 'Do you love her?'

She felt Sam's body tense against hers. 'I loved Charlotte,' Sam said, speaking of Chloe's mum. 'And I loved you. And that's it for me.' He pulled away from her a little so that he could look in her eyes. 'I think that's it for me and love.'

Without thinking Willow reached up and touched his rough cheek with her fingertips.

'Don't let it be,' she said softly. 'Don't let it be the end of love for you. You deserve to be loved by someone good.'

'Don't you?' Sam asked her, his voice low, quiet as they stood in the darkened living room, the hum of the city traffic dashing by outside.

As they gazed into each other's eyes, Willow was dimly aware of the flat phone ringing; had to be a cold caller or a wrong number. No one ever phoned her landline any more.

It rang once, twice, three times and just as Willow was almost certain that Sam was about to say something really important, Daniel's Texan accent filled the room.

'Hey, babe. Have you dropped your phone down the loo again? It goes straight to answerphone. Anyway, this is just your quick pre-naked Monday night call.'

'Is that . . . is that Daniel?' Sam asked, breaking their embrace. Willow rushed over to the phone and picked it up, but the message kept recording.

'Listen, I'm running a bit late with Kayla. I'm seriously going to have to airbrush some tits on her, so can we push it back an hour? If I don't hear from you I'm going to assume yes. Looking forward to getting my hands on that lovely body of yours! *Ciao bella!*'

'What does he mean?' Sam asked. 'What's naked Monday?'

'Um . . . oh, I don't know. Who knows what Daniel ever means about anything,' Willow hedged.

'I didn't realise you still know him.' Sam's eyes dropped momentarily. 'Are you and he . . . ?'

'Friends, we're friends. That's it,' Willow said, emphatically. 'He . . . he helped me out a lot, he was good to me.'

'I bet he was!' Sam's laugh was bitter.

'No, Sam, it was never like that.'

'Sure, well.' Whatever moment of warmth there had been between them evaporated in an instant. 'Look, I'm glad we talked, but I'd better go. I'll say goodbye to Chloe, if that's OK?'

Willow nodded, feeling the chill sweep along the length of her body as he walked away, pulling at her as if he had physically taken part of her with him. Sighing, she went to find India.

India was lying on the bed, her phone in one hand, the other flung above her head like a silent movie damsel in distress.

'Am I sacked?' Willow asked her wearily, discovering at that moment that she rather hoped she was.

'I haven't called Victoria,' India said. 'I called Hugh. He didn't pick up. Of course he didn't. I thought . . . I thought maybe this was all lies made up by Victoria to get me off the hook. I wanted him to tell me I was the only one. Instead I got an answerphone message referring me to his publicist. Perhaps I can get her to tell me I'm the only one. Maybe she has a statement on file for placating his long list of conquests . . .'

Willow glanced over her shoulder; there was no yelling or screaming coming from Chloe's room. What were they doing, Willow wondered. Reluctantly she came into the room and sat on the edge of the bed.

'I'm so sorry,' she told India. 'Victoria told me to tell you what she was planning, but I . . . I didn't. You seemed to be pretty happy . . . I know it was wrong, but I just thought it would be nice for you to stay that way.'

'Cry my eyes out a couple of days ago, cry them out today. What's the difference?'

'The difference is that you would have been prepared,' Willow admitted. 'You would have heard it from me and not the papers, and I could have explained how Victoria was handling things. I wonder who left those papers there.'

'I don't know,' India said unhappily. 'Does it matter?'

'Well, anyway, you are utterly within your rights to phone Victoria and get me fired. She will do it, you know, and she'll put a hit out on me. I'll be toast before next Tuesday.'

'I know that perfectly well,' India said rather archly, sitting up. 'What in God's name she is thinking, hiding me away in this shit hole day after day I don't know. I'm India Torrance. I'm five stars of woman any day of the week, according to *GQ*. What am I doing in this hovel, crying my eyes out over someone who never loved me? What am I doing?'

It was a fair point and one that Willow didn't especially have an answer to.

'Look, I know Victoria moves in mysterious ways but she is usually right about this. And to be fair to her, as far as your future career is concerned she has played it to perfection. A few more days and you will be out of here, all this squalor will be a dim and distant memory and you'll be getting your life back unless . . .'

'Unless I phone her now and demand Blakes,' India said. 'The trouble is, I like you and the shouty pregnant teenager. And I liked the weekend without being prepared. It reminded me of being at home with my sisters. It was nice, it felt real.'

'A little too real, sometimes,' Willow said.

'You forget how nice real life is sometimes,' India said, propping herself up on one elbow. 'So, anyway, I've decided I'm not going to get you fired.'

'Thank you,' Willow said, hearing the front door shut, presumably behind Sam. She had missed her chance to say goodbye again, to regain some of that even keel they'd barely had a chance to establish before Daniel had left his message.

'Was that rugged and handsome man out there Chloe's dad?' India asked.

'Handsome? Don't be sick,' Chloe said, appearing in the doorway. She seemed a little better, settled, which meant, Willow hoped, that she and her dad had parted on reasonably good terms.

'I'm sorry I asked you to look after the baby,' Chloe said. 'I was rushing in, thinking this was a film or something. I shouldn't have just landed the idea on you like that. I should have worked up to it.'

'Don't be sorry. It was such a lovely thought,' Willow said.

'Oh, I still want you to adopt. I'm just saying, there's no rush for you to agree. You can take your time. We've got twelve weeks!'

'Breaking news, I see,' India observed with a watery smile. 'I must say, it comes to something when one is upstaged right in the middle of one's own personal tragedy.'

The three lost women looked at each other for a moment and then finally India got up from the bed, dragging Willow with her.

'Oh fuck it, let's have a group hug and then break open some chocolate. Just don't you two fatties squash me flat.'

Chapter Eleven

'Are you naked under that coat?' was how Daniel greeted Willow as she walked into his studio. As promised, four heaters were plugged in, blasting heat into the set which Daniel had already dressed.

'Here.' He handed her a large glass of wine. 'I figure you're going to need this before we start. You know, shooting Kayla is a nightmare. I mean, she is beautiful, a model. She's got it all going on, the camera loves her and all that jazz. But when it came to doing something a bit different, a bit artistic, she turned *The Three Graces* into a catalogue shoot. This is why she will never make a cover girl. She's got no pizzazz.'

Willow raised her brows, folding her arms in front of her. 'So if the actual model has let you down, there's not much hope for me, is there?'

'Depends,' Daniel winked at her. 'So, are you naked under there, or do you want me to take the fur?'

'Hang on,' Willow gulped the wine down in one go and handed the glass back to Daniel. 'Top that up and you can have the coat.'

'Willow,' Daniel chuckled, 'this is strictly professional. It's not a game of strip poker!'

'I know that! More wine, please.' She paced up and down, glancing around just in case Serious James was hiding anywhere or Kayla had been able to stay on to chaperon after all.

'No need to worry, it's just us,' Daniel said. 'Look, if you're going to back out, do it now, OK? Don't make me light you.'

'OK, OK.' Willow took her coat off.

'That's not quite going to cut it, darling,' Daniel said.

'Well, can't you light me now, with my clothes on? That way I don't have to be naked for ages, freezing my bits off.'

'I can't.' Daniel was apologetic. 'I have to get the luminosity right, bounce the light off your skin.' He took the glass out of her hand. 'There's a screen over there, and a robe. Don't be nervous. Remember what Kayla said? I'm not looking at *you*, I'm just looking at the shapes your body makes.'

'Fine,' Willow said, feeling a thrill of anticipation wrought with anxiety. 'Right, fine.'

'Oh, and, Willow,' Daniel called after her as she headed towards the screen, 'keep the shoes on.'

Willow was grateful that Daniel had not put a mirror behind the screen. That way at least she could keep the image of herself that she had seen in her own bathroom mirror in her mind's eye without having it ruined by good lighting or an accurate reflection. Even wearing the thin cotton robe, she kept her arms over her breasts as she came out, finding Daniel peering into his camera, and messing about with some piece of equipment she didn't recognise.

'Great.' He was very businesslike. 'So you sit here, with your back to me, like so. OK, look over your shoulder at the camera. Hold that for a minute. Great. Robe off.'

Willow swallowed, feeling the heat flare in her cheeks as she slipped the robe off, lifting her bottom a little to allow the robe to fall to the floor in one fluid slither. This would be OK, she told herself. Her back was to him, he would see barely anything, besides her enormous arse.

'Beautiful,' Daniel said. 'The curve of your waist, into your hip. It's perfect. Hold on.'

The next thing Willow knew he was standing next to her, his fingers under her chin as he tilted her face a little more towards the light. Kayla was right, he wasn't looking at her at all, he was only concerned with the light on her cheek. There had been more sexual tension between her and Sam in her flat than there was here.

Willow allowed herself to breathe out a fraction. But only a little. She was still concentrating rather hard on holding her tummy in.

'That's it. Now, you need to bend this arm back a little. Great. Hold it there, while I adjust this lamp . . .' Returning to his camera, he took a few shots as Willow waited.

'Oh, Will, darling, this is looking so good.'

Daniel approached her once more, rearranging a strand of her hair, and stepping back to regard her, his fingers on his chin as he thought. 'Can you remember that exact pose? If you can remember that you can come out of it for a second while I get another prop I want to try out. If not, you need to stay here.'

'I can remember,' Willow said, rubbing the back of her neck as Daniel disappeared into the depths of his studio. As odd as it was to find herself nude, under the glare of the lights, sitting in the middle of this big, almost empty room, she suddenly found that she was totally relaxed. It might be the wine, of course, but perhaps for the first time in her life Willow felt utterly comfortable in her nudity. Daniel looking at her dispassionately down the lens was somehow sexier than if he'd lunged at her the moment she arrived. She was beautiful, he'd said so. He probably said that to every single model that had ever stood in front of his camera but Willow didn't mind that; she liked it. When he said it that way, as if it were a matter of fact, then she felt that it was true.

And it was nice to feel beautiful.

She shook her hair out over her shoulders, tipping back her chin so that she could feel it trail along her back.

'Here we go.' Daniel returned with an armful of cosmetics, which he scattered on the dressing table in front of her, and spent several moments arranging in carefully organised disarray. He was smiling when he turned round, but as he caught sight of her he stopped and the look on his face changed.

All at once Willow felt awkward, uncertain. She felt the fold of her tummy, the dimpling of flesh over her hip. The relaxed sense of beauty she'd briefly enjoyed vanished as Daniel inspected her, his eyes roaming over her breasts, her hips and legs.

Desperate for his observation to be over, Willow prompted him.

'Bloody hell, get on with it, then!' she said, her voice sounding rather strangled. Panic rose in her chest and all of a sudden she didn't want him to want her, to look at her. She wanted Daniel the photographer back: unpassionate, disinterested. This Daniel, the one who saw the real her, scared her. 'I don't care how many heaters you've got on. I'm freezing!'

Blinking as if awoken from a trance, Daniel dipped his head

and turned his back on Willow for a second as he rearranged the cosmetics that he had just arranged, moving them like chess pieces before returning them to almost exactly their original positions.

When he turned round, he was back to his old self.

'You can't hurry art, Will. You should know that. Strike a pose, Madonna.' His voice was easy, playful, as he approached her, but even so, there was a new tension in the air as he tilted her chin this time, pushing his hand into the small of her back to accentuate the curve. 'And this arm needs to go back a little more.'

As he moved her, the back of his hand brushed the side of her breast. Willow closed her eyes as the sensation, even one so slight, shot a *frisson* of excitement through her. She dared not look at him. Nothing about him was discernible now. Had she pleased him, horrified him? Willow could not tell. She only knew that when he'd looked at her and saw *her*, everything had changed.

'Perfect. Stay perfectly still.' Daniel traced the tips of his fingers down her spine, a caress that Willow wondered if she was imagining. She sat perfectly still as his fingers repeated the journey, trailing over her shoulder blades, grazing her waist, brushing over the top of her bottom. She sensed a moment of hesitation before she felt his other hand on her thigh travelling upwards.

'Daniel . . .' Willow felt his fingers creep back up to the nape of her neck, entwine in her hair, sensed his breath on the back of her neck, his other hand rising towards the swell of her breast.

'You feel amazing,' he whispered, and Willow felt his lips closing in on the back of her shoulder. One moment longer and she would be in his arms. This was it. This was exactly how she wanted it.

Only now the moment was here she was terrified of it.

'Daniel!' Willow stood up abruptly, knocking Daniel off balance so that he stumbled and fell against the mannequin he'd positioned, toppling it over. Grabbing the robe off the floor Willow held it in front of her.

Daniel steadied himself and took a breath: he looked utterly stunned.

'God, Willow, I'm so sorry. I thought . . .'

'What?' Willow asked him.

'I thought you wanted me to.'

Willow bit her lip. Until the precise moment that he had touched her she had wanted him to. Only now did she discover that she felt otherwise, and it came as a total shock to her.

'So did I,' Willow said. 'Something's happened to me in the last few days, Daniel. I've changed, or I'm changing. I feel like I've been stuck for years and years in one place, and then I took a wrong turn and I found these shoes – and they are just shoes, I know that – but since I found them everything's changed. I've changed. It's almost like everything I've been wishing for for the last few years has started to come true, and it's too much. Chloe's at home –'

'Little Chloe? Your ex's kid, Chloe?' Daniel ran his fingers through his hair, struggling to keep up. 'Aren't you banned from seeing her?'

'Yes. She found me, and she's fifteen now and pregnant so –'

'What?'

'Yes, I know . . . and I saw Sam today . . .'

'Whoa.' Daniel's expression changed again, becoming a little petulant. 'So how was that?'

'It was quite . . . intense. It ended so abruptly between us, we never had a chance to tie up loose ends, talk it through. We spoke for a few minutes today and I already feel like I understand what happened so much more. I wanted to do this, but I can't be here, like this.' Willow looked down at herself, still sheltering behind the robe. 'Not when they are back at the flat, waiting for me.'

'They? Sam's there too?' Daniel paced, turning his back on Willow long enough for her to be able hurriedly to slip on the robe. He seemed lost in his thoughts for a moment, still trying to make sense of everything Willow was saying. When he spoke there was a hard edge to his voice. 'He's in your flat waiting for you?

'No, it's India Torrance.'

'Willow, am I drunk or dreaming or something? India Torrance, who's been fucking that actor guy, is in your flat?'

'Yes, keep up! She's been hiding out at my place until Victoria got a handle on her story, and that information is strictly confidential, OK?' Daniel shrugged, as if he felt the film star was incidental. Willow took a breath, trying to untangle her thoughts at the same moment as explaining them to Daniel.

'They need me. They both need me so badly, especially now. But what did I do? I came here to take my clothes off for you because I've wanted this, and you, a lot, for a long time now. And you seeing me the way you did, touching me . . . if this was my only chance I didn't want to miss it, I wanted to –'

'To conclude some unfinished business?' Daniel suggested, a little coolly.

'I thought . . . I thought maybe that was what I wanted. But . . .' Willow looked down at her shoes, which seemed so at home with her virtual nudity, '. . . when you touched me I realised something pretty immense.'

'That you love me, or that I repulse you?' Daniel asked, wincing slightly as if either answer might be the wrong one.

'No! Daniel, I realised I want to be a mum.' The revelation came as much as a shock to Willow as it did to Daniel, whose face blanched.

'OK, I'm all for a little bit of love between friends, but I'm not ready for fatherhood yet, you know? Maybe one day . . .'

'No, you nutter,' Willow laughed, relieved to have shocked him out of his unfamiliar intensity, if only for a moment. 'I want to be in Chloe's life. I want to be there for her, I want to be her mum again.' Willow kept talking as she went behind the screen and started to get dressed. 'Do you know, today she offered me her baby.'

'Really? You were right, everything you wish for does come true, sometimes before you've even wished for it. Are you sure those shoes aren't magic? Maybe there's a genie in the sole?' Daniel's voice receded and grew louder as he paced again.

'I don't know,' Willow said, fingering her coat before slipping it on. 'Sometimes I think objects, older things that have belonged to other people, carry a little bit of those lives with them. I don't know anything about who owned these, but maybe a little bit of them has rubbed off on me,' Willow mused aloud as she zipped up her skirt.

'Or maybe a little bit of you has rubbed off on everyone else.' Daniel had stopped just the other side of the screen. 'You are a remarkable woman, Willow. You try and hide it away, but it's always been there. Maybe all you needed was a pair of foxy shoes to strut your stuff in. You've certainly got my attention.'

Willow smiled, pressing her palm against the screen for a second.

'The most amazing thing is that Chloe would trust me to bring up her baby, which means that she still thinks of me as a decent enough person to be a mother. Which maybe, just maybe, means I can build something between us again, if Sam will let me.' Willow smiled. 'Perhaps I can still have a chance to be a mum to Chloe.'

She emerged from the haven of the screen to find Daniel waiting for her, his arms crossed, brows knotted.

'And the baby?' He leaned his head towards her, as if eager to hear her answer.

'I don't think Chloe's thought about the baby at all,' Willow said. 'Maybe not until today, until we saw the scan. I think she made a decision about having it adopted before it was real. Perhaps adoption *is* the best thing – I don't know – but if I'm there with her, and not here taking my clothes off for you, then . . . well, that's the sort of thing a mum does, isn't it?'

'I never thought I'd find maternal instincts in a woman as sexy as hell. Turns out I was wrong.' Daniel approached Willow as she slipped on her coat. He took the lapels of the coat and tugged her closer to him. 'If you think you can be a mum to Chloe, then go for it,' he said, kissing her on the tip of her nose. 'But, Will, sweetheart, two things. I don't know if you can take losing Chloe and Sam –'

'Just Chloe,' Willow protested.

'*And* Sam again,' Daniel insisted. 'And, Willow, my God, you are a beautiful, wonderful, funny, sexy woman. Any man, including me, would be as lucky as hell to have you.'

Willow decided it would be a terrible idea to look him in the eye in case there was more ill-advised touching, so instead she studied his thumbs in the fur of her coat.

'You deserve a life, a husband, a child of your own. You can have those things, if you just let yourself.'

Willow shook her head. 'I can't, Daniel. I can't, you know that. I can't make that work. I've tried. And anyway, what's the big deal? Look at you: you never want to settle down. You've been playing the field for twenty years and you're perfectly content.'

Removing one hand from her lapel, Daniel lifted her chin and made her look at him. 'I used to think so, Willow. I used to think so, but maybe . . .'

Without warning Daniel kissed her, ever so lightly on the lips, pausing for a fraction as his mouth brushed over hers. It was a chaste kiss, almost like a whispered prayer, but it sent a surge of electricity pulsing through Willow, rooting her to the spot.

'Willow . . . I don't really get what I'm feeling right now,' Daniel whispered, his eyes closed. 'I don't know if it's real or just me being me, because you've kind of rejected me here, which usually makes me want a woman more. But I do know that I've got all these feelings churning around in my gut that have maybe been there a long time, and that maybe I've pushed them aside because of . . . well, because you are the only person in the world I am myself with, and I don't want to lose that. So what I'm saying is, I might be a shallow, feckless, awful man or . . . I might be in love with you. I'm not sure which, and I'm not sure that it makes a difference to you either way, but I kind of had to say it.'

Willow caught her breath, trying to take a step back, but Daniel kept her close.

'What I do know for certain is that I am your friend. And I will do whatever I can to help you right now. And maybe, later on, once I've figured this out and you've figured out all your stuff, we might revisit that kiss? See how it makes us feel then?'

Swallowing, Willow nodded, shocked by the suddenness with which Daniel released her, sending her tottering back a step or two on her heels.

'Great. Well, I'll walk you out and get you a cab.' He grinned at her, back to normal Daniel in a snap. 'So I'll see you at Serious James's thing on Thursday. Hey, bring your guests! The awfulness of James's jokes will take their minds off their woes, or push them over the edge, one or the other.'

'I might just do that.'

Daniel opened the door for her. 'One more thing, Willow. You are still my Venus. You don't get out of it that easily.'

As Willow settled back into her seat in the cab, she thought what it might have been like tonight between her and Daniel if she hadn't stopped him. If Chloe hadn't come to her, if Sam hadn't been standing in her flat today, then . . . then it would have been the most perfect moment that Willow could have imagined. But the truth was never that simple between Willow and Daniel. Yes, they had become friends because he lived next door and had a penchant for sponging a drink off her of an afternoon, but they had stayed friends after they had both moved on from that address because of one reason.

After all, it was partly Daniel's fault that Sam had thrown Willow out and told her never to come back.

Becaus it was Daniel that Sam had found Willow in bed with one grey, wet afternoon.

Willow had known that it was just a bit of reckless fun for him from the moment Daniel had pulled her a little closer to him while they were twirling around her living room, drunkenly smooching to *The Greatest Hits of Doris Day*, which Daniel had found in Sam's CD collection. She had known it when, a little bleary eyed and rebellious, he mused aloud about what it would be like to kiss Willow Briars. And she had been under no illusions that this was the beginning of any kind of grand romance when he had led her, unresisting, into the bedroom and pulled the woollen dress she had been wearing over her head.

'Flesh!' he exclaimed with glee as he pushed her back onto the bed, running the palms of his hands over her like he was examining an object rather than a woman. Willow had surrendered quite willingly when, rather awkwardly, he'd yanked off her tights and knickers in one go, and then, whistling through his teeth, had scooped her breasts out of the cups of her bra.

'You are like a confection,' he whispered as he squeezed first one breast and then the other, in turn. 'Pink and white marshmallow.'

It had felt like he'd enveloped her with his kiss, his clothed body covering her nakedness, his mouth covering her face and neck, shoulders and breasts as he pulled away his own clothes, groaning with pleasure when he pressed his own naked skin against hers.

'Like a cloud,' he whispered, moving her thighs apart with one palm.

It was then that Sam had walked in. Willow remembered him standing there like a still from a black-and-white film. It had been a black-and-white day, rain pelting down remorselessly, electric lights on in the morning, Daniel knocking on her door at midday wearing a white shirt and a five o'clock shadow. He'd been carrying a bottle of gin. He'd been bored.

Willow remembered that Sam had stood there, his hand on the bedroom door, frozen to the spot for what had seemed like an age as he tried to take in what he was seeing. She had seen him a fragment of a second before Daniel realised he was there. She'd felt Daniel's mouth on her neck, his hand kneading her breast, his knee pushing between her legs all in that moment, while her eyes were locked with her husband's. Her husband, whom she had loved so much, whom she had always known that she would never be able to keep.

Then Sam acted. He pulled Daniel off her with a strength that Willow did not know he possessed, and literally threw him, naked bar his socks, out of the flat, slamming the door on him. Willow had pulled on her knickers by the time he came back into her bedroom, and stood there holding her woollen dress over her breasts. She remembered it scratching at her skin.

Sam stared at her, his mouth moving, but no words would come.

'I got drunk.' Willow had decided someone should say something. 'It just happened. It was like I wasn't even there.' Willow had known how stupid the words coming out of her mouth were; she hated herself for saying them, even as her lips formed the syllables.

'So he raped you?' Sam advanced further into the room, his tone harshly hopeful, causing Willow to take a step back into the corner, until the backs of her calves pressed against the sharp corners of the bedside table.

'No, no . . . I just . . . I didn't mind either way.'

Sam had run his palms over his face, smearing tears down his cheeks.

'I love you, Willow. I love you,' he'd told her. 'All the shit, all the crap that comes with you. I live with it too, every day. Every day I live with what you told me, and I love you even though I know you don't feel the same.'

'I do . . .' Willow told him.

'How can you?' Sam asked her, and Willow could not reply. 'I thought that even if you didn't love me you might care about me and Chloe. Chloe, for God's sake – hasn't she been through enough?'

Willow had thought of Chloe, of how they'd sat at the kitchen table the previous afternoon, a dank and dark winter Sunday, and created tray after tray of misshapen cupcakes, which they had eaten in one sitting almost as soon as they were iced.

'Sometimes people think you're my mum,' Chloe had said casually, shrugging. 'I don't mind if they do.' And Willow had felt this warmth spread through her chest and something as near to happiness as she had ever known.

'Life is hard,' were the only words she could find for her mouth to form.

Sam shook his head. The way he looked at her – it was as if he was seeing the real her, the woman who did not deserve to be loved. Willow had always known he would one day.

'I want you out before Chloe gets back from school,' Sam had said quietly, turning his face away. 'I don't want her to know anything about this.'

Daniel had not been blameless – of course not – but neither had he been to blame. It was Willow's fault. Willow, who still, after all this time, felt that her body was a worthless thing, a trinket to be cast away lightly for . . . what? That afternoon hadn't even been about her own pleasure, it had been about Daniel's. It had been about a few moments of watching his disconnected desire for her, because when she saw the reflection of that woman mirrored in his eyes, for a moment she felt something.

She hadn't fallen in love with Daniel then. That had been later, in the aftermath, when he had been kind to her. That was a problem Willow had: she often fell for people who were kind to her. 'Pined' was the word Holly used, and she was right. Always seeking approval, always craving kindness, finding it hard to reciprocate.

Yes, they had become friends, almost certainly because Daniel felt responsible. The question was, had they stayed friends because of something more than that?

Holly answered her phone on the first ring, and listened wordlessly as Willow told her everything that had happened that day. Her silence remained long after Willow stopped talking.

'So?' Willow prompted her. 'What do I do now?'

'I don't know what else you can do except show Chloe that you will always be there for her, whatever happens. As for Sam, I don't know, Willow. The way you feel about him can't be summed up in a few words. What I do know is that you should be very careful about getting your fingers burned by Daniel Fayre.' Holly fell silent again.

'You know what I'm like. I'll get it wrong again, I'll hurt Chloe, drive Sam away. I'll lose the only friend I've got other than you. I'm just not a good enough person for all this. Everyone is better off when I'm just . . . me.'

‘Don’t say that,’ Holly said quietly. ‘Please, Willow, can’t this just be the moment you let go of the past? Can’t this be the moment that it’s finally over?’

‘It’s never over, though, is it?’ Willow said. ‘I don’t see that it can ever be over.’

‘It can,’ Holly told her. ‘It has to be.’

Static crackled in Willow’s ear as she listened to the sound of her sister’s breathing, and the sudden wave of panic that had overwhelmed her subsided a little. She reached into her pocket, finding the little locket and clenching it in her fist.

‘You need me,’ Holly said, with an air of finality as if she had come to a decision.

‘No, no – don’t be silly. It was just a moment. I’m fine now.’

‘No, something’s going on and you need me. I’m coming. Give me a couple of days to arrange things here and then I’ll be there.’

Chapter Twelve

Holly is coming, was the thought that woke Willow that freezing Thursday morning. A moment later her phone buzzed against the carpet and she rolled onto her side and fished around for wherever she had left it when she'd wrapped herself up in her duvet and drunk two large glasses of wine in a bid to get to sleep on her less than comfortable sofa.

Finally she found the phone, answering it eyes closed, without needing to see who was calling because she already knew.

'When do you get here?' Willow asked her sister sleepily. 'And what bloody time is it, anyway?'

'It's a tiny bit after six,' Holly whispered. 'I've arranged it all. Gray is coming up to town for some meeting or something, so I've cadged a lift for me and the girls. I thought maybe we could hang out? Do a bit of shopping, be ladies that lunch? You'll get some twin strength and I'll get to have a conversation that doesn't involve puppies, ponies, bunnies or rainbows.'

'Did you say six in the *morning*?' Willow grumbled, rubbing her eyes, struggling to place these first few minutes of wakefulness in the general scheme of things. 'Which morning?'

'Thursday,' Holly said. 'I'd love to see Chloe and maybe Sam, and I was wondering if I might even get a glimpse of India

Torrance. That would be something to tell the WI. It's been killing me not to tell anyone up until now, and just think how the Stepford wives will hate me when I say I know her. Besides, I want to try on your magic shoes. There is a dearth of decent shoes in this town, and nowhere to wear them except for the Harbour Club, and you know me, I've never really been a huge fan of sailors' wives and all their gold trim and horizontal stripes –'

'Holly.' Willow cut her sister off, pushing herself into a sitting position. It was still dark outside, and freezing until the heating clicked on in about half an hour. 'Thank you, I love you, but I am OK. You don't have to come.'

'I do,' Holly said with a certainty that Willow didn't want to argue with. 'Let me be there for you.'

'You always are.'

'Not always. Anyway, I've arranged everything now and the girls are so excited and . . .'

There was a silence. 'And?'

'You need me,' Holly said. 'I can feel it.'

'Can you?' Willow rubbed her eyes. 'I think that, all things considered, I'm actually coping quite well.'

'And you are, but I can feel the butterflies in your tummy. Your life is suddenly full of choices and chances, and I don't want you to –'

'Screw it up again?' Willow sighed.

'Panic,' Holly sidestepped the question. 'Besides, I want to see my sister. I miss you.'

'I want to see you too, but today might be tricky. Victoria called late last night. She's done some deals, sacrificed a few lambs and done a spot of voodoo, and now she's ready to relaunch India into the public eye. I've got to take India into the office in a couple of hours and then try and swing the afternoon off. Chloe's appointment with the social worker is this afternoon. I really want to be here. And I've half promised to go to this comedy thing tonight. I don't have to go to that, I suppose; it wasn't set in stone.'

Willow was surprised to discover a tinge of disappointment at the idea of missing James's big night. There was no good reason to want to go; it would just be a whole lot of weird after her and Daniel's 'moment' in his studio. Potentially love her he might, but not enough – at least not yet – to end things with Kayla. Both of them would be there tonight; and Willow was worried about seeing Daniel again and Kayla being able to see it written all over her face that something had happened. Barely anything at all, Willow told herself, some caresses and a bit of a kiss wasn't exactly grounds for a grand romance. It was more the way that Daniel had looked at her and what he said that lingered in Willow's mind. It had been exciting and passionate, but also noncommittal, which was probably as much as anyone could ever hope for from Daniel. Even so, Willow liked Kayla, and she didn't want to go behind her back.

Holly arriving was a perfect excuse not to go to Battersea, but, Willow realised rather unexpectedly, she would be sorry not to see James. There was something about him that was . . . effortless. Yes, that's what she liked about him. When she was with him she didn't think about what she looked like or what she was wearing or saying, because she was just herself. In many ways it was a wonderful relief.

'Oh, no, don't change anything for me. I know exactly what to do!' Holly sounded excited, like she used to when they were girls planning some adventure that would invariably get them into trouble with their mother. 'The girls and I will get to London about ten, Gray says he can drop us off somewhere behind Oxford Street, we can meet you for lunch and see Chloe. You can go off to see the social worker whilst I take the kids to a flick or something. Then Gray can take them home and I can stay in London with you and get the train back in the morning. We can *both* do the comedy night! Please say yes, Willow. I haven't had a fun night out since . . . since we crept out that night when we were about fourteen to go and see that band you liked in the pub up the road.'

'That's not true,' Willow said, smiling at Holly's enthusiasm despite the early hour.

'It feels like it is! I need a laugh, Willow, and Gray owes me about a year's worth of nights out. Please say I can come?'

'Of course you can come. You can always come, you nutter.' Holly's excitement was infectious. 'I can't wait to see you.'

'Finally there's the twin affinity thing,' Holly chuckled. 'So I'll see you at Liberty at midday, and then if there's time we'll take the girls to Hamleys and whip them into a frenzy of hysteria just in time for the cinema, and then Gray to drive them home.'

'Perfection,' the sisters said in unison, and when Willow put down the phone she felt that unique sense of contentment that came from being close to Holly, a liquid warmth that spread through her bones. Having Holly close was like home returning to her.

Victoria had sent a car for India. Her car, a beautiful old Bentley, complete with her driver and informal bodyguard, David Vickers, who was well into his fifties but looked like he could still take someone down if he had to, mainly because he had a thick moustache and the word 'hate' tattooed on both sets of knuckles.

'It's Victoria's idea of a gesture,' Willow said as she and India peered out of the window, looking at the one-hundred-and-fifty-thousand-pound car sitting on a double yellow line, its hazard lights blinking elegantly, more than a little incongruous on the dirty, crowded, cut-price street, which was the antithesis of the glamorous designer-boutique-lined boulevards it usually glided along. Willow was fairly certain that Victoria had never been to Wood Green. If she thought of it at all it was probably as a lovely villagey part of London, with an actual green, not the tangle of congested roads and concrete, swarming with 'the public', as Victoria referred to anyone who was not her.

'Some gesture.' India peered at the car, her profile perfectly lit by the cold stark light of the white-skied morning. She looked a little gaunt, Willow thought, her famous cheekbones even more pronounced than usual, and it was clear her brief sojourn in the world of the less worthy hadn't done her any favours in terms of restoring that inner glow that the critics raved about. Willow had always thought that the whole 'my body is a temple' thing was a load of nonsense but, judging from the way India looked, it turned out that a diet of fast food and alcohol wasn't very good for you after all.

'It's her way of welcoming you back into your life,' Willow explained. 'The deal for your exclusive interview and photoshoot has been made with *True Glitz*, and not only will you be one hundred thousand pounds better off, you are also now released back into the world, a wronged woman, a poor naïve girl, led astray by an older manipulative predator. Hugh is off the

New Year Honours List, and it looks like he probably won't be expecting a phone call from Richard Curtis anytime soon. After all those exposés, and with more to come, he is officially disgraced.'

India's face remained impassive as she listened, gazing sightlessly at the car.

'It also means there will be press outside the office, who you must not talk to but can let photograph you.' Willow repeated Victoria's orders. 'Victoria said wear grey or black, sunglasses, headscarf, sombre face, sad, regretful mouth.'

India laughed once, turning her back on the window and looking around Willow's humble living room, its two elderly leather sofas, the rickety coffee table piled high with yesterday's plates and glasses, and prints on the walls that Willow had not looked at since she'd bought them as a job lot from Ikea. It was about a million miles away from a suite at Blakes. Shrugging, India turned briefly back to the window and wrote something in the condensation.

Pausing only to kiss Willow on the cheek, she retired to her room and began to prepare for her relaunch.

Willow looked at the window. The words that India had inscribed were already beginning to run and disappear.

'Thank you.'

David did not even turn to look when Willow bundled Chloe into the back of the car. As Victoria's driver-slash-bodyguard he had probably seen a lot more shocking sights in his time than a pregnant girl who had determinedly squeezed herself into a non-pregnant girl's leopard-print dress that fitted so tightly the spots were stretched into stripes across the mound of her belly.

Willow had been careful not to mention Chloe to Victoria, but she didn't want to leave her alone in the flat today, not with the visit from the adoption social worker hanging over their heads. Chloe hadn't said anything since they'd had a call to arrange the appointment, but her young features had tightened almost to breaking point. After spending a few more days around Chloe, Willow could see quite clearly that the girl was doing her level best not to think about her pregnancy at all, something that must be harder to do after the scan and seeing her little boy's face. Now, with the prospect of having to discuss the details of adoption only hours away, she had become quiet, withdrawn. As Willow had helped her get her coat on a few minutes earlier, Chloe had sucked in a sudden breath, pressing her hand to her tummy, presumably feeling the baby moving, but her expression didn't alter and she didn't even mention it.

Since suggesting that Willow took the baby, Chloe had not discussed the prospects of adoption any further with Willow and yet it was constantly present, like a dark cloud insinuating its way between every word she spoke, every breath she took. Willow worried that the enormity of what was happening to Chloe was building like lava in a volcano and that eventually an eruption was inevitable.

Deciding to give away a baby made on an idea of the future that could only be guessed at was difficult for anyone. But for Chloe? Chloe had somehow separated herself from what was happening to her body for months now, and Willow was not the least bit surprised. She'd pushed the changes to her body, all the aches and pains, into one little tiny corner in her mind and shut the door on it. Today the door was bursting open and there would be no containing the truth of what lay behind it any more. Willow knew something of the fear that the truth might engulf you, that it might destroy you, crush you with its intolerable weight. Now there was nowhere to run for Chloe, no delaying tactic or imaginary world to hide in. Today was the day that she had to face the truth.

For the first time since her marriage to Sam had fallen so spectacularly apart, work had become an inconvenience instead of a distraction, and being at Victoria's disposal a chore. Having India to stay hadn't been ideal but at least it had given her what she would never normally be granted: time off to be with Chloe. In any case, Willow did not want to leave Chloe on her own to dwell, so she decided to take the risk of Victoria discovering her and to sit Chloe in reception with a few magazines for a while, gambling on nobody noticing her. Unlikely, in a leopard-print dress, to be honest.

Willow waited for India, who was wearing a light grey cashmere jumper dress over distressed jeans, a white headscarf over her hair, and most of her face obliterated by huge Chanel shades. She had followed Victoria's direction to the letter, even accentuating her sad, regretful mouth with a touch of clear gloss. Shutting the back passenger door on India, who leaned her head against the glass of the window, Willow climbed into the cream leather and real walnut luxury of the front passenger seat, discreetly sweeping off a magazine featuring naked busty ladies onto the floor and under the foot mat, where she happened to know that David Vickers kept his light entertainment.

'Miss Briars,' David greeted Willow formally, as always.

'Mr Vickers.' Willow always returned the greeting with equal civility. After all, they were Victoria's two longest serving staff and between them had either taken Victoria to, rescued her from, or seen with their very own eyes more awfulness in the back of that beautiful Bentley than any living person ever should. Victoria had once implied that David Vickers was ex-SAS and Willow believed her. He had the look of a man who would never be surprised by anything ever again, which was almost the only qualification you needed to work for Victoria.

'And how is our esteemed boss today?' Willow asked, as David pulled the Bentley out into the traffic, stopping a London bus in its tracks, without turning a hair.

'Very pleased with herself, Willow.' David raised a weary brow. 'Very pleased with herself indeed.'

'She has rather outdone herself,' Willow conceded. 'David, I'd appreciate it if you didn't mention my precious cargo in the back there, to Victoria. It's a personal matter I don't want to bother her with it.'

'You know me, Willow,' David said, never taking his eyes off the road. 'I never see nothing, 'less I have to.'

The Bentley stopped a few streets away from the office, just a little way up from Portal Way and Bleeding Heart Yard. Willow curled up her toes in her shoes, wondering if she took that wrong turning again, whether the shop would still be there, or if it was like a retail version of *The Flying Dutchman*, only ever appearing out of the mists once every fifty years or so to accessorise the really needy. Everything that had happened to her since she'd slipped on the shoes had to be a coincidence – a little bit of second-hand patent leather couldn't be that much of a catalyst for change – but as they passed the shady little entrance way to the courtyard behind, Willow knew that at some point she would have to go back, just in case.

As the car slowed to a stop, Willow twisted in her seat to find Chloe chewing on her thumb.

'Can you remember the way to the office I told you from here?'

Chloe nodded. 'Go and sit in reception and just wait for me. If anyone asks what you're doing, tell them you're casting for the next series of *Sixteen and Pregnant*.'

As Chloe was about to exit India covered the girl's bitten-nailed, ruddy hand with her own. 'Thank you for putting up with me,' she smiled at Chloe.

'It's been fun.' Chloe nodded. 'Hanging out with a celeb, no one will ever believe me. Good luck with all the being famous shit.'

India knotted her sad regretful mouth into an approximation of a smile.

'We're going to stay friends,' India told Chloe. 'I promise you. After the dust has settled I'll be in touch to see how you're doing.'

Chloe studied India's face for while, before adding, 'That would be cool.'

Willow watched anxiously as Chloe dragged herself out of the car and headed in more or less the right direction, wondering what incentive the teenager had to do as she was told instead of disappearing into the streets of London to spend one more day in blissful denial. She was woefully underdressed for the weather, in her leggings and dress, a military jacket that would not do up jammed onto her shoulders. A sparkly cotton scarf wound several times around her neck was her only nod to the chill in the air.

No, today would not be a good day to choose to run away and never be seen again.

Photographers and press thronged the steps of the office as they pulled up outside, immediately surrounding the car even before it came to a standstill. Undoing her belt, Willow twisted in her seat, as the first flash bounced off the darkened glass on the windows.

'Are you ready?' she asked India, who seemed composed, almost more comfortable with this moment than any she had spent in Willow's flat.

'I'm ready,' India replied. 'It's funny, you know, I feel like I've been out of the world for the last few days. As if I've been totally lifted off the planet.'

'My flat probably does harbour some alien life forms,' Willow admitted.

'And now I'm back.' Somewhere in the wan, drawn face there was a note of triumph. India took off her glasses for a moment. 'Thank you for looking after me. I mean it. That life out there, with all the money and glitz and hotels and travel, and sometimes even a spot of acting, is wonderful and distracting and I'm more grateful to Victoria than I realised, to know that it's all still there, waiting for me. But even so, it's been a long time since I've felt like I was at home, even if it was someone else's. Thank you for looking after me so well.'

'Really, I don't think I did a very good job at all,' Willow confessed. 'I left you alone, foisted Chloe on you and fed you additives and booze.'

'Precisely.' India reached forward and touched her hand.

'And it was just what I needed. And now I'm ready to greet my public.'

'David?' Willow turned to the driver, who got out of the car, using some of his hand-to-hand combat skills to discreetly elbow a couple of journalists out of the way and make a clear space for India. Used to the press ignoring her whilst at the same attempting to trample her, Willow got out and opened the door for India.

'How are you, India?' someone called out, as India stepped into the cool air.

'What do you think about Hugh Cramner now?'

'How does it feel to know you went to bed with a sex addict?'

'Have you got a message for Hugh's wife?'

Flanked on either side by Willow and David, India kept her head down, her sad mouth perfectly poised, her eyes hidden behind her glasses. She looked the picture of fragile elegance as she mounted the steps up to Victoria's office, and Willow was not in the least bit surprised when the journalist barring her way stepped aside for her and the questions died down into an awe-struck silence.

And then, flouting Victoria's order in a way that only a true star could, India turned and, taking off her glasses, seemed to look everyone who was there in the eye.

'The last week has been the hardest and most testing of my life, one full of heartbreak and regret. Mine is just one of the many lives that Hugh Cramner has trampled on in his selfish pursuit of gratuitous pleasure. Now I have to pick myself up and get on with my future.'

Turning on her heel, India swept into the building with Willow close behind her.

India had played it perfectly and, more than that, had taken that very public moment to let Hugh Cramner know exactly what she thought of him.

As she hurried after India, Willow was relieved to see Chloe slumped on the leather sofa in reception, her face buried in a magazine.

'David?' Willow caught him as they waited for the lift to arrive. 'I don't suppose you've got a minute to keep an eye on that one, have you? I'm quite keen she doesn't wander off anywhere. She can be a bit of a handful.'

David's moustache bristled just as Willow knew it would.

'Willow, I've stormed more embassies than you've had hot dinners. I'm sure I can keep an eye on a slip of a girl for five minutes.'

Nevertheless Willow silently wished him good luck.

The champagne cork hit the ceiling in Victoria's office with a bang.

'You were brilliant, darling, perfect,' Victoria crowed, filling the flutes that Willow held out for her so quickly that the ice-cold liquid ran down her fingers and over her wrists. 'You got the statement that I told you to make spot on. Hughy will be turning in the metaphorical grave of his career, darling!'

India relieved Willow of one of the glasses, sipping through the several inches of froth.

'After everything I thought we meant to each other I just wanted to be able to say something to him, and if he won't return my calls then what else is a girl to do?' India's smile was bright, almost obliterating the pain in her eyes.

'I quite agree,' Victoria said, taking the other glass. Willow looked around for a third glass but there was none. 'Of course, you have to get through finishing the shoot with the bastard, but it's fine, the producers want as little of the cheating scumbag as possible in their film, so his part has been heavily cut, darling. They've given all his lines to that chap who plays the butler . . . anyway, they've whittled down his time on set to two days' shooting, which you can do all in one go, and then you can wash him out of your hair for ever, but it will have to be with Shinerama shampoo, as you've just landed their new campaign, and you've also been offered tissues in Japan – it's fine, they'll pay you a mint and no one important will see it.'

'Great,' India said, handing her glass to Willow, who after a second of hesitation filled it again and took a sip herself.

'*True Glitz* wants you done and dusted for next week's issue, so, Willow, you're taking her to that hotel in Hertfordshire, the one where all the footballers take their mistresses. You have to be in hair and make-up by one and the journo will interview you whilst you're getting your slap on.' Victoria took the champagne bottle out of Willow's hand and, forgetting she had an empty glass, took a swig directly out of it. 'Best of all I've got you back into Blakes for this evening, where they are waiting to accommodate your every whim. David will take you back down to Cornwall in the morning. I'm lending him to you until we've replaced all your staff.'

India began to say something but Victoria cut across her. 'No, I insist. Besides, it's fine. I took on this young actor yesterday, terribly keen but needs some extra income until his career takes off, so I'm going to keep him around to do some bits and bobs for me here and there. He's ever so willing to please, just how I like them.'

'We have to replace *all* my people?' India asked.

Victoria nodded. 'My sources confirmed that bitchy little PA was the one that leaked the story. She had copies of all your texts and emails. And I always think if one has to go it's best to do a clean sweep – you know what staff are like, always in cahoots, the ungrateful little mice – but never fear, I'll lend you Willow until I find someone else super for you. And as for that strumpet, she'll be stuck in Z-list hell for the rest of her natural life. I've already got her running around after the latest ITV3 casualty of war.

'Willow, find me some more champagne, darling. I absolutely have to keep last night's hangover at bay until at least Sunday.'

Willow took the empty bottle, hesitating as she wondered how on earth she was going to brook the subject that she couldn't accompany India to the *True Glitz* photoshoot that afternoon.

'Well, go on then, darling. You know my metabolism can only take a maximum of fifteen minutes sober. Chop chop.'

'Actually, Victoria,' sensing Willow's anxiety, India stepped in, 'I don't want to seem ungrateful but is there someone else who could come with me, rather than Willow? Don't get me wrong, Willow has been wonderful, utterly brilliant. But you know how it is, darling. The last few days have been so intense I could really do with a breath of fresh air, a change of scenery.'

'Bored of Willow? Perfectly fine, can't say I blame you,' Victoria said, marching to the door. 'Lucy! Get in here now!'

India winked at Willow, who mouthed a silent thank you.

'There is one thing I want you to do for me, though,' India told Victoria, who slammed the door just as Lucy arrived outside it.

'Anything, my love. Anything at all,' Victoria lied.

'Give Willow the rest of this week off,' India commanded

rather than asked. 'I think she could do with a change of scenery too. She's been by my side non-stop for days. She must need a rest.'

'Give Willow even more time off? Of course.' Victoria waved her hand like a fairy godmother issuing empty wishes. 'Consider it done, darling. I was just about to suggest it myself.'

'Do you promise me?' India pinned her down.

Victoria looked affronted. 'Do you doubt the word of the woman who's single-handedly saved your career?'

There was a knock at the door. 'Did you want me?' Lucy called uncertainly from the other side.

Victoria opened the door. 'What on earth are you doing out there, girl? Come in!'

'Gosh, sorry.' Lucy appeared in the doorway. 'Oh, Willow, am I pleased to see you. I was just trying to work the copier. I have no idea what all those buttons do – will you show me? Oh, and I think I might have accidentally permanently deleted your Excel account files. It asked me if I was sure and I went to press "cancel" and just clicked on "OK" instead! Random, lol!'

'Stop making noise now.' Victoria held up her hand. 'You are looking after India on her photoshoot, this afternoon. Do not mess it up,' Victoria told Lucy, who squealed most inappropriately. Victoria looked at her the way a cat might eye up a particularly irritating mouse. 'I said stop making noise. Go, ring ahead and make sure they've got all the things that India likes. And as for you,' she turned to Willow, 'I suppose you'd better go home.'

Victoria watched impassively as Willow and India hugged. 'Good luck,' India whispered in her ear. 'I'll leave it a suitable number of days and then I'm offering you the job of my PA.'

Willow's eyes widened but she didn't say anything as India excused herself and followed an endlessly chattering Lucy to her new and improved future.

'So I'll be off then,' Willow said to Victoria.

'Are you sure you can't just put through my expenses before you go, darling? And just book me in somewhere for lunch, oysters for me and Carlos. He gets ravenous, darling. I have to feed him all the time, keep his zinc levels up. And I am still waiting for that champagne.'

'Fine, and then I'm going,' Willow said, pursing her lips.

'Of course you are, darling.' Victoria watched Willow as she picked up the empty glasses by their stems. 'What is it about you? You've changed.'

'In what way?' Willow asked her, a little impatiently.

'I've never seen you actually want to leave work before. I think that for the first time since you've worked for me you've got someone at home you want to see.'

For a moment Willow was almost taken in by the warm tone, the friendly twinkle of a confidante in Victoria's eyes. Then she realised it was just Victoria trying to find out if anyone else had known about India being in her flat.

'Me?' Willow shook her head. 'Rest assured, Victoria, my life is as empty and as lonely as you like it.'

For once it was Willow who was smiling to herself as she outmanoeuvred her boss in one easy step.

'Aunty Pillow!' Jo-Jo spotted Willow first, closely followed by Jemima, the two of them hurtling towards her like mini identical hurricanes, swirls of varying shades of pink.

‘’Lo, Aunty Pillow,’ Jem said, winding her arms around Willow’s waist, halting her acceleration by breaking her face on Willow’s middle. ‘You’ve got on a teddy coat! It’s snugly.’

‘Aunty Pillow,’ Jo-Jo broke into the embrace, ‘Mummy says Hamleys is the biggest toy shop in the world. That’s big, isn’t it? Do they have every single toy there ever was? Do they have penny farthings like when you were young and everything was black and white?’

‘Um, it wasn’t ever actually black and white, and penny farthings were a bit before my time, *and* Mummy’s.’ Willow grinned at her sister, who was hovering, waiting for her chance to say hello. She looked as beautiful as ever, in slim-fitting jeans topped with a cream faux-fur jacket. Willow was always momentarily startled when she saw her sister. It was rather like coming face to face with your own ghost, or rather a parallel life that really should be lived a universe away.

‘I am pretty sure you already have every single toy there has ever been,’ Willow told her nieces, letting them lead her to Holly. ‘I’ve seen your bedroom.’

The sisters embraced, holding onto each other for a long moment, each checking that the other was really there. It was good to see Holly again; strange but not unexpected that she should be wearing a faux-fur coat not dissimilar to Willow’s, and a top underneath an identical shade of blue.

‘Snap!’ Willow said as they both slipped off their coats. She turned round and reached out a hand to Chloe, who was standing well back, mostly looking in the other direction as if she were assessing how easily she’d be able to make a break for it. Reluctantly she edged closer, self-consciously moving chairs out of her way.

'Holly, you remember Chloe.' Willow let go of her sister to slip her arm around Chloe.

'Of course I do. Haven't you grown!' Holly exclaimed, her eyes widening in horror at her comment before the sentence was even fully formed. 'I mean, haven't you grown up . . . I don't mean, you know, I don't mean . . .'

'She doesn't mean that you are fat,' Jem said helpfully. 'Although you are fat. Aunty Pillow is fatter than Mummy. We wish Mummy were fatter, because then she'd be more cuddly, like Aunty Pillow. Your tummy looks hard, though, like a giant beach ball.'

'Yeah, I know,' Chloe said, a little uncomfortable with all the attention that was being directed at her abdomen.

'That's because there's a baby in there,' Holly told the excited girls as Willow pulled back a chair for Chloe to ease herself into. This reunion must seem strange for her, Willow thought. When she had been preparing to marry Sam, Chloe and Holly had spent quite a lot of time together, the three of them shopping for dresses until they had literally visited every single wedding emporium in London, and a good deal of the South-West too. Holly had been delighted by Chloe, and it was partly down to their time together that she'd decided that it was time for her and Gray to start a family of their own. The three of them had twirled about in acres of silk tulle in this very shop, Willow remembered, none of them knowing, on that bright optimistic morning, what lay ahead. Or was that not right? Perhaps Willow had known, perhaps she had always known.

'A baby!' Jo-Jo stared at Chloe's tummy. 'How did it get there? Did you eat it?'

'Um.' Chloe looked at Holly for help.

'God just decided that now was the right time for Chloe to have a baby,' Holly said, making Chloe snort into her hand.

'Yeah, because it got me out of loads of homework,' she told the girls.

'Does it poo in there?' Jem asked. The sisters began to giggle hysterically, one egged on by the other. 'Does your baby poo in your tummy?'

'I think it might do, actually,' Chloe said. 'I skipped over that bit in the book.'

Jem produced a teddy from her little pink rucksack and promptly shoved it up her top. 'I've got a baby pooing in my tummy too!' She made a long, wet raspberry noise that sent Jo-Jo into paroxysms of laughter. Jo-Jo found her own teddy and followed suit.

Holly chuckled fondly as she watched her daughters caught up in each other's merriment.

'Sorry about those two, they are right little hellions,' Holly said, finally taking her moment to embrace Chloe as the girls scampered in and out of the tables, informing anyone who would listen about their pooing babies. 'So, how are you, Chloe?'

'I'm OK, I guess.' Chloe seemed to find it hard to look Holly in the eye. 'A bit tired.'

'I bet.' Holly kissed her on the cheek. 'I know I was when I was about six months gone with those two. It was all I could do to open my eyes, never mind actually get out of bed. You look beautiful, though, glowing.'

Willow watched Chloe, her tightly wrought, pale face and hunched shoulders, and thought her sister was half right. Chloe did look beautiful, but she didn't glow. Rather, she looked like the negative of a photograph. The ghost of a girl that had once been, an image worn away by worry. The urge to protect Chloe from any further hurt clenched Willow suddenly by the heart. Whatever happened, Willow only knew she had to make sure it did not leave a legacy that would always dog the girl, tracking her remorselessly through every moment. Willow made a silent promise that she would not allow that.

'I'm not so bad,' Chloe said, mustering a smile. 'It's easier being pregnant when you're younger. Your body is made for it. The optimum physical age to have a baby is fourteen. I read that.'

'I'm going to be fourteen in a hundred years or something,' Jem said, pausing briefly at the table's edge to suck on a bottle of juice. 'Mummy, can I have a baby when I'm fourteen?'

'Christ, no!' Holly exclaimed. 'I . . . I mean it would interfere terribly with your being a ballerina.'

'Your mum's right.' Chloe smiled at Jem. 'You can't do twirls with a big fat tummy.'

'I suppose not,' Jem said rather seriously. 'I'm only going to be a ballerina on Thursdays. For the rest of the week I'm going to be a stunt quad biker, horse rider, and princess. I'm having Fridays off to go shopping.'

'Cool.' Chloe smiled. 'And what about you?'

Sensing she was being left out of something Jo-Jo joined them at the table, her teddy still *in situ* up her jumper.

'I'm going to be the same as her, but also, too, I am going to be an artist,' Jo-Jo said. 'I am awfully good at painting flowers. So I shan't have Fridays off, but Jem is going to make tea that day and we aren't ever going to get married because we don't like sharing.'

'Yes, definitely don't married if you don't like sharing.' Holly rolled her eyes. 'Honestly, you'd have thought I'd asked Gray to cut his arm off when I suggested he bring us up with him today. He can't bear having the girls in his car. He spends the whole trip telling them not to draw on the windows with their fingers or drop crumbs on the upholstery. Well, of course, Jo-Jo spilled her juice. You should have seen his face!'

Holly complained in the way that wives who not only love their husbands but know that their husbands love them back do.

'Can we go to Hamleys *now*?' Jo-Jo asked, backed up by excited squeals from her sister.

'No, we haven't had our lunch yet!' Holly exclaimed.

'Not hungry,' the twins replied in perfect unison.

'Well, the grown-ups need to eat. Chloe is eating for—'

'I'll take them,' Chloe volunteered. 'I could do with some fresh air and I'm not hungry either.' Willow and Holly exchanged glances. 'I ate about twenty biscuits while I was waiting for you to finish work,' Chloe explained.

'Up to you,' Willow said, looking at Holly.

'The thing is, they can be a bit of a handful,' Holly said. 'Take your eye off them, even for a second and –'

'I won't, I promise,' Chloe said earnestly. 'It's ages since I've been to Hamleys and . . . it'll be nice. I swear I won't lose them. Or sell them, even if I get offered loads of money. Here, you two,' she gestured to the girls, who had peeled off to run around a fashionably dressed mannequin for no particular reason. They flanked her, one either side like two fallen angels up to no good.

'Want to come to Hamleys with me while these two do chatting?'

'Yay!'

Chloe was drowned out by cheers. 'OK, but if I take you there are strict rules.' The twins found Chloe's stern face particularly amusing, but they stilled themselves enough to listen. 'No running away, no running at all, because I can't keep up with this baby in my tummy.'

'Doing pooing!' Jo-Jo giggled from behind a hand.

'Or windy-pops,' Jem added, digging her sister in the ribs.

'No misbehaving of any kind,' Chloe said. 'Can you promise to do that? Because if I lose you I'll be in big trouble with your mummy and aunty.'

'We promise.' Jem was spokesperson for both twins.

'Do you *really*?' Holly sounded a little anxious. 'London is a big place. If you got lost here Mummy might never find you, ever again.'

The girls promised her most sincerely that they would stay close to Chloe and be good, and Chloe promised Willow she would be back in half an hour. Willow and Holly watched the noisy little trio go with some trepidation, both of them silently cataloguing an endless list of terrible things that might happen to their girls on a quick trip round the world's biggest toy shop.

'So shall we order?' Holly said uncertainly.

'We could order or . . . we could follow them at a discreet distance and make sure they are OK.' Willow voiced exactly what her sister was thinking. They scraped back their chairs in unison.

It turned out that they need not have worried. Chloe had each twin firmly by the hand and never let either one go, even to negotiate a long crocodile of identically bobble-hatted foreign students. The twins side-skipped and hopped around Chloe, faces turned upwards as they no doubt questioned her endlessly about her pooing baby.

'Are *you* OK?' Holly asked Willow as they waited by the entrance of the toy shop for the girls to mount the escalators to the first floor.

'Me?' Willow watched the threesome ascend. 'Why wouldn't I be fine?'

'Because, Willow, it broke your heart losing Chloe and Sam, and now they've suddenly turned up in your life it must be . . . painful, odd, nice, unsettling. It must be all of those things that you haven't really said.' Holly hooked her fingers through Willow's, grabbing two pairs of novelty flower-shaped sunglasses out of a bin as they headed for the escalator.

'Do you remember dressing up in Mum's clothes, before – when it was just the three of us in that flat? Do you remember her hats? I mean, she was a single mother, two kids, a cleaning job, and she had loads and loads of posh hats, with veils and silk flowers. Do you remember? You liked the pink one, with the butterflies. I always wore the red. I wonder where she got those hats.'

She put on one pair of the sunglasses and handed the other to Willow. 'It's been ages since we've done any dressing up – go on, for me?'

Willow shrugged and put her glasses on too.

'I mean, doesn't it make you wonder, what if?' Holly said, ducking a little as they reached the top of the escalator. The pair hopped off, shielding themselves behind a ten-foot teddy bear dressed as a soldier.

'What does, hats?' Willow's smile was wry.

'What if you and Sam had rode out the storm?' Holly said carefully.

'What if is the one question I never ask myself. Honestly, seeing Chloe again is the best thing that's happened to me in years,' Willow said as they peered around the big bear's behind, Holly gesturing for her sister to make a dash for the end of the aisle. 'Even in all this mess, just having her close is frightening, exhilarating, brilliant . . . I really missed her, Holly, more than I let myself realise. I can't afford to start dwelling on what if.'

'I know,' Holly said. 'And what about seeing Sam again? How does that make you feel?'

They loitered at the end of the Barbie aisle.

Willow considered lying, but she knew there was no point. 'Confusing,' she admitted. 'I think it would be easier for us to hate each other, and there is a lot of anger and guilt, but I don't hate him and I don't think he hates me any more. I see him and I just want to go bed with him.'

'Willow!' Holly exclaimed, stifling herself at the last minute before they blew their cover.

Ducking down as one of the twins looked up, Willow found a bottom shelf full of tiaras. The two women glanced at each other and suddenly it seemed entirely appropriate for each of them to jam a tiara on her head.

'I remember Mum's jewellery. All that glittering stuff, big chunky jewels – her top drawer was like a treasure chest, wasn't it? Funny, it never occurred to me that there we were, sometimes going to bed hungry, and yet the three of us were all dressed like princesses all the time. I didn't mind it then, and even after everything that's happened I don't mind it now. It was lovely, having a beautiful mum. Feeling like a princess was better than being full. '

Holly realigned Willow's rather wonky tiara. 'Do you realise that we look really quite bizarre?' she said. 'And that security guard thinks we're shoplifting?' Willow raised her glasses and winked at the gentleman in question.

'On Monday I did a naked photoshoot – for all of five minutes, admittedly. Still, sunglass- and tiara-disapproving security personnel hold no fear for me now.'

Holly chuckled. 'You were telling me about wanting to go to bed with Sam?'

'I didn't mean for sex.' Willow rolled her eyes behind the pink lenses of her glasses. 'I mean, I just want to curl up in his arms under a blanket. Sam always made me feel so safe and secure. While I was with him I felt like nothing else could touch me.'

'So, is he still all brooding and sexy?' Holly asked as, still crouching, they peered down the Barbie aisle to see the twins agog at the endless array of plastic loveliness.

'Ooh, look. Wands.' Willow picked up one crystal-encrusted wand that caught her eye and handed another to her sister. 'He is, he is, but he's changed. He used to look like there was nothing in the world that could defeat him, like nothing scared him. That seems to have gone away. I worry that it's my fault.'

'What you did was stupid and thoughtless, and I'm sure you hurt him a lot. But he was the one who couldn't understand why it happened. It was Sam's stubborn pride that lost him the woman he loved. That's what hurt him.'

'Hmm. Would you be so understanding if you found Gray in bed with a naked woman, even if they hadn't had sex yet?'

Holly scowled furiously. 'I would nail him to the floor by his balls.'

'Exactly.' Willow fell silent, wondering how wrong it would be to pop on a pair of fairy wings to top off her ensemble, and then deciding against it. Naked photoshoot aside, she wasn't quite ready for wings yet. A thought that struck her as something of a metaphor for her whole life.

'So now they are back – and, if they stick around, Sam's back in your life on a regular basis – would you, you know . . . try and get back together with him?' As they straightened up, Holly finally asked her the burning question, one that somehow lacked the required *gravitas*, topped off as it was by pink sparkling gemstones, more than a little like the ones their mother used to keep in her top drawer.

'Don't be silly!' Willow couldn't stop herself from giggling, more with relief at discovering the answer than at her sister's get-up. 'He's got a new girlfriend who makes her own pasta, and besides, if I couldn't let Sam love me the first time round, what's different now, apart from that this time he'd know I'd be very likely to ruin things all over again? We'd never trust each other. Oh, and now I feel sad.'

As the girls dragged Chloe on, Willow and Holly followed, stopping to smile indulgently as the twins charged full pelt into a mountain of stuffed toys, cheering as they were engulfed by an avalanche of puppies and teddies.

'I'm pretty sure they're not supposed to do that,' Holly said.

'Get out of there, right now!' Chloe yelled in such a grown-up and authoritative tone that two heads immediately popped out of the fuzz, looking almost contrite.

'It was her idea,' Jem said sulkily, before looking past Chloe and squinting at Willow and Holly. 'Mummy, is that *you*?'

'It would appear so,' Holly said, rather sheepishly taking off the tiara. 'Hey, look what I got both of you!'

'Mummy!' Jo-Jo giggled as she ran up to her mother, closely followed by her sister. 'You look like a princess!'

'Did you get wings too?' Jem asked, gesturing for Willow to bend down so that she could de-crown her. 'All good princesses have wings.'

'What do you look like?' Chloe repressed a smile. 'Apart from like you're on day release for the loony bin and following us. And, by the way, look, I haven't lost them and only caused minor criminal damage.'

There had been a lecture from the security guard and a section manager, and a lot of tidying up before they were eventually allowed to leave the shop, laden down with several guilt-inspired purchases, including baby dolls that pooed. As Willow and Holly walked behind the others, Willow felt a surge of joy at seeing Chloe, swinging hands with the girls, looking happy and relaxed.

'You are, you know,' Holly said, taking her eyes off her daughters for a moment to consider Willow.

'I am what?' Willow asked her.

'Different. I can feel it, even when I'm down in Christchurch. It's hard to explain. It's like you've got something back . . .'

'I've got new shoes,' Willow said. 'And this coat.'

'Those are lovely shoes and it's a great coat, but . . .' Holly's smile wavered, her eyes clouding behind her rose-tinted spectacles. 'Willow, you never talk about what happened . . .'

'There's nothing to say,' Willow countered firmly. 'What on earth is there to say?'

'There is more to say than there are words for,' Holly said, her face serious behind the glasses. 'Look, I'm not trying to drag it all up now. I just wanted to say that . . . there must be a chance for you to be OK. There must be, because if there isn't then . . .'

'Then what?' Willow asked her quietly.

'Then this is a terrible world we live in, where there is never enough good to outweigh all the bad,' Holly said. 'And I couldn't bear that.'

Willow smiled at her sister. 'How can that possibly be true? How can a world where two grown women dress up like demented fairies to go incognito ever be terrible?'

She caught Holly's hand and squeezed it, each sister drawing strength from the other.

After saying goodbye to the girls as Holly took them to the cinema, Willow paused for a moment to look at Chloe. On impulse she took her hand and kissed it, pulling Chloe into a huge hug.

'Oh, Chloe,' Willow said to the pregnant fifteen-year-old in her arms and the little girl she'd left behind, 'I've missed you so much, darling.'

Chloe was silent for a long time and then, to Willow's joy, she hugged her back before whispering, 'I suppose I've missed you too.'

Willow and Chloe waited.

Willow had vacuumed the flat and dusted as soon as they got back from Hamleys, even finding a tin of spray polish under the sink and going at the sideboard with an entire packet of make-up-removing facial wipes. After doing the best she could with her scant cleaning materials, she found some perfume lurking in the bottom of a drawer. It was the gift that Daniel had given her for Christmas last year, telling her in his usual forthright manner that it was exactly the same brand that he'd given the two girls he'd been seeing at the time because it was on three for two at Boots. It wasn't Willow at all – it was flowery and sweet – but even if it had been her kind of perfume she would never have worn it. Still plastic-wrapped and untouched, it served as a timely reminder of exactly how little Daniel thought of her: a walk-on, an extra in his life, whom he rewarded with thoughtless freebies.

Unwrapping the bottle from its cellophane, Willow began to spray it all over the flat. It was funny, she thought as she doused the place in notes of springtime, she had felt much more comfortable loving Daniel when he hurt her in that casual, careless way. She almost preferred it when he wasn't thinking about her, when their friendship was a constant background hum that either one of them could revisit whenever they liked. In her head Willow thought she'd been playing the long game, waiting for him to want her, for the moment of their union. And then on Monday, in a heartbeat, all of that changed.

For the first time Daniel was within reach, and for the first time Willow wasn't at all sure that she wanted him.

Willow paused in front of the dusty mirror that hung over her gas fire, looking into her own eyes for a long moment. There was something else too; when she'd seen Holly today she had felt less different from her identical twin. It was a hard notion to explain, but even with their physical and emotional selves so in tune, for a very long time Willow had felt separated from her sister by the blunt instrument of fate. Their two lives had taken such different, divergent paths, all leading back to one terrible moment in time. Sometimes, even when they were in the same room, hand in hand, Willow would look at Holly, at her husband and children, and feel that they were miles apart. But she hadn't felt that today. Today she had felt like a part of her sister.

'Magic slippers,' she muttered to herself. 'Haunted shoes, haunted by the spirit of a kick-ass super fox who makes men love her when they don't want to . . .'

'Please don't talk to yourself when she's here,' Chloe said, coming out of her bedroom with an actual maternity dress on and her long black hair brushed and shiny. Willow looked her up and down. She'd taken her piercing out and removed most of her eyeliner, making her look a good deal younger, a sight that was simultaneously touching and awful.

'You want to make a good impression,' Willow said.

'Well, I don't want her to judge me,' Chloe said. 'I don't want her to think I'm some idiot kid who got knocked up because she didn't know any better.'

'OK,' Willow said carefully. 'Well. Good.'

'I want her to take me seriously. To realise that I'm not just trying to get out of this. I'm trying to make the best possible life for my baby.'

'I think she will realise that,' Willow said.

'And what about you, do you take me seriously?' Chloe challenged her.

Willow nodded. 'Of course I do.'

'Then have you thought about my idea, about taking the baby?'

Willow shook her head and went over to Chloe, putting her arm around her. 'To be honest, Chloe, I've mainly been thinking about you.'

'The baby is me too, Willow. Please –' The doorbell sounded before Chloe could say any more.

Willow kissed the top of her head. 'That will be your father.'

It turned out that it was both Sam and Tina Ellroy, the adoption social worker from Haringey, who had met on the stairs. Sam stood back, allowing Tina in first. She was a capable-looking woman in her late forties, her hair pulled back under a scarf. She was friendly, though, with a kind voice and a nice smile.

'Tea?' Willow offered after Sam introduced Tina to Chloe.

Willow stood in the kitchen watching as Chloe smiled shyly, while Tina asked her a few general questions about the baby. Chloe looked so young then, younger than her fifteen years, even. All the bluster and determination seemed to have been washed away with her make-up. Willow could tell that she didn't know whether to sit down or stand up, to sit next to Tina or across from her. After a moment, Willow's heart ached as Chloe slipped her hand into her father's, who was standing just as awkwardly as his daughter, their fingers tightening around each other's in silent solidarity.

'Well, shall we sit?' Tina expertly took the lead, taking a mug of tea from Willow. Chloe and Sam sat side by side on the sofa, Tina on the sofa opposite, and after a moment Chloe patted the space next to her, which Willow squeezed into.

'So, Chloe, you are thinking about giving the baby up for adoption,' Tina began pleasantly.

'I've decided to,' Chloe said. 'I'm not thinking about it, I've decided. I am.'

'OK.' Tina smiled at her. 'But just to make sure you are absolutely certain Haringey Council is obliged to ask you a number of questions about yourself, your circumstances and your situation, and then give you all the counselling and support you need to make this difficult choice. Do you understand?'

Chloe nodded. Tina rustled about in her outsize bag for a moment, pulling out a packet of tissues and some lipstick before she found a notepad and, after some further investigation, a Biro, which she scribbled with furiously on the notebook cover to make sure it worked. Judging by the ink-blackened cover, it was a ritual she often repeated.

'So, we've established that you are twenty-eight weeks along, and that your and the baby's health is good. What about your family – any history of health problems there?'

'My mum died when I three,' Chloe blurted out. 'She had a blood clot in her head.'

'She was thirty-two,' Sam added.

Tina nodded, making a note. 'That must have been hard for you both.'

'I don't remember,' Chloe said.

'It was.' Sam stared at the toes of his boots. 'It was very hard.'

Tina wrote something else in her notebook and then looked up at Chloe, smiling brightly.

'Anything else? Asthma, eczema, heart disease, high blood pressure?'

Chloe looked up at Sam, who shook his head.

'And the father?' Tina asked.

Chloe looked blank. 'He's nothing to do with this.'

Tina pulled down the corners of her mouth, a considered expression. 'Although at this point the father does not have any rights over your decision, the Council's policy is to always try to contact the father and involve him as much as possible in the process. Even if he doesn't want to be involved, it is important that we have a name for the baby, if at all possible. It's incredibly meaningful to adopted children to have that route back to their birth parents. It helps them understand where they came from and why they were adopted, gives them a sense of identity. We try to collect as much information now so that when the child is old enough, the circumstances of its birth won't be a . . . black hole.'

Chloe shifted uncomfortably in her seat, her palms passing fleetingly over her bump.

'But it was just this boy, this boy at a party, who I didn't even see again.' She chewed the top of her thumb. 'It was just a one-night thing. I don't even know his name.'

Willow frowned. That was not what Chloe had told her the other day. She told her the boy knew about the baby and wanted nothing to do with it. Why didn't she just tell Tina that?

'Oh, Chloe,' Sam said softly, bowing his head. Willow thought it must be so hard for him to hear this, but he didn't take his hand from hers. If anything, he held on to it more tightly.

Tina tried again. 'You can't remember anything about him, not his first name? You're completely sure?'

'I'm sure, all right? Fuck!' Chloe stood up suddenly, walking to the window. 'This is nothing to do with him.'

'Chloe?' Willow stood up too, as Chloe leaned her forehead against the damp glass. 'What's wrong?'

'I want to get my baby adopted, that's all. I'm not under arrest, am I?'

'It's OK.' Tina smiled. Her tone was reasonable, but her eyes followed Chloe closely.

'Are you trying to protect whoever it was, is that what it is?' Sam pleaded. 'Do you think I'm going to go round there and deck him?'

Chloe turned round, wrapping her arms around herself. 'That is what you said you'd do,' she reminded him.

'No, I mean, yes, but – I was in shock, Chloe. You'd hidden this from me for six months and then suddenly there you are, my little girl, the size of a house . . .'

'Oh, thanks,' Chloe snapped.

'I'm sorry, I didn't mean . . . you're not fat – there's nothing to you.' Sam turned to Tina. 'We've grown apart since she hit puberty, I suppose. We were always so close, in it together, a team. Then she started changing and I stopped knowing how to talk to her or what to say.'

'I see.' Tina continued to scribble.

'I probably just thought it was best to let her get on with it. I was wrong.' Sam shook his head. 'She's a good kid. This mess is down to me.'

'These things happen; they're no one's fault,' Tina reassured him with practised certainty. 'The key now is to manage the situation as best we possibly can and to plan for the future of the baby. Even if you do decide to give it—'

'Him, he's a him,' Chloe said emphatically. 'Even if I decide to give *him* up.'

'Of course. Even if you decide to give him up, then one day any scrap of information you might be able to pass on to him will mean so much. And not just about the father, but . . . what special talents you have in your or the father's family, traits or skills that might be passed down to him. Anything you'd like him to know when he grows up, a letter from you, a photo of you with him. Anything you can do to show him that when you decided to have him adopted it was out of love and not because you didn't care. Because you wanted the best for him and not because you didn't want him. If you are certain that you want to have him adopted then that really is the greatest gift you can ever give your baby.'

Huddled against the rattling windows, Chloe stared at Tina, and Willow found herself worrying that she would be getting a chill on her back from the draughty, rotting window frame.

'Chloe, love,' Sam got up, tentatively approaching his daughter, 'I'm not angry any more, not with you or even whoever it was who . . .' He coughed. 'I want the best for you and for that little one. He is my grandson, after all. So if you want to contact the father, get him involved in this, I promise I won't kick off.'

'I don't want to,' Chloe said quietly, suddenly brittle.

Willow looked from Tina to Chloe, the anxiety in Tina's face feeding Willow's own sense of unease. Ever since she had arrived Willow had seen the lost child in Chloe that she had been herself; now, for the briefest of moments, it was like looking into her own past, and it frightened her.

'He might be a snotty-nosed kid, but he should know. He should know what he's done and at least take some responsibility,' Sam went on with his usual bludgeoning bluster.

'No!' Chloe raised her voice. 'No, I'm not going to see him or tell him or . . . or anything, OK? Because I hate him! I hate him, I hate him, I hate him and he isn't getting anywhere near me ever again! Do you get it?'

'Yes, yes, it's fine,' Tina reassured her. 'Don't worry.'

'Good. Is that it? Because I'm tired. I want to . . .' Chloe gestured vaguely at her room, her skin crawling with naked desperation to be out of the situation.

'That will do for today,' Tina said pleasantly. 'There's no rush.'

'Bye then.' Chloe all but ran into her bedroom, closing the door firmly behind her.

'What just happened?' Sam asked Willow. 'She looked scared.'

Willow, determined not to interfere, looked at Tina.

'She is scared. This is an incredibly scary situation for a young woman to be in and I am concerned,' Tina said, reading over her notes. 'I don't think Chloe is at all sure about this decision yet, and that maybe she hasn't been altogether forthcoming about the circumstances of how the baby was conceived.'

'What does that mean?' Sam pressed her.

'I don't know,' Tina said. 'And I don't think at this point I'm the right person to try and ask her. Look, I see a lot of kids in all sorts of terrible danger in my job. I learn to spot when someone is hiding something, and I'm pretty sure Chloe is. But I also know when there is genuine love and trust between parents and their children.' She smiled at Sam. 'I can see you have had a rocky time – a single dad and a teenage girl is never easy – but that girl trusts you and she loves you. And you.' Tina smiled at Willow as she stood up, collecting her jacket and bag. 'She is so lucky that you two have stayed friends. The number of divorced parents who make it their duty to mess up their children to score points off each other never ceases to amaze me. And for a step-mother to stay so present in her life – well, I can tell it means a lot to her.'

Sam and Willow exchanged glances, neither speaking.

'Anyway, I think we should take the pressure off Chloe for

now. She doesn't have to make any final decisions yet. Even after the birth she has time to change her mind. I do think she would benefit from counselling as soon as possible, though. There's a waiting list but I'll put her on it now, because otherwise the baby will be eighteen before she gets seen, and I suggest you contact her school. They are legally obliged to put together some work for her, even if she's been excluded, that will keep her up to date so that she's not so far behind when she does go back. I'll open a file for her, so that if you need me you can contact me as her personal case worker, but . . .' Tina paused. 'Look, I shouldn't say this – I'm not really allowed to have an opinion – but I didn't get the chance to tell Chloe about all the help and support we have here in the borough for underage mums. If she keeps the baby we can help get her through her GCSEs, put her on parenting courses, help her through college, even university. There are childcare support groups, and with a strong family support network like yours there is no reason why she couldn't be a wonderful mother and have everything in life that you want her to.' Tina shrugged. 'That baby is your blood, your precious cargo, and in this case I'm not sure an adoptive parent would be able to give him a better life than you.' Tina smiled briefly. 'I'd get put up against a wall and shot if the powers that be knew I'd said that. Call me any time. I can't promise I'll always be there, but I will always get back to you as soon as possible.'

When Willow had seen Tina out, she shut the door and turned round to find Sam with his back to her, his shoulders hunched, tense. Tentatively she crossed the room, putting her hand on his back.

'Do you think we did this to her?' he asked, without looking up.

'I think we let her down,' Willow said. 'And I know I let you both down.'

Sam turned and gathered Willow into his arms, squeezing the breath out of her as he tightened his embrace.

'Oh, Willow,' he said into her hair, 'I love her so much, and I don't know how to help her. Why won't she talk about the father? Do you think she doesn't want to keep the baby because whoever it was hurt her . . . maybe even . . . ?'

Sam couldn't bring himself to say out loud what he was thinking, but Willow knew exactly what he was afraid of.

'I think we just need to be there for her. I think she's probably been worrying about everybody except herself – you, the baby . . . even me. Maybe it was too soon to arrange a social worker. Here I am, steaming in trying to be someone I'm not.'

'Someone you're not?' Sam released her a little so he could look at her.

'Her mum?' Willow admitted. 'I've missed her, Sam. There's been this ache in my chest and I thought it was part of me – that I'd always had it and I always would – but when she came back . . . it went. Maybe I'm trying too hard to prove to her how much she means to me.'

'How much Chloe means to you,' Sam repeated the phrase, testing it.

'What we should do is something fun,' Willow said. 'Put a smile on her face. I'm meeting Holly later and we're going to this comedy night in Battersea to see a sort of friend do his first ever stand-up. It's going to be awful – he's not at all funny – but there might be some good people on. I was going to ask you if you minded me taking Chloe, but I've got a better idea. Why don't you come too?'

Sam pursed his lips a little. 'Me? Go to a comedy club?'

'That's such an insane idea, is it?' Willow attempted a winning smile that somehow seemed to hit home.

'OK,' Sam said, half smiling. 'Fine then, why not? I'll drive, you'll kill us.'

Willow's face fell.

'I'm joking, Will. Your driving isn't that bad. Nearly, but not quite.'

'Daniel will be there,' Willow said quickly, thinking of the back of Daniel's hand on her breast, the heat of his breath in her hair. She was really, really keen that Sam didn't find out about that, sensing that, even though their relationship was long over, even the hint of something more between her and Daniel would put paid to any chance of friendship between them.

'Oh.' Sam's face clouded over. 'Of course, you're still friends.'

'He'll be there with Kayla, his girlfriend, she's a model. Does that mean you won't come?'

Sam shook his head. 'Look, I'm a grown-up. And if you and Daniel are close and you want to stay in Chloe's life then I've got to be grown up about this too.'

'You're sure?' Willow asked him.

'Are you sure you want me to come?' Sam asked her.

Willow looked up at him, his familiar face, the lines and creases she hadn't been able to stop looking at every chance she got. She missed him too, not just Chloe. She missed the love she'd once felt for him with every beat of her heart. But she knew that to have him in her life now she would have to be prepared to accept a lot less than he had once been willing to give, and perhaps that would be worse than not having him at all.

'I am sure,' she smiled.

Sam hesitated and then, reaching out, he picked up her fingers lightly in his.

'I never thought I'd say this, but it's good to see you, Willow.'

Chapter Thirteen

The Dog and Bone, Cheyne Walk, was one of those pubs that had once been called something traditional and prosaic like the Red Lion or the White Swan, but which some large corporation had given a trendy facelift to, pushing out the regulars in favour of bringing in the young, part of that makeover including Funny Thursdays. It was in the upstairs room of this polished and corporate pub that Serious James was to make his debut as a professional stand-up comedian. Willow feared for him.

'Up-and-coming comedy talent, it says here,' she said as she scanned the names that had been chalked on the board outside the pub. 'Oh, look, here's James!'

James's name had been tagged on right at the bottom, squeezed in so tightly that whoever had added it had been forced to write it round the corner and up the margin.

'You really shouldn't be in a pub,' Sam grumbled pleasantly, his hand on Chloe's shoulder.

'I don't think anyone's going to ask me for ID, Dad,' Chloe said, patting her belly. 'Besides, it's not as if I'm going to be getting tanked up, is it? At least another three months before I can get drunk again!'

Chloe treated Sam to a cheeky grin, and Willow smiled

inwardly. It was so nice to see the two of them this way, relaxed together, and it was even nicer to be with them to be part of it, however much on the periphery. She watched Sam from behind as he insisted on buying all of their tickets, including Holly's. She had hugged him hard when they had met back at the flat, instantly dissolving any residual tension there might have been about the fact that he'd thrown her sister out into the rain. Willow loved Holly for that, for understanding that peace with Sam was so much more important than principle, even though she knew, had she asked it, Holly would quite happily have clocked him one with the nearest blunt instrument.

Having Holly, Chloe and Sam in one place was the nearest thing to perfect that Willow had experienced for a long time. She felt stronger, and something almost close to happy. She closed her eyes for a second as she stood in the cold outside the pub and tried to remember the last time she'd been truly, purely happy. But the memory would not come, barricaded as it was behind the locked doors that Willow refused to open, shut in the darkness with thoughts she would not allow to surface. She snapped her eyes open again, shuddering, but not against the cold. Don't spoil this, she told herself, as she watched Holly punch Sam lightly on the shoulder as she teased him about something. Let this moment be what it is, let it be good.

Finally the queue moved in through the double doors and Willow followed the others up the stairs. Holly waited for her at the top, while Sam and Chloe went to look for a table.

'I think he's still a dish,' Holly whispered in her ear. 'I actually fancy him a bit more now.'

'You fancy Sam?' Willow whispered back, appalled.

'We are twins, darling – of course I'm going to fancy the same men that you do.'

'Well, I don't fancy Gray,' Willow retorted.

'Neither do I!' Holly told her cheerfully. 'I mean, of course I do, but not in the same way as I used to. Graham and I have been together so long there aren't any surprises left.'

'That's not a bad thing,' Willow said, looking around the room. There was a small platform stage with a single microphone standing in the middle, a spotlight trained on it, and a small PA to one side. 'To be with a man for all those years, who loves you and whom you love. That's what it's all about, right? That's a wonderful thing.'

'Will!' Daniel stood up, waving them over, his smile quickly fading as he saw Sam, who'd found a separate table with Chloe and had been trying to catch Willow's eye.

'Yes, it is wonderful,' Holly agreed as she turned her gaze from Daniel to Sam. 'But not nearly as interesting as every man you meet suddenly falling for you! Did you see Daniel's face then? He's jealous!'

'Nonsense,' Willow said. 'He's competitive. It's a whole different thing.'

'Come over here and sit with us,' Kayla insisted. 'Bring your friends over too.'

Willow caught Sam's eye, hoping her expression was apologetic. After a moment, with Chloe dragging him by the hand, the two of them arrived at the table, where, after some judicial chair borrowing and shuffling around, they were all seated, Daniel on her right and Sam on her left. Catching Holly's very amused expression, Willow could not have been more grateful for the large gin and tonic that Sam handed her.

'Sam.' Daniel reached across her lap, extended a hand to Sam who, jaw clenched, took it.

'Daniel.'

'Hey, kiddo,' Daniel grinned at Chloe, greeting her the way that he always used to.

'Hello.' Chloe's response was reserved, to say the least. Willow didn't think Sam had ever told Chloe all the details of why she'd left so abruptly, but she was no fool. Even then she must have noticed that her stepmother and her neighbour had left the building at the same time.

'Interesting times, huh?' Daniel said, nodding at the bump.

Chloe shrugged, turning her back on Daniel as she looked in the opposite direction in the most perfectly executed snub. Willow could not help but be rather proud of her.

If an awkward moment had been about to develop, beautiful, insensitive, thoughtless Kayla trampled all over it with her usual aplomb, leaning right across the table to shake hands with the newcomers.

'Hi, I'm Kayla, Daniel's girlfriend.' Kayla smiled beautifully for Sam, who was treated to a glimpse of her small but perfectly formed breasts beneath the scoop of her cream knitted minidress, just before the sweep of her treacle-coloured hair swept forward over her shoulders, and covered her modesty. She looked divine, Willow thought, feeling rather uncomfortable in the jeans that should have been too small and a rather low-cut top that she had put on and taken off three times before coming out, caught between worrying that either Sam or Daniel would think it was for his benefit, or thinking that she looked middle-aged. Eventually the plunge neckline had won out, but only because she had run out of time.

How Daniel could possibly think of her as being on the same planet in terms of desirability as Kayla, Willow did not know. She remembered when he had first met Kayla, a model on a shoot he'd been working on. He'd sent Willow dozens of texts telling her the details of his attempts to seduce Kayla, asking her for tips and advice and for a long time Kayla had resisted him, telling him that it was her policy never to date photographers as it might affect her work. Of course, Daniel always wanted what he could not have, and his pursuit of her had been relentless. Willow had never asked exactly what Daniel had done finally to win Kayla over, but she remembered receiving a text from him in the early hours one morning that simply said, 'Job done.'

'How awful do you think he'll be, Willow?' Kayla asked Willow cheerfully. 'Do you think it will be like on *X Factor*, when you want to rip your eyes out in embarrassment?' She turned to Sam. 'Do you know I once had to pretend to be a singer for a video shoot, wearing nothing but a roll of gaffer tape. That smarted when it came off, I can tell you! In a nice way, though.'

Kayla giggled, and Sam blushed, coughing into his pint.

'Perhaps he won't be so bad. He can even be quite funny sometimes,' Willow said, wondering where James was now and if he'd climbed out of the window in the gents and run away, which was exactly what she would have done.

'Funny? Are you sure, Willow?' Kayla jiggled in her seat. 'I'm excited. I just hope people aren't too mean to him. He was bullied at school, you know. Standing up in front of these people and getting a laugh is like his own private Everest.'

'Bullied?' Daniel chuckled. 'How do you know?'

'That night you passed out on tequila in the summer, James and I had a long dark night of the soul,' Kayla told him.

'Everyone took the piss out of him because he lived with his aunt and wore eyeliner, or something.' She leaned a little closer to Willow. 'That's when he told me that he thought you were the most interesting woman he'd ever met. I was a bit offended. I thought I was bound to be the most interesting woman he'd ever met.'

'James wore eyeliner?' Daniel was aghast. 'In Texas if you're a man who wears eyeliner it's a shooting offence.'

'Hang on, isn't he your friend? Why don't you know this stuff?' Willow asked.

'Male friendship is not based on the knowledge of shit. It's based on the ability to talk shit. I've got you, Willow, if I ever want to talk.'

'And me,' Kayla said, under the ripple of applause that greeted the MC coming on stage. 'And me, Daniel!'

Daniel ignored her. 'He's on first, poor bastard.'

Daniel looked over at Willow and smiled. It was a different sort of smile from usual, a secret one.

If Kayla or Sam had seen she was certain they would know exactly what it meant: it meant trouble.

'If he's here then he must be quite good, surely?' Sam said, his voice tense.

'Bless you, Sam.' Daniel's smile was patronising. 'But you don't know Serious James; he's never been knowingly funny in his life.'

'Oh God, I feel embarrassed already. I don't want to look, but I do.' Kayla grinned at Daniel, putting her hand on his knee. Deftly he picked it up, squeezed it and put it back in her own lap.

'And now give it up for comedy's funniest accountant, James Baker!'

Serious James shuffled onto the stage and stood behind the microphone, looking very much like he wished that he could hide behind it. The room fell silent and Willow estimated he had about a minute before the crowd started to get restless. Still he said nothing. He stood there, in a pair of unfashionable jeans and a pink shirt that he'd tucked in, his too long scruffy blond hair all over the place.

'I'm depressed,' he told the crowd suddenly, breathing into the mic.

'So am I now you've turned up!' someone heckled from the back. James ignored him.

'Loser,' Chloe muttered quite loudly. 'I'm missing telly for this.'

Willow bit her lip, just willing James not to be terrible.

'I'm in love,' James told them, seriously. 'I'm in love with this woman, but she doesn't love me back.'

'She's got taste!' someone yelled; the crowd chuckled.

'I'm not sure, but I think it's bad if the hecklers are getting better laughs than the comic,' Holly observed cheerfully, sipping gin through a straw with the gay abandon of a married mother on the loose for the first time in months.

'She doesn't even know that I love her,' James went on, taking the mic off the stand and walking a little closer to the crowd, which, Willow thought, was tantamount to a Christian calling, 'Here, kitty' to the lions in ancient Rome. 'The problem is when I'm around her I can't seem to speak.'

'Shame she's not here now!'

James's smile was rueful. 'Who says she isn't? And I'm talking love here, not lust.'

The crowd whoooed as one, and Kayla reached over the table

to tap Willow on the knee. 'He's talking about you, you know.'

Willow shook her head, suddenly very aware of Daniel and Sam flanking her as she took a large mouthful of gin.

'It's not like when your penis is doing the thinking, you know, when you meet a fit girl and it keeps transmitting these thoughts to your brain that if you're not very careful you know will come out of your mouth before you can stop them. You know, like when it goes, "Ask her to have sex with you, ask her to have sex with you . . ".' There was a slight titter at the back of the room. 'And, let's face it, we don't have to be in love with a girl to think that, do we, huh? We don't even have to like her.' Willow breathed out a sigh of relief as laughter rippled around the room. 'Or necessarily be in the same room . . .'

No heckles this time, just some goodwilled chuckles.

'No, this is love, this is proper love. Because not only is she as beautiful as she is lovely, she's all those other things the love of your life is supposed to be. Funny and clever and brave and feisty. I love her.' James looked pained, which seemed to make the crowd laugh. 'Trouble is, I don't know how to tell her. I know that really the goods should speak for themselves.' He gestured up and down the length of his body. 'I'm a sexy guy, right? I think we can all agree on that.' Willow smiled, the crowd was warming to James, and his lovelorn persona. 'But I want to impress her – she's the kind of girl you want to impress. I want to show her things that will make her gasp in wonder.'

'Show her your dick!'

'I said make her gasp in wonder, mate, not disappoint her. But the thing, the one thing I really want to do is make her laugh.' James was silent for a moment, his pathetic expression enough this time to raise laughter.

'The trouble is, I'm not a funny guy. My day job is as an accountant. I can't exactly whisper in her ear,' James put on a sexy and, for some reason, French accent, 'did you know that if you file your tax return online by the thirtieth of September the Revenue will work out what you have to pay for you?' He looked at a pretty girl sitting near the stage. 'Are you turned on?'

She giggled and nodded.

'Oh, cool. Maybe I will try it.'

This time even Chloe chuckled.

'So I've decided that as soon as I get her alone I'm going to ask her out. You know, when it's just me and her. But I can't seem to come up with a good enough reason for her to want to spend any time alone with me. I thought about asking her to dinner, but that's just too much pressure. I mean, that's an hour where you are sitting across a table from someone trying to be fascinating. My brain will be trying to be funny and my penis will be trying to get me laid, and at some point my mouth will fuck up and I'll say, don't you think it would be hilarious if we had sex in the toilet, and she'll throw wine at me and storm out and then . . . then it will be *much* harder to marry her.'

This time the laugh was studded with a smattering of applause.

'Is he really talking about you?' Sam asked.

'I'm pretty sure he isn't,' Willow said, uncomfortable. 'It's an act, isn't it?'

'Because I love this woman, I love her. Do you understand me, I love her.' James cocked his head to one side. 'Starting to sound a teensy bit stalkerish, I know, but I am completely sincere. Yes, I have only met her four times, *but* they were the best four ten minutes of my life and if you add them up, that's like *nearly* three-quarters of an hour and I defy anyone in this room to say that you can't fall in love in forty minutes. Especially if you're drunk.' There were cheers and wolf whistles. 'But I'm not drunk . . . yet. I'm stone-cold sober and I am in love. It is a bit of a worry that she doesn't seem to want to be around me for longer than ten minutes at a time, I grant you. But that's OK. Accountants are very efficient, we can get a lot done in ten minutes . . .'

Willow looked around her. The fifty or so people in the room were all engaged with James, all smiling and laughing. His humour wasn't obvious, he didn't have joke after joke lined up, really he was just having a conversation with them, but it was one that they seemed to want to have.

'So I invited her here tonight to see me in action, impress her with my razor-sharp wit.' James paused for a long moment, unafraid of the silence. 'I'm going to start any minute now.'

'Where is she, then?' a rather drunk woman demanded. 'Ask her out!'

The crowd applauded and cheered.

'He's going to ask you out in front of all these people,' Kayla said, clapping her hands like a delighted child. 'You are going to be really embarrassed, Willow!'

'Fuck, is he? Nightmare!' Chloe sat up suddenly, wide-eyed.

'Is he?' Sam asked, his shoulders squaring.

'He'd better not,' Daniel warned.

'Why not?' Kayla asked him. 'Daniel, why not?'

'Of course he isn't going to ask me out, don't be ridiculous . . . he wouldn't.' Willow hoped desperately that she was right.

'Er, Willow?' James said her name in the microphone.

'Oh my God,' Holly said. 'He is as well.'

'I knew it!' Kayla was triumphant.

'Please will you have dinner with me after?'

The single spotlight that had previously been focused on James swung onto her, the intense light dazzling her instantly. Willow tried to shield her face from the light but still she couldn't see. All she could feel was someone's hand on her shoulder, another person touching her leg, like she was being pushed or jostled.

'Willow, I really think you belong to me.'

From a distance she heard Holly speak as if her voice was lost somewhere inside Willow's head.

'OK, this is stupid. Can't you see she doesn't like it? Let her go, I think she could do with some air.'

'What you need to understand,' James's voice altered, echoing deeper and darker in her head, a voice that belonged to someone else, 'is that you belong to me now. No one will ever love you the way that I do.'

In a heartbeat Willow was paralysed, her heart racing, fear and anxiety coursing through her veins.

'Willow?' She heard her sister's voice, felt concerned hands all over her. 'Look, get that bloody light off her,' she heard Holly snap.

Everyone was looking at her. Willow was afraid to open her eyes. Everyone could tell, everyone knew . . . and there was nothing she could do to stop it.

Then the spotlight snapped off and the room fell mostly into darkness, except for the lights behind the bar.

Pushing her chair back, Willow shoved her way free of the table and stumbled towards the door, cheers and wolf whistles following her as she practically fell down the stairs, throwing herself out into the freezing night, gasping the cold in, even though the chill made her lungs contract.

What had happened? Which moment had filled her with this panic? The light in her eyes, the hands on her legs, the tone of voice? No, it had been the words, the words that reminded her of something long ago, something whispered in her ear: 'I own you now, Willow, you belong to me. Never forget that.'

'How could I ever forget that?' Willow whispered to herself. 'I never can.'

Steadying herself against the rough wall of the pub, Willow concentrated on the cars swathing through the rain and muck, their red brake lights blinking into the distance, the lights of Battersea Bridge shining like beacons, lighting a way across the dark, dirty river. How foolish she had been to think that shoes, a coat and a grubby bit of metal might be all the armour she needed to be out in the world. As soon as she tried, as soon as she made an effort to join the human race, something would always happen to remind her of all the reasons why she couldn't.

Willow turned away as James appeared, her coat in his hand.

'Your sister wanted to come, and your ex-husband and Daniel are more or less on the verge of forming an alliance in order to kill me, but I asked them to let me apologise first . . .' James struggled for words. 'In my head that was really witty and romantic, charming and sweet. I had no idea you'd be quite so horrified. I'm so sorry, Willow. I'm so . . . fucking mortified.'

Willow steeled herself, before turning to take the coat, drawing it around her and buttoning it up against both the cold and him. James fell silent, taking a packet of cigarettes out of his jacket pocket and lighting one. 'I wasn't joking up there, not about any of it, but especially not about knowing what to say. I never know what to say, I never get it right. I don't read people or signals right, ever . . . but I want you to know that . . .' James said nothing for a long time, his mouth working, but no words emerging. Desperate to be allowed to leave, Willow took the lit cigarette out of his hand and took a drag on it, inhaling too quickly so that the acrid smoke made her cough and choke, and she remembered the scent of pipe smoke hanging in the hair above her head.

'Look, it's not your fault. Most girls would have loved that. I'm just . . . I've got . . . issues.'

'Having a spotlight shone in your eyes and being discussed in public issues?' James asked her. 'Because, now I come to think of it, I think most people have those issues.'

Willow said nothing. It was all she could do to concentrate on smoking and not throwing up.

'I've got issues,' James told her, babbling on regardless. 'I've got more issues than *Playboy*. I can't go for a poo if I'm not at home, I say "poo" and I'm forty . . . I can't stand the sound of other people chewing, it makes me want to vomit, and I can never tell what another person is thinking even if it's written all over their face. And I only stopped stuttering when I was twenty-one after several very expensive sessions of speech therapy that I paid for by working in a fast-food restaurant. Honestly, you want to try standing in a stripy apron and saying, "Do you want f - f - f - fries with that?" I'm issue led. I'm issue boy. I've got more hang-ups than . . . I can't think of a punch line.'

Willow rubbed her hands across her face. 'Look, it's fine – you haven't done anything wrong, James. I had a bit of a trauma as a child. I'm mainly fine now but sometimes I get flashbacks when I least expect them and I panic.'

'Oh God, really? What, a car crash or something?' James asked.

'Something like that.'

'Fuck.' James ran his fingers through his hair. 'Fuck. I am a twat. I should have realised that my debut on stage is not the right time to ask a girl out. Why do I never get these things right? It's my destiny to live alone, you know. I can't be trusted with other people.'

Willow mustered the hint of a smile. 'You were good, though. People liked you, right up until the part where you publicly humiliated me.'

'Christ!' James kicked the pub wall and then winced. 'Fucking boating shoes, how did they become fashionable?'

'I'm not sure they did,' Willow told him, stubbing the cigarette out on the wall.

'What does make you laugh?' James asked her suddenly. 'I mean, if me breaking my toe, kicking a wall in a pair of mid-life-crisis canvas shoes that should only ever really be seen on the teenage members of an indie band doesn't, then what does?'

Willow shrugged. 'I don't know, funny stuff. You, you made me laugh tonight.'

'No, I didn't,' James told her. 'I was watching you out of the corner of my eye the whole time. You smiled, you looked at other people laughing, but you didn't laugh. I've met you a few times now, Willow, and I've never ever seen you laugh.'

'Don't be silly. I do,' Willow said, unsettled. 'I laugh all the time.'

Just then the pub doors burst open and almost all of the

people that Willow knew bundled out in something just short of a posse.

'Right, twat, your five minutes to grovel is up. Now get away from my sister.' Holly, rather fortified by her large gin, barged her way between James and Willow, hands on hips. 'Are you all right, baby?'

'I'm fine,' Willow said, with some surprise. It was true. She was fine. Usually when those moments overtook her it took an age for her hands to stop shaking, her heart to stop racing, for sick nausea to abate to functional levels again, but James had turned up and distracted her with his talk of issues and his stupid shoes and his declaration that she never laughed. And now she thought about it, Willow found that she couldn't remember the last time she had laughed. Not just belly laughed, rolled around on the floor laughed, but even chuckled, even politely.

'Right, we're going home.' Sam beckoned to her. 'Come on, Willow.'

'You are a dick,' Chloe menaced James, determined to get her boot in. 'Willow wouldn't go out with you if you were the last man on the planet.'

'I'm fine, you know.' Willow held up her hands. 'Just a bit embarrassed. It's not James's fault I freaked out.'

'It is his fault. It is your fault, mate,' Daniel said. 'How many times have I told you, you are better off not saying anything to anyone?'

'That's a bit harsh,' Willow frowned.

'I'm sticking up for you, Will!' Daniel exclaimed, crossing in front of Sam to stand close to her. 'You OK?' he asked her in a low voice.

'I'm fine!' Willow pushed him back. 'Holly, I laugh, don't I?'

'Course you do, when things are *funny.*' Holly scowled at James, an effect that was somewhat lessened by her bloodshot eyes.

'Right, when was the last time you saw me laugh? Today, right? In Hamleys, when the girls were rolling around in the soft toys and we dressed up like fairies. We all laughed, didn't we?'

'I didn't,' Chloe said. 'And actually, neither did you. You smiled – you smile a lot, Willow.'

'So Holly and the twins were on the point of getting thrown out of Hamleys for teddy assault and I didn't laugh, did I? I don't think I laughed,' Willow said. 'When did I stop laughing?'

James watched her, his breath visible in the chilly air.

'You need to get some rest,' Sam said to Willow, nodding at his car.

'I'll take her home,' Daniel offered.

'No, I don't want to go home. I want to go for a walk.'

'Sweetheart, come on. Let's get you home.' Holly put her arm through Willow's.

Willow shook her head. 'Here, take the key, go back with Chloe and Sam. I'm fine. I just need some time.'

Holly frowned, but she knew better than to press Willow any further.

'But how will you get back?' Sam asked.

'I'll take her,' Daniel repeated.

'Yes, we will,' Kayla interjected. 'Poor Willow, I don't suppose you're used to attention, are you?'

'I think you should go home, babe.' Daniel patted Kayla's shoulder. 'I'll look after Will. She needs an old friend right now.'

'But I . . .' Seeing the look on Daniel's face, Kayla stuttered into silence.

'James,' Willow said as everyone fussed around her, 'will you come for a walk with me?'

James blinked. 'Me? If you're sure?'

'I am. Come on, let's walk across the bridge.'

She tried to leave, but Sam put his hand on her arm, stopping her. 'Explain to me why I don't just take Chloe home,' he said.

Willow paused. 'Because I don't think the three of us can be together at your place. And that's what Chloe wants right now: the three of us together.'

'And what do you want?' Sam asked her.

Willow eased her arm from under his hand. 'Right now I want to go for a walk with James and talk about laughing. And the last time I checked, nobody here had the right to tell me to do any different.'

'I'm not actually sure there is anything else on the other side of the bridge much,' James said, struggling to keep up with Willow as she marched purposefully towards Battersea Bridge, her heels clicking rhythmically on the pavement. 'You know, apart from the power station and some houses and stuff. Oh, and South London. I've heard it exists . . . never been there myself. Not one for travelling.'

'I grew up by the sea,' Willow said. 'I don't think you realise how much a part of you it is until you see some water and suddenly you just want to go and stand next to it, feeling it moving beside you. We don't have to go across the bridge. I just want to get to the middle.'

'OK. These shoes weren't really made for walking, but what the lady wants . . .'

'If I weren't wearing vintage heels I'd almost feel sorry for you, in your . . . plimsolls.' Willow smiled at him, slowing her pace. 'So all that stuff on the stage. The bit about being in love with me, wanting to marry me – all that was an act, right?'

'Yes, no, I don't know – which would you prefer? I'm easy either way.' James attempted a winning smile, but Willow wasn't looking at him.

She stopped as they neared the centre of the bridge, leaning her face into the wind and peering down into the depths of the dark water of the Thames snaking silently by below them.

'Because you should know that now is precisely the worst moment of my life to be asking me out for a date. I have a pregnant ex-stepdaughter, whose father is my ex-husband, a man who I still really care about, and who I'm trying to work out some sort of relationship with; a crazy boss who owns my soul; and things between Daniel and I have been a little weird since he saw me naked and thinks he might be in love with me.'

'He tried it on, didn't he? I knew it!' James kicked the iron railing of the bridge, swearing loudly and wailing, 'Why don't I wear real shoes!'

'It's because I'm wearing these magic shoes,' Willow said. 'Ever since I got them I've been irresistible to men.'

James looked at her feet. 'They are very sexy shoes, but it's not because of that. I've known you since before the shoes and I've always found you irresistible. And Daniel has been talking about you that way since I've known him. He told me that you two had . . . unfinished business.' He held up his palms as Willow's eyes widened. 'He didn't give me any details, he just implied that once something happened between you. He talks a lot about whether the moment has passed, if it's too late to go back. He seems to feel rather responsible for you, which for Daniel is quite possibly the nearest to making a commitment he will ever get.' James leaned his chin on the cold painted railing. 'I obviously think it would be a terrible idea for you to get together with Daniel, but he is my friend and, for what it's worth, I do think Daniel cares about you more than he's ever cared about anyone. If you *really* want to know what I think . . .'

'Yes?' Willow looked at him.

'I think that's what's stopped him from trying to pick up wherever it was you two left off. He knows himself too well, and you are the one person he wouldn't want to hurt.'

'What a terrible collection of fuck-ups we are,' Willow said, turning back to gaze at London, spread out before them, sparkling against the crystal-clear night sky. 'Do you think this city is full of people like us, holing ourselves up in our little bolt holes, afraid of talking to anyone else, touching anyone else in case it gets too messy?'

'I do, actually,' James said. 'I used to be pissed off about always being the outsider – you know, the nice boy who kept himself to himself and then ended up blowing up the school – but then I realised everyone is the same, I'm just more obvious about it than most.'

'Is that why you wore eyeliner to school? To be more obvious?' Willow asked him.

'No, I wore eyeliner to school to look like Robert Smith of The Cure. It wasn't my fault I was the only stammering Goth in Bolton.' He bit his lip. 'Funny, you know, I got the shit kicked out of me day after day for years, but I always got up every morning, I always backcombed my fringe and put my eyeliner on and I always went back. I used to think, one day they will see the real me, and they'll realise that I'm actually quite a nice bloke. They never did.'

'It sounds awful,' Willow said. 'Being trapped in a situation you don't know how to get out of. Knowing every day that something terrible will happen. That sounds bad.'

'It was quite bad, I won't lie. But look at me now, I'm a kick-ass accountant; they can't take that away from me.' James waited, perhaps for Willow to laugh, but she didn't.

'So can I ask about the car crash? It must have been awful. Did . . . did someone die?'

Willow watched him in the light of the bridge lamps for a second, his earnest grey-green eyes filled with genuine concern. She could tell him the truth about her past, but if she did, experience had taught her that he would never be the same way with her again. There were few people besides her mother and her sister who knew, but a week or so before she had married Sam she decided she had to tell him. Willow felt that it was only fair. After all, he was the man she was going to marry, to share her life with. He deserved to know everything about her and that wouldn't be possible if she kept a secret of such magnitude from him. Holly had tried to talk her out of it, telling her she should just enjoy her happiness, not taint it with the past, but she had been adamant, determined. Certain that telling him would wipe a slate clean, prepare her for a fresh, new, clean life.

She had cooked his favourite meal, Yorkshire hotpot, and opened a bottle of really good wine. She'd lit candles and put on a nice dress. In retrospect, perhaps creating the air of romance hadn't been her best decision, but even then Willow was trying to soften the blow she was about to deal.

Willow didn't know what she had expected, but she had been

stunned by Sam's reaction, stunned and frightened. He had been angry – no, furious – filled with impotent rage, turning over the table, sending the hotpot sliding over the polished boards. That night he wasn't able to look at her or touch her, and, worst of all, when Chloe came in, rubbing her eyes, to see what the fuss was about, he'd stepped in front of Willow, barring her way, saying he'd put Chloe back to bed himself. It was as if he thought she might still be tainted.

The next morning things were awkward and distant between them, and Willow was fraught with the old certainty that all of this was her fault, that she'd brought it on herself. Of course she didn't deserve to be happy or loved; she was unlovable. On the second night she had cried alone in bed while Sam sat up, staring into the fire and polishing off a bottle of whisky. It seemed to Willow that, in seeking to break down the very last shade of separation between them, she had crowbarred them apart, ruining her happiness with Sam before it had even begun. Then, on the second morning, five days before their wedding, Sam had come and sat on the edge of the bed and told her he was sorry, and Willow felt utterly bereft as he laid his head on her shoulder and wept. Willow remembered wishing that she could cry with him, but no tears would come.

Perhaps if she'd never told him then their marriage wouldn't have always been polluted with the truth, tainting everything, until that rainy afternoon when Willow, immune to emotion, had let Daniel take off her clothes.

James was awkward and uncertain, a bit of an oddball and a geek, but she liked the way he was with her and the way she was with him. The last thing she wanted was for that to change.

'Yes, someone died,' she said, telling him a half-truth.

'Is that why you don't laugh?' James asked her.

'I didn't know I don't laugh, so I don't know,' Willow said.

Tentatively James leaned close to her until their cheeks were almost touching. 'I would love to see you laugh,' he whispered softly in her ear, his hot breath warm against her skin.

Smiling awkwardly, Willow took a sort of sideways step back, turning her head away from him, but James didn't seem offended. Shrugging, he bounced on his toes. 'You know what, I think I've actually got frostbite. These fucking shoes, I only wore them to impress you. Seriously, what grown man wears plimsolls?'

'Where do you live?' Willow asked him, nodding at the constellation of lights on the north side of the river.

'Off the King's Road,' James said, rather proudly. 'In a mews cottage.'

'Impressive,' Willow whistled.

'I know, but it's not mine. I'm house-sitting for this bloke I know who's currently avoiding the tax man in the Cayman Islands. He does something very mysterious with gold.'

'A lot of men would have lied about that,' Willow observed. 'A lot of men would have pretended it was their place, to try and seduce a girl.'

'I know, and I would have, but I'm distracted by the near certainty that when I take these plimsolls off one of my little toes is going to come off with it, and you don't strike me as the sort of woman to go for a nine-toed man, no matter how loaded he is.'

'Take me back to your house for a drink,' Willow instructed him.

'Really? Back to my house? For a drink? Me and you?'

James's incredulity was endearing. Willow tried to remember when she had ever been liked first by a man, before liking him. It might have been never; usually all of her romantic entanglements, bar the very fleeting ones, had been based on her secret adoration from afar. It made a pleasant change to be the object of desire.

'Yes, it's . . . what, a twenty-minute walk? Didn't you tell about fifty people that all you wanted was to be alone with me? Here's your chance.'

'Well, yes but . . .'

Willow had already started walking.

As was often the way with the very rich, the man who owned the million pounds' worth of mews cottage that James was staying in had questionable taste. There was a coffee table made out of a white porcelain dolphin topped with smoked glass, white leather sofas and a life-sized, rather pointy-breasted statue of a nude reclining in the hallway. Willow felt a huge swell of affection for James as he walked in and hung up his jacket on one nipple, without giving the monstrosity a second glance.

'You think that's bad,' he told her. 'The headboard of the bed is a giant gilded swan. *A swan.* Impossible to read a book comfortably when your headrest is a metal swan.'

She followed him into the living room where he eased off his shoes. 'Thank God, it's just a blister,' he told her. 'My dreams of becoming a dancer aren't over yet. So what can I get you?'

Willow watched by the door as he went to a mirrored drinks cabinet that lit up as he opened the doors and peered in. 'I've got some blue shit, some green shit, some pink shit and . . . oh, there's whisky. Would you like some whisky? It's a twenty-five-year-old single malt, apparently. Probably quite nice – I wouldn't know. I'm more of a cider man, myself.'

'Yes, please,' Willow said, slipping her coat off and crossing to the window where she looked down the narrow cobbled street. She heard the clink of ice in glasses and a moment later James handed her a glass. Willow took a sip, enjoying the heat of the spirit on the back of her throat, spreading warmth all through her. It was nice here, lost in this new life with expensive and ugly *objets d'art* and a man who thought she was wonderful.

'So you are remarkable,' James said. 'Somehow I knew it when I first met you. Do you remember?'

Willow looked rather hard at a small brass model of two bulls copulating.

'At Daniel's?'

'At Daniel's studio, about a year ago.' James's smile was distant. 'There I was with a glass of very cheap wine, stuck in the middle of a crowd of people who I had no idea how to talk to . . .'

'I thought that was everyone.'

' . . . and there you were. You walked in the door and it was like you absorbed all the light and then reflected it back times a billion. Like a sun. I mean, you are beautiful, right, and stacked, but it wasn't just that I noticed. It was your . . . strength. I looked at you and the first word that came to my head was "remarkable". I thought you were remarkable, and now I know why. Willow . . .' James coughed, 'I was wondering . . .'

'Would you like to have sex?' Willow asked him.

'Pardon?' James's face froze. 'What?'

'I said, if you like we could have sex now. I like you and I know you like me, and that's what you want, isn't it? To have sex. You said on stage tonight your penis would be telling your brain to ask me for sex . . . and I don't mind if we do it. It might even be quite nice.'

'You don't mind?' James repeated.

'No, I don't mind if you want to have sex with me.' Willow put down her glass and went to him, winding her arm around his neck and pressing her breasts against his chest. 'You want me, don't you? You want sex?'

James stiffened. 'I . . . yes, of course I do. But not . . . not like this. This isn't you at all, what are you doing?'

Willow's arms dropped to her side as James gently guided her two steps away from him.

'This isn't you, Willow,' he said gently. 'This isn't about you wanting me. I'm pretty sure you don't want me at all. So tell me, what's going on?'

'How do you know what I want?' Willow asked him. 'How do you know what is or isn't me? You know nothing about me, you've made up this fairy tale in your head about poor Willow, asleep for a thousand years, never to wake until her handsome prince comes along to make her laugh. That is a joke!' She backed away as she spoke, her pride stinging from the rejection, draining the last of her whisky. 'Why bother with all the crap, James, all the talk and the romance and the words? It all boils down to the same thing. You want sex. And I don't mind. What's so bad about that?'

'Willow, I want you – of course I want you, you're stunning – but I want you to want me, for it to mean something. And I don't know if that's possible but I do know I'd regret stuffing up any chance of getting to know you properly by jumping into bed now. Also that metal swan puts me off. It's got this beady glass eye that seems to follow you wherever you go.'

Willow dropped her glass, hearing its lead weight thud on the polished wood floor, and turned on her heel, picking her coat up on the way out.

'Wait, Willow. I'm sorry. I always make a joke at the wrong time . . . Willow!'

Willow slammed the door shut behind her, dragging her coat on as she headed towards the King's Road. It took less than a minute for a cab to approach, and when she climbed into the back she finally had a moment to think.

She felt as if her being, her fabric, was being pulled apart in every direction. This was what happened when you let yourself connect, let other people into your heart and life again. She had wished for this, every solitary tube journey home on dark nights, every awkward kiss goodbye from a man she never intended to see again, every lonely meal for one on her lap in front of the TV. Whether she had been conscious of this or not, she had wished for it. For Chloe, for Sam. For Daniel to want her and, more than anything, to feel the way she had for a little while with James that evening. To feel like the woman she should have been.

The bitter truth was that when it came to it, she simply didn't know how to be that woman, just as she didn't know how to be a mother or a wife. And James was right, she didn't laugh. She hadn't laughed since the day she left Chloe.

For almost thirty years she had been a prisoner to the past, its hungry fingers ceaselessly finding and reaching for her, no matter how much she tried. How could she be there for Chloe, or her sister? How could she ever be free of it unless she wrenched herself free at last? Holly had been begging her for years to try to break free, and now for the first time in all of the thirty years, Willow not only knew that she must, she knew that she could.

Her decision made, she reached for her phone to call Holly. It rang just as she took it out of the bag.

'It's time for me to go home,' Willow said.

'If you are sure,' Holly replied. 'I'll be with you. You don't have to be afraid.'

'But I will be,' Willow said. 'I will be.'

Chapter Fourteen

'Time off?' Victoria looked at Willow over the top of her fake glasses. 'I beg your pardon?'

'I need some time off some . . . compassionate leave.'

'Some . . . say again?' Victoria cocked one ear towards Willow.

'It's my mother,' Willow lied. 'And you did technically give me the rest of the week off anyway, in front of witnesses. It's just I might need a bit more time. Off.'

'Dead?' Victoria began thumbing through her diary, ignoring Willow's reminder. 'Can you be back by Thursday?'

'No, she's not dead and I can't be back by Thursday. I need to see her. She's ill.'

'Ill, darling? Cold, flu, cancer – give me some details, sweetie. I need to know how – what was it you said? – how "compassionate" I need to appear to be.'

Victoria was irritable, and Willow wasn't surprised. Officially Willow was owed weeks in unclaimed leave, which she could take whenever she liked, but Willow had felt it only proper that she ask her for some more time off in person. Now she had made the decision to go home and see her mother she couldn't delay it. Any hesitation and she was certain she'd put it off again, perhaps for another thirty years. But the word on the office grapevine was that Lucy had got everything wrong on India's photoshoot, offended both star and photographer, and did nothing very much more than get in the way, trying to cadge freebies off Wardrobe. In the meantime another one of Victoria's clients had been 'mugged' whilst walking his dog on Hampstead Heath, returning home to his wife not only with no wallet, but also, most mysteriously, with no underwear either. Some bright and probably underpaid spark at the local police station had leaked it to the press and now Victoria was working out how to spin the news that TV's most wholesome hunk had a thing for desperate young men.

'I don't know what the fuss is about these days,' she'd been grumbling to herself when Willow appeared in her doorway. 'If you are gay, you are gay. What's the point of pretending otherwise? Unless you are in a boy band, obviously.' Looking up to find Willow, she didn't miss a beat. 'Where *have* you been, darling? I need you to find me a mugger who also steals underwear from heterosexual men, and then pay him to give himself up. Chop chop.'

The news that Willow had only popped in and was rather hoping not to be back again for a week at least came as something of a blow.

'Mum's got multiple sclerosis,' Willow said rather quietly.

'On her deathbed, is she?' Victoria asked, resentfully.

Willow hesitated, considering telling the truth, which was that the disease ate away at her mother year by year, her mobility, her hearing and, most recently, her sight, but that actually, with the kind of care Holly and the team of nurses, which Gray provided for her to keep her in her beloved house, there was no reason why she wouldn't live for another twenty years, if she could stand it that long. Everyone admired her English-lady refusal to let anything so trivial as a neurological disease stop her from entering her plum jam in the village fête. And when it did strike her down, as it had recently, she never let depression defeat her. In many ways she was a brave, resilient woman, a woman who deserved to be loved, and Willow did love her. But she hated her too, with a bitter poisonous fury that meant that to be in a room with her for longer than an hour was almost impossible. To admit to hating one's mother wasn't something Willow found easy to do, but it was easier than it should have been because, of course, the truth was her mother hated her back.

However, she was not anywhere near to being on her deathbed.

'Yes, the doctors think she might be,' Willow said, pressing her mouth into a thin line.

Victoria's sigh was long and theatrical. 'You'll have to find me a temp who knows how to use basic office equipment and a reason to fire that bloody awful Lucy. Honestly, darling, never ever employ the child of a friend. That girl is good for only one thing, and I don't want to repeat what it is.'

'A temp I can do before I go, but a reason to fire Lucy . . .' Willow stopped. 'As much as I hate to say it, she is good on the phone and easy on the eye. Matilda in reception is going on maternity leave in a month . . .'

'Matilda is pregnant? Who's the father?' Victoria perked up.

'I imagine it's her husband,' Willow sighed. 'Why not transfer Lucy there for some training? If she complains tell her you're letting her learn the job from the ground up, like you did.'

'Well, I did spend a lot of my early career lying down, that's true,' Victoria mused. 'OK, you can have a week off. Any longer and I may fire you.'

'Thank you.' Willow bowed her head.

'And, um, are you OK?' Willow was about to reply when she realised that Victoria was more ticking off items from a list than actually enquiring after her welfare. 'Sorry for your loss, anything I can do let me know, take all the time you need . . . I don't mean that last bit. You have a week.'

Chloe and Holly had been waiting for Willow the previous night when she'd arrived back at the flat, sitting side by side on the sofa, watching some reality show that Chloe was addicted to.

'Cow! Why would you marry her?" Holly was exclaiming as Willow let herself in with the spare key she kept hidden in the landing picture rail. 'She looks like a fucking outsize meringue.'

'Nice mouth,' Willow said.

'Oh, good,' Holly got up and came to kiss her. 'What happened?'

'You know what happened,' Willow said. 'I've decided that I've got to go home. I've got to see Mum, I've got to face her. I can't go on like this, Holly. I wreck everything I touch. I'm stuck in this fat, stupid body, never being me. I don't even really know who I am and I don't want to always be this way. I want to be free of it, once and for all. I want a chance to laugh.'

'Er . . . who are you now then?' Chloe asked her, peering over the back of the sofa.

'Not the sort of person who stays married,' Willow said. 'Or who is always there, no matter what, for the people she loves. I'm the sort of person who hides away, a half-person who wishes for what she can't have and then runs away from it when it's hers. I'm the sort of person that almost dragged poor sweet James into bed against his will and then blamed him for knowing that that was really the last thing I wanted.'

'Oh, bloody hell, aren't you too old for sex yet?' Chloe was disgusted.

'Oh, Will.' Holly was not surprised. 'The walk didn't go exactly as planned then?'

'No, it went better. He sees me the way I want to be. I liked being with him – he's interesting and sweet, and not all bluster and ego. I wasn't second-guessing myself, or trying to be thinner or funnier. Considering he pretty much humiliated me in front of a room of strangers I really, really like him.'

'Really?' Chloe looked disappointed. 'More than Dad?

'I love your dad, Chloe,' Willow said sadly, 'and I think he cares about me too. But I'd be lying to you if I said that there was a chance that we'd ever get back together.'

Chloe was silent for a second. 'Well, good,' she said. 'That would be a nightmare.'

Holly put the kettle on while Willow went and sat next to Chloe, winding an arm around her neck and kissing her on the forehead. 'You and me, however, we can definitely get back together. For good.'

'Weirdo,' Chloe retorted, but she was smiling.

'So how did you go from being yourself with James to attempting to press-gang him into sex?' Holly asked. Her eyes met Willow's across Chloe's head.

'I don't know,' Willow said. She didn't want to say out loud that this was often how it had been with her. Through her late teens and raucous twenties she had been the party girl, the girl who was just looking for a good time. Boys had loved her for that, and she had embraced the persona right up until the moment she'd met Sam. And after the divorce, her encounters had been more discreet and personal, never crossing from that physical part of her life into the rest of it. But always it had been about sex, because sex was the only way Willow really knew how to communicate with a man. There had been so much that she wanted to say to James. She'd wanted to flirt with him, tell him stories and make him laugh. But when she thought about it, it seemed impossible, so she went to her default setting instead. Sex was a language she understood.

'Poor James, he very sweetly said he thought more of me than that and I stormed out.'

'Gay!' Chloe exclaimed.

Holly handed her a cup of tea, squeezing into the last remaining space on the sofa.

'So tomorrow we're going on a road trip, just like we used to. Do you remember? As soon as we got our licences, we'd wait till Mum wasn't looking, then we'd get Ian's shitty old Rover out of the garage and drive and drive.'

Willow smiled, remembering their reckless high-speed journeys to anywhere that wasn't Christchurch, Holly a little less brave than she was but never willing to let her sister go it alone. Sometimes they'd dodge school and drive along the coast to Bournemouth first thing in the morning, spend the day frittering away in the amusement arcades the cash they made from their Saturday jobs, and the evening trying to get served in various pubs. Once they'd been so successful they'd got too drunk to drive home and had slept the night on the beach. Their mother had screamed at them for a solid hour when they arrived back the next day, and Willow remembered the relief of realising that she didn't have to care any more. What could her mother do to her now – now that Willow didn't care what Mummy thought of her any more? From that point on it had become her mission to wind up her mother as much as she could. Looking back, Willow regretted those last few months at home, but not because of the bitter rift that grew between her and her mother; because of Holly's attempts to overcompensate by becoming a better daughter in direct correlation with Willow's disintegrating behaviour. And also because if there had ever been a chance again that Imogene Briars would have seen her daughter as the girl she had once loved, it had died then, before Willow had even turned eighteen.

'We'll be like Thelma and Louise,' Holly said, 'only without the shooting and driving-off-a-cliff part, plus I've got to pick the girls up at three fifteen.'

'Am I coming then?' Chloe asked bluntly. 'Only I don't remember the pregnant chick in *Thelma and Louise*.'

'Of course you are,' Willow said. 'A break by the sea, a stay in Holly's house – it's just what you need. Some space to think. I haven't asked Sam, but I don't suppose he'll mind.'

'He might want to come too,' Chloe said. 'Tonight he said he missed me.'

'Well, he could come down for a few days. I'll have run out of bedrooms, but the Captain's Club is lovely,' Holly said brightly. Willow loved her for her optimism, loved her for putting on enough of a brave face for both of them. Only Holly and Willow knew what this trip was really about. And Willow wanted to keep it that way.

'Sandy beach or stony beach?' Chloe asked.

'You can catch a ferry from Mudeford to the nicest, sweetest, sandy beach in the world ever, complete with candy-striped beach huts,' Holly told her. 'When we were little our mum used to take us there after school. Sometimes it would be just the three of us on this tiny little beach, endless blue sky, warm yellow sand. It was perfect, wasn't it, Will?'

Willow nodded. 'It was.'

'You will, of course, freeze to death if you go out there in this weather, but it is lovely.'

'OK then, I'll come,' Chloe said as if her answer would have been any different for a stony beach.

Sam had arrived on the doorstep the following morning just as Willow got out of the shower. Assuming it must be the postman with a package she opened the door a crack, wishing she was wearing rather more than a large towel when she let him in.

'Are you OK?' he asked her.

'I'm fine,' she said. 'I just needed a bit of space from . . . my past, to get some perspective.'

'And did you?'

Willow stood on the carpet in her bare feet, the chill of the morning radiating off Sam making her shudder. 'No, but what I did realise is that I can't get away from . . . the things that happened. I need to face up to it, Sam. I need to conquer it, I suppose.'

Sam nodded. 'What can I do?' he asked.

'You have enough on your plate,' Willow said.

'I blamed you for what happened to us,' he told her, 'but it wasn't your fault, it was mine. I should have been helping you do this years ago. You trusted me with the truth and I threw that back in your face. No wonder you turned to someone else.' He shuddered visibly. 'I have a lot on my plate, but you are part of it. So please tell me there is something I can do. Because if there is then I think helping you will really help me.'

Willow nodded, steeling herself for what was to come. 'I want to go to Christchurch, to try and talk to Mum,' she said.

'Are you sure? Are you ready?'

'I don't suppose that I will ever be ready, but what else can I do? It seems like the right place to start. I'd like to take Chloe. I know I shouldn't rely on her and I promise not to involve her, but having her near inspires me. She makes me brave. Besides, Holly's house is such a lovely place, it will be good for her too, I think. A break from everything here, a place to think and perhaps clear her head.'

Sam hesitated. 'I need some time too, some time to get closer to Chloe. I'll take a few days off. That way Chloe and I get time together, you get time to talk things over with your mum, and if you need me I'll be close.'

Willow nodded.

'And then?' Sam asked her.

'And then?

'What if going home, seeing your mum, talking about it doesn't help? What then?'

Willow closed her eyes for a moment. 'I have no idea.'

'Well, whatever it is, let me be here for you, Willow. Please.' Sam took a step closer to her. 'It's pretty shoddy that it took my daughter getting pregnant and running away to bring us back together. I wasn't prepared for how I'd feel when I saw you, for how much I missed you and regretted . . . how I handled things. It took a lot for me to let myself fall in love again after Charlotte died. And when I found you with . . .' He swallowed. 'I'm not proud of myself, Willow, when I think about how I pushed you away at exactly the moment I should have been protecting you. You were lost and trying your best with a husband that didn't talk about anything that mattered. I shut myself off, I let you drift, and that was wrong. So let me be here for you now. Let me get back some of the self-respect I once had.'

'Sam,' Willow breathed, 'don't say that.'

'It's true.' He shrugged. 'It's how I feel. I want to be your friend. For me, it's, well, it's a matter of honour.'

Towel or no towel, Willow had put her arms around her former husband and hugged him. 'Oh, Sam,' she'd said, 'that is so you.'

Having wrung her leave from Victoria, Willow left the office with Lucy *in situ* behind the reception desk, and a very efficient temp called Marlene, who Willow regularly employed as she used to be a psychiatric nurse and was never surprised by anything. Besides, anyone who could authoritatively diagnose Victoria as a narcissistic sociopath was OK by her, even if she did pop a Ritalin or two along with her morning tea.

Feeling purposeful and focused as she was, it came as something of a shock when she walked right into James on Golden Square, treading heavily on his poorly shod toes and sending him staggering back a step or two, ricocheting off a lamppost.

'Oh!' Willow exclaimed, backing away from him and into another pedestrian, who swore at both of them. 'James?'

'Sorry, sorry,' James apologised through his pain. 'I know what it looks like and it's true, I am stalking you.'

'You're stalking me?' Willow blinked.

'Just a bit. I thought about not hanging around outside your office and waiting for you to come out so that I could pretend to bump into you but, well, I just didn't want last night to be the last I ever saw of you,' James explained.

'You didn't think about going down the email or phone call route?'

'I didn't want to give you the option of screening me out. When you think about it, a bit of light stalking is quite romantic.'

'I have to go,' Willow said uncertainly. 'I'll call you.'

'Wait! I know, I know, Daniel is right, I am awful with people. I have no idea how to relate to them at all.' James looked bereft. 'I mean, a beautiful woman offers me sex and I turn it down. What kind of weirdo am I?'

'James!' Willow nodded at the passers-by, who were turning their heads as they caught snatches of his less than covert conversation.

'See, sorry. What I'm saying is, of course I should have gone to bed with you. I'm an idiot and you are a strong independent woman who knows what she wants. I'm just stuck in the late twentieth century with this foolish notion that one should get to know a girl emotionally and intellectually because then the physical stuff will actually mean something. Also, while I'm on the subject, you really took me off guard. I wasn't ready. I hadn't changed the sheets on the bed in a week and I thought there was a good chance I'd left yesterday's pants on the swan's head . . .'

Willow stared at James wide-eyed.

'Should I stop talking now?' James said.

'I would if I were you,' Willow said.

'Sorry.' He winced, as if he were just hearing the words that had come out of his mouth on a ten-second delay. 'I'll be off. Take care, yeah?'

'James.' Willow stopped him with a hand on his arm. 'I'm sorry for throwing myself at you. It was completely out of order, and you know what, turning me down was the nicest thing you could have done for me. You are a gentleman, a strange, bizarre and mildly disturbing gentleman.'

'Really?' James rallied a small smile.

'Yes, because of you I didn't wake up this morning full of self-loathing,' Willow said. 'That was a good thing.'

'Oh . . . I see. Right. Not *entirely* sure how to take that.'

Willow took a breath. 'I've got to go away for a few days. I'll be honest, I can't work out if I like you or not, but if you haven't totally gone off me by the time I get back maybe we could have dinner?'

'Dinner?' James's face lifted and then fell instantly. 'No, you won't want to.'

'I do, I will – I'm suggesting it,' Willow said. 'I'm asking you out, James.'

'But you don't know the whole picture.'

'What do you mean?' Willow asked him.

'Daniel's broken up with Kayla,' James said. 'He told me this morning. He's broken up with Kayla so that he can give it a go with you.'

Chapter Fifteen

'Aunty Pillow again!' Jo-Jo flung open the door and wrapped herself around Willow with the abandon that only four-year-olds know. Bending down, Willow scooped her up, hugging her tiny frame into her body and whirling her around until she giggled.

'Me too, me too!' Jem protested, clinging at her skirts. In a moment Willow had one twin under each arm, spinning until she made them all dizzy and they ended up in a pile of nieces and aunt on Holly's small, perfectly manicured front lawn. Chloe was giggling, leaning back on the car that Willow had hired, courtesy of Victoria, although her boss didn't know it yet.

'Er, hello? Any chance of a greeting for your mummy?' Holly laughed, scooping up one girl and then the other. 'You know, the one that gave birth to you.'

'You're always here,' Jo-Jo said. 'Aunty Pillow is a treat.'

'You're squishy, Aunty Pillow,' Jem said, hugging one of Willow's ample arms as she clambered to her feet. 'Like a bouncy castle!'

'I'm like a what?' Willow feigned horror. 'Well, *you're* stinky!' She held her nose as she planted a kiss on the cheek of each twin before surrendering them each a hand.

'Willow.' Graham appeared at the door, rather incongruous in a frilly apron, and a business shirt rolled up to the elbows, his hands apparently covered in flour. He leaned towards Willow and kissed her on the cheek. 'Thank you for bringing my wife home at last.'

'Oh my God, I was gone for a day and a half!' Holly exclaimed, rolling her eyes at Willow.

'You said work at home for a day, the girls will be no trouble,' Graham grumbled amiably. 'How am I going to explain to my boss that the costings aren't done because I've been making cupcakes.'

'Fairy cakes, Daddy!' Jo-Jo rolled her eyes, an exact replica of her mother.

'Daddy is a terrible chef,' Jem told Chloe, dragging her from the car and towards the front door. 'He got eggshells in the cakes, which are still nice but a bit crunchy.'

'Added fibre,' Graham said, deadpan.

'If you looked after us, Aunty Pillow, then we wouldn't get crunchy-bit fairy cakes, would we? Or have to worry about our five a day, or sleeping, because you are fun.'

'Mummy is very keen on us sleeping,' Jem explained to Chloe. 'I expect you will want your baby to sleep too and not always be going, "Waaaa! Waaa! Waaa!"'

The twins giggled and the baby impression fast became a rhythmic chant. Seeing the fond resignation on Holly's face, Willow briefly wondered if this was what it had been like for her mother looking after the pair of them when they were this little, only alone and without any money. She must have breathed a huge sigh of relief when she met Ian; she must have told herself that now everything was going to be all right.

'Girls, girls!' Holly had to raise her voice to make herself heard over the din. 'Why don't you show Chloe her room?'

'I will, I will,' Jem said.

'I will. That's not fair!' Jo-Jo wailed.

'You both can,' Holly told them, shaking her head at Graham. 'Go on, and make sure you show Chloe where the bathroom and the towels are.'

'And after, we'll show you our room, which is the nicest room in the house because it is a colour. All the other rooms are white but Daddy said we were allowed a colour and so it is pink, which is our favourite,' Jem explained.

'Pink? You do surprise me,' Chloe said as the girls led her in.

'Do we? What colour did you think it would be?'

Willow watched as the girls led Chloe inside the four-storey white timber-built town house which sat on the edge of the estuary looking out over the placid waters of the river. It was a beautiful house, full of light and open spaces, like a negative image of the dark cluttered home Willow and Holly had grown up in. Whenever Willow visited, which was rarely, she felt like it was doing her good, like a sort of psychic battery was charging her with renewed life, energising off Holly's serene vigour.

'Sorry to descend on you, Gray,' Willow said, nodding in the general direction of where Chloe was probably now being regaled with princess paraphernalia.

'Don't be silly, it's fine. I knew when I married a twin that whatever was ours was mainly Holly's and therefore also yours. Besides, it's really good to see you, Willow, especially if you can take over the baking.'

'Hark at him. Anyone would think he was a househusband!' Holly cuffed him lightly on the shoulder, before embracing him.

Willow hung back a little, watching with familiar envy as Holly and Graham, arms around each other, walked into their beautiful home. Holly had always been so good at being with people, so good at loving them and being loved. Willow and her sister were the same people, cut from the very same cloth. Yes, fate had dealt them each a very different hand but surely she had it somewhere within her to be the same quietly content peaceful person. Squinting a little, Willow tried very hard to imagine that it was she and Daniel arm in arm, ribbing each other fondly, but somehow the picture didn't come into focus.

Willow had left James rather awkwardly in the street outside her office, unsure how to react to the news that she had yet to hear in person from Daniel. The fact that he had ended things with Kayla was not only huge, it was important because it was so different from his usual *modus operandi.* Normally he ignored a girl until she finally gave up and went away, and always the women in his life overlapped, the old and the new constantly crisscrossing the threshold of his flat in carefully choreographed slots. If he had really formally finished with Kayla, sat her down and said that it was over between them, and if he had really done that because he was serious about being with *her* . . . well, the thought made Willow's head spin, which was perhaps why she had left James standing in the street after he'd unloaded his bombshell, walking off at a rate of knots before realising that she was going in the wrong direction for the tube. On her way back she had crossed the road, staying close to the buildings in case she should run into James again, and sure enough, there he was in his long black coat, and white and black plimsolls, sitting outside a café on the other side of the street, staring miserably into a paper cup of coffee. Willow had stopped and thought about going across to him, but what would she say? If Daniel had left his girlfriend for her, then that changed everything, but, for now at least, Willow was not exactly sure how. Nor did she have the time to think about it.

So she didn't cross the road and speak to James, as much as she wanted to do something to lift his solemn face out of his coffee cup. But then neither did she answer the phone when Daniel rang, deleting his message without playing it. Everything, *everything*, even the possibility of being in an actual relationship, was on hold at least until she got back, and possibly far beyond.

'How do you do that?' Willow asked Holly as soon as Graham disappeared to clean himself up. 'Be married so effortlessly?'

'I don't know, really,' Holly said. 'I'm lucky, I suppose.'

'It's not luck. It's like wherever you go there is harmony.' Willow smiled. 'You just seem so easy with people, even Chloe. As soon as you spoke to her, she relaxed. How do you do that?'

'You do it too,' Holly insisted, curling her arm round Willow's waist.

Willow stopped, turning to look into Holly's eyes. 'I'm scared, Holly.'

Holly hugged her tightly before leading her inside. 'I know. Just think, don't turn back now. There are so many good things waiting for you, Willow. What you need now is the courage to believe you deserve them. And before you can find that you need to face down the past. I'm not saying that suddenly everything will be OK, but if you can face it, look it in the eye, then maybe you won't have to run from it any more.'

'I've tried to talk to Mum before. She never wants to listen.'

'I know,' Holly said, a touch exasperated, possibly with their mother, possibly with Willow, probably with both of them. 'The way she has treated you will never make sense to me, and I think that what really scares her is that it won't make sense to her either. I try not to believe in fate – the idea of it terrifies me – but with Chloe back in your life, and you ready to join the human race again, it *feels* like now is exactly the right time to talk to Mum. We were laughing the other day about our picnics on the hill. She misses you.'

Willow was silent.

'God knows, I don't understand why she is the way she is with you. It makes me . . . it makes me seethe, when I think about it. But she's getting old, Willow, and this last attack, it's really hit her hard. She looks diminished, smaller, almost, like she's fading before my eyes. If you could just talk to her, if we could just . . . make sense of it all before it's too late. I'm sure that's what she wants too. She must do, mustn't she? Otherwise she'd be inhuman and I can't, I won't, believe that.'

'Do you really think that it's possible for me and Mum to make peace?' Willow asked hopefully, feeling a little braver already.

'I do.' That was Holly all over, putting people at their ease, pouring oil on troubled waters, setting aside the doubts and fears she must also have in her quest to help everyone else feel like the world was a good place to be, even when it wasn't.

'When do you think I should go?' Willow asked as she followed Holly up the stairs to the first-floor kitchen. With a huge window facing the estuary, the kitchen took up one entire floor, shiny white units surrounding a white tiled floor, white dining table and chairs and a long white sofa positioned to face the view. Willow went immediately to the ceiling-height window, resting her forehead against the cool glass as she took in the scene: a series of flat planes, the sky, the River Stour flowing into the sea, the receding land, slashed here and there with the vertical masts of the sailing boats dotted along the horizon. This was home, Willow thought as she felt her heart settle back where it belonged. This landscape, the endless steel-blue sky, the low horizon. This was the place she loved more than any other, but it was only in Holly's house that she felt able to admit it, to admit that the place where she loved to be more than any other was also the place that hurt her the most.

'I normally go in twice a day,' she heard Holly say behind her, filling the jug from her coffee machine with water. 'Her sight's all but gone at the moment. She can't do anything for herself so I've got the nurses coming in, one day, one night. They're really good, getting her up and dressed, doing her meals. But she's not impressed. You know what she's like. She thinks I'm letting her down by getting help. Hell, I think it.'

'There's only so much you can do, Holly,' Willow said. 'You've got the girls to worry about. And Graham's away a lot. You can't nurse her twenty-four hours a day and look after your family. You mustn't feel guilty about that.'

'But I do,' Holly sighed. 'I do.'

Holly came to stand next to Willow as the coffee machine began to rumble and gurgle behind them. Willow felt Holly's hand slip into her own and for a moment the pair enjoyed that unique feeling that only came when they were together, that moment of wholeness.

'I know I shouldn't feel like I do. I mean, she's sick, she's *so* sick, Willow. And it must be so frightening to wake up virtually blind. The first I knew about it was when she called me from the hospital, the day it happened. She'd been in Ian's study for some reason when the attack came on. There's still a phone in there, thank God, and she managed to get help. She said everything went completely dark for a while. She didn't know what time it was, or even if she was alive. When I got to the hospital she was sitting up in bed, treating one of the nurses like a housemaid. Still she looked so . . . small. Like a bag of bones.'

'Oh God, Holls, I'm sorry.' Willow squeezed her fingers. 'I never ask you about any of this stuff and you never tell me.'

'So I spend all day and night at the hospital,' Holly went on, 'and there's an MRI, and the tests and the scans, but we all know what it is. It's the MS cutting off another piece of her. And I can't help thinking, what if it's for ever this time, Will? What if her sight doesn't come back?'

'It will,' Willow said. 'That's always the way it is with Mum. It will come back. She's as hard as nails. She'll go on for ever.'

'I hope so.' Holly's voice caught with the threat of tears. 'What would I do if she . . .' She pressed a hand to her mouth. 'I need you two to be OK before that happens. I love you both so much.'

Fear, anxiety, hope and longing jostled in Willow's chest for her attention. There was no point in delaying what came next. But still she wasn't quite ready, not yet.

'Have you got the photo album handy?' Willow asked Holly suddenly.

'Always.' Holly brightened, reaching up to a cupboard above the fridge and rooting about for a moment before bringing out all that remained of their lives as small girls, living alone with their mother. It was a shiny plastic-covered photo album, illustrated with an early eighties photograph of a cornfield at sunset. Willow remembered her mum bringing it home from Woolworths, smoothing her palm over the image before telling her two girls that she was going to make a book all about them. They'd spent the whole afternoon sorting out envelopes of photos of them from birth onwards, carefully sticking them into the album with little tacky squares, making up captions that made them squeal with laughter.

Skipping a little, Holly took the album over to the white sofa, patting the seat for Willow to join her. Sitting side by side, they opened the cover to see the first page, full of anticipation even though they had pored over the photos a thousand times before.

'Willow and Holly naked on a rug,' Willow smiled, running her finger over the curved back of herself as a baby, probably about four months old. 'Remember how we cracked up when Mum wrote "naked"?'

Holly nodded. 'And here we are at about one. We must have just been walking.' Holly pointed at a pair of toddlers, hand in hand, dressed to the nines in smocked coats and ridiculously ornate little knitted bonnets that tied under the chin, the ribbons finished with woollen pompoms. 'Fashion models go for a walk' was written underneath in her mother's careful handwriting. 'Look at us, look at our little hats. You know, I think that's why I've got a phobia about pompoms to this day.'

'This one is my favourite,' Willow said.

It was a cutting from a local newspaper, with the heading 'School Nativity Shows off its Christmas Stars!' It was one of the few photos that had the three of them in, Willow and Holly in their angel costumes, their mother kneeling between them, an arm around either girl, kissing Willow on the cheek. For a second Willow closed her eyes and felt the touch of her mother's lips on her cheek, smelled her scent, heard her laughter, saw the sparkle of pride in her eyes as she stood up and applauded her girls, who after all had done nothing very much more than stand on the stage and remember to say 'Lo, behold!'

'The best times,' Holly said, resting her head on Willow's shoulder. 'All here in this book, safe for ever.'

Willow nodded, leaning over to look a little closer at the face of the child that was now lost in time. Had she let that little girl down by growing up the way she did? Willow didn't know the answer, but she knew one thing: she could delay seeing her mother no longer.

'Coffee's done,' Holly said, getting up to go and pour it.

'I'll have a coffee and then I'll go and see her,' Willow said.

'I'll come,' Holly offered immediately.

'No, no, don't be silly. Stay here with the girls. Have a break from worrying for a bit.'

That faint vertical line between Holly's eyebrows deepened into a valley.

'Have you thought about what you're going to say or how?'

'I don't know,' Willow coughed. 'I'll work up to it, I suppose.'

That didn't seem to ease her sister's concern. 'Are you sure you're OK to go on your own, to the house?' Holly's anxiety vibrated strongly through her words. 'You hate going to the house.'

'I know but . . . it's just a house, and I'm a grown woman. I can cope with a building.' Willow heard the keys rattling in the locks of the closed doors in her mind and she knew that Holly heard them too. What she mustn't do – what she *absolutely* mustn't do – was let those doors creak open.

'She *has* missed you,' Holly said, brightening a little. 'I heard her bragging about your important job the other day. She is proud of you. She does love you.'

'I know,' Willow said, pressing her hand against the glass, as if she could touch the cool clean sky. 'And I love her. That's what makes it so hard.'

The house that Willow and Holly had done most of their growing up in was impressive, one befitting that of a bank manager back in the seventies and eighties when being a bank manager was still a job with the kind of *gravitas* that commanded respect.

From the front, which wasn't really the front, but the side of the house that happened to be the only aspect that overlooked the road, it looked like what might be a three- or four-bedroomed house of indeterminate age, with a bleak grey pebble-dash facia and a heavy, black-painted front door that looked too old and too big for the building. In fact the house was late Georgian and spread out along the banks of the river, mostly unseen from the busy road that was now lined with takeaways and estate agents'. It was a secret house, with a delicate wrought-iron first-floor veranda that overlooked the old abbey, and a long narrow and leafy garden where Willow and her sister had spent many happy hours skipping in and out of the shadows, lost in an imaginary world that lived and breathed around them.

The house even had its own private jetty, the same little wooden boat still secured to it, quietly rotting away. Ian had devised a system of ropes and pulleys so that he could let the twins drift quite safely out into the middle of the river to fish on a summer's evening, never with much of a prospect of catching anything, but quite content to sit side by side in silence, watching the flies hovering above the water, the sinking sun turning the water amber, until their mother called them to go in to bed, and Ian had to winch them in again, like two little fishes themselves, snared on barbed hooks.

As Willow took the short walk from Holly's house to her mother's, along one of the many branches of the Stour that wended in and out of the town, and across the stone bridge by the ruined abbey, she put off thinking about the moment of arrival. Instead she decided to occupy her mind with the mystery of the shoes that seemed to sparkle with every step she took. She had no proof that they had had the same owner as the coat that flapped so incongruously around her body in the sedate seaside town, and the locket nestled in the pocket. The three objects felt as if they must somehow be connected, as if, when together, they vibrated with some kind of resonance, with familiar memories. Willow watched the sun dazzle as it danced on her shoes and, as she had so often done as a little girl returning home from school, she daydreamed away the journey, imagining what it would be like to be the woman who had once walked in these shoes. Perhaps she had lost her childhood sweetheart to the Great War, left only with the token that he gave her, handmade in the trenches. Maybe she'd danced away the pain through the roaring twenties, finding her smile again in these beautiful shoes until finally she'd met and married a man who cared enough for her to give her a fine fur coat. A man whom she'd loved for ever after, even though she'd never forgotten her first love.

It was a flight of fancy, a daydream – but for a moment Willow could almost picture the woman's face, smiling at her, whispering a word that Willow couldn't quite hear.

And then suddenly she was there, standing outside the outsize front door, its crevices grimed with dirt and dust. Her heart clenched, at once fossilised by dread.

Finding it impossible to control the shaking that gripped her muscles as she stood in front of her mother's house, she was unable to decide if she was trembling with fear or rage. Willow closed her eyes and thought of Holly, felt the touch of her hand and heard the admonishment that she knew her sister would say if she were here.

'She's only a sick old lady,' Willow told the door. 'She can't hurt you.'

Unable to hesitate for any longer she fumbled for the key that she still kept on her, slid it into the grimy brass lock and turned it, pushing open the slightly sticky, ill-fitting door.

The hallway was a long cool dark passage, travelling the length of the house and opening out into a Victorian glasshouse where once her mother had obsessively grown tomatoes for the chutney that she religiously entered into the WI competitions. The last time Willow had visited there were only a few withered vines in dry dusty pots remaining. Willow could see the haze of light at the dark corridor's end; the sunlight dancing outside the glass suddenly felt another world away.

On her left was the formal sitting room, curtains always drawn, and on her right the formal dining room with French doors that overlooked the river, a room only ever used at Christmas and Easter. Also on her left was the staircase that rose to the first floor where Mum and Ian's bedroom, with that lovely veranda, overlooked the river. There was the guest room, which now welcomed the night nurse, and, at the back of the house Ian's study, which as far as Willow knew had remained exactly as he had left it on the day he died. His hidy-hole, he'd called it. A place to get away from all the women, he'd joked.

And then another staircase to the second floor, the attic rooms. A twin pair of rooms for twin girls, who'd begged to share when they'd first moved in, a request that their mother denied, unable to believe that they wouldn't finally each want a room, not to mention a bed, of their own.

Just before the conservatory, the kitchen, stone floor, large and square – a room that was always cold, even though it was flooded with sunshine – and before that the 'television room', as her mother had rather grandly called it, echoed across the hallway by the music room, so named because of the rickety upright piano that nobody could play, leaning drunkenly against one wall.

Willow stood on the doorstep, feeling all the empty rooms beckoning her, doors creaking inwards. If the nurse hadn't appeared at that moment she might very well have turned round and left.

'You must be Willow! The other twin, here at last!' The nurse had a clipped, possibly Eastern European accent, coupled with a warm smile. 'Don't stand there, come in, come in. Mum will be pleased to see you!'

'Sorry, I was just . . .' Willow looked longingly over her shoulder at the busy road.

'I know, you must prepare yourself. A sick parent is hard for any child to cope with, even a fully grown one. I'm Magda, I'm the day nurse. I've washed Mum, helped her dress. She's very particular to look nice. She ate a little breakfast. I talk, talk, talk all the time to her, so she tells me to shut up, says she doesn't know what I'm doing coming over here, stealing all the jobs. I tell her that's the EU for you. She is not amused.' Magda laughed. 'I don't mind, I don't mind. Now she is in her chair in the sitting room, listening to the TV. She thinks maybe she sees a little more light today, I don't know, perhaps she does. The doctor says improvement will be slow, if there is to be any. So, do you come in?'

Willow looked over Magda's shoulder, down the long dark corridor. 'Actually I just remembered . . .'

Without warning Magda took both of Willow's hands and held them in her own. They were cool and smooth, like marble. 'You are upset and worried for your mum, but you mustn't be. She is a strong woman, the MS is nothing to her. You know, it won't kill her. She will live to see your children married, I promise you.'

'Thank you,' Willow said, so touched by Magda's concern that she wanted at least to appear reassured.

'So.' Magda tugged gently at her hands, easing her over the threshold. 'Come and go and see her then!'

Reluctantly Willow slipped her coat off her shoulders, a crop of goose bumps springing up on the tops of her arms. Outside she had been too hot with the coat on; in this house she was too cold without it. She looked down at her shoes. Even they had lost their glimmer and dulled in the shadowy interior. Hanging her coat on the banister, in exactly the way her mother would disapprove of, she advanced along the hallway to the television room. On the other side of the door she could hear some cooking show burbling away.

'Nonsense,' she heard her mother mutter. 'Whoever heard of stir-frying broccoli? What has the world come to?'

'Hi, mum,' Willow said, pushing open the door.

Her mother smiled at her voice and Willow felt a rush of warmth flood her chest. She always forgot that she loved her mother until she saw her.

'Willow.' Her mum lifted her head, looking in the direction of her voice. 'You might have come sooner. It comes to something when a mother has to go blind to get a look at her daughter.' She held out her hand and Willow went to her, taking it and sitting on the old leather stool that had always been in that room, placed at her feet, probably by Magda.

'I know, I'm sorry. It never seems like the right time. Work keeps me so busy. But you look well, considering.' Willow spoke tentatively, carefully placing every word. It was so long since she'd even talked to her mum, let alone seen her, that she felt every second that ticked by was fraught with danger. Imogene Briars was very good at small talk, at passing the time of day. It was when you tried to breach those ramparts of good manners and appearances that things began to fall apart, and yet that was exactly what Willow was here to do.

Willow studied her mother. She had looked much worse in the past than she did now. Her long silver-blonde hair was neatly brushed and shining, and Magda had dressed her in some comfy trousers coupled with a pastel blue T-shirt that brought out the colour of her sightless eyes. Willow supposed she expected her mother to look a lot less healthy, wizened and bent over, her eyes perhaps milky white. It was a relief to see her looking human, happy even. But that was an odd thing about Imogene that both sisters had noticed. She always seemed happier and more relaxed just after the illness had struck, as if the tension of waiting for an attack could be forgotten, for a little while at least, now that the worst *had* happened.

‘I feel well. It’s just my flaming eyes,’ Imogene said, tapping the centre of her forehead with her forefingers. ‘Goodness, of all the things to go. I don’t mind the pain, you know that. And the legs and what have you, flailing about is always a difficulty, but I cope. But this, this is almost too much.’ Imogene squeezed her fingers. ‘I’m glad you came. Your sister’s been useless. Got the nurses in straight away. She’s barely been here. She thinks because that husband of hers has got money that writing a cheque will solve everything.’ She lowered her voice. ‘I don’t want foreign nurses looking after me. I need my own family. My own flesh and blood.’

‘Holly does all that she can, you know that, Mum. She’s got the twins to look after.’

‘The twins. I had twins to look after. I was much younger than you two are now, and all alone before I met your stepfather, and I didn’t have money. I still did it, though.’

‘I know,’ Willow said, knowing it was pointless explaining that life back then, when it had been just the three of them and an electric meter, was much simpler than it was for Holly now, despite all the material comforts she had. For one thing, Imogene didn’t have a sick mother to try and look after. Willow and Holly had always wondered why their life was so short of grandparents, and quite soon after Ian and Imogene were married they had taken it upon themselves to look for evidence. All that they’d found was a letter, brief and to the point, informing Imogene that she was not to come home again, or to try to contact her family. At the time neither sister had been able to imagine what sin could possibly have been committed to be so totally excluded from her family. They had been horrified on their mother’s behalf and, after carefully returning the letter to the drawer in which they'd found it, they had been especially nice to her, careful not to play up or upset her for several days. Much later, Willow had come to the conclusion that in 1970 an unmarried and pregnant daughter was much more of a scandal than it was now. How would her mother react if she knew Chloe were here, if she knew her situation? Willow thought. She should be full of sympathy and understanding, but Willow would have been surprised if that were the case. Imogene had covered up her early shame and indiscretion with years of respectability and properness that she clung on to above all else. Willow and Holly never knew who their father was – they had never wanted to – but whoever he was he had long ago become obsolete, eclipsed by the man their mother had married.

'Still, it is hard for Holly, with Gray away so much, and the girls are a proper handful.'

'Those children are angels,' Imogene protested. 'Thank God they've got your looks and not their father's; man looks like a boiled egg. I suppose at least if I never see again I won't have to look at him any more.'

'Besides –' Willow went on, suppressing her smile. Imogene's loathing of Holly's husband was legendary, and entirely fictional. The old lady couldn't be more thrilled that one of her daughters had married a rich man; she just would rather die than admit it – 'if it wasn't for the nurses then you'd be in hospital now. You wouldn't be able to be at home. Graham's money means you can stay here, in your home.'

'Sometimes I think I can hear him, you know,' Imogene said suddenly, her sightless eyes rolling towards the ceiling.

'Graham?' Willow asked, uneasy.

'No, stupid. Him, my Ian. I think I can hear him in his study, pacing up and down, moving things around. Sometimes I wake up in the middle of the night, still wondering where he is, after all these years. I go in there and look for him, but he's never there.'

Willow was silent, watching a TV chef beat an egg with practised aplomb.

'So how is *London*?' Willow's mother stressed the word with some venom. 'Are you happy?'

'Happy?' Willow was taken off guard by the direct question.

'I just hope you're happy now, that's all. Finally,' her mother said, the tone in her voice shifting just enough to make Willow's insides clench.

'Yes, I like it. It's interesting.'

'But still no boyfriend.' It was a statement, laced with disappointment and edged with spite.

'Well, I don't want to rush into anything . . .' Willow stumbled over her own inadequacy.

'You're not getting any younger, Willow. Your sister left it late to have her two, but even if you get pregnant tomorrow, you'll be sixty when your children graduate college.'

'They might not go to college,' Willow said.

'Probably not, not if they take after you.' Imogene's face had clouded, and Willow knew that the grace period was fast coming to an end.

'You could have stayed married,' her mother accused her. 'You had a chance to stay married, even after the affair.'

'It was hardly an affair,' Willow said, letting her mother draw her into a downward spiral of recrimination. 'But I couldn't, there was no trust any more. I couldn't stay in that marriage knowing how it was . . .'

'It's that poor girl I feel sorry for. Lost not one but two mothers in her short life. What's that going to do to a child?'

'I feel sorry for her too,' Willow said quietly, secretly thinking she knew exactly what it was like not to have a mother to turn to.

'But that's you, isn't it? That's you all over, Willow. Never stuck to anything, not like Holly. Never cared about what you destroyed.'

'That's not true.' Willow's throat tightened on each word as her mother nudged her ever closer to the precipice.

'It's because you're cold,' her mother went on. 'Heartless. Always have been.'

'I'm not heartless, Mother, and if I find it difficult to connect to people it's because . . .' Willow took a breath. 'Mum, I don't laugh, did you know that?'

'What are you talking about?' Imogene frowned.

'I'm not sure when I stopped – if it was weeks or months or years ago – but there is no joy in me. I'm broken inside.'

'Nonsense. In my day there was no such thing as stress. We just got on.' Imogene felt for the remote control that was on the arm of her chair, turning off the TV. Perhaps a minute of near silence, except for the ticking of the wind-up clock on the mantel, filled the spaces between them. Who wound it now, Willow found herself wondering uneasily. It had always been Ian's job.

'Mum, I want to be better. To be happy. To be able to connect with people, the way that Holly does. I want to be better. I'd like to meet someone and have children.'

'Try visiting your mother more. That would be a start.' Imogene fidgeted in her chair, turning her head towards the door as if she were hopeful someone might come through it.

'What I'm trying to say is, I want to heal,' Willow said. 'I want things to be OK between us again, for it to be like it used to be. Holly and I were looking at the photo album before I came out. I was so happy then. Maybe it was just the three of us, and perhaps we didn't have much, but you made us feel so loved, all the time. Loved and special.'

'Well,' Imogene said, as if not sure how to take the compliment. 'Well, that's what a mum does, isn't it?'

'I know. You've taught us both a lot about motherhood.' Willow took a breath, steeling herself to find the right words to go on. It almost felt as if she were sightless too, feeling her way through the conversation with her fingertips, trying to tease the right words out. Perhaps there were no right words, perhaps she just had to take a step into the darkness and trust that she would land somewhere.

'Mum, I need to talk to you about what happened between us. About what happened with me and Ian, and the way things have been since you found out. I know you didn't want to face it then. That's hard for me to accept, but I suppose you didn't want to believe something like that. Perhaps you felt guilty.' Willow felt fear tightening her throat, but still she went on. 'But, Mum, what happened, it's shaped the whole of my life, it's made me a lesser person than the one I should have been. Nothing can ever make it completely better, but if you . . . if you would just accept what happened, if you would just be my mum, I think it would be like having a ton weight of stone lifted off my shoulders. I miss you, Mum. Please, please, now at least, could you admit that you knew the truth, you knew what was happening with—'

'Don't. You. Dare.' Her mother lifted one finger in warning, just as she had done when Willow was a little girl, a warning that was, as often as not, followed by the back of her hand.

Willow sat on the little leather footstool, every space inside her, her mouth, her nose, her eyes and ears, clogged with impotent emotion that she couldn't even name, that she only knew was smothering her.

'It was you,' Imogen said. 'You ruined everything. You drove him to an early grave, you know. You killed him with your lies.'

Willow shook her head, her mouth opening but no sound coming out. She stood up abruptly, tipping the stool as she stood, heading for the door.

'I'm sorry. I thought perhaps we could talk honestly –'

'Oh, that's right, walk away. Walk away,' Imogene crowed.

Willow halted in her tracks.

'What do you expect me to do, Mother? Do you expect me to stay here and listen to this? I *loved* him, God help me!'

'I expect you to live your life like a grown woman and stop blaming everything on other people.'

'I'm going,' Willow said, her hand on the door. 'I'll tell Magda to make you dinner.'

'You will never be happy!' Imogene's voice rattled in the empty hallway as Willow headed towards the front door, grabbing her coat off the banister, her mother's taunts echoing after her. 'You don't deserve to be happy, you deceitful little bitch. You poison everything you touch!'

Magda was on the other side of the front door, smoking a cigarette when Willow tore it open.

'Excuse me,' Willow stumbled over her, struggling to regain her composure. 'Goodbye.'

'You won't stay longer?' Magda asked as Willow pushed past her. 'Too difficult to see her like this? Perhaps you need some time, yes? And come back.'

Willow didn't answer. Head down, she marched furiously away from the house, her cheeks burning, her eyes stinging with fury, all the anger and the fear and confusion crowding her vision with shadows, her locked doors rattling, threatening to burst at the hinges. Only once she had crossed the river did she stop, on the bank opposite the house. She looked at the window of Ian's study, her heart in her mouth. Was he still there, pacing and moving things around? Arranging his desk chair in just the right place so he could see her reflection in the mirror when she sat in it. So he could get the perfect view.

In an instant Willow's knees buckled beneath her and she sank to the ground, surrendering in terror to the locked doors that sprung open all around her with a cacophony of crashes. Covering her head with her hands Willow could not stop the past tumbling on top of her, threatening to crush her with its unbearable weight as the horror, the awful horror of everything that she had endured, engulfed her.

And then there was the palm of a hand on the back of her neck, and then Holly's arms around her, her voice in her ear soothing and soft, and her shoulder to lean on as she gathered Willow into her arms and helped her to her feet. Willow knew there were people looking, she could sense them, as she buried her face in her sister's hair.

'My sister has been taken ill,' she heard Holly say as if she were very far away. 'Please excuse us.'

Willow let Holly guide her, the unbearable panic subsiding with each step that took her further from that house, pushing each heavy oversized door shut in her head, one by one. Finally Holly bundled her into the cool, quiet calm of her house.

'The girls . . . Chloe,' Willow sobbed as she sank onto the

bottom stair. Holly shut the front door on the world, locked, bolted it and then slid on a chain. 'They mustn't see me like this.'

'Chloe's taken them down to the harbour to feed the swans. It's OK. We can talk. Let it out, Will. Tell me.' She led Willow upstairs to her favourite window and directed her at the view. 'Was it very bad?'

'She hates me,' Willow said. 'She will never believe me.'

'She hates us both,' Holly replied.

'But me more. She hates me more. She blames me. She blames me for what she will not admit is true,' Willow said. 'She hates me for something that she says never happened.'

'We know the truth,' Holly said, her eyes on the horizon. 'I never doubted you, not for a second.'

'Why me?' Willow said. It was almost a whisper. 'Why me?'

'I don't know. We'll never know,' Holly replied gently. 'I wish it had been me.'

'Don't say that.' Willow turned to look at Holly, her reflection, her sister's face wrought with the pain she knew was engraved on her own. 'The only thing that makes it bearable is that it wasn't you.'

'I used to be so jealous,' Holly said, repeating verbatim a conversation they had had again and again. 'Of you and him and your little chats. I was jealous, Will. The thought of it makes me sick to my stomach.'

'I never told you.'

'But still, I should have known. I'm your twin. Perhaps I did know, I just didn't want to look.' Holly covered her mouth with the back of her hand, suppressing a retch. All three of them had adored Ian, from the moment he came into their lives. It wasn't only their mother who was besotted with his tall good looks, his sense of fun or the way he took control, made order out of the chaos of their lives. Without knowing it they had all missed having a man in their lives, and Willow wanted to please him, she wanted him to like her. She sought him out, knocked on the door of his den, interrupted his work to talk to him. But he was never cross, he was always interested in whatever she had to say, he laughed at her jokes. Willow looked forward to seeing him and even though she knew it irritated her mother, she followed him around like a besotted puppy. Which was why, almost a year after he'd married her mother, when he closed the door on his hidy-hole and put his arm around her waist and asked her if she would like him to kiss her, she had said yes please.

'I didn't want you to know. I wanted to keep you safe. He said . . . he said if I ever told anyone, no one would understand; he said Mum would make me leave, that she'd be angry. He was right, wasn't he?'

'He wasn't right about anything. He was a monster. Mum knows it, she just can't bear to admit it. And so she attacks you, not because she hates you but because she's ashamed.'

The women held each other then, one melding into the other, holding off the past in a long embrace that secured, at least for now, the doors that kept the terrible truth at bay.

The truth that, when Willow was nine, Ian had come into her room one night, shutting the door behind him.

Chapter Sixteen

'I like Chloe,' Jem said later that night as Willow tucked her and her sister into bed. 'She can cross her eyes and touch the tip of her nose with her tongue. She told us a story.'

'Did she?' Willow said, brushing Jem's fringe off her forehead, which she promptly smoothed back down. 'What was it about?'

'About a duck,' Jo-Jo told her. 'A fuzzy duck.'

'That sounds like Chloe,' Willow said.

'Are you OK, Aunty Pillow?' Jem asked, patting Willow's cheek rather more firmly than necessary. 'Your eyes are red and puffy – did you cry? Did you fall over?'

'I didn't fall over, but I did cry a bit. I'm fine now, though,' Willow told them.

'Who made you cry?' Jem looked concerned.

'No one. I just felt a bit sad. Not any more, though! It's impossible to be sad when you have two such delightful nieces.' Willow smiled for them, and they seemed reassured.

'Is it because you have to go back soon and you will miss us?' Jem asked, solemnly.

'Yes.' Willow nodded, resting her cheek for a moment on the small girl's tummy. 'I will miss you very much.'

'You should visit more often, Mummy says it all the time.' Jo-Jo yawned, patting Willow on the head.

'Mummy's right, I should,' Willow agreed, basking in the warm glow of the pink fairy lights that adorned the ceiling of their tiny room, the smallest in the house. The girls had picked it themselves at the age of two and showed no sign of wanting to move out. They enjoyed their proximity, something that Willow and Holly understood perfectly. Holly had never suggested the girls might want a room each, even though the house had plenty. If and when they were ready to be apart, she always said, they'd let her know.

'Aunty Pillow?' Jem reached out for Willow's hand. 'Are you famous?'

'No,' Willow smiled. 'No, not at all.'

'That's a shame.' Jem turned her head away, signalling that she was ready for sleep. 'Famous people are better.'

'There is no one in the world who is better than your mum,' Willow said.

'Yes, Mummy is the loveliest mummy that there has ever been, even when she makes us eat greens and . . .' Jem drifted away before completing her sentence.

'Night-night, Jo-Jo,' Willow whispered to her other niece.

'Night-night – and don't be sad any more, Aunty Pillow. We shall love you, come what may.'

Holly had made crab and chilli linguine, and was tonging it onto plates when Willow came down from putting the twins to bed. She sat at the shining glass-topped white table and Holly filled one of her over-sized designer wine glasses to the top with something very cold and white. She repeated the action for herself, before pouring a glass of sparkling water for Chloe.

'Gray won't be joining us,' Holly said as she sat down opposite Willow. 'He's having dinner at his desk. Says it's something vital for work, but I think he's just scared of all the women in the house.'

'Dad called,' Chloe said. 'He's only just leaving London so he's going to check straight into the hotel when he gets here and come for breakfast tomorrow.'

'It's nice that he's taking the time to come down here, to be with you. It shows how much he cares,' Holly said, glancing at Willow.

'It shows how much he wants to control me,' Chloe grumbled.

'That's not what he's doing,' Holly told her gently. 'He's trying to look after you, like he always has. The trouble is, you've changed and he hasn't. He hasn't quite realised yet that you need a different sort of looking after now. He'll get there.'

No one spoke for a moment or two. Chloe twirled her pasta around her fork, first clockwise, then anticlockwise, playing with her food, occasionally glancing at Willow, no doubt taking in her swollen lids and pinched, puffy face.

Oddly enough, Willow felt utterly calm. For a little while, at least, she knew she would feel like this; she would feel serene and peaceful and . . . relieved. Because, as painful as her visit to her mother, to that house, had been, it had released everything that had been building up inside her since the last time she had been forced to confront what had happened, like blowing a pressure valve – all the anger, sorrow, grief and guilt. All the thoughts of what might have been if she'd done something or said something different; of what kind of person she might have been if her mother had never taken them into the bank to ask for an overdraft. If she hadn't been so full of herself or made herself stand out to get his attention. If she hadn't liked Ian so much, if she hadn't wanted him to like her. If she hadn't said, yes please.

The battle that Willow fought on a daily basis was between her child's mind and her adult one. Now, in the present, she knew well enough what had happened to her. Although she'd never been able to bear the idea of counselling, of talking things through with some well-meaning stranger, after the divorce forced her to consider how the past was influencing her life now, she could say with some certainty that she had been groomed. That Ian had spent months preparing her for what he wanted. She knew that those two words had been put in her mouth, without her realising. Willow knew all of that perfectly well in her adult mind, but it was the child's mind, the little girl who didn't know or understand what was going on until it was all too late and there was no way out, that was the voice she had to fight to keep locked away. The voice that told her it was her choice, her fault, that she had wanted it to happen, that she had made it happen.

All these toxic background thoughts that polluted her head on a daily basis, often without her present mind even registering them, had spewed out of her in a frenzy of emotion.

Holly, who felt every beat of anguish with her, had held her in her arms as they stood before the window and let her cry until she saw Chloe and the twins trailing back along the shore, pockets bulging with what was no doubt another precious collection of stones. Then she had pushed Willow's hair back from her forehead, lifted her chin and kissed her, telling her to go and wash her face, the girls were coming back.

Previously, that would be that. They wouldn't talk about what they never talked about for as long as possible, and for a few days, perhaps even for a week or two, there would be a feeling of acceptance, of a slate wiped clean. There would be the potential of a fresh start, of the future spreading out before them like a blank page, as the tide of their fury swept back out to sea. Usually Willow was resolved to enjoy these times, these rare periods of calm between the storms that almost always raged in her heart. And here, at her sister's house, where Holly had laboured so faithfully to make a home free from anguish, was normally the perfect place.

But not this time, because when she looked at Chloe she knew that one thing had changed, at least. She was not prepared to go back to London stuck in the limbo her stepfather had put her in all those years ago. This time she would be free of him; she would not let him ruin the rest of her life. To do that she needed to make her mother face the truth, no matter how much it hurt her. And this time Willow thought she knew how.

'I'm not sure I can eat this,' Chloe said at last, her voice small as she pushed the plate away. 'It looks nice and that, but I . . . isn't seafood a bit dodgy for unborn babies?'

'I don't know. Do you know, Holly?'

'I think crab's OK, actually, but now I come to think of it, the last thing you need is chilli, you poor thing. You'll be up all night with acid reflux! I'll make you something else. It won't take a moment to whiz you up some tomato and basil, is that OK? I can pop some rocket on the side.'

'I don't really like rocket,' Chloe muttered, avoiding looking at Willow. 'I mean, have you got any chips in the freezer? Or toast?'

'Don't be silly, you need fresh food in your condition. Won't take a moment.' Holly bustled around, busying herself with tearing up fresh basil, adding chopped tomatoes and olive oil to a pan.

'Being pregnant sucks,' Chloe said finally, taking a sip of her water. 'I really fancy a glass of wine.'

'Really, don't you just think it's amazing?' Holly beamed as she set a fresh plate of pasta in front of Chloe. 'That little life, growing away inside of you. One day soon they'll become a person, a noisy, opinionated, sleep-refusing, wonderful, loving, clever little person. And you'll be watching to see if she or he has your smile, your laugh, your frown.'

'The girls have got your frown,' Willow and Holly said simultaneously, chuckling at some private joke.

'It's wonderful!' Holly beamed at Chloe.

Chloe swallowed, her jaw tightening. She dropped her gaze to the pasta she still didn't eat.

'Oh God, I'm being tactless, aren't I?' Holly said. 'I just don't think, that's my trouble. Oh God, Chloe, I'm so sorry.'

'It's OK,' Chloe said. 'It's just, well . . . I won't know what he's like, if he's noisy or annoying. Or has my frown. I won't know it at all, will I?'

Chloe pushed her plate away from her, which Holly automatically pushed back. Willow watched, fascinated, to see how her sister dealt with this moment, desperate to learn from her.

'Well, you don't have to decide right away,' Holly said, shuffling her chair closer to Chloe and taking a knife and fork to the younger woman's linguine. After a few diagonal slices she loaded up a fork and all but made engine noises as she piloted it towards Chloe's mouth. 'Either way, you still need to eat. Open.'

Chloe obliged, chewing dutifully until after Holly plied her with one or two mouthfuls more, her mind caught up with her body in understanding she was hungry and she took the fork and began to feed herself.

'I can't have a baby, I'm fifteen,' Chloe said, between mouthfuls. 'I mean, obviously biologically I can. But it's not . . . how would I cope? I wouldn't, would I? I'd want to be fifteen. I'd want to be young and I'd have this baby. Neither of us would be happy.'

'It would be hard, that's for sure, but with support from your family, from Sam . . .' Willow and Holly exchanged glances. 'I'm not saying that adoption isn't the right choice, I'm just saying it's important that you know it isn't the only choice.'

Chloe shook her head. 'Can you imagine Dad looking after me and a baby on his own? He can't even look after himself, his only kid is a problem child, he's down two wives already, and the next one in line is a total bitch. In fact, even if he did want me to keep the baby, she wouldn't let him. She'd send it off to a children's home or something.'

'Really?' Holly said mildly. 'You make her sound like a fairy book wicked stepmother. Is she *really* that bad?'

It had never occurred to Willow to ask Chloe that question. She simply thought that Sam's latest girlfriend must be as awful as Chloe described her. Perhaps that idea suited her just as much as it suited Chloe to think so. No one ever wanted to feel that they'd been replaced by a better model, even when, in her case, it was pretty inevitable.

'Well, whatever she's like right now it's your job to think

about the rest of your life and which path you can most easily live with. The path where you trust your child to someone else to bring up, or the path where you make the decision to be a parent. What's most important is finding the way that is going to cause the least amount of damage, for both you and the baby.'

'Blimey, when did you take a degree in psychoanalysis?' Willow asked Holly.

'I read,' Holly said, unable to look at Willow directly. 'I'm interested in finding ways of letting go, of being free of the past. You know, finding a way to heal.'

'The thing is,' Chloe said, 'I do sometimes think about it. I think about him, the baby. About me and him together, and I get this really weird feeling of wanting to hold him so badly. And I think how amazing it must be to love a person that much and for them to love you too, and I have this idea in my head that we'd be like a little team, him and me against the world. But . . . but what if I don't love him? What if I look at him and all I see is his dad and then . . .' She looked up at Willow, her dark eyes full of fear. 'What if I hate him?'

'Oh, Chloe.' Holly covered Chloe's hand with her own and Willow got up, coming to put her arm around the girl.

'Do you think you'd hate him because you hate the father?' Willow asked her.

Chloe nodded.

'It wasn't just some random boy at a party, was it?' Willow said.

Chloe shook her head.

'Who was it, Chloe?' Willow asked her, ever so gently.

'It wasn't like I didn't want it, or that I'm not almost old enough,' Chloe said. 'It wasn't like I didn't go after him, because

I did. He kept saying no, that it was a terrible idea, that it mustn't happen. But everyone could see the way we felt about each other, everyone said that the tension between us was amazing! It wasn't just in my head – everyone thought it, all my friends. And then one day it just happened. One minute we were talking and the next we were kissing and it was so amazing, it was brilliant.'

'Who was it?' Willow asked.

'He said that he'd tried and tried to ignore his feelings but that he couldn't any more and that if I wanted to be with him I had to understand that nobody could ever know. And I was fine with that, I liked it.' Chloe was adamant. 'It's not like I didn't know what I was doing.'

'Chloe, who was it?' Willow asked again.

'Mr Jacobs,' Chloe whispered, lowering her lashes. 'Ed, Ed Jacobs – my music teacher at school.'

'Your teacher?' Holly gasped.

'Yes, but it wasn't like he was a perv. He's twenty-four, not much older than me at all really. He said that as soon as I was old enough I could leave school and then we could be together and no one could stop us. We had it all planned out. I was going to do my A levels at college and then he was going to support me through university. I mean, he loved me, he really, really did and then . . .'

'And then?' Willow asked.

'I got pregnant. I don't know how – we were so careful – but it happened and he . . .' Chloe swallowed, 'he changed overnight. Suddenly it was like he hated me, like I'd deliberately set out to ruin his life, wreck his career. He went from being so lovely and sweet to . . . it felt like he was controlling me. He wanted me to get an abortion, he made the appointment and everything, forged a letter from Dad to get me off school, said I had to make out I was sick. He had it all planned and suddenly I felt like I was being smothered and controlled and I didn't want that. So I told him I wasn't going to do that and he went crazy, screaming and shouting at me. He said if I told anyone about us he'd . . . well, he threatened me.'

'He did what?' Willow said very quietly, very softly. 'How?'

'He said he'd make sure the whole school knew what a slut I was, how easy I was. That the baby could be anybody's. That I'd lied about us, made it all up because I was a psycho little bitch. That I could say what I wanted, but no one would believe me, and anyway, even if they did, my dad would hate me and I'd lose all my friends.'

Willow bit her lip, her eyes meeting Holly's. There would be a time and a place to deal with Mr Jacobs but it wasn't now. The last thing Chloe needed now, as she was teetering on the brink of coming to terms with her pregnancy, was someone to go wading in all guns blazing. Not yet.

'Well, he was wrong about that,' Willow said. 'If you wanted to you could prove that the baby is his as soon as he's born. It's a simple test to show paternity.'

'Really?' Chloe asked. 'Like on *Jeremy Kyle*?'

'Exactly,' Willow said. 'But look, is it because of this man that you decided to give the baby up for adoption? Is it only because of him that you don't want to keep it?'

Chloe thought for a moment, pushing her half-eaten plate of food away from her.

'At first I just didn't want to do what he wanted, and then after I left school I tried not to think about it for a while. Then it kept growing and growing, and I knew that I had to tell Dad, but I didn't know how. So I decided to find you. Dad keeps everything in files in his office, so I went in there while he was at work and picked the lock on his filing cabinet with a paperclip. I really did!' Chloe was momentarily distracted by her fledgeling skills as a criminal. 'Everything is in there – everything. There's even a file on me. I found a little bag in it with my first ever haircut and my hospital tag . . . Anyway, there was a file marked "Willow". It's where he keeps your wedding photos, things you sent him, cards and stuff, and the stuff about the divorce. There was a solicitor's letter that had your address on it. I copied it out and Googled it. That's how I found you. I didn't have a plan. I wasn't expecting to run into you outside your house. I was trying to find out if you were still there, and then there you were. In the street.'

'You said that you came to me because you are like me. What did you mean?' Willow asked her.

'I don't know really.' Chloe looked embarrassed. 'I think I meant that you knew what it was like to make a mistake. You slept with Daniel.'

'You knew about that?' Willow was shocked. 'And we didn't actually have sex.'

She neglected to mention that it was probably only because Sam had walked in on them.

'It was hard not to know. After you left, Dad was in pieces, crying all the time. I was frightened; I mean Dad, crying? I couldn't imagine it, it's like . . . well, you know, when your dad cries that's like the end of the world, isn't it?'

'I imagine it is,' Willow said.

'And then one night Daniel came round. I was supposed to be in bed but I could hear raised voices and then them talking about you. Well, I didn't know where you'd gone or why Dad was so upset so I got out of bed and crept to the front door. They were standing in the corridor, yelling, but in whispers. Daniel was worried about you. He was saying Dad had overreacted, that what happened wasn't your fault, that it was all down to him. He said that you loved Dad, and that what happened had been a silly mistake and that it had meant nothing to you. He said if Dad had an ounce of sense he'd take you back. Dad said he'd drop dead before he took any advice from Daniel.' Chloe shrugged. 'I knew there had been some sort of argument between the three of you, but as far as I was concerned Dad was in the wrong, Daniel said you were sorry, that it was his fault not yours. I couldn't understand why Dad wouldn't make up with you, and of course he wouldn't explain it to me. And in all these years since, I've been angry about it, angry about him taking you away from me. I just didn't get it, and what really upset me was that half the time, neither did he. When I was looking for your address I found the divorce papers. They had Daniel's name on. It said adultery.'

Willow let out a long breath, feeling her shoulders and chest deflate.

'I didn't know that,' Holly said. 'I didn't think he'd called it adultery.'

'He wanted it to be over quickly, and his solicitor said that was the quickest way.' Willow turned to Chloe. 'There was never an affair with Daniel. It was a one-off thing, and it didn't get as far as sex. I don't know why I let it happen. I regret it every single day. I'm so sorry you had to find out about it, about me, this way.'

'It's OK,' Chloe said. 'It was actually a relief, sort of.'

Willow looked up at her.

'Dad's never been the same since you went, and I'm pissed off about that. I'm pissed off that you just left me. But . . . I woke up in the middle of the night, soon after Ed finished with me, and it hit me like this massive slap in the face. He used me, he led me on. He flirted with me and made me believe that things were real between us. But really he just wanted a bit of fun that wasn't going to interfere with his life. That's what I was to him. I felt so stupid. What a fucking stupid little girl, to let him – that pig – be my first. And now this?' She cradled her belly in her arms. 'It's not fair that one silly mistake can ruin the rest of your life, is it? I mean, I'm young, I'm a kid. How is it fair that trusting in someone, believing in someone, can be your only chance, your last chance? At least when I came to you I knew you'd understand that people sometimes do the wrong thing, even when they don't mean it. And that sometimes it's not just something you can move on from.'

Willow shook her head in wonderment as she listened to Chloe, reaching out to stroke her long dark hair back from her face and cup her cheek in the palm of her hand.

'You are an incredible girl,' Willow said. 'I think your dad should be so proud of the young woman you've become. To deal with all of this for so long, all on your own, and to have the kind of insight and perspective on it that you do . . . I think you are amazing. I never knew your mum, but I think she would be so proud of you.'

'Really?' Chloe's black eyes filled with tears. 'Do you really think that, because all I ever think is how much I've let her down.'

'No, no,' Holly said, her voice uncharacteristically hard. 'All you've done is be a fifteen-year-old girl. You are the one who's been let down.'

'What you need to be certain of is the decision you are making now,' Willow said. 'Nobody would blame you for deciding that adoption is the right step for you and the baby. But it has to be because that is really what you feel is right, not because you're scared of the father, or angry at him. This is about you and your child, no one else.'

'Willow is right,' Holly said. 'I promise you when you hold your baby in your arms the love you feel is times about a million the love you feel for any man. It eclipses everything else. The circumstances of how he came about, all the trouble and pain won't matter any more because he is yours and you are his, and that is all that counts.' Holly smiled. 'I'm not saying it wouldn't be a tough road ahead for you if you kept him – you are so, so young – but I do promise you that if you did decide to keep him all you would feel for him would be the most powerful, wonderful love.'

Willow found tears filling her own eyes as she listened to Holly talking about her experience of motherhood.

'It's true,' Willow told Chloe, leaning down so that her forehead touched Chloe's. 'Holly is right.'

'How do you know?' Chloe asked her.

'Because when I saw you standing outside my flat that is *exactly* the way that I felt.'

Chapter Seventeen

The rare gift of autumnal morning sun streamed in through the window, revealing a chink of perfect blue sky as if Holly had arranged that only beautiful weather should be permitted outside her beautiful house. Willow stretched, feeling the clean cotton sheets shift beneath her bare skin. She was in the second-best guest room this time – Holly had put Chloe in the nicest room – but it was still like Buckingham Palace compared to her own flat, a place where a person could have a clean mind, free of clutter and shadows. On the rare occasions that Willow came to visit she resolved to give her own place exactly the same treatment as soon as she got home – after all, she must have it in her to be the serene competent woman her sister was – but somehow it never happened.

As she sat up in bed, feeling the heat of the September sun trapped and magnified by all the glass, warming the skin on her bare back, she made the resolution again. Before anything else Willow slipped on her shoes and immediately felt better. Pulling a shirt on, she went to the window and breathed in the horizon. Today looked like a good day to start again; today looked like a day when it might be possible to ditch the ballast of the past and sail away up into the sky. Maybe today it would be possible to be free, to leave those locked rooms behind for ever. Maybe, just maybe, this would be the time when the shadows didn't drag her back again.

Only before she could do that, she would have to open at least one locked door. And to do that she would have to go back to her mother's house.

Sam was sitting at the kitchen table when Willow came down, doing his level best to make conversation with the little girls, something Willow knew he had once been very good at.

'Do you like scrambled eggs?' Jem was asking him, nose delicately wrinkled as Holly served him exactly that on toast. '*I* think it looks like when you've got a cold and snot comes out.'

'Jem!' Holly exclaimed. 'Try to remember you are a lady!'

'I'm not a lady, I'm a child.' Jem's response was equally exasperated.

'Now you come to mention it . . .' Sam said, regarding the eggs quizzically. Then he grinned and winked at the girls. 'Lucky I love snot! Yummy!'

The girls giggled hysterically, tucking into their own eggs with renewed vigour.

Willow was both pleased and worried to see Sam sitting at the table. Chloe needed him here, Willow was sure of that. Equally, though, someone would have to tell him about Mr Jacobs and Willow was pretty sure that it was going to have to be her.

They had sat up a long time last night, Gray entering at one point and then, sensing the situation, tactfully leaving them again as he had done without complaint over the entire span of his relationship with Holly.

The three of them talked around and around the choices that Chloe had, the older women desperately trying neither to lead nor push her in any direction, simply to help her order her thoughts, to make sense of them, but the more they talked the less clear Chloe seemed.

'Can't you just tell me what to do?' she had begged Willow at one point. 'Whatever you say, I'll do it, I promise. And then I won't have to think any more.'

'The worst thing about growing up is that there are some things you have to decide for yourself,' Willow told her. 'And this is one of them.'

Eventually Willow had taken Chloe to bed, tucking her into an expanse of clean white cotton, like she used to when Chloe was a little girl, leaning over and kissing her forehead.

'Holly is going to have a nightmare trying to get all that mascara off her sheets,' she chided Chloe gently. As she went to leave, Chloe caught her hand, pulling her back to sitting on the bed.

'Do you think Dad will hate me, for what happened with Ed?'

'I think your dad will be angry and he has a right to be,' Willow said honestly. 'I think that it will be difficult and painful, and that you'll have to tell a few people what happened. But I think you also know that you need to tell the truth. It must have felt like a very grown-up romance to you, and perhaps it was. But he should have known better. What he did was wrong.'

'Yeah, but only because he was my teacher. I mean, what if he was a bus driver, or a . . . mechanic. He wouldn't lose his job then, would he?'

'No, I suppose not.' Willow could see how much Chloe was struggling with what had happened. Even now, even after Ed had let her down so very badly, she didn't want to think badly of him, or of their affair. He was her first love, she didn't want that memory to be sullied by scandal. Bleakly, Willow doubted that that was possible.

'The thing is, he's chosen to work with children, and to abuse that trust placed in him by the school and the parents is unforgivable. As beautiful and as grown-up as you are, you are still legally underage. And he was fully aware of that, otherwise he wouldn't have been so intent on bullying you to cover it up and save his own skin.'

'I really thought he loved me,' Chloe said softly. 'He looked at me like he loved me. When I was with him I felt like I existed.' She sniffed. 'Willow, there's something I'm worried about, but I don't know how to say it.'

'What?' Willow asked.

'Well . . . have I been abused? I mean, I haven't have I, because like loads of girls have sex at my age, don't they, with older boys, out of choice? It wasn't abuse, was it, because I wanted it, and I wanted him? I know what he did was wrong and the way he's treated me is shit, but it's not the same, is it?'

Willow bit her lip, tears confusing her vision for a moment. She turned her head away, searching very carefully for the right words to say. To be impartial, rational, reasonable at this exact moment was almost impossible, but Chloe had enough to deal with already. Instinctively Willow knew she had to tread so carefully so as not to leave any more scars for the girl to bear.

'Willow? I'm sorry, I don't want to make you cry.' Chloe propped herself up on her elbows, putting her hand on Willow's shoulder. 'It's just that when I said about what happened to you and Holly it sounded . . . well, it sounded wrong. And I've never thought that it was wrong before. I mean, stupid and hurtful and messy, yes, but not wrong. And I don't want to feel like that. I don't want to be weirded out, because that would do my head right in. Did Ed "abuse" me?'

Willow took a breath. 'I think that Ed Jacobs abused your trust. I think he took advantage of your youth and that he has behaved terribly in a way that will lose him his job, most likely. You've had your heart broken, darling, at the age when you most want to believe in love. And for you the consequences are a little more concrete than just the pain and listening to sad songs on your iPod. But the way you feel now won't last. The best thing you can do for you and your baby now is to look to the future and live your life because, whatever you decide, your life will be full of joy and happiness, and pretty soon what happened between you and him won't matter at all. I promise you that.'

Chloe seemed satisfied by her answer, pulling Willow down to kiss her again.

'I'm sorry I've turned out to be such a massive pain in the arse,' she told Willow.

'Oh, Chloe, you've turned out to be the most wonderful person I know,' Willow told her.

Sam smiled at Willow as she sat at the table opposite him and was promptly offered a plate of snot by Jo-Jo. He looked a little better, Willow thought. He looked like he might be growing into the maelstrom that had whipped up around him out of nowhere, rising to the challenge. He'd never been one to leave a gauntlet lying on the ground, Sam had always said. Willow remembered how looking at him used to make her catch her breath, how every time he touched her she would catch on fire. The love she had for him was still there, but it was muted now. The love she had once thought might save her was worn almost entirely away.

It wasn't Sam's fault, somehow Willow seemed to know that now. There was only one person who could rescue her and she was wearing a particularly lovely pair of vintage shoes.

Willow's insides tightened as she thought of how angry Sam would be when he found out about the baby's father, but in a way she also thought that was a good thing. Finally there was something fatherly he could do for Chloe.

'Gray's gone already, off for a day of sailing with his cronies,' Holly said pouring coffee. 'Magda called. The night nurse said Mum had a very bad night, little sleep. I said I'd go over this morning, take her some of those fairy cakes, hey, girls?'

'Grandma can't see at the moment,' Jo-Jo explained to Sam. 'She is a bit poorly. So we're going to take her cakes and do her a dance.'

'And some singing, as she can't see,' Jem added. 'Grandma loves our singing more than anything in the whole world.'

'I'll come too,' Willow said, smiling at the girls.

'Really?' Holly looked uncertain.

'Yes. I might not visit Grandma. After all, I wouldn't want to distract her from your singing.' She grinned at Jem. 'But I think there's something I want in my old bedroom. Something I left there, so I thought I'd pop and have a look for it.'

'Are you sure?' Holly asked anxiously. 'What is it?'

'I think I must have blocked it out, until last night, talking to Chloe. It was then I remembered . . . there's something that I hid in my room. Proof,' Willow said, 'for Mum.'

Holly's face was immobile, wrought in a static expression of dismay.

'I don't know, Willow. She's old and ill – do you really want to do this?'

'I want my mum,' Willow said, shrugging simply, thinking of how Chloe had needed her last night. 'I haven't had her for twenty-five years, and I want her now. I think this is the only way.'

'She's down the road,' Jem said.

'Mummy's got her phone number,' Jo-Jo added.

'Thank you.' Willow smiled at them. 'Sam, will you come with me? I might need a hand.'

'Of course,' Sam said.

Just then Chloe appeared in the doorway, her hair tousled into a frenetic bird's nest, the remnants of yesterday's make-up smeared across her eyes. She had the look of a warrior princess, a chariot-racing queen ready for battle.

'Daddy,' she said with a sweetness that belied her dishevelled fierceness. Wordlessly she padded over to where he was sitting and, standing behind him, put her arms around him and kissed him on his stubbled cheek. 'I missed you,' she said.

Sam blinked, looking over his shoulder at her, turning his neck rather awkwardly so that he could kiss her back. 'I missed you too,' he said, his tone a mingle of surprise and pleasure.

'I like it here by the sea, though,' Chloe said, stealing a piece of toast from his plate and then going to lean on the kitchen counter next to Holly, who was buttering more toast. 'It feels free, less cluttered.'

'Yes, my hotel's very nice too,' Sam said, watching Chloe as she helped Holly load the dishwasher.

'Maybe we could go for a walk later. I can show you the swans; there are millions of them.'

'What's happened?' Sam asked bluntly.

Willow, Holly and Chloe all avoided looking at him.

'Hmm?'

'Sorry?'

'Nothing.' They all responded in unison, exchanging furtive glances.

'Something has happened that Chloe is worried might get her into more trouble and you two know what it is.' Sam took a breath. 'What?'

'Girls, run along and get dressed in something lovely for Grandma,' Holly said brightly.

'Why, she can't see us?' Jem said, crossing her arms and sitting back resolutely in her chair. 'I'm not brushing my hair if she can't see us.'

'She can see bright colours, and besides, you know Grandma always likes you to look nice. And Jem, Grandma will *know* if you haven't brushed your hair. Go on, you can wear anything you like, even your best party dresses.'

'Oh, goody,' said Jo-Jo, scampering for the door.

'I'm wearing trousers,' Jem grumbled as she followed her sister, scowling sideways at her mother. 'And a hat.'

'Well?' Sam stood up, crossing his arms defensively. 'What now?'

'Look,' Willow said, 'sit down. Frowns at dawn aren't going to do anyone any good, are they?' Sam sank back into his chair.

'Holly, you go and help the girls get ready. Chloe, you'd better go and strip your bed, get the sheets in the wash before those make-up stains set.'

'But I—'

'Go on.' Willow nodded firmly at the door and, abandoning her half-eaten piece of toast on the table top, Chloe went.

'What is it?' Sam asked her urgently.

'Before I tell you I want you to remember something,' Willow said. 'What Chloe needs now is her dad at her side, telling her he will be there for her, come what may.'

'I know that,' Sam said. 'That's all I want. Willow, what is it?'

'Good, because what I'm about to tell you is going to make you very, very angry.'

Willow could feel Chloe's eyes on her back, watching from her bedroom window, as she half walked, half ran after Sam down towards the water's edge. He'd taken off as soon as she finished talking, struggling briefly with the sliding doors that opened out onto the back garden and led down to the river, desperate to be free of the information that Willow had just burdened him with.

He whirled round as Willow approached, taking backward steps to escape her.

'I don't care what you say,' he warned her, shouting into the brisk wind that had whipped up the rain that was now falling, snatching his words out of his mouth and throwing them back in his face.

'OK, if that's what you want to do, but—'

'There is no but here, Willow.' Sam's face was contorted with fury and disgust. 'He used my little girl, he tricked her into sleeping with him, he got her pregnant and then abandoned her to save his own vile skin. I will pound his stupid fucking face into the ground. I sat opposite that man at parents' evening. I sat there and listened to him tell me what a wonderful daughter I had when he was . . . I am going to kill him.'

'We will both kill him,' Willow said, grabbing both of Sam's hands and steadying him. The sharply playful breeze grabbed at her hair, blowing it into her mouth and eyes. 'We will both see he gets exactly what he deserves.'

'What kind of man am I?' Sam said, shaking his head in despair. 'I couldn't protect her, I couldn't protect you. I'm useless.'

'Sam, don't say that.' Willow leaned close to him and dropped her voice.

'It's true. I'm not the man you thought I was, Willow. I'm not the man *I* thought I was. Do you know what I felt when you told me about your stepfather?' Sam said, turning his face away from her. 'I felt sick with disgust. But there was no one I could kill for you, no one I could make pay for what he did to you – he was already dead! It just ate away at me and every time I looked at you . . . I got these images in my head and I couldn't bear it. I felt like someone had poisoned everything. He wasn't there to take the blame so I . . . I blamed you.' He wrenched free of her grasp. 'That's the kind of man I am. That's why I didn't take you back, not because I couldn't get past what happened with Daniel, but because I was in no way good enough for you, Willow. And now . . . and now this?' Sam shook his head, incredulous. 'It's like a punishment.'

'It's not,' Willow said. 'For Chloe this was a forbidden romance, like *Romeo and Juliet*, secret and exciting. When he stranded her the way he did she was hurt and confused. She didn't know which way to turn, or what to do. But you should have heard her last night. She now has a very clear picture of what happened in her head, she understands completely, and I think . . . I think if she thought you would be able to cope with it, then I think she might keep the baby.'

Sam looked up into her eyes. 'Really?'

Willow nodded. 'Yes, Sam, I do. If she knows that she's got us there to back her up, I think she would. And I haven't said as much to her, but in my heart I think that she should. That social worker was right: between us we can give both her and your grandchild the kind of start in life they deserve. We can be there for them both. You said you wanted to help me, you said it would make you feel honourable again. Well, I feel the same about Chloe. I love her, I just want to help her. And as much as I would really like to see you knock seven bells out of that scumbag, it won't help anyone – not Chloe, not you or the baby. Of course we need to go to the school, and soon. But at the moment Chloe feels safe and centred. Let's make sure she stays that way.'

Almost physically restraining himself, Sam nodded, glancing back at the house. Chloe might have been watching them but it was impossible to tell: the rolling rain-encumbered sky filled every window with its reflection.

'I know you're right,' Sam said. He closed his eyes, clenching his fists. 'I just really want to hit someone.'

'Me too,' Willow replied.

'You know, when you told me that the bastard who hurt you was dead, I was disappointed,' Sam said. 'I would have killed him for you, you know. I would have.'

'I know,' Willow said. 'And sometimes, as crazy as it sounds, I wish that he were still here too, because it's only now that I am strong enough to look him in the eye and explain to him exactly what he did to me. But I can still face him, and I can still be free of him. That's why I'm going back to the house today and that's why I need you with me, Sam. I don't think I can do it without you.'

Sam nodded. 'So what now?'

'Go back to the house, find Chloe and hug her, and tell her

you love her and that whatever she decides you will be there for her.'

'It could never be any other way,' Sam said.

'I know, and so does she, really. She just doesn't know that she knows it.'

Willow and Sam waited on the doorstep of her mother's house as Holly followed the girls inside. A moment later Magda came out, unlit cigarette in hand.

'You're not going in?' she asked Willow, smiling at Sam and offering him her hand to shake. 'Hello, I'm Magda, I'm the day nurse.'

'I'm Sam, Willow's . . . friend,' Sam said, hesitating as he tried to pin down the nature of their relationship. It seemed to come as something of a small revelation to him.

'Friend?' Magda laughed, waggling her cigarette at Willow. 'He is very handsome man, you should make him more than a friend.'

'How's Mum today?' Willow asked.

'Good. The doctor comes this afternoon, but she was telling me the colours on TV, so, God willing, I think this sight loss will pass, or at least not stay as bad. She is making me pick up plums and apples from your garden ready for cooking, so I think she feels OK.'

'That's good,' Willow said, eyeing the sliver of darkness pervading through the crack in the partially open front door. Every step of the way here she had been so determined to do this, to unlock every last door and search out Ian's ghost. But now she was here, she was afraid again. She was a lost and lonely frightened little girl.

'You go and see,' Magda said. 'Go, see for yourself.'

'I think I'll let the twins have the limelight for now,' Willow said. 'I've got a few matters I need to sort out upstairs. We'll just nip up there and grab a couple of things first.'

Shrugging, Magda pushed open the door and stepped aside to let them in.

Willow looked up the stairs, her heart racing, and took a step back, walking into Sam's chest.

'One step at a time,' he whispered in her ear. 'I'm here.'

The fourth stair up creaked. Willow remembered for two reasons: because she and her sister always used to skip over it if they wanted to sneak in or out without their mother listening, and because Willow would lie in bed counting the creaks. The first creak would be her mother going up to bed. The second creak would be Ian.

Now, as much out of superstition as anything else, she stepped over the fourth step, wincing as Sam trod on it behind her. As she reached the first landing Willow stopped. Her mother's bedroom door was half open, a pale watery light cast across the rose-print wallpaper, which hadn't been changed in thirty years. After a moment's hesitation Willow pushed it open and walked in. It was a beautiful room, perfectly proportioned, high ceilings and the original doors that led out onto the veranda, but it was so cold. Not in temperature, although today there was a chill in the air, but in atmosphere. This was a room without love, Willow thought, looking at her mother's neatly made bed, a purple hot-water bottle sitting in between the pillows. How had Ian loved Imogene, Willow wondered. Had he ever loved her at all? Had he taken her in his arms and kissed her, and if he had, did she ever sense in the dark that there was something else, something much darker still lurking in the shadows? Willow caught her own reflection in the mirror over the fireplace. She looked pale and drawn, for the first time in a long while she could see the contours of her cheekbones. For a moment, the mirror became like a portal through time, and it was almost like looking at her mother staring back at her. How lonely she must have been, Willow realised. How lonely for Imogene to be wooed into a life of married respectability only to find her husband withdrawn and distant, cut off from everything, even her own children, by his controlling behaviour. For the briefest of moments, Willow almost understood what it had been like to be Imogene back then, their eyes meeting across the decades. And then it was gone and Willow knew where she had to go next.

'Are you OK?' Sam asked.

Willow nodded, reaching out for his hand and gripping it tightly. She led him over to the next room, Ian's hidy-hole.

'This was his room, his study where he worked and pursued his hobbies.' Willow put her palm flat against the door, feeling her breath shorten and tighten, her heartbeat accelerating. 'He liked to spot wild flowers, to press them and keep them in a book,' she told Sam, imagining Ian sitting at his desk, his head bent over some book or other, the light from the Anglepoise lamp on his desk reflecting off the bald spot on the top of his head, his thick-framed glasses sitting on the end of his nose. 'I thought I was the bee's knees because he let me come in here and look at his collection.' Willow snatched her hand away from the door as if it had suddenly scalded her. 'And then afterwards, after he started, well, it happened in this room too. "Willow, come and look at my new flowers," he would call out. Holly would be so upset, feeling so left out that he liked me more than her. And I would pretend I hadn't seen him, or heard him, or that I had something better to do. But Mum would always make me go. I suppose she thought it was nice, that he was taking such an interest. And she hated her kids to seem rude or ungrateful; she'd always brought us up better than that.'

Willow felt Sam standing very close behind her; she felt his arms encircle her shoulders.

'And so you went?' he asked.

Willow nodded. 'I want to go in, I want to see that it's just a room. That's he's not in there, that it can't hurt me. But I don't know if I can. I wanted to be strong enough, but I don't think that I am.'

'I am,' Sam said. He kissed Willow on the cheek and then released her, opening the door before she could stop him. Willow gasped, the air dragged out of her lungs in a single second. He was there, for a moment, in the half-light that ebbed through the drawn curtains, he was there, sitting at his desk, smiling at her.

Willow, come and look at this.

And then he was gone. Instinctively Willow wanted to back away, but Sam reached out a hand to her and after a moment she took it, stepping into the room. It was small, lined with books, the desk still cluttered with his things: albums, a desk diary from the year he died, the Anglepoise lamp, which had somehow been shifted into a broken disjointed angle, as if it were trying to escape the otherwise perfectly preserved room. Willow looked around her. The room seemed much smaller than she remembered; the leather-topped desk Ian used to sit her at looked small, innocuous. A thick film of dust covered everything except, on his desk top, four finger streaks dragged across the surface. They must have been from when her mother had come in here to call for help. Back when she was nine, it was a sign of Ian's importance that he had a phone extension in his office, back when hardly anybody had two phones in their house. The beige plastic phone with the old-fashioned dial seemed like a relic now, but then it had served to add to his authority.

'You know,' the intrusion of Sam's voice made her jump, 'the chances are there will be something hidden away in here – photos, maybe. Something to show what kind of person he was. If we look, I bet we'll find some evidence.'

Willow looked at the locked desk drawer, the set of keys still hanging innocuously from the lock. There was a small safe on the shelf behind a stack of box files that Willow thought perhaps nobody knew about apart from her. After Ian had died, Willow thought there might be money in it, a secret stash, enough for her to be able to take herself and Holly away. It had taken every ounce of courage she had had to come into the room, to search for the combination, but whatever bravery she had deserted her as soon as she crossed the threshold. She had not known the combination then and she would not search for it now. All these years on Willow wondered what exactly Ian did keep in a secret safe that even her mother didn't know about. Whatever it was then, it was only right that those secrets, too, had their final resting place, a place of solitude and peace. Willow had no inclination to disturb them, dragging them out into the light to be violated again.

She let go of Sam's hand for a moment and looked around the room.

'There is nothing in here, no ghosts,' she said, to the room at large as much as to herself. 'Nothing in here but dust.'

She waited for Sam to leave and then, looking around one last time, she shut the door, both here, in her mother's house, and in her mind. Now she had gone back Willow knew that that door would no longer rattle, demanding to be opened, and perhaps for the first time since Ian had died she finally understood that she would never hear him calling for her again. A sense of relief drained through her, dragging the almost unrecognised constant nag of fear that had grated on every single inward breath she had ever taken and stripping it away from her blood and bones, until, standing there on the landing outside Ian's hidy-hole, the realisation finally hit home.

I am safe, Willow thought, looking up the stairs to her bedroom. I am safe.

'Come on,' she said to Sam, feeling emboldened by the sensation. It had been a long, long time since Willow had gone to her old room, and if she'd had to in the past she made a point of staying in it for as little time as possible, never sleeping there since the day she left home. Now Willow stopped at the top of the staircase. Turn left and you went into her room, turn right and you entered Holly's.

Had Ian ever stood there and made that choice, Willow wondered. Did he toss a coin, or draw a lot? Was there something that he saw in her that wasn't in Holly, some vulnerability her sister had not shown? Willow did not know, and she was burdened with the truth that she would never know, but there was nothing to be gained by wrangling over questions that would never be answered. It was what it was. Let it go, part of her said. Let it go.

As much as Willow wished for that to be possible she knew that it was not. When something was as much a part of you as the colour of your hair or the pitch of your voice, you couldn't let it go, no matter how you might wish it. But perhaps, perhaps she could acknowledge the damage that had been done and let it rest. At least, Willow thought, as she looked from Holly's door to her own, at least she could be glad about one thing.

How glad she was that he had left her sister alone.

Steeling herself, Willow marched to her bedroom door and pushed it open with enough force to send the knob thudding into the wall. How her mother used to shout at her about that dent in the wall. Willow smiled to herself, pulling the door back and running her fingers over the dip.

'Funny,' Sam said, nodding at a single poster of a boy band still just about Blu-Tacked to the wall by one corner.

'Hey, they were all the rage once,' Willow said, crossing to the wall and smoothing the poster back into position. 'See this one, in the boots? I used to daydream that I'd bump into him on the high street and that he'd whisk me away from all this.'

'So what's in here?' Sam asked her. The rest of the room was bare, the wardrobe was empty, the bed thankfully gone, the ghostly outline of the furniture that had once been there embedded in the grubby pink nylon carpet. Willow turned a slow circle, looking around, taking in every corner, every shadow. Then abruptly she kneeled on the floor.

'Willow?' Sam said. 'Are you OK?'

Willow nodded, drawing her coat around her. 'Ian told me he loved me more than anyone else in the world. He said that I should feel special, chosen. That he would always look after me. It started when I was nine. I got my first period when I was twelve and he didn't want me after that. And the terrible thing is that, as relieved as I was, I also felt rejected, betrayed. Part of the reason I've struggled so long to come to terms with it is the disgust I have in myself for feeling that way. After he was . . . over me, he didn't look at me or speak to me directly again, not for three years. It was as if he were disappointed in me for growing up. I became angry and literally hateful – full of hate for him, for my mother. The only person I could bear to be with was Holly. Poor Holly, constantly trying to keep the peace, trying to understand. I didn't tell her until after Ian had died, but as soon as I did it was like she had always known, she just hadn't been able to bear it. Holly believed me right from the start. Mum didn't.'

Willow leaned forward, running her hands over the rough surface of the cheap carpet.

'I don't understand how that's possible,' Sam said, kneeling next to her. 'How can a mother hear her daughter say those things and refuse to believe it?'

Willow shrugged. 'I don't know. Maybe because I waited three years to tell her, maybe because I lived with him all that time and said nothing. Maybe because she already knew. I don't know why, but I was wild and getting wilder. As soon as he died, it was like this pent-up fury in me that I'd been pushing back down burst out. And with it, all the pain and the hurt. I did every single thing I could think of to hurt my mother, to punish her. Everything. And all the while all I wanted was for her to open her arms to me, to hold me and tell me that everything would be OK.'

Willow's voice broke on the last few words, and she bit down hard enough on her lip to taste blood.

Sam reached out for her, but she didn't move, keeping her head bowed as she sat perfectly still, waiting for the wave of emotion to pass her by. Eventually Sam let his arms fall back to his sides. After perhaps a minute, Willow lifted her head.

'I wanted her to believe me, to believe her daughter, so I never showed her the one thing that would prove it. In fact, I succeeded in forgetting about it until last night when I was talking to Chloe. I want to do everything in my power to make sure she is free to be happy for the rest of her life – that's what a mother does, isn't it? It was at exactly the same moment I thought that that I remembered the proof.'

Sam looked ashen, his face filled with fear.

'What is the proof, Willow?' he asked.

Crawling on her hands and knees to the small fireplace, Willow hooked her fingernails behind a loose piece of skirting board, pulling it back just enough to be able to slide two fingers behind it. Looking up at the ceiling, she felt around for a second or two and then, finding her quarry, pulled it out. It was a folded piece of paper.

Willow held it out to Sam, who took it reluctantly.

'Ian wrote me a love letter.'

'So anyway, I'm going to be the angel and the Virgin Mary.' Jo-jo was at her grandmother's knee as Willow and Sam walked into the room.

'You are so not!' Jem said. 'She is so not. We don't even start at big school till Jan-yew-airy. Do we, Mummy?'

'No,' Holly said carefully, eyeing Willow as she walked into the room. 'But Janet says you're going to do something Christmas-ey at pre-school.'

'Pre-school!' Jo-Jo wailed. 'I don't want to be a cracker again!'

'I liked being a cracker, because when you get pulled you go POP!' Jem giggled, and Willow watched her mum's face soften and smile as she listened to her grandchildren.

'Your mummy and aunty were angels in their school nativity,' Imogene said, her face lit by the memory. 'It was their first Christmas at school, so they were about five and they had all these golden curls, just like you two. So lovely they were. I had to make their costumes out of bed sheets. Not old ones – we didn't have any old ones. We just had one set of bed sheets, so I cut them up and made tunics, and we slept on the mattress until the January sales.' Imogene chuckled. 'I made halos out of coat hangers and a bit of old tinsel my neighbour gave us. Luckily they were the most beautiful girls anyone had ever seen so it didn't matter that their costumes were so shoddy.'

'What does shoddy mean?' Jem asked.

'Will you make us our outfits, Grandma?' Jo-Jo asked.

'As long as my peepers are working by then, of course I will.'

Willow watched the little tableau. Her mum looked so happy; even with the pain and stress of her disease, having her grandchildren here transformed her totally. The love she felt for them, the joy they brought her, was palpable. Willow fingered the letter, still folded in her hands.

'Hello, Mum,' Willow said.

'Hello, dear,' Imogene replied cheerfully, as if nothing had happened between them. 'I wondered how long you were going to be loitering by the door.'

'Hello, Imogene,' Sam said. 'It's Sam, do you remember?'

'Sam! Of course I remember.' Imogene glowed. 'Holly has

been telling me all about you and Chloe, a baby on the way, I hear.' Imogene paused. 'Don't be too hard on her, Sam. I was not so much older than her when I fell pregnant with these two. My parents wouldn't have a bar of me. I almost left the babies on the hospital steps – perhaps I would have but the two of them, even when they first came out all bright red and squalling, they were like two peas in a pod. Anyway I made the walk there, but I think I would have died on the way home, so I went in, let them take care of us. Oh, it was a terrible scandal, I can tell you, but I got through. Me and my twins, we got through.' Imogene turned her head towards where she could make out Sam's shadow. 'It would have been easier with my mum behind me, though.'

Willow turned away, the painful irony shooting through her. 'Shall I make tea?' she said.

'Magda's making it,' Imogene said.

'Mum, I need to show you something,' Willow said. 'Can we talk? Alone?'

'Alone?' Imogene was surprised. 'Are you going to take my little songstresses away from me?'

'Just for a minute,' Willow said apologetically. 'I have to do this.'

Holly stared at the piece of paper in Willow's hand. 'Are you sure that you have to?' she all but begged.

Grimly, Willow nodded.

'Come on, girls,' Holly said. 'Let's help Magda find some biscuits and if you're good you can have a go on Grandma's piano.'

The cheers draining out of the sitting room left only tension and foreboding in their wake.

‘I’ll stay,’ Sam offered and Willow did not protest.

‘Mum.’ Willow sat down on the leather footstool, meeting her mother’s eyes. Imogene’s vision had improved enough for her to be able to focus on her daughter. ‘You know what I want to talk about . . .’

Imogene physically recoiled. ‘Not this again! Willow, you are a grown woman – when will you stop needing to make things up to get attention?’

Willow’s hand clenched on the letter, its thick fold biting into the palm of her hand. From across the hall the disjointed sound came of an out-of-tune piano being bashed indiscriminately.

‘The thing is, I know how hard this is for you but . . . Mum, the way you talked about me, me and Holly then. When you made our angel costumes?’

‘What about it?’ Imogene asked stiffly.

‘Do you remember the little girl I was then?’ Willow asked. ‘Do you remember how I used to make you laugh, always be into everything, always in trouble but never naughty? Because I remember how loved you used to make us feel, Mum, that as long as we had each other we didn’t need anything else in the world.’

Imogene was silent for a long time, looking into the crackling fire.

‘Of course,’ she said. ‘I always did my best for you.’

‘I know you did. And I know that you were so happy when you married Ian. We were happy too. Everything seemed perfect.’

‘It was perfect,’ Imogene persisted. ‘It was.’

‘Mum, when did she go?’ Willow asked.

‘Who? What do you mean?’ Imogene shifted in her chair, the

crashing of the piano keys growing louder and more ebullient next door.

'The little girl I used to be. When did the happy, funny, mischievous little girl you knew go, and the sullen, shy, quiet one appear? Do you remember that happening? Did you notice?'

'Of course I noticed. Ian said –' Imogene stopped herself.

'What did Ian say?' Willow forced her mouth to form the question, even though saying his name in this house seemed dangerous, as if somehow it might evoke him.

'You were nine. Ian said you were jealous. He said you weren't used to me having someone in my life and that you'd get used to it eventually. He said it was best to let you get on with it.'

'Is that what you thought?' Willow asked her.

'Yes, because it was the truth!' Imogene's voice was high, brittle.

Willow pinched her nose between her thumb and forefinger, desperate not to have to say what she was about to, not to have to unfold the letter and read it out loud.

'When I was in his office, when he called me up there to look at something, do you know what he was doing, Mum?'

'It wasn't like that. *He* wasn't like that,' Imogene persisted. 'I was his wife – don't you think I would have *known*? If what you said was true, I would have known.'

'He was. He was like that and he did those things to me. Under your roof, when you were in bed or in the kitchen, or in the garden with Holly. He did them to me, to the little girl that you loved.'

'No, no, don't.' Imogene pressed her hands over her head. 'Don't say that.'

Willow glanced up at Sam, standing taut by the door, her

resolve wavering. He nodded once, and Willow understood his meaning. *Go on.*

'I have something that proves it, something I haven't looked at in decades, something I tried really hard to forget.' Willow began to unfold the letter. 'I don't want to read this again, Mum. I don't want to say out loud the words that he wrote here, but I have to. I have to do something . . .'

Imogene reached out, her hand searching for Willow's.

'Don't.'

'Don't?'

'You don't have to.'

Willow stared at her mother. Imogene's expression was unreadable. 'Why not, Mum?'

'I honestly thought he was telling the truth,' Imogene said after a moment, so quietly Willow almost didn't hear her, afraid to speak or breathe or move. 'Do you honestly think I'd have let him go on hurting you if I'd known?' She shook her head. 'I didn't know, Willow. It wasn't something you looked for, or really understood then. It was a joke – a dirty old man in a raincoat hiding in the bushes. It wasn't a bank manager, it wasn't a husband. It never crossed my mind . . . I swear to you I didn't know what he was doing.'

'But you do now? You believe me now? Why now?' Willow asked her, a confusion of relief and anger flooding through her.

Imogene went on, talking almost to herself, looking inwards, examining the past in her mind's eye.

'I knew something was wrong between him and me. I knew he was withdrawn and cut off. I thought it was because of you two, because he couldn't love another man's children. Because you especially didn't seem to want to be anywhere near him. He said he'd make a fuss of you, spend extra time with you. He said I wasn't to worry, he'd bring you round. I didn't know, I promise you. I believed him.'

Tears tracked silently down Willow's face, running into her parted mouth so that she could taste the salt.

'I loved him, you see,' Imogene said. 'I loved him with every bit of me. I wanted him to be happy, I wanted to be the perfect wife, to make his home a haven for him. To have everything just so. And I thought that's what he wanted too. I noticed a change in you, but children do change when they are growing up.'

'You never asked me,' Willow said. 'You never asked me what was wrong. Why?'

'Perhaps I was afraid of the answer. Perhaps I sensed something but I was too afraid to look, to ask,' Imogene said brittlely. 'Then when he died, one minute you were inconsolable and then the next, you'd tell me . . . unspeakable things. How could I believe that of the man I loved, the man I brought into your life?' Imogene's voice cracked and broke. 'You were such an angry girl, so nasty. I'd lost my husband, all I had left were you two, but you weren't there. I felt like you drove him away at the end, and that you were taking Holly away from me too.'

'You didn't know? Not then?' Willow asked, incredulous.

Imogene shook her head.

'When then?' Willow sobbed.

Reaching out, Imogene put her hand on the back of Willow's head, stroking her hair.

'I wasn't in bed when this episode struck, I was in Ian's office. It was the middle of the night and I woke up, and I could just hear all the emptiness around me. I could feel all the empty rooms and I missed him so much. So I got up to sit in his room, like I told you. I've done it before. Not often, but every few months I just go in there and I sit. I was sitting there, looking around – I had the most terrible headache, the start of this bother, I suppose – when I saw his diary. It was sitting in the top drawer of his desk, bold as brass. Not hidden or anything. Funny, after all those years of not touching a thing I just wanted to see his handwriting. I thought it would be a business diary, but it wasn't, it was a personal diary.'

'About me?' Willow asked, sickened.

'No,' Imogene shook her head. 'It was written in the year that he died, the year, thank God, he was too sick to go out. It was about the neighbour's daughter. Do you remember her? Of course, she'll be all grown up now, but then she was about eight. I remember the day he met her. She'd called round to collect a ball that had come over the fence. He'd shown her the summerhouse.'

'Did he . . . ?'

'No, but in his diary he wrote about her, he wrote . . .' Imogene pressed her fist to her mouth. 'He wrote terrible things, Willow. Oh, Willow, Willow, I'm so sorry. I just couldn't bear it to be true. I didn't want it to be true and it was. All these years I've pushed you away. All these years I've called you a liar. I really believed that's what you were, and it was there all that time. All that filth he thought and did, written out in those neat little letters. All those years I should have been there for you, gone for ever.'

Willow folded in on herself, her head dropping to her knees, her arms cradled over her head.

'When you came I wanted to say something, but I couldn't. I couldn't face myself.' Leaning forward in her chair, Imogene reached for her daughter, bending forward as far as she could, pulling Willow towards her and into her arms. 'And you will never be able to forgive me. You should never forgive me, Willow. I won't ever forgive myself.'

Willow heard the door shut quietly as Sam left, and the old piano fell silent. Willow didn't know how long she stayed there with her head in her mother's lap, Imogene stroking her hair as they talked, but the sun sank behind the trees and Holly and the girls left long before Willow raised her head.

'I can't die now,' Imogene said, eventually making Willow sit up and look at her.

'You're not going to, are you? What's the doctor said?'

'I don't think I'm any more likely to die now than I was yesterday,' Imogene told her. 'But what I mean is, I can't die, not until I've made you realise that I have always loved you, just as much as I loved that little angel in her bed sheet dress. That never went away, Willow. And I can't die until I come to terms with the fact that . . . I should have protected you and I failed.'

Saying nothing, Willow sat up.

'Where is it? Where's the letter?' Imogene asked.

After a moment Willow pressed it into her mother's hand.

'Starting tomorrow, I'm going to get rid of everything – everything – in this house that ever belonged to him. I'm going to burn it. And I'm going to put the house on the market. It's much too big for me now. I'll get a smaller place, somewhere modern, no stairs. A little flat, like the one we used to have, and maybe sometimes you will come and stay. But starting tomorrow – no, starting now – I'm going to make sure that there is not one trace of him left on this earth to hurt you.'

Leaning forward, Imogene threw Ian's letter into the fire, and

Willow watched it curl up and blacken in the flames. What had haunted her for so long turned to ashes in seconds.

'This is a beginning,' she said to Imogene. 'It's a new start between us. And that is more than I ever hoped for.' Bending, she kissed her mum on the forehead.

'Willow.' Imogene hesitated. 'I love you, darling.'

'I love you too, Mum,' Willow said simply. 'Look, would you like me to stay here tonight?' She was aware that this near-empty building didn't hold any terrors for her any more.

'Goodness, no. I don't need any fuss. The night nurse will be here. She's very nice. Scottish, if you know what I mean.'

Willow did not know what her mother meant, but she did know that when she finally pulled on her coat, every bone in her body ached, her mouth was dry and she felt something new, something so faint it almost wasn't present. She felt possibility. Possibility opening up a future for her that for the first time ever might go anywhere she wanted it to.

Chapter Eighteen

Willow slipped her coat off her shoulders and looked in the bedroom mirror. She ran her hand over her waist and hips, turning this way and that as she appraised herself. Her body hadn't changed, she thought, not really. Perhaps she had lost a few inches here and there. There had been too much to do and too many people in her flat of late to be able to sit and watch TV with her bra off whilst eating a takeaway meant for two. Her clothes were a little looser, they fitted better, but she was still a very curvy woman who wouldn't see the right side of a size fourteen without some serious dieting. The curious thing was that as Willow observed the swell of her breasts and the rise of her hips, she didn't mind any more. Gone was that nagging dissatisfaction that she was not the size her sister had always been; gone was the feeling that her true self was slathered in self-inflicted fat, a punishment for her own irreversible failing. Instead, Willow felt a little breathless as she took in her reflection, because it occurred to her, exceptionally late in life, that she was actually rather beautiful.

Willow smiled down at her shoes, her faithful companions since all of this had begun, always gleaming faintly as if they were made from a piece of Van Gogh's starry sky.

Willow took the shoes off and looked at them. Everything had changed the moment she had slipped them on her feet. It was almost as if . . . She mused for a moment on the possibility that there was something more to the shoes than their sheer beauty and perfect fit: the mysterious shop that had appeared out of nowhere, the possibly mad, possibly insightful old shopkeeper who might be an oracle or a shaman, or maybe just a lonely old lady. And yet everything, everything had changed from the moment that Willow slipped on those shoes and put on her coat. Suddenly wishes came true, Chloe came back, Sam forgave her and Daniel . . . well, if James was to be believed Daniel wanted her at last. There had to be something, some catalyst that set off this miraculous chain of events. Surely it couldn't be something as fanciful as a pair of magic shoes.

Willow remembered then that there was one other thing too: the locket that had been nestling quietly in the coat pocket since she'd put it there, half forgotten in the midst of everything else. Impulsively Willow reached into the pocket and found it. Suddenly it seemed very important to know what was inside.

Chloe had gone home with Sam for dinner. He was bringing her back to sleep later, which Willow knew pained him, but the fact that she wanted to spend any time alone with him at all was a gargantuan leap forward. Chloe's relief when Sam had reacted in a measured and calm way to the news about the baby's father had been palpable. It wasn't so much his anger over what Chloe had been drawn into that the girl had been so worried about, Willow realised as she had watched the two of them chucking lumps of stale bread at the scores of swans in Christchurch harbour, it was what Sam thought of her that

Chloe was so afraid of. Willow didn't know what words were spoken between father and daughter in the hour they spent alone together after she'd told Sam about Mr Jacobs. But whatever it was, it had put a light of belonging back in Chloe's eyes and they had gone on to talk about what the future might hold for them both.

For a moment, as Sam's car had pulled away this evening, Willow had felt a spasm of panic, suddenly afraid that she wouldn't see either of them again. And then she remembered she didn't have to be afraid any more. Of course they would come back. It was a novel sensation, the expectation of good things happening, rather than the certainty of bad. Willow thought it might take a while to get used to.

So Willow had her flat truly to herself for the first time in what felt like an age. Leaping up off the bed, she took a few steps in her stockinged feet before feeling naked and slipping her shoes back on.

Going to the kitchen, she rooted about under the sink for a while until she found a little tub of jewellery cleaner she'd bought to try to revive a pair of silver earrings that Chloe had bought her one Christmas, but had never been able to bring herself to use. Taking the edge of a much neglected duster, she carefully began to clean the locket, careful not to rub too hard at the image of the king's head and the partial inscription '*GEORGIUS V DEI GRA BRIT OMN REX*' on one side, and on the other a lion rampant, almost rubbed away entirely, the date of 1915 only just visible. The king's shilling, Willow thought to herself, wondering if at least one of these two coins had been handed over to whoever made this locket on the day that he signed up.

Patiently, Willow rubbed until she had got as much of the blackened tarnish off the locket as she could. It gleamed faintly as she turned it over in her palm, and then, holding her breath, fearful of breaking the makeshift hinge and clasp, Willow slid one fingernail between the edges of the coins. She gasped as the locket gave way, opening slightly. Ever so gently she eased the sides apart.

Inside she found something quite unexpected. She'd been hoping for a photo, or a lock of hair. But instead there was a tiny scrap of yellowish material. Tipping the fragment into one palm and placing the locket carefully on the table, Willow inspected it more closely. It was a tiny square of silk, cut into about a half-inch square. Once white, now yellowed with age, it had been folded into an even smaller square. Carefully Willow smoothed it flat in her palm. Still faintly visible, written in copperplate handwriting, in what must be pencil, was one single word.

'Courage.'

Who the message had been intended for Willow would never know. Perhaps for a young man going to meet his fate in the trenches, or for his sweetheart left to hold the fort alone, but at that moment it seemed as if it had found its way through space and time, and life after life and hand after hand, to come to her, because it was a message that meant everything to her. For so much of her life Willow had been afraid. Fear that insinuated its way into every heartbeat and every breath. At the back of every thought, every decision made and action taken, it had been there, an insidious parasite feeding off her, eating away the person she should have been. Going back to her mother's house, facing head-on what she could never change, had finally banished that disease from Willow altogether. Courage was what she needed at this exact moment, and if she could find the courage to greet whatever the future might hold with a hopeful heart, then the rest would surely be up to her.

Meticulously Willow refolded the silk and eased it back into the locket, gently pressing it shut until it clicked. Returning to her bedroom, she pulled open the top drawer in her dressing table, rooting through a tangle of jewellery, until she found a silver chain she hadn't worn in years. Slipping the locket onto the chain, she fixed it around her neck, reassured by its cool weight at the base of her throat.

Courage. Willow had a new watchword.

A flash of unfamiliar colour now caught her eye on the windowsill. She'd spent so little time in her bedroom recently that she'd forgotten the stacks of books and the little china dog that she had also brought home from the shop. Suddenly convinced that these objects too must have some significance, Willow rushed over to the pile, picking the dog up, turning it over in her hands, peering at it, and getting rather excited when she shook it and heard a faint metallic sound grazing its insides. After much careful tapping and tipping, she eventually teased its hidden treasure out of a hole in its base. It turned out to be a paperclip. Smiling, Willow picked up the books one by one, with titles like *Her Heart's Desire* and *A Lover's Promise*, none of which seemed to be significant. She thumbed through the pages, looking for something – a lost photo, a love letter, notes written on the yellowing paper. But there was nothing but years of dust taking flight. Sitting down on her bed, Willow gathered the books into a pile and hugged them to her chest, her heart lightened by the knowledge that not everything meant something. Some things just were. After a moment she flopped back on her bed, opening one of the books at random and began to read.

Her solitude was abruptly interrupted by the door buzzer. Sighing, Willow went to the door and picked up the intercom.

'Willow? At last! Where have you been, woman? It's Daniel. I need to see you.'

Pressing the buzzer to let him in, Willow put the front door on the latch, took a couple of steps back and then reached for the locket around her neck and waited.

She had absolutely no idea how she was going to feel about Daniel until she saw him in the flesh.

Courage.

'There you are.' Daniel beamed as he came in the door, carrying an oversized bunch of peonies. He stood looking at her. 'There is my Willow. You haven't returned my calls, my emails, my anything. Talk about hard to get. It's been driving me mad!'

'I've been away,' Willow said, feeling suddenly rather reserved around the man she'd devoted every moment of daydreaming to for the last five years.

'Yeah, I know, with Sam.' Daniel looked disgruntled. 'So, is it back on with you two now?'

'No,' Willow said. 'No, not that way. We care about each other a lot, but no. There isn't any way back there for us.' She shifted from one foot to the other.

'Oh. Oh well, these are for you,' Daniel said as if he'd just remembered the flowers. He thrust them at Willow, who took them, burying her face in their sweetness, grateful for an excuse to step away from the door and the uncertain greeting, and look for a vase.

'So how do you feel about not getting back together with Sam?' Daniel asked her as she filled a vase with water.

'I feel good about it,' Willow said. 'I mean, I feel good that Sam and I are friends now. There were a lot of unsaid words festering between us, a lot of things that we've finally had a chance to resolve. In the end it turned out that it wasn't so much how we felt about each other as how we felt about ourselves that came between us. It's funny, if it hadn't been for Chloe running away I don't think we would ever have spoken again, and yet here we are, in the middle of all this, and somehow it feels like a family.'

'A family.' Daniel nodded. 'I guess that's modern life for you; whatever works, right?'

'Right.' Willow nodded, taking extra care in placing the peonies in the vase, positioning them on the table, hopeful that the flowers might ward off what she knew was coming.

'I hear you saw Serious James just before you went,' Daniel said.

How much did he hear, Willow wondered? Did he hear about her trying to sleep with Serious James? She didn't think so. James didn't strike her as the kiss-and-tell type.

'He said that he'd told you.' Daniel was edgy, nervous. He looked so handsome it made Willow's stomach ache, and yet she still, still didn't know how she was going to react when the moment came.

'Told me?' Willow hedged uncomfortably.

'About me and Kayla. We're through!' Daniel waited, as if for a reaction, and when none was apparent, went on, 'For the first time in about twenty years I am totally single. Not a woman in sight.' He spread his hands, palms raised as if to make the point. 'I am completely free.'

'Oh? And how do you like it?' Willow asked him, finding the courage to look him in the eye.

'I hate it, Willow, I hate it.' Daniel's eyes met hers. 'I want to be with you. I need to be with you, Willow. It's you, it's you, it's always been you.'

In one stride he closed the space between them and took her in his arms.

Willow luxuriated in his kiss, in feeling the soft billows of her body clash with the hard contours of his, one strong arm securing her to him, around her waist, the other in her hair. She closed her eyes and let the moment wash over her, as if each second was a day, a month, a year. A single kiss to satisfy years of yearning, because as soon as Daniel had taken her in his arms Willow had known what she previously could never have guessed. This wonderful, passionate, beautiful kiss was to be their last.

Daniel Fayre was not the man for her.

'Oh, Willow, darling,' Daniel muttered, his fingers pulling at her shirt, easing it out of the waistband of her skirt.

'Daniel, wait,' Willow said, trying to block his hand.

'I can't wait. I've been waiting all my life for this,' Daniel said, kissing her neck as he fumbled for her skirt. 'Since I saw you that day you posed for me, my Venus, when you looked so delicious, I haven't been able to get the thought of you out of my head. You just don't know what the sight of a woman like you does to a man. It's like finding a glass of cool water after forty days and nights in the desert . . .'

'Daniel!' Willow stopped him by gripping his wrist firmly enough to make him look at her. As soon as he caught her expression his face fell.

'No way,' he said, allowing her to remove his hand from her entirely. 'You're not telling me that you don't feel the same way? Not now, Willow. You've been in love with me for years – did you think I didn't notice?'

Willow bit her lip. 'I have.'

'See?' Daniel grinned. 'I was thinking and thinking about it while you weren't answering your phone to me, and you know what I realised? I've been afraid of the strength of it, and the massive importance of what it meant. I was too scared to admit my feelings. That's why I didn't do anything about it, Willow. That's why I kept going out with all those models.'

'Oh, that's why.' Willow found herself smiling.

'What's so funny?' Daniel asked. 'I'm declaring love here, sweetheart. Try and take it a little more seriously, OK? I'm giving you all my best lines.'

'I know,' Willow said. Reaching out, she touched Daniel's beautiful cheek, tracing his perfect jaw line. 'I heard you say the stuff about the drink of water in the desert to Kayla.'

'I didn't . . .' Daniel faltered as Willow dropped her hand from his face. 'Well, even if I did, that's got nothing to do with this. Willow, you are real, you are the only real person in my life and the way I feel about you won't go away. Because it's real, it's really, really . . . you know . . . real.'

'The thing is, I think that real is actually the last thing that it is,' Willow said. 'I think suddenly things got a bit heated between us because there was nakedness, and Sam was back on the scene, and you must have known that James was preparing to woo me in the worst possible way in history, because he would have told you. Things were over between you and Kayla already, and I'm . . . well, I was a banker, wasn't I? Good old reliable Willow. You could always rely on me to be there, in love with you. Unless, of course, I suddenly got back with Sam or fell for Serious James.'

'Serious James,' Daniel chuckled. 'Not my idea of competition.'

'And all of that coincided with me getting a very sexy pair of shoes. Which basically added up to making me, Willow Briars, impossible for you, Daniel Fayre, to resist. You don't love me, Daniel. Actually, that's not fair. I think you kind of do, but not in the way you think you do.'

'But I do . . .' Daniel looked confused, as if his brain could not compute what was happening. 'I do feel that way about you, Willow, I do.'

Willow hesitated, crossing her arms as she chose her words very carefully. The truth was that, after all this time, she could not believe what she was about to say.

'Daniel, even if you do feel that way about me, the problem is I don't feel that way about you. I don't love you, Daniel.'

'But you do, you do, you always have,' Daniel said, bemused.

'I don't think so. I think I pined for you and I wanted you. I think I thought it was love but . . . it was more of a needing, wanting, hunger kind of thing. I loved you because I knew you would never love me, and . . . well, this is hard for me to say, but for a very long time now I haven't really felt like I am very worthy of being loved.'

Daniel stared at her, aghast.

'Are you crazy? You're the best person I know. And not just now, not just recently when you've got all sexy and in demand. I mean always. You have always been the best person I know, the person I know who most deserves all the things you deny yourself. Including a piece of this hot hunk of love, you know what I'm saying?'

'I do know what you're saying, and I'm saying no thank you, thank you very much for asking.'

'I don't understand,' he said. 'Willow, it's me, it's Daniel saying you and me babe, how about it?'

'I know. I look at you and you are so very handsome that I think I must be crazy, but I know I'm right. We became friends out of a whole mess of confusion, but even though I've been torturing myself over you all of these years, your friendship has meant a lot to me. I want us to be friends, Daniel.'

'Ouch.' Daniel covered his belly with his hands as if he had just been punched. 'You're giving me the "let's be friends" speech, when we haven't even had sex? If you're going to give me the "let's be friends" speech then the very least I deserve is some sex.' The glint in Daniel's lovely eyes was all the proof that Willow needed to know he wasn't heartbroken. 'Come on, Willow, don't be the one woman in the world I'll never have.'

'I think that is exactly the woman I am.' Willow smiled brightly at him. 'Now do you want a cup of tea?'

It was getting on for ten when Sam and Chloe came back. Daniel had been texting Kayla even before he'd finished his tea, and instead of feeling hurt or vaguely surprised Willow had felt relieved. The moment of madness that had started on a wet afternoon five years ago was finally over and now they could just relax and enjoy each other's company.

'Nice dinner?' Willow asked as Chloe collapsed awkwardly onto the sofa, holding her palm over her belly.

'Well, there was no rocket, so it was a start,' she grumbled amiably, grinning at her dad.

'It was a very nice dinner. We talked a lot, didn't we, Chloe?' Sam smiled at Willow. 'All this time we thought we were at odds with each other, turns out that actually we think the same way about most things.'

'Yes, we do.' Chloe's face became serious. 'We talked, and I went over and over everything with Dad and he's behind me a hundred per cent.' Chloe and Sam exchanged glances of solidarity that warmed Willow's heart, even as the anticipation she felt gripped her.

'I've decided what I'm going to do, Willow,' Chloe said, hauling herself up into a sitting position.

'Right.' Willow felt her heart race, her hand reach up and close around the locket.

Chloe smiled. 'I'd really like to stay here with you, until the baby is born.' She looked at Sam, who nodded for her to go on. 'And, well, Dad and I have talked and . . . I think adoption is the right way to go,' Chloe said.

'Oh.' The word, more like a sigh, escaped from Willow before she could stop it, her heart plummeting downwards. 'Well then, you know I'm here for you, to support you through every minute of it.'

'Yes, I do know that,' Chloe said. 'Which is why . . . I'm going to keep the baby and you are going to adopt me. If you don't mind?'

'What?' Willow's jaw dropped open as she watched the hopeful smile that lit up Chloe's face.

'Please, please don't think I'm mad,' Chloe said, the words tumbling out of her. 'I've talked it through with Dad and we phoned that nice social worker. She actually picked up the phone, which she says must be a sign, because she's hardly ever at her desk and she was about to go home . . . but, anyway – it *is* possible, it *is* totally legal – you can do it. I can be adopted until I'm eighteen, and you don't have to be married to Dad, you just need his consent and mine. And then, Willow –' Chloe's eyes shone – 'and then you could be my mum and I could be your daughter, and this little chap, well, he would make you a granny. I was going to try and gloss over that part but . . . .' Chloe stared at Willow's frozen face. 'Willow! Please, say something?'

Willow looked at Sam, tears brimming in her eyes, shaking her head. 'Is this real?' she asked him. 'Me adopt Chloe? Wouldn't you mind? Adoption – it's a massive thing. And, Chloe, you know I feel like you are my daughter. I always will. We don't need a piece of paper to make it true.'

'I can't think of anyone I'd rather have to officially always be there for my daughter,' Sam said. 'If it's what you both want then I'm happy.'

'It is what we both want,' Chloe said, taking Willow's hands and looking into her eyes. 'Because it's not just a bit of paper. It's proof. Proof that you are my second mum and I'm your daughter.'

Willow nodded, smiling. 'Can I really be this happy?'

'You can,' Sam nodded. 'You really can. And it's about time, too.'

'Please say yes,' Chloe pressed her.

'Oh, Chloe, yes, yes, nothing in the world would make me happier!'

And kneeling down in front of her daughter, Willow held her in her arms and she laughed and laughed.

She laughed out loud for joy.

Epilogue

'Where are we going again?' James asked Willow, covering her gloved hand with his as they strolled arm in arm through the first few flakes of snow. 'I'm pretty sure if you buy any more baby clothes that kid's going to need his own crib.' He chuckled. 'See what I did there? Crib? Like a gangsta pad and a baby bed, like a play on words? I'm hilarious, aren't I? Seriously, though, how much of a pay rise did Victoria give you with that promotion?'

'The very least that she could get away with to stop me from leaving her and going to work for India,' Willow smiled.

As good as her word, India had come into the office on her last trip to London before going out to LA and informed Victoria that she was offering Willow the job of her PA. When she named how much she intended to pay her, Victoria had blanched white in horror, offering to match the pay rise and make Willow a junior agent on the spot. After much hand-wringing, and umming and ahhing Willow had told India that she was loyal to Victoria, that as much as she loved and respected India, there was no way she could leave the woman who had done so much for her, a response that had even Victoria looking quite moved.

What Victoria did not know, what she would never know, was

that India had come to the flat to offer Willow the job and, having found that she rather liked being in one place with all the people that she loved, Willow had regretfully declined. Which was when India came up with the plan to secure her promotion, a plan that worked like a charm. It turned out that she and a world-famous film star had become rather good friends and that quite soon Chloe's baby would have the most famous godmother in the world.

'I am so proud of you,' James said. 'Do you know how amazing you are, exactly?'

'You are the most amazing man I know,' Willow told him fondly, pausing to kiss him under a streetlamp. She'd been kissing Serious James for the best part of three months now, and the sensation was always the same: a wonderful spread of heat that began in her lips and languorously wended its way through her limbs in a wanton build-up of passion. Willow was certain that it was now time to do a little more than kiss James, but she hadn't told him that yet. Three months of kissing James had taught her that it was best to take him by surprise in these matters. The less time he had to worry about things, the less nervous he would be, and the most wonderful revelation that Willow had discovered about her new boyfriend was that he really was the most remarkable kisser.

Goodness only knew what delights that hideous swan bed would hold for her, and Willow knew that she didn't want to wait any longer to find out.

'Can I just say that your photo was the most amazing piece at the whole of that exhibition we just went to?' James asked her, smiling fondly to himself. 'You looked stunning. I must say, Daniel did an incredible job on that shoot.'

Yes, really incredible, Willow thought, considering he'd only taken a few frames before the ill-advised touching and kissing. She was glad though, that despite everything, he'd used her photo as the centrepiece of the exhibition, especially when she saw it, blown up to almost life size and in pride of place in the centre of the gallery. Looking at the image of sumptuous sexuality that he'd created was nothing like looking at herself, but it did make her see that everything she thought was wrong about her body was also right. It just depended on which way you looked at it.

'I've got to say, it does a man good to walk into a place with officially the most beautiful woman in the world on his arm.'

'I hardly think so,' Willow laughed. 'But I love it that you think so.'

'And I love you,' James said suddenly. 'Oh fuck. Fuck. I said it, out loud, in the street, in the snow . . . shit. I was trying to pretend to be all blasé and not feel impossibly romantic and not blurt out that I am totally and utterly and irrevocably in love with you in this cheesy and clichéd rom-com fashion. And now it's too late.'

'James . . .' Willow giggled.

'I know,' James went on, 'we can pretend you didn't hear that. Let's do that; let's pretend you didn't hear me telling you that I love you and then in a few weeks, after some masterful love-making – well, some lovemaking – I'll tell you again . . .'

'James!' Willow's chuckle evolved into a laugh.

'At a completely cool and original time. Like maybe at the meat counter in the supermarket, or at the dentist's or, oh, I know, when I'm on stage . . . or maybe not. That didn't go down so well last time . . .'

'James, will you shut up!' Willow laughed, tears freezing on her cheeks.

'God, I love you even more when you laugh,' James said, suddenly serious. 'And I don't even care about the clichés.'

'Good,' Willow said. 'Because hearing you say that on this snowy December evening makes me very, very happy indeed.'

Willow took advantage of James's delighted silence to guide him off the main road and down Portal Way, to where Bleeding Heart Yard opened out into a tiny square.

'Are you going to mug me?' James said. 'Is that why you've brought me here?'

Willow said nothing, leading him around the solitary snow-garnished willow tree, which somebody had taken the trouble to lace with glittering fairy lights, until the glow of the only shop window in the square was visible, a single spotlight illuminating the display. The grimy door was firmly shut, and the handwritten 'Closed' sign was on display.

'You've brought me to this dark and probably dangerous place to show me a closed shop? I love your eccentricity, Willow, but now you are starting to slightly scare me.'

'Look.' Willow nodded at the display. A battered and moth-eaten old fur coat was draped rather grandly over some upturned boxes, and at its hem, positioned with the toes turned in, as if they were about to click three times for home, were Willow's magic shoes.

'Oh, your shoes. You've given your shoes away.' James looked perplexed, sweetly trying to hide his confusion from Willow because he sensed that even though he didn't understand it, it was very important.

'Not away,' Willow said, grabbing the lapels of his coat and pulling him close to her. 'I've given them back. Because I don't need them any more. They are waiting for the next person.'

'That's brilliant,' James said.

'Because,' Willow went on, looking into his eyes, 'Serious, wonderful, lovely, incredible James, for the first time in my life I am totally and utterly happy. And because I love you, too.'

'Oh.' James was quiet for a moment. 'Oh, Willow.'

It wasn't the first kiss they shared, bathed in the golden glow of that single spotlight in the secret little square of Bleeding Heart Yard, but it was the kiss when each of them finally knew that they would never stop kissing each other as long as they lived.

A little later, as Willow and James headed back to the tube, arm in arm, her head resting on his shoulder, he remembered something else.

'What about the locket? Did you give that back too?'

'I gave the locket to Chloe,' Willow said. 'The bravest girl I know.'

Acknowledgements

I count myself exceptionally lucky to have worked for over ten years with the same fantastic editorial team at Arrow, Kate Elton and Georgina Hawtrey-Woore. It's a very fortunate writer who gets the benefit of these two brilliant women's insight and skill for so many years, and I thank them and the whole Arrow team for their tireless support and dedication.

It's also been ten years since I first met my fantastic agent Lizzy Kremer, who has, over those years become not only a good friend but also an invaluable asset to my life as a writer. Lizzy, thank you so much for always being there with a compliment sandwich!

Thank you also to my dear friends who are my inspiration, my sounding boards and most loyal supporters, Katy Regan, Peigh Evans, Jenny Matthews, Margi Harris, Kirstie Robertson, Catherine Ashley, Cathy Carter, Rosie Wooley and Sarah Darby.

Also Joanne Wilcock, Ian Wilcock, Claire Gordon, Jaydee Parry, Ragna Brent, Jayne Pickard, Kayla Staniland, thank you all.

During the year it took to write this book I got married, so I'd like to thank my husband Adam Evans, for all his love, ideas, feedback and support, and of course my brilliant, wonderful, incredible children who inspire me every day.

If you liked *THE OTHER SISTER*, then why not try

WE ARE ALL MADE OF STARS

Also by Rowan Coleman

'Oh, what a gorgeous book this is - it gripped me and wouldn't let me go. So engaging, so beautifully written – I loved every single thing about it' Jill Mansell

'What a lovely, utterly life affirming, heart-breaking book *We Are All Made of Stars* by Rowan Coleman is'
Jenny Colgan

Turn the page for a sneak peek . . .

Dear Len,

Well, if you are reading this, it's happened. And I suppose that I ought to be glad, and so should you. We've both spent such a long time waiting, and I could see how much it was wearing you down, as much as you tried to hide it.

Now, the life insurance policy is in the shoebox in the bedroom, on top of the wardrobe, under that hat I wore to our Dominic's wedding – remember? The one with the veil you said made me look like a femme fatale? You might not; you drank too much beer, and four of Dominic's friends had to carry you upstairs, you great oaf. It's not much of a payout, I don't think, but it will be enough for the funeral at least. I don't have any wishes concerning that matter. You know me better than anyone else will. I trust you to get it right.

The washing machine. It's easy, really: you turn the round knob clockwise to the temperature you want to wash at, but don't worry about that. Just wash everything at forty degrees. It mostly works out all right. And you put the liquid in the plastic thing in the drum, not in the drawer. I don't even really know why they have those drawers any more.

You need to eat – and not stuff you can microwave. You need to at least shake hands with a vegetable once a week, promise me. You always made the Sunday night tea – cheese on toast and baked beans on the side – so I'm sure you'll be able to keep body and soul together if you put some effort in. I expect at first lots of people will feed you, but you'll need to get a cookbook. I think there's a Delia under the bed. I got it for Christmas last year from Susan, and I thought, what a cheek!

Len, do you remember the night we met? Do you remember how you led me on to the dance floor? You didn't talk, didn't ask me or anything, you rogue. Just took my hand and led me out there. And how we twirled and laughed – the room became a blur. And when the song stopped, you kissed me. Still hadn't said a word to me, mind you, and you kissed me right off my feet. The first thing you said to me was, 'You'd better tell me your name, as you're the girl I'm going to marry.' Cheeky beggar, I thought, but you were right.

It's been a good life, Len, full of love and happiness. Just as much – more than – the sadness and the bad times, if you think about it, and I have had a lot of time to think about it, lately. A person can't really ask for more. Don't stop because I've stopped; keep going, Len. Keep dancing, dancing with our grandchildren, for me. Make them laugh, and spoil them rotten.

And when you think of me, don't think of me in these last few days: think of me twirling and laughing and dancing in your arms.

Remember me this way.

Your loving wife,

Dorothy

PROLOGUE

STELLA

He was a runner. That was the first thing I knew about Vincent.

One hot July, four years ago, I saw him early each morning, running past me as I walked to work, for almost three weeks in a row.

That summer I'd decided to get up before seven, to enjoy the relative quiet of an early north London morning on my way to start a shift at the hospital. I was a trauma nurse back then, and there was something about the near stillness of the streets, the quiet of the roads, that gave me just a little space to exhale before a full eight hours of holding my breath. So I walked to work, sauntered more like, kicking empty coffee cups out of my way, flirting with street sweepers, dropping a strong cup of tea off to the homeless guy who was always crammed up against the railings by the park, working on his never-ending novel. It was my rest time, my respite.

At almost exactly the same time every morning, Vincent ran past me at full pelt, like he was racing some unseen opponent. I'd catch a glimpse of a water bottle, closely cropped dark hair, a tan, nice legs – long and muscular. Every day, at almost exactly the same time, for nearly three weeks. He'd whip by, and I'd think, there's the runner guy, another moment ticked off on my journey. I liked the predictability. The flirty street sweeper, the cup of tea drop, the runner. Sort of like having your favourite song stuck in your head.

Then one morning he slowed down, just a hair's breadth, and turned his head. For the briefest moment I looked into his eyes – such a bright blue, like mirrors reflecting the sky. And then he was gone again, but it was already too late: my routine was disturbed, along with my peace of mind. All day that day, in the middle of some life-and-death drama or in the quiet of the locker room, I found the image of those eyes returning to me again and again. And each time it gave me butterflies.

The next morning, I waited for him to run past me again, and for normality to be restored. Except he stopped, so abruptly, a few feet in front of me and then bent over for a moment, his hands on his knees, catching his breath. I hesitated, sidestepped and decided to keep walking.

'Wait ... please.' He took a breath between words, holding up a hand that halted me. 'I thought I wasn't going to stop, and then I thought, sod it, so I did.'

'OK,' I said.

'I thought you might like to come for a coffee with me?' He smiled – it was full of charm; it was a smile that was used to winning.

'Did you?' I asked him. 'Why?'

'Well, hoped, more like,' he said, the smile faltering a little. 'My name is Vincent. Vincent Carey. I'm a squaddie, Coldstream Guards. I'm on leave, going back to the desert soon. And you never know, do you? So I thought … well, you've got lovely hair – all curls, all down your back. And eyes like amber.'

He had noticed my eyes – perhaps in that same second that I noticed his.

'I'm a very lazy person,' I told him. 'I never go anywhere fast.'

'Is that a weird way of saying no to coffee?' I liked his frown as much as his smile.

'It's a warning,' I said. 'A warning that I might not be your kind of person.'

'Sometimes,' he said, 'you just know when someone is your sort of person.'

'From their hair?' I laughed.

'From their eyes.'

I couldn't argue with that.

'Mind if I walk part of the way with you?' he'd asked.

'OK.' I smiled to myself as he fell in step next to me, and we walked in silence for a while.

'You weren't kidding about being slow,' he said, eventually.

The second thing I knew about Vincent was that one day I was going to marry him. But the first thing I knew was that he was a runner.

Which makes it so hard to look at him now: his damaged face turned to the wall as he sleeps, and the space where his leg used to be.

CHAPTER ONE

HOPE

I can't sleep. I can never sleep these days – not in here, anyway, where they don't let it be truly dark, not ever. But it's not only that; it's because I can't stop thinking about how I came to be here. I know, of course: I caught something – a bug, bacterial, which is dangerous news when you live with cystic fibrosis. I almost died, and now I'm here, in this place where they never really turn the lights out on the long and painful road to recuperation. I know that, but what I don't know, what I want to know, is *how*. I want to know precisely the second that little cluster of bacteria drifted like falling blossom into my bloodstream. I can't know, of course, but that doesn't mean I don't want to or that I can stop thinking about it. The frustrating thing about my condition is that I have a lot of time on my hands to think, but not a lot of time on the clock to live. Time moves slowly and quickly at the very same time – racing and stretching, boring and terrifying. And you can live your whole life with the idea of mortality – that one day it will be the last day – and still never really know or care what that means. Not until the last day arrives, that is.

I was at a party, when Death came to find me.

I hate parties, but my best friend Ben made me go.

'You can't stay in all your life,' he said, dragging me out of my room and down the stairs. 'You are twenty-one years old, nearly twenty-two. You should be out every night, enjoying the prime of your life!'

'*You* are in your prime of your life; I'm most likely middle aged,' I told him, even though I knew he hated me referring to my short life expectancy this way. 'And anyway, I could. I could stay in all my life and listen to Joni Mitchell and read books, and design book covers, try and work out the solo of "Beat It" on my guitar, and I'd be perfectly fine.'

'Mrs K.?' Ben dragged me into the living room, where my parents were watching the same old same old on TV – some police detective, who drinks too much and lost his wife in a bitter divorce, chasing down some psycho-killer. 'Tell your daughter: she's a twenty-one-year-old woman. She needs to go out and have fun! Remind her that life is for living, and not for sitting alone in her room reading about how other people do it! Plus it's all the old crew from school, back from uni now. We haven't been together in ages, and they are all dying to see her.'

Mum turned in her chair, and I could see the worry in her eyes, despite her smile. But there was nothing new there: she'd been worried for every moment of my twenty-one years, constantly. Sometimes I wonder if she'd wished she could change my name, after I was diagnosed as a baby and the situation was officially hope-less, but it was too late by then; it was a name that already belonged to me – a cruel irony that we both have to live with now. My poor darling mum, she had enough on her plate. It wasn't fair to make her decide if I went out or not, because she'd spend the rest of the evening worrying either way, and later she would have torn herself to pieces with blame. So, making my own decision, that was one of the things I did right that night. It was just the choice that was wrong.

'Oh, fine, I'm coming out, I'll get changed.'

Ben grinned at me and sat down on the bottom stair, and I thought of him there, in his skinny jeans, an outsize jumper sloping off one shoulder, jet black hair and eyes lined with smudges of Kohl, as I rifled through my wardrobe, looking for something, anything, that might even nearly equal his effortless cool. It wasn't fair, really – that little odd duckling, the boy that the other kids left out or pushed around, had suddenly grown into a sexy, hip swan. We had used to be lame kids together. That was how we came to be best friends; it was part of the natural process of banding together, like circling our wagons – greater safety, even in our meagre number of two, than being alone. Him: the skinny, shy kid with the grey collars and worn-down shoes; and me: the sick girl.

I don't think it was then that Death entered, when Ben came into the house, though it could have been. He could have left a trace of a germ on the bannister or the damp towel in the downstairs loo. It could have been then, but I don't think it was, because near-death by hand towel isn't even nearly fitting enough.

I dressed all in black, trying to hide my skinny frame with a skater skirt and a long top, and wondered how many other girls my age longed to put weight on. I rimmed my eyes with dark eye shadow and hoped that would do the trick.

The moment we walked in through the door, and the wave of heat and sweat and molecules of saliva, which I know are in every breath I take, hit us, I wanted to go home. I almost turned around right then, but Ben had his hand on the small of my back. There was something protective about it, something comforting. And these were my friends, after all. The people I grew up with, who were always nice to me and did fun runs in my name. Who I could sit and have a coffee and a laugh with; who would always find something for us to talk about, while carefully avoiding those potentially awkward questions like, 'How's it going? Still think you'll be dead soon?'

'Hopey!' Sally Morse, my sort-of best female friend from school, ran the length of the hallway to engulf me in a hug. 'Oh shit, it's so good to see you. You look great! How's it going? What's new? You're like an entrepreneur or something, aren't you?' She hooked her arm through mine, briefly resting her head on my shoulder as she led me into the kitchen, and I noticed the slight pinkness around her nostrils: the remnants of a cold.

'I'm OK,' I told her, accepting a beer. 'I started designing book covers for people, and it's going quite well.'

'That's so cool,' she said happily. 'That's so totally cool because, you know, really university is a huge waste of time; there are no jobs out there, and you end up in loads of debt – it's a very expensive way to get laid and drunk. I emailed you loads, but you're shit at replying. Too busy, I suppose, being a businesswoman.'

She paused for a moment, scanning my face, and then dragged me into a hug, filling my face with a curious combination of lemon- and smoke-scented hair, and I hugged her back. I'd thought I didn't miss any of that: the people I once saw almost every day for most of life. I'd told myself that, anyway, but it turned out that I did. I was happy to see her in that moment, happy I had come. Perhaps it was then, perhaps in that little moment of optimism and nostalgia, in the midst of that hug, I'd inhaled my own assassin. I hope not. Although it would be just like the universe to try and undo you when you are happy, because in my experience the universe is an arse.

But the good thing about being amongst my old friends was that there was no need to explain – no need to have the eternal prologue of a conversation when I tell them about the CF, and they look sad and awkward in turn. It was a relief to be amongst the people who have been preparing for my exit, almost since the very first moment I made my entrance into their lives.

It wasn't long before Sally was tonsils-deep in some guy who I thought she'd most likely brought with her, because I didn't know him, so I made my way through the mass of people, looking for Ben.

'Hope!' Clara Clayton shrieked, planting a glossy kiss on my cheek. 'It's so good to see you! If you're here, that means Ben is here, and I want to see him. Bloody hell, he's grown up hot ... Hey, are you two ...?'

'Hello, Hope,' said Tom Green, the school heartthrob for so many years, and now no less sweet, blonde, or strappingly broad-chested. 'How are things? How are you doing?' He was still awkward, polite, kind, tall – all of the things about him that used to make me swoon when I was thirteen years old, though not anymore, I was interested to notice; now I thought he was lovely but sort of dull.

'I like your look,' he said, with some effort. 'Really... cool.'

As I made my way through the party, cigarettes being hastily put out as I approached, I relaxed. I felt at home here, amongst friends. I felt like a twenty-one-year-old woman at a party. I relaxed, and that was probably my mistake.

It could have been in any one of those miniature reunions that Death made its move, during that long hour of leaning in too close to people while they told me what degree they got, and what they were going to do next. It might have been then, or it could have been when the taxi driver coughed all over the change he gave me on the way over. But I don't think it was.

I think it happened when Ben kissed me.

Because, let's get this straight, I spend most of my time in my bedroom in my parents' house pretending that designing a few book covers is a proper grown-up career, and reading books, lots of books. And a man kissing me would definitely be the cause of my demise in a Victorian novel.

I'm prone to dwelling. I'm a dweller.

*

Ben was drunk, in the way that only he gets drunk, which is not at all, then all at once. And he'd gone from being uber-cool to dancing and laughing and spinning, and hugging, and playing air guitar, and chatting up girls, who lapped up his nonsense, while I stood in the corner of the room, watching him, smiling despite myself. He loves to think he's cool – the guy in the rock band, the 'I don't give a toss about you' rock star – but it doesn't take very much for him to be his great big dorky self: the boy I used to know. The one who'd fill his pockets with worms to save them from other boys stomping on them; the guy who might look like he could snack on bats' heads by night but who is an assistant manager in Carphone Warehouse by day.

Suddenly, he careered into me, grabbing hold of my shoulders, and we both fell back onto the sofa laughing – him a little too hard, and me a little too politely.

'You are such a dick,' I told him, reasonably fondly, though.

'Then why am I your best mate?' he asked me, winding his arm around my shoulder and pulling me even closer to him, fluttering his ridiculously long brown lashes.

'Oh, shut up,' I said, screwing my face up as he rubbed his cheek against mine, like an over-friendly dog. I made my move to protect him from himself, which was to make him think he was protecting me, which meant he'd stop drinking quite so much, so fast. 'You know what? This party, it's not really doing it for me. I think I'm going to go home. Will you take me home?'

'No, don't go!' Ben grabbed my face in his hands and made me look into his eyes, squeezing my mouth into a frankly ridiculous pout. 'You're always leaving places early. Stop leaving me, Hope. When are you going to get that I hate you leaving me behind? I want you around all the time.'

'Don't be a twat,' I'd said, although hesitantly, because the way he was looking at me just then was angry and hurt all at once. It was hard to read, and I am not a fan of ambiguity. Just for a moment, for the briefest of seconds, I glimpsed that perhaps something about the way he was acting tonight had to do with me.

'Just don't go,' he said.

'But Ben, I ...'

Which was when he kissed me.

I mean really kissed me. Ben, who I had known since I was five years old. Ben, who once waded into a patch of nettles to carry me out. Ben, who'd held my hair and made small talk while I hawked up globules of mucus, during my nightly coughing rituals. Ben kissed me, and it was a real kiss, urgent and hard, and with his tongue. It was physical, and awkward, and it took me by surprise, because I'd never been kissed like that before, with this kind of force or, well, *need*. As he pressed me back hard into the sofa, suddenly I felt like I couldn't breathe. I panicked and I pushed him away.

'Shit,' he said. 'I'm really drunk. Sorry. Sorry, shit.'

I got up and went to the bathroom. Flounced is probably a better word – I flounced off to cover my confusion, feigned fury and offence. I spent a long time looking at myself in the mirror, looking at my kiss-stained mouth. Somehow I knew that everything had changed, and that it wasn't going to be for the better.

When I came back, Ben had passed out on the sofa, his head lolling back in the cushions, his mouth wide open.

I got a taxi home alone and was in bed before midnight.

When I saw Ben the next day, he said he hardly remembered anything and told me to never let him drink again. He didn't mention the kiss, and I still have no idea if he has forgotten, or if he'd rather just not talk about it.

A week after that, I was admitted to hospital with a bacterial lung infection.

The pain, the pain, and the gasping for air, and the desperate need all the time for there to be more of it, took up most of my energy, but not all of it. There was a moment, just one, of perfect clarity, when I heard the doctor say to my mother, 'It's touch and go, I'm afraid.'

And I thought, I am not ready. I am not ready yet.

I made it, I'm still here, still alive, almost ready to go back to life. I won this round. But I can't sleep, you see, because even though I can't know, I want to know. I need to know the exact moment that I let Death in, and I can't sleep – because what if I'm not ready the next time it finds me?